Coming Home for Christmas: Three Holiday Stories

Enduring Light

Marriage of Mercy

My Loving Vigil Keeping

Her Hesitant Heart

The Double Cross

Safe Passage

Carla Kelly's Christmas Collection

In Love and War

A Timeless Romance Anthology: Old West Collection

Marco and the Devil's Bargain

Softly Falling

Paloma and the Horse Traders

NONFICTION

*On the Upper Missouri: The Journal
of Rudolph Friedrich Kurz*

Fort Buford: Sentinel at the Confluence

Stop Me If You've Read This One

Doing no Harm

Doing no Harm

CARLA KELLY

SWEETWATER
BOOKS
AN IMPRINT OF CEDAR FORT, INC.
SPRINGVILLE, UTAH

This is a work of fiction. The characters, names, incidents, places, and dialogue are products of the author's imagination and are not to be construed as real. The views expressed within this work are the sole responsibility of the author and do not necessarily reflect the position of Cedar Fort, Inc., or any other entity.

ISBN 13: 978-1-4621-1738-3

Published by Sweetwater Books, an imprint of Cedar Fort, Inc.
2373 W. 700 S., Springville, UT, 84663
Distributed by Cedar Fort, Inc., www.cedarfort.com

LIBRARY OF CONGRESS CATALOGING-IN-PUBLICATION DATA

    Kelly, Carla, author.
   Doing no harm / by Carla Kelly.
      pages cm
    Summary: After a celebrated career in the war against Napoleon, Captain Douglas Bowden moves to a small fishing village to escape military life and put his medical skills to good use.
   ISBN 978-1-4621-1738-3 (mass market : alk. paper)
   1. Physicians--Great Britain--History--19th century--Fiction. I. Title.
   PS3561.E3928D65 2015
   813'.54--dc23
                       2015032097

Cover design by Rebecca J. Greenwood
Cover design © 2015 by Lyle Mortimer
Edited and typeset by Melissa J. Caldwell

Printed in the United States of America

10 9 8 7 6 5 4 3 2

*In memory of Edward Jordan "Bud" Hagan (1916–2008),
M.D., former US Navy surgeon serving with the First Marine
Division at Cape Gloucester, Peleliu, and Okinawa, 1943–45.*

*When I interviewed Bud Hagan to write his memoir, nei-
ther of us knew that he would become the model for Douglas
Bowden, Surgeon [retired], Royal Navy. It was easy to write
about an honorable military doctor because I knew one.*

"The physician must . . . have two special objects in view with regard to disease, namely, to do good or to do no harm."

—HIPPOCRATES
found in *Of the Epidemics*, Book 1, Section 2

Chapter 1

*W*HAT SAY YOU, CAPTAIN? TIME'S wasting. You come well recommended, and I agree with the Navy Board. The war is over, but we still need hospitals. Aye or nay?"

After twenty-five years at sea fighting in a global conflict, Surgeon Douglas Bowden, Royal Navy, wasn't an easy man to surprise. He was surprised now. He sat back in Admiral Sir David Carew's uncomfortable chair for guests—or was it a chair for uncomfortable guests?—and considered the offer.

Maybe he was silent too long.

"Starting tomorrow!" Sir David glanced at his calendar. "May 6, 1816."

"Assistant superintendent here at Stonehouse?" Douglas asked and almost winced with the stupidity of his query.

"Where else?" the admiral snapped, his patience obviously at an end. "This Stonehouse, not the one in Siam! Don't try me, lad."

Maybe it was the "lad" that decided the matter. *I am a full-grown man and a competent surgeon*, Douglas thought,

1

wishing the slight didn't rankle, not after all these years. *I am not your lad. My father was only a cooper in Norfolk, but I am still not your lad.*

"I think not, Sir David," Douglas replied, noting with silent glee that it was the physician's turn to look startled. "I believe I will relinquish my warrant, instead." He hadn't forgotten all his manners. "Thank you for the offer."

Evidently Sir David wasn't accustomed to being turned down flatter than a ship's biscuit. "Twice your current salary!" he sputtered. "A house on the row here!"

Douglas hesitated. Perhaps he had been hasty. He had nothing against making money, and a house on the row would certainly announce the habitation of a man at the top of his profession, someone worthy of note.

"You'll be considered a gentleman!"

Sir David Carew had thrown out his final incentive. He sat back, folded his arms, and glared at Douglas.

That, you old rip, is the very reason I will never take this position, Douglas thought, his mind made up by Sir David's last dangled carrot. Just the saying of it told him that prissy old Davey Care-Less would never consider him a gentleman and an equal, even if his surgical talents far eclipsed most physicians' abilities.

Douglas stood up. "Alas, Sir David, I cannot oblige you, kind as your offer is. I will surrender my warrant to the Navy Board when I pass through London and be on my way tomorrow." He extended his foot and made a proper bow to the physician. "Thank you for the consideration. Good-day."

He closed the door while Sir David's mouth still hung open in amazement. Douglas stopped by the yeoman's desk, laughing to himself at the scribe's equally wide-open mouth and staring eyes. He must have heard the whole exchange.

"Am I the first sea dog to lift my leg on Sir David's shoes?" Douglas whispered, his eyes merry.

"Very nearly," the yeoman whispered back.

They both ducked involuntarily when something—perhaps a medical text—crashed against the closed door.

Douglas put on his bicorn and walked into the main hall of the administrative block at Stonehouse, the Royal Naval hospital between Plymouth and Devonport. He glanced into various offices as he headed toward the main door, noting that many of them were empty now.

There was a time . . . He stopped, remembering the activity in the building when Napoleon stomped all over Europe, and nothing but the Royal Navy's wooden walls kept him from jumping the Channel for more mischief. Boney had called England a nation of shopkeepers. Had he seen the paperwork flying about, he'd have called England a nation of clerks.

Douglas stood for a longer moment outside the main door, admiring the symmetry of the ward blocks, separate buildings on either side of Admin, connected by graceful colonnades. He had served a brief, involuntary six months at Stonehouse only because he was supposed to be recuperating from a falling mast after a nameless skirmish on the blockade. A month of pain between his shoulders was followed by more pain, as he rose up from his sickbed too soon and assisted the overworked Stonehouse staff. Such was war.

Thinking of his stay, he pulled his cloak closer against cold rain and hurried along the walk to Ward Four, where he had worked. The door wasn't locked, so he went inside, sniffing stale air only, without the overlay of body stench and putrefaction.

"What are you doing?" he asked himself. He walked up the stairs to the first floor, scene of his own incarceration for a month because the officers' block was crammed to overflowing, and his eventual residency for five more as he worked there.

The cots were still in place, and so was the ward nurse's

desk. Douglas Bowden looked from empty cot to empty cot, remembering each wounded seaman—those who lived and those who didn't. It was much the same ordeal he put himself through each night before he slept as he did a mental inventory of some of his more memorable cases and anguished over the men he could not save. And then the dreams followed.

He had asked a fellow surgeon once if he dreamed that way too. The surgeon's reply was a deep sigh, followed by a massive change of subject. Douglas never asked again.

But everyone was gone now. "How about that?" he said out loud as he turned around and went more slowly down the stairs. No smells, no moans, no screams. Why did he still hear them?

Ward Block Five appeared to be occupied. He thought about going inside just to see if he knew the attending surgeon, but it wasn't necessary.

"Doug! I see old Davey Carew did call you in. Aye or nay?"

Captain Owen Brackett stood in the doorway, umbrella in hand. He motioned Douglas inside. The rain pelted harder, reminding him that England in May was a saucy minx, teasing with the bloom of spring one day and striking back with cold rain the next.

They shook hands. Brackett must have spent his whole career at Stonehouse, which was to the advantage of numerous wounded men, Douglas knew.

"'Tis nay, Owen," Douglas said, with a shake of his head. "I couldn't bring myself to take the offer."

"Which was . . . ?"

"Assistant superintendent."

"I turned him down too," Brackett said. "I have my eye on a private practice in Ashton, Kent, and we leave in two weeks. Aggie's idea, and I didn't argue. You ever marry?"

"Never on land long enough to convince some poor lady of my nonexistent charms."

The other surgeon held his umbrella over them both as they continued toward the street. "You can't be a day over forty-five," Brackett told him. "You'll find a willing widow somewhere."

Douglas winced. "I'll be thirty-seven next Tuesday."

"Beg pardon." Brackett recovered quickly and laughed. "Nothing like a constant sea voyage to age a man, eh? You need a little wrinkle salve, that's all."

Douglas smiled at his friend. "I have all my parts, howsomever. I'm thinking about a practice, too, some-place where I cannot see the ocean."

"You know that won't work."

"Certainly it will," Douglas assured him. "I'm weary of water."

Brackett shrugged. He gestured to one of the row houses that the admiral had touted as a main attraction for continued employment in the Royal Navy. "Come inside for luncheon? Aggie will be happy to see you."

Douglas should have said yes. He had nothing more pressing on his schedule than a walk in the rain to Plymouth. He could have hired a hack, but he suddenly longed to be alone as he contemplated his unrelenting wartime career and the unease that peace was bringing.

He begged off, after promising Captain Brackett that he would drop him a line in Ashton when he was settled somewhere. Precisely where, Douglas had no idea yet, but Brackett didn't need to know.

The dockyards still bustled with activity, and always would as long as England needed a navy. Quieter now, the hospital would still function. The turmoil of war had left in its wake a certain sadness that went beyond death and suffering. Douglas did not understand his feelings, except that peace was already proving to be onerous. He knew he could not bear to stay much longer in Plymouth, unwilling to see the worn-out ships—masts and sails gone—placed in ordinary. They were now as superfluous as he was, and he didn't relish watching the end.

He stood another few minutes at the dry docks, which gave him the most concrete indication that the war was over. Of the three docks, a keel had been laid in one, and the other two graving docks were empty. He wondered if the shipwrights and carpenters had retired like him or if they had been dismissed. The ropeworks lay idle.

Improbably, the two miles to Plymouth through still-busy streets cheered him. He was unused to the nearly forgotten pleasure of walking and walking in any direction, unimpeded by a ship's railing. True, he had walked up and down the deck, mulling over this wound, or that amputation, or that scrofulous tumor until he either solved the problem or wore himself out. He knew exactly how many steps in any direction were his allotment on the average frigate of King George.

Satisfied, Douglas watched people at work, laborers passing, children arguing, women hawking fish. He saw ordinary life through new eyes, since it was not ordinary to him.

Once back in the Barbican, that rabbit warren of medieval narrow streets and buildings so old they leaned, Douglas went directly to Carter and Brustein's counting office.

He was ushered in with all usual politeness and welcomed in a few minutes by David Brustein, looking older and grayer than Douglas remembered, but didn't they all? David introduced him to his son, Solomon, a youth still, but evidently learning the family business that began when the late Jonathan Carter took on a Jewish clerk, name of Ezra Brustein.

"Yes, another generation coming up," David said. "How may I help you, Captain Bowden?"

Only a bare half hour served to assure Douglas that his prize money earned through the years was chugging along sturdily and growing his funds at a pleasant rate.

David leaned back in his chair and laced his fingers across an ample chest. "I predict that you will be able to live quite comfortably on the interest alone, Captain, until you are at least one hundred and twenty." He looked heavenward. "God willing."

They laughed, the satisfied sound that men of means can make. Douglas left a few minutes later, his inside breast pocket heavy with sufficient for his needs until such time as he found a permanent home. He bid them a fond good-bye, still amazed, somewhere down deep, that a cooper's son could have done so well. Maybe Napoleon had been good for something, even if the price had been extraordinarily high.

He arrived at the Drake in time for late luncheon, which he knew Mrs. Fillion had held back for him. With fewer officers lingering about the premises these days, she couldn't afford to be less than obliging to latecomers.

After a peek in the empty cardroom, where he reflected on the death of the perpetual game of whist that had lasted through a generation of war, Douglas seated himself in the dining room. Mrs. Fillion started him with her excellent soup, hot and flavorful and worlds better than anything on board ship.

"Leek soup?" he asked, supremely pleased.

"I know how you men like it," she said.

She hesitated a moment, and while she hesitated, Douglas gestured to the chair beside him. Mrs. Fillion was no lady, but she had manners.

"Well, Captain?"

"I turned him down."

"I thought you might."

He appreciated the kindness in her eyes. Maybe they understood one another. Mrs. Fillion had begun her career at the Drake as the scullery maid, and now she owned the property. He had joined the Royal Navy as a loblolly boy, feeding the wounded and emptying urinals. He knew how far from his station in life he had risen, compared to some of the titled officers he had served with. His modest status mattered nothing to Mrs. Fillion, after he saved her second son from pneumonia. Too bad that he died at Trafalgar, but that was war.

He could unbend with Mrs. Fillion. "Trouble is, I have no particular plans, beyond finding a place to live far from the ocean."

She had the same look on her face as Captain Brackett when Douglas had mentioned his miniscule plans.

He waved it away and beat her to the point. "I do not require a view of the ocean to be entirely happy," he assured her.

"We'll see," was all she said.

Chapter 2

*A*FTER A BEASTLY NIGHT, TOSS-
ing around because the bed did not sway
from side to side and his dreams had followed him to Plymouth, Douglas packed his duffle. He
folded the letter of resignation he had written to the Navy
Board and placed it carefully in his inside breast pocket.
He looked around to make sure he had forgotten nothing
and closed the second of several doors on his Royal Navy
career.

Over supper last night, Mrs. Fillion had agreed to keep
his sea trunk in her storeroom until such time as he found
an agreeable place to live, at which event she would send
it to him.

The storeroom had turned him melancholy, lined as it
was with other men's sea trunks, dead men who had left
the Drake for the Channel and died in the service of poor
King George.

"What should I do with these?" Mrs. Fillion had
asked. "When a relative contacts me, I send them on, but
it's been years now."

I could easily have been one of these, he had thought, as

his neck hairs did a little piping jig. No surviving family, no wife, and no children. By the hand of Providence, he had survived the war a generation long.

"Hold an auction, and give the proceeds to the orphanage here."

She nodded. "I expect to hear from you in a month with a direction."

"Aye, Mrs. Fillion," he said and kissed her cheek. "Count on it."

He caught the mail coach two doors down and did not look back as the coach traveled up the hill, away from the Barbican and the port that had figured so prominently in his life and in the life of the nation. Instead, he thought of Plymouth's history as a Royal Navy port and wondered what future surgeons in future wars would think about this cheeky little town that held so many of his memories.

He couldn't ignore the semaphores lining the coastal road. He remembered when the arms on the semaphores wagged their signals up the coast and eventually to London and Portsmouth, bearing news of ship returns and departures, battles won or lost. The arms hung idle now. What was so important in 1816 that needed more speed than a man on horseback or the mail coach?

Douglas leaned back against the lumpy horsehair cushion and closed his eyes, wishing he had wings to fly him away from the tug and pull of Plymouth and the Royal Navy he was so bent on leaving. He felt a deep hole in his heart and knew that he grieved for the loss of many friends and companions, and many ships, and so many dead that he could not save. He hoped his face did not show his sorrow. The mail coach was full, and he did not relish pitying looks.

He opened his eyes to see an old woman sitting opposite, her expression so kind. As he returned her gaze, she leaned forward across the narrow space separating them and patted his knee.

"I lost a husband and son to Napoleon," she whispered, tears glittering in her eyes. "I think you have lost too."

He nodded, unable to speak, but reassured in a way he had not imagined possible. She did not pity him; she understood him. Maybe there would be a village somewhere that would understand and let him just be its surgeon. He closed his eyes and slept, worn out after a sleepless night, and countless other sleepless nights stretching back twenty-five years. When he woke, a Catholic priest sat in her place.

London was much as he remembered it, busy and crowded, the streets reeking with the stink of horse manure. That was one virtue of the sea life—yes, the ships smelled to high heaven too, but it wasn't horse poop.

He secured a hotel frequented by fellow officers and took his letter to the Navy Board. The clerk sighed to see it and looked at him over smudged spectacles.

"Captain, who in the world will take care of our sailors?"

"Someone other than I," Douglas said cheerfully. "I take it you have been dealing with many of these?"

"The number is legion," the clerk said. "Sir."

He was sent to another office, where a second overworked man stamped approval to his desire to sever himself from the Royal Navy; then he sent Douglas on to yet another functionary intent upon changing his mind.

"Captain Bowden, you have no idea how many surgeons have decided to swallow the anchor," Captain Bracewood told him. With reluctance, as though the stamp was too heavy to lift, he suspended it over Douglas's written resignation. When one pleading look went nowhere, Bracewood sighed the sigh of centuries as he stamped, initialed, and dated the letter.

I am a free man, Douglas thought, even as he tried to look properly sympathetic. "Look at it this way, Captain: perhaps there will be another war soon."

That didn't go well. Captain Bracewood's face turned an amazing color not ordinarily found in nature, and he pointed to the door. Douglas snapped off as fine a salute as he had ever executed, did an about-face, and took the hint.

He stayed another week in London, visiting a tailor recommended by his last captain. He commissioned three new civilian suits, more shirts, some ordinary trousers, and a low-crowned beaver hat that he thought looked stupid. He was so used to the intimidation factor of his lofty bicorn that he felt like a midget from Astley's Royal Amphitheatre, which he also visited. He kept one good uniform to be buried in eventually.

A morning at a balloon ascension was followed by a visit to the shabby sheds that housed Lord Elgin's famous marbles. He stayed a long time, walking around the pieces and remembering a visit to Athens when the statues were still in their proper places high up in the Parthenon.

A night in Drury Lane Theatre observing the great Edmund Keane portray Othello had charged his tired brain but mainly served to remind Douglas of his own time spent in Cyprus, doing what he could during an outbreak of diphtheria. Most of his patients had fared no better than Desdemona, which meant he added those Cypriot corpses to his never-ending list when he was supposed to be sleeping.

His most enjoyable bit of tourism took him to the British Museum solely to look at poor dead Sydney Parkinson's magnificent watercolors drawn in Australia and South Sea islands, during one of Captain Cook's voyages. He had to ask a bored clerk to let him see the delicate little beauties, stored in the nether regions of the museum. Douglas admired the exquisite drawings and felt some of the tension leave his shoulders. They reminded him of better times at sea, including a lengthy stopover in Otaheite, with its lovely women. They were not the stuff of nightmare, thank the Almighty; quite the opposite.

When he collected his new clothes at the end of the week, Douglas had to agree that even if he didn't cut a dashing figure—too many wrinkles, hair too gray at thirty-seven—at least he was comfortable, especially in the trousers. Who knew that really good tailors could actually add a little extra fabric to whichever side where a man needed more room?

Then it was back to the mail coach, with his new clothing and the old smallclothes and nightshirt folded carefully into an equally new traveling case. He wore one of his new suits, since his navy days were done. His boat cloak remained useful and would probably never wear out. Back went his one good bicorn into its hatbox, and everything else into his duffel bag. He wore the beaver hat but with regrets.

As usual, he carried his capital knives and medical kit in the same battered leather satchel, which he rested on his lap when the coach was crowded, and set next to him when it was not. All his worldy possessions except for a trunk and box of shells were right there on the Royal Mail, going who knew where.

The rain had let up. He sat back and enjoyed the beauty of an English spring as the coach rocked its way north. The swaying never bothered him, even though one of the passengers turned green and threw up into his hat. This misdemeanor set off a small child and required the coach to stop and the driver's assistant to sluice out the interior. Such was travel.

It was pain in his hinder parts that finally caused Douglas to surrender several days later at Pauling, a village high in the Pennines. He got out, stretched, and looked around, wondering if this was the place for him. Under the discreet protection of his boat cloak, he rubbed his backside, thinking that perhaps he could stay here a few days and make a decision. He had seen a quantity of pleasant villages in the last few days; when had he become so picky?

Wisdom acquired during his journey encouraged him to seek a public house away from the inn where the mail coach stopped. He found such a place in the next block, which fulfilled the requirements of relative silence, and from the odors emanating from the open door, good victuals.

A clean room on the second floor, followed by a meal of stuffed quail and tender asparagus that nearly reduced him to tears, affirmed his choice. He followed it with ale the golden color reminiscent of the hair of a woman he knew in the Baltics, and then local cheese, one piece after another until he almost hurt himself.

Since the sky still held some color, he did what he usually did and climbed the nearest hill. He stood at the summit and looked in vain for a glimpse of ocean. He walked down, nodding his head, and then retired to his bed, made cozy with a thoughtful warming pan. His dreams were no worse than usual, but certainly no better.

He slept through the sound of the mail coach leaving and woke to more kitchen fragrances. The innkeep had said something last night about thick slabs of bacon and shirred eggs with cheese. Douglas smelled bread and put his hands behind his head, thinking of a piece the size of a Portuguese roof tile, slathered with butter.

He stayed two more days in Pauling, walking the countryside. When Douglas inquired, the innkeep told him with a sorrowful shake of his head that there was no physician or surgeon any closer than ten miles.

"You don't look pieced out and ruinated, sir," the keep ventured.

"I'm as healthy as they come," Douglas assured him. "I'm a surgeon just retired from the Royal Navy and looking for a place that needs a doctor."

"We're it, then, sir," he said, his expression brightening. "Wait'll I tell the missus and the vicar!"

"Hold off, man. I haven't quite decided," Douglas cautioned. "Just give me another day."

He used that day to walk by a deserted stone house, two stories, just across the street from the inn. He even went around back to look in the windows, gratified to see sound floors. He could have an office, waiting room, and surgery on the main floor, and he suspected two bedchambers upstairs, one for him and the other for a patient who might require closer observation.

When he inquired at the inn, the keep told him that the local magistrate owned the house. He gave Douglas directions to the man's house and looked at him expectantly.

"Tomorrow is soon enough to decide," Douglas warned him.

"You don't rush into things, do you, sir?" the keep asked.

Douglas thought of all the surgeries and frantic first aid on a bloody deck that he had rushed into. "On occasion I do," he said. "I've never owned a house or set down roots before."

The keep pushed a glass of golden ale toward him. "Tomorrow's soon enough."

Douglas didn't argue. He drank slowly, savoring the bright taste of the ale as he rolled it around his mouth. Something in the back of his brain suggested to him that he should be more eager to visit the magistrate, now that he had found the perfect setting for the rest of his life's work.

After supper—shepherd's pie with crust so flaky that he ate too much—Douglas walked up the tallest hill again, wondering why he kept doing that. Pauling met every need. Why this blasted hill? Still he climbed.

The same view met his gaze, rolling hills, covered now with the white blooms of hawthorn, sheep, and little lambs capering about on stiff legs, without even a glimpse of the ocean.

Suddenly he knew. Both Mrs. Fillion and Captain

Brackett had been absolutely correct. He tipped his head back to look at the sky and laughed at his folly.

"Douglas Bowden, you are a fool," he said out loud. A ram on the other side of the fence glared at him. "You can no more live without a view of the ocean than a dolphin."

That was it, plain as day. He came down the hill more slowly, shaking his head over his own idiocy. When he came in sight of the inn, he hoped that the innkeeper had kept his word and not said anything. Douglas reckoned he hadn't. Good publicans could generally be trusted with all manner of drunken secrets, or in his case, stupid ideas.

As it turned out, the man hadn't breathed a word. Douglas asked for another glass of ale and told the keep to pour one for himself. Elbows on the counter, Douglas offered his confession that he would be more likely to grow gills than live without a view of the ocean.

His drinking companion took it philosophically, which meant another glass for each of them.

"What now, sir?" the keep asked, after a discreet belch.

"I'm not one to backtrack. It's bad luck," Douglas said. "Thoughts?"

The innkeep looked at the spout. "Are you still shouting?"

"Aye. Pour away."

He topped himself another one and drank, leaving foam on his upper lip. "Keep going north and then turn a bit west."

"That's it?"

"Aye. Scotland."

Douglas blinked. "That's the best you can do?" he teased as the fumes tunneled into his brain. Getting up tomorrow was going to be a sore trial.

"If Scotland can't cure what ails you, you're hopeless, sir."

"What ails me, my good man?"

"Too much peace all at once."

Chapter 3

*H*E CROSSED THE SCOTTISH border in the rain, which, all things considered, was appropriate. He had heard rumors about Scottish weather from the first luff of the Corinthian, when they were stuck without wind in the South Seas and sitting practically bare in their smallclothes on the deck years back.

"Nobody in my village would believe this much sun," the luff had said. "I swear it rains every day at home. Thank the Almighty that I joined the Royal Navy and discovered sun." He had laughed and turned over, to toast the other side. "Did'ye not know that God is Scottish? Frugal with the sun."

Douglas smiled at the memory as the coach bowled along. He had left the Royal Mail behind in Carlisle and trundled his goods into a less colorful bonecracker that took him to Gretna Green, a town famous for marriages over the blacksmith's anvil. He looked around with interest, but no one appeared to be lined up for matrimony.

He spent the night at Dumfries. In the morning, this innkeep, in his well nigh impenetrable brogue, informed him of an even smaller carriage headed south to Dundrennan and on to the Gatehouse of Fleet on Solway Firth. The helpful man may have suggested other routes, but Douglas was already having second thoughts about trying to live and work where he could barely understand the natives.

Still, the clouds lifted to show off the Firth of Solway. Douglas saw little fishing boats, nets stretched behind them, trolling the cold water. He felt his whole body relax and his respirations slow down because he knew he was watching salt water again.

Luncheon in Dundrennan was a hurried affair, with the coachman itching to make up time lost lollygagging behind a flock of sheep. Douglas ate what looked like a pasty, all crisp and light brown, but with the disturbing taste of liver, mutton, and oats that he knew he would be belching up for at least a week.

He checked Scottish food off his mental list. He had eaten far worse in his years with the fleet. *I could stand by a window in my dining room, eat this loathsome fare, and still have a view of the ocean*, he thought, which made him smile.

Before they left Dundrennan, he asked the coachman if the little town had any physicians.

"Och, aye! Twa. And aren't they always going after each other's patients?" the man exclaimed. "They've divided the town clean in half!"

Douglas crossed Dundrennan off his mental list as he began to wonder if Scotland was a good idea after all. "Tell me, please, about the other towns on this route?"

He shrugged. "There's Wilcomb, a bonny place if you don't mind smugglers; Castle McPherson, ditto; Whitby, where the people are daft, half of them; Edgar . . ." He stopped, as if trying to think of something kind to say about Edgar. "Smells like fish." He brightened. "Miss Grant's Tearoom." He leaned closer. "I've seen grown men weep over her lemon curd, although I am partial to orange marmalade."

"I've never considered settling in a place just because of a tearoom," Douglas joked.

"I suppose many a man has said just that," the coachman joked in turn. His face turned serious then. "Nay, not Edgar for you. It's a poor fishing village. You'd mentioned physicians. Lad, if you're in need of one, you'll die before ye find one close to the likes of Edgar." He rubbed both his thumbs and forefingers together. "Doctors need money like us all."

"No money in Edgar?"

"Nay. A physician there would get no more than herring and neeps in payment."

Douglas gave the grimace that he knew was expected of him, but didn't cross Edgar off his mental list. He could at least try Miss Grant's lemon curd on some toast so the stop wouldn't be a total waste.

The coachman glanced at his timepiece and evidently discovered he had no more time to discuss Scotland's more obscure destinations. He hurried three old ladies into his carriage and asked Douglas to help him heave his traveling case and duffel on top, where they were strapped down. He shook his head over the odd-shaped hatbox with the Royal Navy fouled anchor embossed on the side. "What in blazes is this?" he asked as he tied it down.

"My bicorn. I'm recently severed from the Royal Navy," Douglas said. "Looking for a place to settle down."

"And ye came here?" the coachman asked in amazement. "Laddie, good thing I warned ye about the fish and rain and poor folk." He chuckled and climbed into his box. "Weren't you listening to me?" he called down.

Maybe I should consider Whitby, where only half the people are daft, Douglas thought, wondering why a reasonably intelligent man should suddenly turn stupid once out of the Royal Navy. He seated himself next to one of the ladies, a thin one, who still frowned at the space his medical satchel took up. He sighed inwardly and put it on his lap, vowing to travel north to Glasgow tomorrow and inquire about passage to Canada.

Still, he found his gaze lingering on the view outside the little coach's window: low hills that particular shade of green that meant spring in the British Isles, a sight he had not seen in years. To look the other way meant to watch the firth, which would do for the ocean. He saw fish and kelp drying on racks and children running along the shore barefoot, for the most part, even though the air was chilly and damp. *Tough people, these Scots,* he thought.

The hour lacked half to noon when they turned slightly north and paralleled a river. They crossed on a stone bridge that arched so prettily over the water. The arch was pronounced enough to suggest that fishing boards could likely travel underneath.

Still training north, the carriage bumped over a marginal road for another vertebrae-compressing mile, then slowed. He tried to peer ahead and was rewarded with the view of a village, nothing as charming as Dundrennan, with its competitive physicians. This was a sturdy, no-nonsense-looking town, but with pastel-colored stone houses that surprisingly reminded him of the Italian coast.

He looked at the thin woman seated next to him. He hadn't said a word to her or any of them, because they hadn't been introduced, but he asked, "Is this Edgar?"

She nodded, and no more. He tried his luck again. "And the river?"

"Dee," she said, either marvelously frugal with words, or determined not to speak to an upstart she didn't know; probably it was both.

He smiled inside, wondering that if it had been the Albemarle River if she would only have said "Alb," figuring that was all courtesy demanded.

"Home of Miss Grant's peerless lemon curd?" he asked the other travelers in general, idly wondering if any of these serious-faced ladies would unbend.

One of them opened her mouth—whether to reply or shush him—when the coachman pulled to a sudden stop. Douglas looked out the window, drew in his breath, and was out the door before the wheels quit rolling, already yanking at his neck cloth.

A woman far gone in pregnancy stood in the road, screaming for help, as she carried a boy too big to lift, but whose oddly bent leg spurted blood.

"Set him down," Douglas demanded.

The woman stared at him with terrified eyes, almost as though she did not understand what he demanded. When she made no move, Douglas grabbed the boy from her and laid him in the road, swiftly tightening his cravat two inches above the wound where a snapped bone protruded. The boy, pale as milk, stared at him, then quietly fainted.

"I'm a surgeon," he told the woman as she tugged at his arm. "Leave me be!"

She understood him now. She sank down beside him, her bloody hands to her face. "I've been telling and telling my man to fix the stone steps to the cellar, but does he ever do anything but drink?"

By now, heads were popping out of store doorways. They drew back in as a man staggered toward Douglas, a stick in his hand, which he slammed down on the woman's back, shouting in a language Douglas recognized as Gaelic.

Douglas leaped to his feet and grabbed the stick, forcing the man backward until he fell down in a sodden heap and made no move to get up. Douglas handed the stick to the woman, probably the drunkard's wife. "Use it on him if he makes a move."

"I daren't," she said softly.

"I wouldn't mind," the coachman said as he got down from his box and took the stick from her.

Douglas turned back to his unconscious patient, relieved to see that his jury-rigged tourniquet had done its duty. He took a long look at the compound fracture.

"I can reduce this," he told the boy's mother. "Which is your house?"

She pointed to a stone building with an unpainted door open and hanging onto its hinges for dear life. She struggled to her feet until Douglas gave her a hand up. Disturbed, he looked around at the small crowd, wondering why no one offered to help.

"What's the matter with people here?" he asked the coachman in a low voice.

"No one lifts a finger for Highlanders," he replied. "Nobody wants them."

"I was better off at sea," Douglas muttered under his breath. He picked up the boy and carried him toward the hovel faintly disguised as a house.

The mother hurried ahead of him and opened the door wider. He stood on the threshold, stared at the filth within, and turned around.

"Madam, I wouldn't put a dog in there," he snapped. "The poor beast would die of infection."

Uncertain what to do, he walked back to the coachman. "Do you know . . . is there someplace clean in this pathetic village where I can treat this child?"

The coachman shook the stick at the man lying on the road, who was beginning to groan. "Wouldn't know, sir. I just drive through to the Hare and Hound. It's a noisy inn. You wouldn't want to tend him there."

"Can anyone here tell me where to take this boy?" Douglas asked, pitching his voice to hurricane strength, a voice used to shouting orders to be heard above the roar of cannons and the shrieks of wounded men on a bloody deck.

"Only one place for you to take Tommy Tavish," one hardy soul told him, stepping out from the growing crowd. "'Tis Miss Olive Grant's Tearoom."

"Where?"

"Follow me."

Chapter 4

*J*T'S A RARE DELEGATION, COMIN'
down the road. I don't think it's luncheon they'll
be after."

"My goodness, you're right," Olive Grant said to her
customer.

Olive brushed her fingers against her spotless apron,
the lace one she changed to once the luncheon simmered
on the hob or roasted in the Rumford. She stepped into
the doorway, door open to receive diners, now that the
weather had turned warmer, and stared at the crowd
coming her way.

Only an imbecile would have gaped in wonder, and
Olive was no imbecile. A swift glance took in a tall man
carrying a limp child in his arms. She looked closer at the
bloody bandage, the foot turning in a direction not generally achievable, and then bones. She gulped and spoke to
her scullery maid, not taking her eyes from the strange
parade coming closer.

"Maeve! Take that piece of canvas from the scullery.
You know the one. Put it on the little bed upstairs. Hurry
now!"

Olive took a deep breath and stepped outside in time to hold the door wider as the tall man came inside. Because staring at the wounded child made her queasy, she looked at the man instead. What she saw reassured her. There was nothing in his expression of terror or worry, merely calm competence. She let her breath out slowly, less afraid.

"Someone told me this was the cleanest place in town," he said by way of introduction.

"Next to Lady Telford's big house, I daresay this is true," she said, gesturing toward the stairs. "First door on the right."

He didn't hesitate to move swiftly up the stairs, calling over his shoulder, "Hot water, please, and towels." She held her breath, but he ducked just in time to avoid banging his head on the turn of the stairs.

She hurried to do as he ordered and nearly ran into Mrs. Tavish, eyes wild and hands and face bloody. Olive took the woman by her arm and steered her in the direction of the kitchen, ignoring disapproving glances as she wished some of her fellow townsmen were less judgmental.

She sat Tommy's mother down and reached for a cloth dipped in the hot water that Maeve, bless her reliable heart, had already poured into a deep basin. Olive squeezed out the towel and pressed it to Mrs. Tavish's face, thinking to herself that there was as much grime as blood. The woman held the cloth to her face, taking comfort from the warmth.

Olive turned to Maeve. "Pour her tea and make her tidy," she ordered. "I am going upstairs."

Olive put several towels in the crook of her arm and picked up the basin. Minding her steps, she hurried up the familiar stairs, avoiding the squeaky treads from habit, and entered the room.

The tall man had taken bandage scissors to the unconscious boy's trousers. Olive set down the basin on the little table beside the bed and draped the towels over the headboard. She saw the man's open leather satchel, which had other scissors and tools she didn't recognize, or possibly chose not to.

"I am Olive Grant," she said. "And you, sir?"

"Captain Douglas Bowden," he said without turning around. "Well, no, I am merely Douglas Bowden now, but I am a surgeon."

He turned around then and gave her such a direct look, the kind of earnest inquiry she hadn't seen since her father was alive.

"Are you squeamish, Miss Grant?" he asked.

"Aye," she admitted, but then set the record straight. "However, I do not flinch from duty." *Honestly, Olive,* she thought, exasperated with herself. *You sound like a ninny.*

He smiled then. "I could have used a plain speaker like you during the war and saved myself enormous amounts of time. I need you now. Will you please keep the twist tight on my neck cloth?"

She looked at his neck, then realized he meant the bloody scrap he must have tightened around the boy's leg.

She would have been embarrassed, but he wasn't going to let her. "I don't think any amount of laundry soap will ever make this clean again," he told her, entirely at ease. "Put your fingers right by mine. Underneath them now. Keep up the pressure on the knot."

Their hands touched and she tightened her grip when he let go.

"Excellent!" he said and rummaged in his satchel. He was even humming, which made her smile, even as she kept her grip on the ghastly tourniquet and wished she did not have to contemplate the bone ends protruding from torn skin.

"Are you going to have to . . . to . . . oh, my . . . amputate?" Better to know now, even if he thought her an idiot because her voice squeaked.

"Not if I can help it," he said cheerfully.

25

With a clink of metal on metal, he pulled another pair of scissors from a cloth pouch he unrolled with one hand. Olive gasped and looked away from the saw and knives even longer than those in her kitchen, and probably sharper.

"My capital knives," he said. "I won't need them, except for this little bistoury. Hand me a small towel."

She did as he asked with her free hand. He spread the towel by the boy's leg and set the little curved knife on it, and the scissors.

"What . . . what . . ." Her mouth just wasn't working.

"I'm going to lengthen this laceration a little, then snap that bone back in place. Young ones fare better from this sort of injury. Then I'll start suturing. Hmm. Reach under my arms and see if you can find a bodkin about four inches long."

She did as he asked, closer to a man than she had ever been in her life.

"There it is. Here now." He teased her bloody fingers away from the improvised tourniquet and twisted in the steel bodkin, anchoring it with strips of bandage plaster. "It'll stay in place now. I need your hands."

Olive looked at him, struck again by his pleasant attitude, as her stomach did little flops. He even seemed to be enjoying himself.

"At least you introduced yourself," she grumbled, which made him laugh.

"You don't do surgery here more than once or twice a day?" he teased, which had the effect of slowing down her racing heart and steadying those hands he thought he needed.

"You, sir, are trying me," she said. "What do you want me to do?"

He pulled out one thin steel instrument with two hooks on the end. "Tenaculum," he said as he handed it to her. "Go around on the other side of poor little Tommy Tavish and pull back the skin."

She did as he said, tears in her eyes, fearful for Tommy. "I'm hurting him," she whispered.

"He's unconscious," the surgeon reminded her. "If he comes around before I'm done, and I'll work fast, just drop the tenaculum and hold him down."

He must have seen the fear in her face, because Mr. Bowden or Captain Bowden or whatever he was put his free hand over hers and squeezed. "You're a bonny lass," he said, "and that's all the Scottish I know."

She had to laugh, her fear shoved back into a dark corner. The tenaculum tidily held back the skin. She watched in growing admiration as the surgeon worked quickly, every move decisive. She gasped when he snapped the bone in place and dabbed at the blood where he pointed.

She was aware that Maeve, her eyes huge, had come into the room, carrying more water in a brass can. The surgeon must have seen her from the corner of his eye.

"Aha! I need you too. You are . . ."

"Maeve Gibson," the child quavered.

"Maeve, Maeve, what a pretty name," Douglas Bowden said. "If I had a daughter, I would name her Maeve, but I would need a wife first, all things considered."

Maeve put her hand to her mouth and giggled, the terror leaving her eyes. Olive looked at the surgeon, wondering how he knew just what to say.

He turned to Olive. "Can you spare a bed slat?"

"Take one from the end of my bed," she told Maeve.

The child darted from the room and returned in a few moments with the length of wood.

"Excellent!" Douglas Bowden said as he continued to dab gently around the black sutures. "Is there a crowd assembled downstairs, my dear?"

"Tha wouldn't believe the size of it," Maeve declared.

"Take this slat and find a capable-looking man. I can recommend the coachman, if you're at a loss." He turned to Olive. "My dear, do you have an ax in your woodpile?"

"Indeed I do. How long do you want the splint?" Olive said.

"Twelve inches, for one, and three times that for the other. Maeve, can you do this? All of Scotland is depending on you."

The scullery maid flashed him a smile and tore down the stairs with the slat.

"You are a remarkable manager of people," Olive told him.

"I get what I want," he replied, all complaisance, because he meant it. "He's coming around, Miss Grant. It is Miss, isn't it?"

"Indeed it is."

Why that should have made her face go warm, Olive Grant couldn't have said. She was thirty years old and long an antique virgin. No need to feel embarrassed about her lot in life. She turned her attention to Tommy, who was starting to moan now and tossing his head.

"Just sit down by his head and put your arms around him," the surgeon said simply. "Just hug him. It feels so good when someone is terrified."

By the time Tommy opened his eyes, Olive's arms were tight around him. He was dirty and smelly, with hair so greasy that she should have been repelled. She felt Tommy's long, shuddering sigh, followed by a sob, and then silence, as the surgeon put his hands gently on both sides of the boy's face.

"You've been as brave as men I have cared for in the middle of battles," Douglas Bowden said. "Tommy Tavish, you're a wonder. Just hold still now, that's a good lad."

Maeve pounded up the stairs, followed by Tommy's mother, moving slowly, exhausted with such effort in her late pregnancy. Olive ran next door to her own room and brought back a chair. Mrs. Tavish sank down gratefully, her face a study in worry and fright. Tears filled her eyes, but she remained silent.

"Can you spare a sheet?" the surgeon asked. "I have bandages, but I need more."

Olive sent Maeve to the linen closet. In a moment, Olive was ripping one of her lovely sheets into three-inch-wide strips. Working with sure hands, careful not to hurt Tommy, Mr. Bowden bound the splints in place, the smaller one inside Tommy's leg, and the longer one outside, going all the way from his ankle nearly to his armpit.

"I can't move," Tommy said, fearful again.

"Precisely," Mr. Bowden told him. "After a few days like this, if all is well, I'll get a smaller splint for the outside."

"But if I can't . . . how can I . . ." Tommy's face grew red.

"Not a worry, lad," the surgeon told him. "I'll take care of you."

Olive felt her eyes fill with tears then, because she knew this stranger, this confident, capable man she hadn't known an hour ago, would do exactly that. She couldn't help her tears then, but Mr. Bowden took it all in stride. He motioned her closer. She stood up and walked right under his outstretched arm.

He hugged her, and then Maeve on the other side, both of them in tears.

"Watering pots," he murmured. "Just watering pots. Do all Scottish women remain firm in the crisis and fall apart later? I like that order of things."

Chapter 5

*N*O ARGUMENT; HE DID LIKE that. How Miss Grant managed to smell so sweetly of vanilla scent, even after embracing as filthy a little boy as he had ever tended and in a room awash with blood, Douglas couldn't have said. Long experience had taught him to take what came, with appropriate rejoicing.

She freed herself quickly from his impromptu embrace, but she smiled, so he knew he had not offended her. She touched his heart when she went to Tommy with a clean cloth dipped in warm water from the brass can and wiped his face, his dirty neck, and then his arms, crusted with what looked like fish leavings. *Tommy must be a dock boy*, Douglas decided.

"May I fetch him some food?" she asked.

Tommy's eyes had been closing. At the word *food*, they opened and he nodded. Douglas saw the hunger in them, which even eclipsed the pain of a compound fracture. *How to do this without shaming the lad?* Douglas thought a moment.

"Tommy, I know you hurt, and I am going to give you a sleeping draught," he began. "When did you last eat?"

Tommy glanced at his silent mother. "I don't remember," he said finally, the words dragged out of him.

Douglas considered his little patient, an independent being, unlike the men of the Royal Navy, who had to take what he dished out. He looked into the boy's eyes again, and suddenly knew what he was doing. It had nothing to do with him but everything to do with his mother.

"I know you're hungry, and so is your mam," Douglas told him. "If you can stand the pain for a little while, we can probably convince Miss Grant to bring up some food for you and your mother. Draughts and food don't mix well."

Douglas saw the deep gratitude in Tommy's eyes and found it difficult to continue. Good thing he needed to make a slight adjustment to the splint just then, an adjustment precisely long enough to allow him to collect his feelings.

"That's better. Can't leave these little things untended," Douglas said finally. "If you eat something now, you and your mam, you'll have to wait another hour before I give you that sleeping draught. Personally, I think that best, if you can manage the pain, lad."

"I can manage," the boy whispered.

"Excellent." Douglas knew better than to look at Miss Grant, so he fiddled with that splint again. When he finally looked in Miss Grant's direction, she was gathering up bits of bloody lint that needed no attention at the moment. *What silly beings we are*, he thought, grateful for human kindness.

Miss Grant was obviously made of sterner stuff than he had thought, considering her reluctance around blood. She turned to Mrs. Tavish. "I have so much to do. If my scullery maid and I bring some food up here for you and Tommy, could you feed him while we are busy elsewhere?"

Perfect, he thought, *perfect. The two of them can eat without an audience watching them wolf down a meal.* "I will echo that, Mrs. Tavish." Douglas indicated the scissors, suturing needle, bistoury, and catgut. "I'll take all this downstairs while you eat and I wash my instruments. They must be cared for immediately. Will you help us by feeding Tommy?"

Mrs. Tavish nodded, her eyes less haunted. He saw something in them of anticipation and maybe even hope. He doubted supremely that anything good had happened to her in years. *Let it be a handsome bit of food, Miss Grant*, he thought.

Miss Grant clapped her hands. "Brilliant! Maeve and I will only be a few minutes. I so appreciate your help, Mrs. Tavish. Come, Maeve." She left the room with her scullery maid.

Moved to the depths of his heart, Douglas gathered together the untidy pieces of his profession and put them in the leather satchel. "I'll be up in an hour with that sleeping draught," he said, and he left the room. He gave a nod to Mrs. Tavish. "Mind he doesn't gulp his food. I'm relying on you."

He saw the poor woman straighten her back. "I can take care of my son," she said with a touch of pride, probably another emotion in short shrift in the Tavish household.

Grateful for the ladies, he went downstairs slowly. His heart softened again to see a dining room full of people eating, served by what looked like friends who had come to gawk a bit, then stayed to serve meals to Miss Grant's customers, in lieu of her absence. He went into the kitchen in time to see the proprietor dabbing at her eyes as she loaded two plates with more food than either Tavish had probably seen in donkey's years.

"A little less on each plate. I try not to overfeed starving folk," he admonished. Strange that he thought he knew her heart already, and so he told her. "Miss Grant, I have not known you outside of an hour, but I am confident you will find a way to give Mrs. Tavish more to eat. I hazard a guess that you are probably even a bit of a bully, when it comes to nourishing the starving."

She nodded, tears in her eyes. "Do you ever want to help the whole world, Captain?" she asked.

"Only my entire life," he assured her. "We'll start small here in Edgar."

What in blazes am I implying? he asked himself, horrified, as Miss Grant and Maeve covered the plates with cloths and left the kitchen. Hungry himself, he looked in the largest pot and salivated to see meat, onions, and potatoes in a brown sauce. He found a bowl and spoon and helped himself.

"You're useful and you cook," he said softly. He finished and left a handful of coins on the serving table.

He stayed in the kitchen, nodding to the earnest ladies serving Miss Grant's noontime meals to what probably constituted her usual clientele, older men and women of modest means who relied on the capable woman with the soft heart. He didn't see more than small coins left on tables.

Miss Grant and Maeve came into the kitchen in short order. She quickly put the scullery maid to work gathering dishes from the dining room and then sat down at the serving table. He watched her struggle, and then handed her his handkerchief.

She kept the cloth to her face for a long moment and finally blew her nose. "Mrs. Tavish couldn't even wait until we left the room. Oh, Captain, she almost fell on that food!" She put her hand to her mouth until she gained some control. "And Tommy—he's in such pain, but he is hungrier."

"It's a poor village," he said.

He took a liberty and got another bowl from the cabinet. He filled it with stew and set it in front of Miss Grant. "You're an excellent cook, by the way," he told her.

"Just a simple stew for the middle of the week," she replied, but he heard the pride in her voice. "I cook mainly for pensioners, Highlanders who aren't too prideful, and the odd visitor who drops by and saves a little boy's life."

"So I am the odd visitor," he teased.

She laughed. "Oh, you know what I mean!" Her face grew serious and she set down her spoon. "I do not know where you are going, Captain, but I do hope you can remain here a few days for Tommy."

"Certainly I will," he replied, startled that she would think anything else. She blushed and he realized she had never had any dealings with doctors. "It's what sawbones do, Miss Grant," he explained. "I would no more leave now than walk barefoot on spikes."

"Thank you," she said simply and picked up her spoon again.

"Highlanders?" he asked. "Here?"

"They were dumped on Edgar two years ago, and no one quite knows what to do with them. I feed some, but the others are so proud, or shamed." She shook her head and he saw her frustration. "We don't understand them."

Dumped here? Douglas realized he knew nothing about Scotland. He left Miss Grant to eat in peace and went through the dining room, looking for the coachman. One of the diners told him the man was long gone. His luggage had been left in the tearoom's snug entry hall.

He stood for a long moment in the open door, looking at Edgar, with its lovely pastel-painted stone houses and businesses. Just beyond, he watched the fishing boats near the mouth of the River Dee, but on the seawaters of the Firth of Solway. He saw the ruined castle on the hill and a mansion a little closer to the village. A bell in the church tower rang two times. He watched a woman pruning her roses, nodding to a passerby on the other side of the low stone wall surrounding her tidy house. He looked up at seagulls wheeling overhead, then swooping down to the dockside to join the squabble of other gulls waiting less than patiently for the fishmongers to gut and clean the catch.

It was a village ordinary and poor, if people like the Tavishes existed, and pensioners found it cheaper to eat at Miss Grant's Tearoom than manage their own kitchens. Probably things were better in the approaching summer, when little garden plots could be tended and provide some variety from what he suspected was a diet of oats and fish. Winter would be the hungry time, but he imagined this village at Christmas, when there would probably be carols sung and some kindness shown to the poor from those only slightly better off.

He shook his head. Edgar would never do, of course, but he wasn't going to leave until Tommy was better. He would find a more prosperous village farther on. Still, the apple trees were in bloom in Edgar, and he did like the sound of the gulls. He saw little girls skipping rope and chanting a rhyme he couldn't quite hear but which reminded him of his own dear sister, dead from childbirth, these ten years. He noticed other little girls standing in the shadows, just watching, not invited to jump rope. Perhaps they were Highland children.

Captain Douglas Bowden, surgeon, late of the Royal Navy, looked around and saw a simple village, one of thousands he had done his best to keep safe from Napoleon, and it touched his heart. "We did it for you," he said to the distant little girls. "We would do it again."

Thoughtful, he walked into the street and then back the way the coach had come. Tommy Tavish's father still lay in a sodden heap, snoring off a monumental drunk as chickens pecked around him. Douglas came closer and toed him. Nothing. He squatted by the man's head and put practiced fingers to a filthy neck, hunting for a pulse. He found it, and thought it almost a pity that such a man would sober up and likely get angry because his put-upon wife committed some non-existent infraction that war-ranted a kick or a slap, never mind that she was greatly pregnant. Punishment would follow dreary punishment until the end of their already sorry lives.

He stood up and found himself looking at whom he thought must be the constable, from the truncheon he carried. "What do you do with a man like this?" Douglas asked.

"Lately I just leave him in the street to come to him-self. Sometimes it rains—this being Scotland—and I hope he will die of t'lung ailment." The constable shrugged his shoulders. "A man can hope, anyways. Hasn't happened yet, though."

"I have to salute your plain speaking," Douglas said. "Can a man like this be put away somewhere to rot?"

"Sadly, no," the constable answered, with a sorrowful shake of his head. "He would have to kill someone . . ."

He let the sentence trail away, but Douglas felt the unspoken chill. And who would die except his wife and son?

The constable seemed like a fount of realism. He could stand candid conversation. "At sea, someone could drop his worthless hide overboard during a night watch, to no one's regret," Douglas said. "Don't think it hasn't happened."

The constable nodded. "The coachman, he told me you were Royal Navy, asking about doctors and such." He peered at Douglas. "You patched up young Tommy. Stay here, laddie. We have a need."

"I'll stay here until Tommy feels better," Douglas hedged.

The constable nodded, evidently philosophical as well as realistic. He stuck out his hand. "Let me at least thank ye for what you've done."

They shook hands and Douglas continued to the Tavish hovel. He opened the door and stood a long while, contemplating the ruin within. *I was better off at sea*, he thought, wondering where a surgeon would start in a backward place like Edgar, or even if a surgeon—not him, of course—would have any power to deal with a sorry sack like Tommy's father.

He heard scratching under a pile of reeking bedding and wondered for one terrible moment if there were other Tavish children hiding and hungry. To his relief, a rail-thin black pup nosed his way toward daylight and wagged his tail, ever optimistic in that way of dogs of a certain age.

Douglas held out his hand, and the pup edged toward him, suggesting to the surgeon that Tavish senior had already applied some well-placed kicks to the little fellow to cow him. In another moment Douglas rubbed the pup behind his ears, which made his tail wag at a velocity that nearly overset him.

Douglas debated about eight seconds whether to leave the little beast to the tender mercies of Mr. Tavish, who probably would have no memory of where his terrified family had gone and react accordingly. He made an executive decision, picking up the pup and tucking him in his arm.

"Miss Grant, you have just acquired an eventual watchdog," he said.

Chapter 6

*H*IS WAS A THOUGHTFUL WALK back down the High Street to Miss Grant's Tearoom, encumbered as he was with a no-hoper pup without a single thing going for him, who still managed to wag his tail. The encumbrance came with the realization that Miss Grant might not care for a dog on the premises, especially one as bedraggled as the Tavishes already in temporary residence.

He held the dog out for a better look. "I will tell Miss Grant that you leaped into my arms to escape bears," he said, glancing around first to make sure that no one stood close by to hear him talking to the malnourished little scrap. "You could use a bath and a haircut." He chuckled. "Come to think of it, so could I."

He had second and third thoughts about his impulsive act. Since Edgar was a small village, there wasn't time for fourth thoughts before he opened the door to Miss Grant's Tearoom. "Here goes, you mutt," he whispered. "Look sagacious and competent."

"You're talking to a dog," was Miss Grant's first

comment, as she eyed the trembling little beast in his arms. "And he doesn't smell good."

Oh, what now? he thought, not knowing this freckled woman well enough to throw himself on her mercy, especially as she was already housing his first patient in Edgar. And there he went again, implying that Edgar was going to be his future home.

He took a closer look at her in better light than upstairs and was instantly charmed. "My stars, Miss Grant, you're heterochromatic."

He could have slapped his head, but he chose honesty, since nothing else was going to succeed.

"I am an idiot too," he said. "All that means is that you have a . . ." He looked closer, because it wasn't so obvious. ". . . a blue eye and a brown one: heterochromia."

She stared at him, and then laughed. "I never knew it had a name. There was an old herb woman in Edgar once who crossed the street to avoid me."

"It's certainly not contagious," he said, happy she was ignoring the pup squirming in his arms now. "Although if that had happened six hundred years ago, you might have been burned at the stake. A pity, but there you are."

She shook her head, her heterochromatic eyes merry. "Captain . . ."

"Mister . . ."

". . . Mister Bowden, is this what passed for small talk in your ship's wardroom?"

"No. Only in Stonehouse, where surgeons congregate and have as little small talk as I." He looked down at the pup. "I stopped at the Tavish's miserable house just as this pitiful specimen burrowed out from under truly nasty blankets." He remembered his own childhood. "Miss Grant, may I keep him?"

She didn't try to hide her smile, so he knew she must have used the same ploy on her parents, years ago. "Only if you promise to take care of him."

"I couldn't leave him there. He's as thin as the rest of them, and I don't think Mr. Tavish will be inclined to charity, when he finds his family gone."

"Set him down, Mr. Bowden. I think he . . ."

They watched as the nameless pup sniffed the air, probably breathing in wonderful fragrances from the kitchen, even though the luncheon hour had long passed. But no, another sniff, and he headed for the stairs, doing his purposeful best, even though he wobbled with hunger and ill-use.

"He's a loyal little brute," Miss Grant said softly. "He's starving, but he's trying to find his boy. Pick him up, Mr. Bowden, and take him upstairs. I will find some kitchen scraps and follow you."

Douglas did as she said, marveling yet again at the kindness of women. He opened the door quietly to see Mrs. Tavish dozing, and Tommy squinting at the ceiling as though he ached even to open his eyes all the way. He glanced sideways, in too much pain to even turn his head.

"Looks like I'm not a minute too soon, lad," Douglas whispered. "I brought you a friend."

He set the pup down on Tommy's bed, hoping the critter wouldn't jostle the boy, but trusting in the kindness of dogs.

His trust was not misplaced. After a sniff of the splints, the pup heaved a sigh that shook his skinny frame and curled up on Tommy's good side, well within reach of the boy's hand, which came down heavily and stayed there.

"How is it they know?" Miss Grant said from the doorway, bowl in hand. She set it on the bed, close to the pup, who fell on the food almost as eagerly as the Tavishes had devoured their meal. "What's his name, Tommy?"

"Duke," the boy said through clenched teeth. "After Wellington."

"That's a lot of name for not much," Douglas said as he washed his hands and dried them on a towel which Miss

Grant, thoughtful woman, had brought upstairs with her. "You have the makings of an excellent pharmacist's mate," he told her.

Miss Grant rolled her heterochromatic eyes at him. "I am no nurse! Your small talk truly leaves a great deal to be desired."

"It's not likely to change," he admitted. "I am thirty-seven and set in my ways."

She was a tease. "I would have thought you older, Mr. Bowden," she told him, taking back the towel and draping it over the footboard to dry.

Joking or not, she knew just what to do when he approached the bed with a glass of dark liquid in his hand. She put her hand behind Tommy's head and raised him up so gently that he scarcely had time to groan. Down went the draught, and not a drop spilled.

"That's it for now," he told Tommy, his hand on the boy's forehead. "You're going to sleep for a long while, and when you come up, I'll put you under again. You need to sleep and heal."

Tommy nodded. A few minutes later, his eyes closed, and Douglas felt his own relief.

"Will . . . will he die?"

Douglas turned to see Mrs. Tavish watching them, her eyes troubled. He knew it was time for plain speaking.

"He will die if he returns to the miasmic air and foul humours in your house," Douglas said. He moved to take her by the arm and help her to her feet because she was struggling to rise. She shrank back in the chair, telling him worlds about her own treatment by the lump of sodden carrion probably still snoring on the High Street.

"I shouldn't stay here. Joe will miss me."

He stepped away from Mrs. Tavish and let Miss Grant help her to her feet.

"Do you have a place you can stay until Mr. Tavish . . . feels better?" Miss Grant asked.

"Aye. My neighbor Mary Cameron," Tommy's mother said. "She's done it before." Big sigh. "And probably will again, mind." Her eyes turned wistful. "We were neighbors back home in the glen."

"Mrs. Tavish, you would be better off leaving such a man," Douglas said, unable to help himself.

"He's my husband," was her quiet reply. She bent over Tommy awkwardly and kissed his forehead, and then went downstairs. When the door closed so quietly, Douglas felt his heart sink.

Douglas didn't even want to look at Miss Grant. "Sometimes I am ashamed of men," he said, embarrassed.

Miss Grant tidied Tommy's bed, apparently not willing to look at him, either. "We keep hoping that Joe Tavish will catch his death some night . . ."

"There's no . . . no . . . squire or man of consequence to deal with someone such as that man?"

"No laird," she said. "Lady Mary Telford lives in that large manor near the old castle, but she is English and doesn't concern herself with us."

She gave him a hopeful look. He knew he had to squelch any designs on her part. He was not the man to change things in Edgar. Useful as he might prove, he had no standing in a village such as this, where even useful new arrivals were probably considered foreigners forevermore.

"Miss Grant, I have no intention of staying in Edgar any longer than to see Tommy on the mend," Douglas announced, feeling remarkably foolish, for some reason. He had barked orders to pharmacist's mates and other surgeons for years, but he felt painfully like an ungrateful idiot.

To his relief, if not strictly balm in Gilead for his conscience, Miss Grant took his declaration in stride. "We are all grateful that you were here this day to save a little boy's life," she assured him.

She had the cutest freckles, freckles all over her face

and what he could see of her neck—little faded freckles that must have been much more pronounced when she was a child, but now a shade just this side of charming. Coupled with her heterochromia and deep red hair, she was a colorful woman. What was that word . . .

"Ephilides!" he exclaimed. "It's been nagging at me since I first saw you."

Tommy stirred. Miss Grant took Douglas by the arm and led him out to the landing. She stared at him and then gave him that patient look he had seen once in a great while, since he had never spent much time on land to observe the fair sex.

"You're so kind to suffer this fool gladly, Miss Grant. Ephilides is the scientific word for freckles." *I've done it again*, he thought in desperation. Might as well blunder on so she will be glad to see me leave. "You have as charming a set of ephilides as I ever hope to see." *There. Call me an idiot to my face.*

To his amazement, she clapped her hands in delight. "Heterochromia and ephilides? Da always said that my eyes were evidence that God Almighty has a rollicking sense of humour. Mam told me that a host of angels kissed me and freckles are the result. It's *bricíní* in Gaelic, by the way."

"You must think me an idiot," he said in apology.

"Since we are into plain speaking, I think you remarkably kind to help Tommy Tavish," she said simply. "Certainly we wish you would stay, but Edgar isn't for everyone."

"It's for you, though?" he asked, grateful to have bumbled through his lack of manners, and in addition, be given an easy exit from the village.

"I'm needed here, and it is my home. Now then, Mr. Bowden, will you be wanting to stay here tonight?"

"If it isn't too much trouble."

"Will the room across the hall do?"

Her offer sounded sensible, except that a more martyr-like approach to Tommy Tavish's care might further atone for his blunders. "Better I sleep in his room. He might be afraid if he wakes up alone."

"Very well, then," she said. "I need to see to dinner. There are usually only a few pensioners, so it is mainly soup and bread." She started down the stairs, so he followed. "I suggest you take a walk around my little village. As villages go, it is modest in the extreme, but there are some of us who love it."

He did as she suggested, shutting the door on Miss Grant and her charming tearoom. The lowering clouds had cleared away to demonstrate that southwestern Scotland did have blue skies. Hand in his pockets, he walked the length of the High he had not traversed yet, which took him past the posting house name of the Hare and Hound, the ubiquitous Presbyterian church, and what looked like a combination tobacconist and lending library. On a whim, he stuck his head inside to inquire about the annual fee for borrowing books and was pleasantly surprised.

A smaller road angled away from the High in that manner of village roads, which meandered where people did, and eventually turned into actual byways. He remembered such roads from his childhood in Norfolk, spent largely in his father's workshop and barrel yard, helping make kegs of all sizes, many intended for the holds of Royal Navy ships.

The only boy with two older sisters, he had left home in shocking fashion. The death of his mother had rendered him melancholy, but with no one to discuss the matter. Papa just worked harder, his face more set, and the vicar in his local parish reminded him that he and others in Norfolk, at least, were born to trouble as the sparks flew upwards.

It wasn't enough to assuage a twelve-year-old boy's heart. The day Papa entrusted him to take a load of kegs to the Great Yarmouth docks was the last day he saw his father. He fulfilled his assignment, sent the money carefully wrapped and addressed to Nahum Bowden's Cooperage in Walton, Norfolk, and offered himself to the Royal Navy.

He was given the choice of powder monkey or loblolly boy, and he took the latter, because medicine interested him. Dumping emesis basins and urinals began his hard school, but his absolute, unyielding calmness in the face of terror moved him quickly to pharmacist's mate. One year in a Spanish prison rendered him nearly fluent in the language, which eased his escape and reunion with the Royal Navy's White Fleet, off anchor on blockade duty.

On the surprising endorsement of a fleet physician, after five years, he spent two years in London Hospital, learning the trade he practiced for the duration of Napoleon's wars. He was skilled, talented, and footloose now.

Walking felt so good. Why seeing water still meant so much to him, he could not have said. He climbed higher up the road, moving aside for wagons, horsemen, and one carriage. When he came to a spot where the road widened, he turned to look down on Edgar. He watched the docks and the fishing vessels, clouded now by competing gulls, which meant the day's catch was ashore.

He studied the High Street until he located the tearoom. A small figure in the back garden, probably Maeve, was pulling laundry off the line. He admired the graceful arch of the stone bridge that crossed the River Dee, and the ruined castle on the opposite height from where he stood. Miss Grant had mentioned a manor of sorts belonging to an Englishwoman, and there it was, easily the most elegant building in town. Just this side of the Dee, he noticed a smaller two-story stone house, painted a soft yellow. No smoke curled from the chimney, even though it was approaching suppertime, and the windows had no curtains.

Maybe the house was empty. Maybe he could start a practice in Edgar. Two rooms on the bottom would suffice for an anteroom-office and a surgery, and there was likely a kitchen, which would be useful for the pharmacology part of his business. He could live upstairs. He reminded himself that he had entertained this same fiction in Pauling.

He convinced himself he had better keep looking, once Tommy Tavish was this side of death and not in danger of infection. A larger, more prosperous village probably waited just around the bend in the land. What was the hurry, anyway? He had leisure for the first time in his life. He could take a carriage or even a post chaise all the way to John o' Groats, at Scotland's rooftop, and travel down the other side.

"That's what I will do," Douglas informed the lupines just poking out for their first view of spring aboveground.

Even so, he took a coin from his pocket and tossed it in the air. "Heads I remain here only a week," he said as he flipped George III over and over. Sure enough, buggy-eyed George stared up at him on the road. Douglas chuckled, pocketed the coin and headed down the road, wondering why he flipped the coin. His plans hadn't changed, and a faulty coin toss wouldn't have mattered. What, three or four days for Tommy to be well enough to leave behind?

Chapter 7

*T*OMMY WOKE ONLY LONG ENOUGH
to ask for a urinal, mutter something, pluck at his
arm, and swallow another sleeping draught. The
pallet Miss Grant had provided was surprisingly comfortable. Douglas thought of other nights standing on a
sand-covered deck in his surgery to keep from slipping on
blood, and decided quickly that Miss Olive Grant's tearoom was vastly superior.

I do not miss that, he thought, to no surprise. Once
Tommy's needs were met, he returned to sleep, only to
wake hours later with a soft hand on his arm. His muscles
tensed, but he did not move.

"Miss Grant?" he whispered finally, not sure if he
should be chagrined or pleased that she was touching him.
She seemed much too proper for what sprang immediately
to mind.

"You were calling out and muttering in your sleep,"
she whispered back. "Is there something I can do for you?"

"No, I . . ." He stopped, and indulged in the truth. "I
have bad dreams." He took a deep breath and said something he never thought he would say to anyone, let alone a

lady he barely knew. "Would you mind awfully just keeping your hand on my shoulder until I return to sleep?"

What on earth was he asking? He closed his eyes in the deepest humiliation, ready to cry, except he was too old for that, too long at this war business.

She said nothing, but increased the pressure of her hand on his shoulder. He didn't mean to, but his head seemed to naturally incline toward her hand. The last thing he felt was his shoulders relaxing. When he woke next, it was morning.

He took a deep breath and smelled wonderful fragrances from the kitchen below. Shame covered him as he remembered what had happened last night, and he knew he could never go downstairs again in this lifetime.

"Sir? Sir?"

Douglas sat up, instantly alert. He looked into brown eyes about on the level of his own brown eyes. He got to his knees and automatically put two fingers on Tommy's neck and then smiled.

"I am going to live?" the boy asked in all seriousness.

"Your regular pulse would indicate precisely that," Douglas replied. He felt the boy's forehead, which was cool. "Are you hungry?"

"I could eat a seagull, feathers and all," Tommy assured him, which made Douglas laugh.

"I don't think it will come to that."

Douglas got to his feet and stretched, fully confident that his days of sleeping on a pallet were numbered. A young surgeon could do it, but he wasn't a young surgeon anymore. "I'll get you something from downstairs after you do your duty with this."

Tommy obliged him, muttering something about being perfectly capable of standing up.

"Not yet, you're not," Douglas replied. "Two more days with this extra-long splint, and then we'll see. Steady as you go."

Douglas took a long look at his surgical handiwork, relieved to see no redness. He sniffed the bandage. Other than the fact that Tommy Tavish was long overdue for a bath, there were no telltale signs of rot.

"Would you at least let me sit up?" the boy asked.

"That I will do and we'll see how you like it."

Gently he pulled Tommy into a semi-recumbent position, listening to the boy's sharp intake of breath and barely stifled groan.

"Maybe not just yet. Agreed?"

Tommy nodded with no argument. He closed his eyes when Douglas lowered him down. "Me mam?"

"She said she was going to stay with a Mrs. Cameron. Is she . . . will she do?"

Tommy nodded again. "She's a good'un. Me da?"

"Hard to say, lad. Let me get you some food."

There was nothing else Douglas could do but go downstairs to the kitchen. Had there not been a patient involved, he was certain he would have gathered his belongings together and slunk out the front door, never to be seen again in Edgar. He took a deep breath and opened the kitchen door.

Her red hair gathered into an untidy topknot, Miss Grant was just preparing one of six loaves of bread for the oven. She smiled at him, not a hint on her face of embarrassment. Her cheeks were rosy, but the kitchen was warm.

"How is our patient?" she asked, and somehow that made all the difference. She was inviting herself into his world, and he was happy to let her in.

"Wanting some food," he replied. "Said he could eat a seagull, feathers and all."

"Too fishy for a convalescent," she said. "Tell him I said no. Baked oats will do, with cream on top. Some for you too? I have boiled eggs, as well. That's what my breakfast crowd likes. Sit a minute."

He did as she asked and felt his face grow warm when

she sat across from him. With no hesitation, she took his hand in hers.

"Don't worry, Mr. Bowden. How on earth could anyone go through a lifetime of war and not have a bad dream or two?" She released his hand and just looked at him, her face so pleasant, even with freckles and funny eyes. He couldn't think of a time he had seen such kindness, which made her face nearly beautiful.

"Thank you," he said quietly. "If . . . if that happens again, just leave me be. I'll wake myself up and go back to sleep."

She shook her head slowly. "Not under my roof you won't," Miss Grant said, her voice low and full of emotion. "My father was a minister, and he didna raise me to ignore suffering."

Douglas swallowed. "It's not much suffering, not in the great scheme of things."

He tried to turn his nighttime anguish into a joke, but she wasn't buying it.

"Not under my roof," she repeated, but softer now. "Let me fix a tray for Tommy and you."

She did an odd thing then, something he never expected. Without a blush or qualm, she took him by the chin and held his head steady so she could look into his eyes. "Do we understand each other?"

He nodded and she released him.

"This will not come up for debate or discussion again, Mr. Bowden." She shook her head, as though vexed with herself. "You must think me a dreadfully managing sort."

"I wish you had been my pharmacist mate in any number of battles," he told her, which did bring out the red in her cheeks, making her even more colorful. "Done and done, madam. How about that food, and handsomely now."

Miss Grant laughed and moved quickly to do his bidding. He poured some coffee and filched a piece of cold toast.

"Try my lemon curd on it," Miss Grant said as she sliced two squares of baked oats and poured cream over them.

He had no plans to ever argue with Miss Grant again, so he did as she said, which meant he ended up licking the knife too. He had never eaten anything so good in his life. "Magnificent," he said. "The coachman mentioned it yesterday. I was skeptical because I have been nearly three days in Scotland and my taste buds died when I crossed the border."

"Wretched man," she joked, which made him smile, because she rolled her Rs even better than other Scots he knew. Maybe it just sounded better, coming from a lady.

And so it was with good humor and calm heart that he took a tray of food upstairs for a brave boy and a man beginning to suspect that peace had its perquisites.

But he had forgotten about the horribly named Duke, who looked at him, ever hopeful, when he came into the room with the tray. "Oh," was all he said, because Miss Grant came up the stairs right behind him with a bowl of scraps.

She held it under Duke's twitching nose, his tail wagging rapidly, and then walked with it into the hall and down the stairs, the pup in hot pursuit. "I'll bring him back when he has had a turn in the garden," she called, making it sound for all the world like Duke was a valued guest who needed to take the air.

"Amazing lady," Douglas said as he set the tray on the bedside table and helped Tommy into a sitting position.

The boy was so hungry that he forgot his pain. He wolfed down the baked oatmeal and inhaled the blood pudding Miss Grant had added. He looked around, still hungry, at the same time Douglas declared that he couldn't eat another bite and offered the remainder of his breakfast to the boy.

"Life is hard for you, lad," Douglas commented, knowing he did not ask a question.

"Aye, mister," the boy replied. "Me mam . . . Sir, please."

"I'll go find this Mrs. Cameron and see how she fares. Do you have a direction?"

"Behind me house and over one," the boy said as he finished the last of Douglas's blood pudding and leaned back, exhausted.

Without a word, Douglas gave him a lesser draught, lowered him down again, and sat beside Tommy until he gave a long sigh and surrendered to poppy sleep. Douglas sat there a moment, knowing that he could leave Edgar right now, and Miss Grant would keep Tommy Tavish alive. He closed his eyes and smiled over the heterochromatic beauty that a woman with red hair, almost a burgundy color, and faded freckles, blue and brown eyes, and a nose just shy of being labeled masterful could possess. He had no argument with her figure, which he would characterize as comfortable, an attribute probably most pleasing on a cold Scottish night. He already knew she had more brains than a roomful of females. Oh hang it, likely more gray matter than most men.

"But I swore an oath and she didn't," he told the sleeping boy. He paused another minute, knowing he had more than fulfilled his oath, as far as his unexpected stay in Edgar warranted. "All right then." For the second time in as many days, he took out that same coin and flicked it, stepping back so it would land flat and not roll. "George, if I see you, I am free to leave."

Again, the coin landed with George staring bug-eyed up to the ceiling. And again, he pocketed the coin and went down out the door to find Mrs. Tavish.

She was precisely where Tommy had said she would be found, also staring at the ceiling, her face a sickly pallor and with eyes so hard he knew what had happened even before Mrs. Cameron ushered him into the hovel.

Mrs. Tavish lay so still that he went directly to her bed and pressed the back of his hand against her neck. Her pulse was slow and thready, and probably only still beating because she looked like a woman with a grievance.

"I'm sorry, Mrs. Tavish," he said softly. He turned to Mrs. Cameron in sudden anger, even as the logical part of his own brain told him he was inappropriate. "Could you not have called me, at least? Perhaps I could have done something!"

Mrs. Cameron didn't suffer fools gladly. She seized his arm with a surprisingly strong grip and jerked him to the corner of the room, so he could stare down at a baby so small and thin that no art of the surgeon could have changed the outcome.

He had the good sense to apologize, even as he pulled back a surprisingly clean towel to take a good look at what happens to a malnourished infant from a malnourished mother.

"I doubt my friend Rhona Tavish has had a decent meal in two years," Mrs. Cameron said, her voice low with emotion. She stuck her face in his. "Mister or Captain or Surgeon or whoever you are, does it ever shame you to be a man?"

"Almost on a daily basis," he replied, which made the woman lower her eyes and step back.

"My boy?" he heard from the bed, even though Mrs. Tavish spoke no louder than a whisper.

"Tommy will live and walk again, Mrs. Tavish," Douglas said, returning to her bedside. "What would you like me to do with your daughter?"

How was it possible for even tears to look exhausted? Touched almost to his heart's core, he who had seen so much, Douglas dabbed at her eyes.

"No money for *cladh*," she whispered. "No potter's field either, please no."

Where did all his nerve come from? "Miss Grant has a pretty little garden behind her house. Do you . . . do you have a name for your daughter?"

"Call her Deoiridh—pilgrim—for she was a pilgrim passing." Mrs. Tavish sighed and slept.

Miss Grant, I am going to keep trying your good will, it appears, he thought. He turned to Mrs. Cameron. "This nice towel, please. I'll get you another."

Mrs. Cameron nodded and went to work shrouding the tiny body. She bound it neatly with cloth strips, offering no protest when Douglas lifted the bedcovers and examined the sleeping Mrs. Tavish.

"You took good care of her," he said finally. He reached in his pocket and pulled out three coins that made Mrs. Cameron's eyes widen. "Buy food for both of you and there will be more."

She put the feather-light infant in his arms and he turned to go. He stopped and handed the child back. "One moment."

In a fury, he crossed the noisome yard into the Tavish's ruin of a house, where Mr. Tavish, sober now and eyes burning like two coals, sat at the table.

"A man takes care of his family!" Douglas shouted, wondering whose voice was so menacing, before he realized it was his own. "I have no power to do anything to you, but take this!"

He picked up a stick by the door, probably the stick that Tavish used to beat his wife and son, and cracked it against the side of the man's head. Tavish grunted, shrugged it off, and slammed Douglas to the ground. The last thing the surgeon remembered was a foot crashing into his ribs, and his own fervent relief that Tavish must have pawned his very boots for one more drink. Shoes would have cracked his skull.

Chapter 8

OLIVE GRANT LEARNED OF MR. Bowden's slow and painful walk from one end of the High Street to the other from one of her pensioners who often dropped by early to pay for his luncheon with fuel for the kitchen stove. The man didn't mention the small bundle the surgeon carried, but he was old, and his eyesight cloudy.

Olive wiped her hands on her apron and went to the door. She took the four steps in two steps and ran to the surgeon, who just stared at her with tears in his eyes and held out the bundle, beseeching her.

She gulped and took the baby, tucking it in her arm as though the child lived. She touched Mr. Bowden's face, wincing when he winced. "I can send Mr. McCullough here for the constable," she said.

"No need. Tavish will just say I struck him first, and I did." He gave his side a gentle pat. "Don't think my ribs broke, but I need to lie down."

"Mr. Bowden, I have no patience with brawlers," she told him, which made the surgeon smile.

"I haven't heard such a tone since my own mother caught me smoking."

"That's a bad habit," she said, matching him for calm. "I trust you gave it up."

"From that day on."

A gesture summoned two diners, who put a hand on either side of Mr. Bowden and helped him into the tearoom. Olive considered the matter for a small moment and pointed to the stairs. "Across the hall from Tommy Tavish," she said.

"I don't mean to turn your home into a hospital ward," Mr. Bowden said.

To Olive's ears, at least he sounded apologetic. He also sounded deep in pain. She sat him down and unbuckled his shoes, then carefully swung his legs onto the mattress. The others left the Spartan little room, but Olive wanted an explanation. She didn't have to wait long.

"I'm no brawler," he began. "I'm not good at it."

"That is patently obvious."

He sighed, which made him wince. "I doubt Mrs. Tavish's baby even drew a breath," he said. "Tiny little malnourished thing. I made some remark to Mrs. Cameron that she should have summoned me, and I got the tongue-lashing I deserved." He sighed again. "No physician or surgeon would have made a difference, even had they been able to afford one."

"And that fired your anger," Olive told him.

"Oh, aye. I wanted to pound Tavish into the soil." Mr. Bowden managed a little laugh, which made him press his hand against his ribs. "Alas, he was sober this time, and I couldn't compete." Even the head shake that followed such a statement made him clench his teeth in pain. "He even robbed me. Turned my pockets inside out, and what did I do but groan?"

"I will definitely summon the constable," Olive said and turned toward the door.

He grasped her hand and raised up on one elbow, while sweat popped up on his forehead. "No, no. Don't do that. I have a strong suspicion that Mr. Tavish has already left for greener pastures. Good riddance to him." He lay down and crossed his hands on his chest, which made Olive laugh.

She stopped laughing when he told her what he had promised Mrs. Tavish.

"I'll send two of my pensioners to dig a wee hole beside my flower garden," she promised. "I can find a small box. I even have a shawl that will make a good lining." She thought of the Highlanders and one lady too proud to come in for food. The woman could sew anything on short notice, and Olive could stretch out her project to include three meals a day for many days. "I know a seamstress for that lining."

"Excellent. Is Tommy awake?"

Olive went to the door and stood there, watching the steady rise and fall of the little boy's chest. "No, thank goodness."

He motioned her back to the bed, and she looked down on a pair of single-colored eyes filled with masterful resolve. Just a glance at his eyes told her all she ever needed to know about Mr. Bowden's determination. She doubted that any man he could even remotely save would dare die.

"I think I did a foolish thing," he began.

"Even more foolish than thinking you could brawl with a man taller than you and maybe a bit younger?"

"It remains to be seen," he said, then closed his eyes in sleep, falling back on that refuge from pain used by all of the Almighty's creatures, from garden gopher to the king of England probably. She watched, her curiosity aroused, and then left unsatisfied as his breathing became regular.

The noon meal brought out more people than usual because Edgar was not a village prone to much excitement. When something out of the everyday happened, the event became a matter of prime importance. Twice she had to add more potatoes to the soup to make it stretch.

"Joe Tavish is gone!" the constable declared, over soup and oat bread. "We owe the good man upstairs on his bed of pain a rousing three cheers!"

The huzzahs resounded, shivering the very window glass. Olive bit her lip to keep from laughing, as she wondered if the sleeping surgeon had suddenly been jerked awake.

"What good thing can we do for the surgeon?" one of Olive's regular dishwashers asked.

Perhaps let him sleep in peace, Olive thought and stifled her laughter with her apron. "I don't think he's staying in Edgar much beyond seeing Tommy on the mend," Olive said. She was never one to gild any lilies, a silly expression, indeed.

"We could take him our ailments and appeal to his better nature," a woman announced.

"And pay him with what?" a one-legged fisherman asked.

Silence. As everyone looked at her, Olive Grant wondered when she had become Edgar's chief magistrate (ex officio, of course).

"I'll have to think about this," she told her friends, touched to her heart because they already relied on her for at least one good meal a day. She made an open-handed gesture. "I really will ponder the matter."

Think she did, once she had sent round a note to the seamstress, along with her mother's shawl and the box. She stood a long time at the window, wishing for summer. She felt old and tired, wondering what she could do to convince the surgeon to stay in Edgar. Nothing came to mind.

Douglas woke later with his rib cage aching and pounding like a drunkard's head. With no small effort, he pulled up his shirt and probed his own ribs, happy to feel no more give than usual. He took a shallow breath, and then a deeper one, and then another until he reached the limit of his endurance. He wouldn't be running any races soon, but at least he could breathe well enough. He hadn't the courage to ask Miss Grant to tape his ribs. He had imposed enough.

He heard a whine and looked toward the door to see scrawny little Duke eyeing him, then retreating to Tommy's room, then returning to cock his head and wag his tail.

"You're obviously smarter than I am," he told Duke. "Go tell Tommy I will be there in a moment." When the dog immediately returned to the room across the hall, Douglas couldn't help smiling.

He made a face when he sat up, but at least he didn't cry out. The footboard of the bed was tall enough to lean on, so he made it to his feet, where he stood, blinking for a moment, trying to remember where he was.

The memory of the humiliating beating administered by Tommy's father made him frown and then regret even the movement of his eyebrows. He touched the eye that throbbed and understood why his vision was faulty. *Good thing I swallowed the anchor and left the Fleet*, he thought. *I could never live this down in the officers' wardroom.*

Walking was easy enough, if he moved slowly. He leaned against the doorframe to Tommy's room. "What'll it be, lad?" he asked. "The pisspot? Some luncheon?"

Tommy gaped at him, his mouth open. "Sir, your eye!" he exclaimed. "Maybe you should sit down."

"Oh, no. I'm on my feet after some effort, and I shall remain upright. First things first."

The matter of easing Tommy was quickly accomplished, with the boy alert enough now to manage the earthenware jug himself. By the time Tommy was tidy, Miss Grant came up the stairs with a tray holding two bowls and bread. She looked at both of them and pointed to the chair.

"Sit, Mr. Bowden," she ordered.

He did as she commanded, knowing enough about women to be certain his life would run smoother if he obeyed. To his amusement, he noticed that Duke sat too.

She handed Douglas a bowl of lamb stew and a spoon, then dipped a slice of bread in it. She did the same for Tommy, after helping him into a sitting position. There was even a smaller bowl for Duke, the smart dog.

As she helped Tommy, Douglas watched his patient, pleased to see that his color had returned and his eyes were alert. *More alert than mine*, he thought, and wondered, *What must you think of me, Miss Grant?*

Miss Grant quickly proved herself kinder than he deserved. "Don't berate yourself, sir. All day people have been stopping by to ask me to thank you for ridding Edgar of a bad egg."

She colored and put her hand to her mouth. "Oh, I . . ."

Tommy proved to be brighter than all three of them. "Did my da give you the black eye?" he asked Douglas.

Douglas nodded. "We had a bit of a brangle. He won."

"Me da is the bad egg?"

"Aye, laddie. I can't deny it," Olive said quietly.

Tommy frowned and returned his attention to Douglas. "Sir, you would only try such a thing if he made you very angry, think on."

Just tell him, Douglas thought. *Let's get it over with.* "He did make me angry. In the first place, I suspect he was the cause of your accident and not what your mother said."

"Aye," Tommy said, his voice barely more than a whisper. "I didna move fast enough for him, and he has this stick. Did he . . . did he do something to me mam?"

Suddenly there was no tough boy, but a child with tear-filled eyes.

"Not as such, Tommy, but I must tell you: your mother was confined last night and your little sister did not live."

Miss Grant sat on the bed and held out her arms, gathering to her heart a boy in tears. She spoke to Tommy, but her eyes were on Douglas. "Your mam is well, but weak from hunger. Mrs. Cameron is taking care of her, and we are taking care of you."

How lovely that sounded to Douglas. He looked into Tommy's face and saw a near tidal wave of relief wash over him. The boy's shoulders relaxed and he rested his head against Miss Grant, who held him close.

"We are taking care of you, indeed," Douglas said. He touched Tommy's head. "Your mother wanted us to bury your little sister in Miss Grant's pretty backyard."

"With a headstone and everything?"

"Headstone and everything," Douglas echoed, thinking of so many burials at sea. He didn't think he sounded ragged and needy, but Miss Grant spoke up so promptly that he wondered.

"You can pick my flowers, when they bloom, and leave them for her. There's already a little bench where your mam can sit," Miss Grant said. "I can't think of a lovelier place."

Tommy seemed to turn inward. He lay back down and looked beyond Miss Grant into another time and place. Douglas had seen such a look on any number of patients, hardy veterans of battle. "Lad?" he asked.

Tommy opened his mouth to speak, then closed it. He looked from Douglas to Miss Grant and took a deep breath. "Miss Grant, I stole a blanket off your line last fall. I think you left it out to air. I'm sorry."

Douglas glanced at Miss Grant, knowing Tommy was ripe for a scold. Miss Grant was made of kinder fabric, apparently.

"Did you take it because you were cold, Tommy?" she asked, her voice quiet but not one to be ignored.

"We had a long winter," he said simply.

"Aye, we did," she agreed. "Did you wrap up tight in it?"

He nodded. "It smelled of something wonderful."

Douglas thought of his visit to the Tavish hovel, where nothing smelled wonderful.

"It's called lavender," Miss Grant said. "This summer I will put you to work gathering lavender heads. Perhaps your mother can help me make lavender sachets. I like to keep one under my pillow."

Well done, Miss Grant, Douglas thought.

"On board ship, he'd have been flogged senseless for theft," Douglas told her, after a lesser administration of laudanum put the boy under again.

"And what did that ever accomplish?" she asked as she helped him across the hall to his own bed.

"Very little," Douglas admitted. "I patched up some torn backs but I could not do much for their spirits. Don't let me make you blush, but upon my word, Miss Grant, you are amazing."

She blushed anyway, and tried to wave away the compliment. His laugh turned into a groan that took her right out of her embarrassment and back to the practical woman he already appreciated.

"This state of affairs will not do, Mr. Bowden," she said, all business again. "Your ribs might not be broken, but you know you will feel better if I wrap them."

"I won't deny it," he said. It was his turn to blush.

"Don't let me make you blush, sir," she teased. "I have seen a rib cage before."

Without a word, he unbuttoned his shirt and let her help him out of it.

"Where, in particular?" she asked.

He pointed to the spot in question. "The extra strips from your sheet are next to my medical bag, where you will also find little clamps in a small box that remarkably says 'clamps.'"

She went across the hall and returned with the items in question. "My goodness, Mr. Bowden, I am not the only colorful person," she said, and there was no disguising her amusement, even if he could not see her face. He knew she was staring at his back. "What on earth is it?"

"That, Miss Grant, is a Fiji islander's interpretation of a medical caduceus. And, yes, I was far gone, wasted, and three sheets to the wind. And young too. Why else would a man get a tattoo?"

"A dare, perhaps?" she asked. "Did it hurt?"

He laughed and groaned. "Not at the time! Once the kava wore off, I was in agony for a few days."

"I hope you learned a lesson," she said, sounding so Scottish that he couldn't help smiling.

"I did. Madam, that is my only tattoo. You may search far and wide, but you will find no more," he said firmly.

"I didn't intend to," she said. "Where do I start? Your ribs, I mean."

She was still smiling as she wound the sheet bandage around him, pulling it tighter at his orders, until he was satisfied. She helped him into his shirt, buttoned it for him, and told him to lie down.

He surrendered happily to someone else's doctoring. He watched her roll up the rest of the sheet bandage, impressed with her kindness. She turned to leave the room. "Miss Grant?"

She looked back at him, waiting.

"You have seen both my tattoo and my ribs," he said, wondering if she might slap his chops even harder than Tavish had, but determined to forge ahead anyway. "I realize that our acquaintance is brief, and I won't be here long, but perhaps you could call me Douglas, all things considered."

She had pretty, even teeth that showed to great advantage when she laughed.

"And I am Olive," she said. "Close your eyes for a while now. I have work to do. Douglas."

Chapter 9

ON THE THIRD DAY OF DOUGLAS'S enforced sojourn in Edgar, tiny Deoiridh Tavish was buried in Miss Olive Grant's own christening gown. "I am thirty years old and unlikely to need it for a bairn of my own," she said quite frankly to Douglas, who wondered about shortsighted Scottish men. *Not my business*, he thought. *Moving on soon.*

The delicate lining of the little box had been anchored in place with the tiny stitches of a true seamstress. Douglas almost had to smile to see the pride on the face of the old woman who had done the stitching.

"Lovely work," he said to the old antique, who blushed, to his delight.

"Now how would you know about good stitching?" she teased.

He held up his hands. "I'd almost wager that I have thrown in as many stitches as you have. I'll call mine sutures. Yours are neater though, and mine were generally sewn on a bobbing deck."

He thought she might chuckle at that, but she patted his arm instead. "Good lad," she murmured. "Took a mighty toll though, eh?"

"Not really," he told her. "I'm alive and quite a few of those men I stitched are too."

She looked at him as she might look at an equal, and he was flattered all out of proportion to the occasion. And then she told him something that made him understand the wisdom of women.

"It's in your eyes, lad. They tell a different story."

She said it quietly and patted his arm again, before turning to Miss Grant, who held the baby. Douglas had a sudden urge to find a looking glass, which he laughed off. He tried to remember the last time he had really looked into anything beyond a shaving mirror and came up empty.

When all was ready, Douglas carried the pitifully small coffin upstairs, so that Tommy, awake now and more alert, could bid hail and farewell to his sister.

The boy had cried to go downstairs and into the garden with the others, but Douglas had firmly vetoed his request. Olive solved the problem by commandeering two of her pensioners, who held Tommy upright by his window so he could watch the simple burial.

Mrs. Tavish must have been in the tearoom's backyard before, maybe stealing blankets with Tommy, because she had chosen her daughter's plot well. The hawthorn bushes had begun their blooming, along with some brave daffodils. Summer here would be a choice place to rest on the bench and think about Deoiridh's brief pilgrimage through a hard world, rendered easier because her time had been so short.

Olive had first thought to ask the minister to do the burial, but he had refused. "It's not consecrated ground," Olive had fumed when she came back from St. Barnabas. "'Use the pauper's field,' he told me. "Wretched man! My father would never have done that, were he still the minister in Edgar."

"Hardly matters," Douglas told her. "I've heard twenty-five years' worth of quarterdeck sermons by any number of captains. Let me recommend Job chapter 19, verses 25–26."

"You must know it by heart."

"Aye." He closed his eyes, remembering far too many burials at sea. "I can recite it from memory."

"And I'll have a verse too. Perhaps I shall sing."

So it was that tiny Deoiridh Tavish, her brother watching from an upstairs window, received a lovely burial in a beautiful garden. The minister might not have deigned to attend, but the yard was full of Olive Grant's pensioners grouped around the flower garden and the little hole.

His ribs pained him too much to lower the box into the grave, but two of the old men he was beginning to recognize did the honors, carefully tamping down the dirt. Olive Grant nodded to him when it was his turn and he stepped forward, thinking of so many other times.

"'For I know that my redeemer liveth, and that he shall stand at the latter day upon the earth. And though after my skin worms destroy this body, yet in my flesh shall I see God,'" he said, wishing all funerals could be in such a lovely setting.

He stepped back into the circle of mourners and Olive Grant took her turn. He admired her hair, all orderly now, and the handsome plaid draped over her shoulder. As she began to sing, he felt a tiny bit of callous chip away from his heart, never mind that such a thing was medically impossible.

He shouldn't have worried about the tears coursing down his cheeks. A surreptitious look around showed him to be in good company as Olive Grant sang Handel's lovely alto solo from *Messiah*.

"'He shall feed his flock like a shepherd; and He shall gather the lambs with His arm, and carry them in his bosom, and gently lead those that are with young.'"

She sang, her voice pure and true. She clasped her hands at her waist, economical and tidy, and cocked her head slightly to one side, her eyes so kind. Douglas felt his own battered spirits settle down. For the first time in forever, his high-held shoulders, always tense, slowly relaxed. He knew something wonderful was happening to him; what it was, he had no idea. If he had been the creative type, he would have thought an august, cosmic hand had just turned a page in his book of life, leaving behind the pages of war and tumult. But he wasn't the creative type, Douglas Bowden reminded himself.

All was calm when she finished, even the gulls by the fishing boats silenced for once, giving smaller spring birds the chance to be heard. When Olive looked in his direction, he patted his heart, which made her tear up, for some reason.

The old people filed away until just the two of them remained in the garden. Douglas heard the upstairs window close, so he knew Tommy Tavish was back in bed.

"Thank you for doing this, Olive Grant," he said. "I've been nothing but a bother to you since I came to town."

"I daresay Tommy Tavish would call you a blessing," she said. She knelt and patted the little mound among her spring flowers, flicking away an imaginary weed and smoothing down the soil. "I believe I will plant blue flax here, and perhaps some heather."

"I promised Mrs. Tavish a headstone," he told her. "Who should I see?"

"Will McCorckle, two doors down," she said quickly. "I would say that we have been the bother to you, Mr. . . . Douglas Bowden."

"If that is so—and I do not believe it for a minute—I'll give Tommy two more days and—"

"And then what?" she finished. "Send him back to starvation? And Mrs. Tavish? What of her?"

"It's your village, not mine," he said quickly, and then was immediately ashamed of so cavalier a comment. "Oh, I didn't mean—"

She had turned away, and he didn't blame her. *It isn't my problem*, he thought and felt the tension return to his shoulders. He didn't know what to say, so he watched the pleasant sway of her skirt instead.

She stopped walking but did not turn around. When she spoke, her voice was still kind. "If you feel up to it, Mr. Bowden, take a walk around Edgar and really look. Supper will be at six of the clock, as usual. Don't overexert yourself, though."

He did as he said. *She called me Mr. Bowden*, he thought, irritated with himself. *And so I was, drat the matter.*

He didn't expect to see anything different from his previous sorties up and down the High Street, most memorably running with a bleeding boy in his arms, and more recently staggering back to the only refuge he knew in Edgar, wounded himself because he had never been much of a fighter. If the Royal Navy had required men like him to board enemy vessels with a cutlass in hand, Englishmen would probably be speaking French now.

The thought made him smile and then laugh a little, driving away those carrion birds that circled ships after battle in places like the China Sea and flapped around him in his dreams. He touched his bound ribs, pleased to feel no worse than he expected. His eye and cheek would be a colorful green soon, and then purple, but it would fade.

It was that time of the afternoon when even a quiet village like Edgar grew even more silent. The sun warmed the cobblestones and the few dogs about were content to loll in the warmth and give him no more than a passing glance, almost as if they were already used to him.

He walked to the little bay and stood there, seeing distant sails of fishing boats returning. He counted no more than ten boats on the horizon, a smaller number than the expansive docks were originally built for. This was no busy fishing port any longer. Where had the men and ships gone?

He stopped at Mrs. Cameron's house, thankful he had remembered to put more coins in his pocket for the two women. Mrs. Tavish was sitting up in bed now. She gave him a ghost of a smile and took his hand when he told her of Deoiridh's funeral.

"I'll see to a small headstone before I leave Edgar," he promised her. "Maybe her name, dates, and a little verse?"

Mrs. Tavish nodded.

"Any verse in particular?"

"Miss Grant will know," Tommy's mother whispered.

"I expect she will," he replied, touched at everyone's reliance on Olive Grant. "Tommy is doing well. I will probably shorten his splint tomorrow and let him sit up. We might even take soap and a cloth to him."

Poor Mrs. Tavish didn't know what to say to someone such as him, even as simple and ordinary as he knew himself to be. She had likely been cowed and abused all her life. Mrs. Cameron curtsied as he handed her more coins and assured him she was buying nourishing food for them both. He probably could not expect more.

And then he was out the door. A cautious glimpse inside the Tavish house showed no evidence of the man. *Good riddance*, Douglas thought and continued his walk.

He walked beyond the village in the direction he had come only two days ago. His attention had been claimed by Tommy at the time, but now he looked and was saddened by what he saw.

He saw a small dry dock, something familiar to him from years of pulling into Plymouth and Portsmouth, where the dry docks had been massive and always full of ships in various stages of construction or repair. This one lay idle and empty with its two brickworked cradles, or graving docks, and bilge blocks and hinge-shores holding up nothing. The gates of one coffer dam were closed and sound, though, allowing no water inside the enclosure. Also closed tight was what he assumed was the machine shed, probably housing pumps and wheels and stays that could be thrust from the brick frame cradling the infant ship and kept level so the builders could do their work.

He walked onto the dock, peering down at the brick-work, impressed with its soundness. The dry dock with its way, down which a finished vessel would slide into the sound, would never have been large enough for a frigate or a ship of the line, but he knew a yacht or a similar-sized craft could be built most handily here.

Where was everyone? Was this what Olive Grant wanted him to see? Did she expect him to wave a wand and have a work force appear?

The fishing fleet was coming up the bay's estuary now. He watched the boats with their clouds of seagulls. Soon the herring and whatever else was caught in these waters would be swung onto the dock and into troughs, where people such as Tommy and his mum would clean, scrape and gut, and prepare for larger markets. The gulls would hang about for the scraps and the day would end.

There appeared to be no other revenue source in Edgar. No wonder the little village was on starvation rations. *This still isn't my problem*, he assured himself.

True or not, he walked back more slowly, savoring the sight of the pretty little village still keeping up appear-ances, rather like an old lady from a good family who had fallen upon hard times.

He stopped at the dock to watch the first boat swing its nets over the gunwales, where the catch was guided into the troughs. Women and children stood ready with their knives. He thought he would buy some fish for Miss

Grant, maybe as a peace offering for being stupid and unmindful. It couldn't hurt. He made his way carefully down the slippery ladder.

He recognized the first woman because he had removed a fish hook from her little son's wrist. She had brought the squalling, squirming lad to Miss Grant's Tearoom the evening of that first long day. It had been the work of mere seconds to poke the barb the rest of the way through (not a popular option), cut it off, and withdraw the shank.

"I'd have done it meself," the woman had assured him, "but I was worried about them wee blood channels."

"Vessels," he had corrected automatically. "'Twas wise of you to bring him to me."

The boy had given him a kick in the shins for his pains, something Douglas was not used to from his years in the fleet, but it hurt less than his eye or his ribs did now. The fishmonger had been less pleased with her son, but it was easy enough to convince the woman that the kick was a natural reaction from a little boy who didn't understand strangers messing with his arm.

Her name. Her name. What was her name?

She seemed to know what he was thinking. "'Tis Mary," she said, as she picked up a knife as wicked as any blade he ever owned.

"How did you know I couldn't remember?" he asked, curious.

Her answer both put him to shame and gave him a resolution. "Not many folks take an interest in us Highlanders," she said with no malice. "We're easy to forget, but it's Mary Patterson."

"I stand reproved and corrected," he told her. "Mary, how is your boy?"

"In trouble as usual again, but with no shooting red streaks, which you told me to look for," she replied promptly.

"Then you've done the job," he replied. "Mary, I know you're busy, but I have a question."

"Then ask it," she said, her eyes on the fish piling up.

"That dry dock. What happened?"

She gave him that patient look that seemed to be the sole purview of women. Miss Grant had already used it on him a time or two. "I've only been here two years, with the other Highlanders, but it was Boney."

"Napoleon? I don't understand."

"Captain over there says it was a bonnie dry dock, with some twenty men working, and a few boys," she told him as she picked up the first fish. "War comes, and they could make more money in Glasgow shipyards."

"All of them?"

"Aye. The ones who didn't leave for t'dry docks took the king's shilling, or joined your own Royal Navy, or were bludgeoned into service by the press gangs."

He understood Edgar's bleak prospects, but he had to ask. "And no one returned?"

Mary shrugged and her hard eyes softened for a brief moment, so brief that he would have missed it, if he hadn't been concentrating on her face, determined to remember her name now. Just that little glimpse into her heart told him she had lost someone to the war.

"No one returned. All dead or working elsewhere." She gave him a shrewd look then. "I'll wager you went to sea because of Boney too."

"Sort of," he told her, coming closer. "My mam died and Da was too busy for me. I was twelve."

She gave him a look of empathy that bound them together—ordinary folk, whether surgeon or fishmonger. "Ye understand then. It was our lot, too, same as yours." The look turned faraway and reminded him of Tommy Tavish. "'Course, we were driven from our homes. Didna want to come here."

She had reduced all his years and skills to her own

level. Cooper's son or fishmonger, maybe this was his village. He nodded to her and started up the ladder, uneasy with the idea because he had no plans to stay.

"Hold there a moment, sir," Mary said, widening the gulf again with "sir." A few quick strokes, a rustle of paper, and she handed him two gutted fish, neatly packaged and bound with twine.

"I shouldn't."

Her expression dared him to refuse. "Ye fixed my wee lad," she reminded him. She waved her wicked knife in front of her, reminding him forcefully of the times he had done the exact same thing to threaten squeamish sailors.

Douglas took the fish from her.

"It's not enough, is it?" she asked, and he heard the anxiety in her voice.

"Quite enough, Mary," he told her, wondering where, on a simple stroll through a village, he had picked up a lump in his throat. "I'm paid in full."

With a wave of her hand, speckled now with iridescent fish scales, she turned back to her work.

"I am not staying here," he muttered under his breath, fully aware that his resolve was almost as slippery now as the waterfront. Tommy Tavish needed to heal quickly.

Chapter 10

WHAT D'YE THINK OF OUR CAPTAIN Bowden?"

Simple question, so there was no reason for Olive Grant to pink up. Her seamstress might be fooled.

"I'm thinking he won't be staying much longer," Olive replied. She gave the evening stew another turn about the pot with her spoon. "He seems immune to the charms of Edgar."

The seamstress laughed and then gave another proprietary pat to the buns before putting them in the Rumford. Olive watched her with real pleasure, happy to have traded delicate stitching on her mam's shawl to line the Tavish baby's box, in exchange for meals. With any luck, Olive could spin out the debt owed for the stitching into a week of meals before the old lady grew suspicious. Mostly, Olive wished that Annys Campbell would privately convince herself that tea and toast once a day didn't measure up to hot meals. That way, they could both overlook the matter and not speak of it again, as the meals continued. It was the Scottish way.

"No, no, not Edgar! What do you think of our doctor?" the seamstress persisted.

"He is kind and good at what he does, but he is a terrible brawler," Olive admitted.

They both laughed at the folly of men in general and Douglas Bowden in particular. Olive pushed a cup of tea toward Annys and followed it with shortbread topped with lemon curd. To her relief, Annys gave a little sigh and took a bite.

I have you now, Olive thought, inwardly pleased.

"He must stay," the seamstress insisted.

"I wouldn't know how to coerce him," Olive replied, which earned her a fishy look from Annys Campbell, almost a what-is-the-matter-with-you look. *What is the matter with me?* she thought and knew the answer immediately. Her parents had raised her to be useful, not ornamental. Experience and observation had taught her that men seemed to prefer the ornamental ladies.

Annys finished her shortbread and spread lemon curd on another piece. "This is going upstairs to Tommy," she announced. "I can sit with him as well as you."

"By all means, Annys," Olive said. "Take along some kitchen scraps for Duke, if you will."

"If he is up to it tomorrow, there will be soap and water for Tommy Tavish," Annys declared.

"And the longer you are here, the more you will eat," Olive whispered as she watched the old woman make the turn in the staircase with more energy than yesterday.

Since Maeve was washing dishes, Olive took her own cup of tea to the window and looked out on Edgar's odd pastel perfection, which belied the need and want behind those curtained windows.

She turned her attention to the High Street and watched Douglas Bowden's gradual progress from the docks, gradual because he was stopped over and over by village folk. He stopped once to lean over the stone wall and speak to Cora MacDonald, who—according to Olive's late father—prided herself on her roses to the point of worship. Well, never mind. Papa had been of strong opinion concerning pride and how it inevitably went before a fall, although not in Cora's case. Olive had decided years ago that Cora's roses were exempt from Biblical injunction.

And hark, she gave Mr. Bowden a handful of blooms, after wrapping the thorny stems in paper. He tucked them in the hand that already carried a paper-wrapped object, which she suspected and hoped was fish.

The next stop took him to the McLarens' stoop, where Matthew McLaren came out with another package. The McLarens kept a Jersey cow. With any luck, it would be butter in payment for the surgeon's effort, only that morning before tiny Deoiridh's funeral, in removing a growth that otherwise marred the loveliness of wee Carlie McLaren's face. He had done that bit of surgery tidily in Olive's small sitting room, where the light was best. He had clamped the child between his legs, and whistling what sounded like a sea ditty, took a flick with his bistoury, and did the deed. He threw in a single stitch before she even had time to cry.

"Now stop at the Rutherfords and get me some eggs," she said, and laughed, because the Rutherfords were about the only family that hadn't dropped by the tearoom for medical consultation. No eggs.

He made the rest of the distance with no interruption, a half-smile on his face. Before he reached the tearoom, he turned back to stare a moment at the docks. His shoulders rose and fell, and Olive wondered what he had learned there.

He did have nice shoulders and a pleasant, hip-shot way of standing, which placed him squarely on a pitching deck. She wondered if he would always balance himself that way and decided that he would.

And I am wasting time admiring a man from the back, Olive scolded herself, even as she smiled, too, certain that if her late father knew of such a thing she would be scolded. She smiled because she thought perhaps her late mother would be standing beside her admiring, too. All this led to a moment's pleasant reflection of their similarities before the door jangled and the man in question came inside.

"We have made a haul," he announced, which pleased her and embarrassed her at the same time. Such a statement seemed to promise more than she knew he likely intended.

With a flourish, he set the packet in twine on the table by the window where she stood. He untied the knot with dexterous fingers—he did have surgeon's hands, no mistaking—and showed the fish.

"You remember that simple hook extraction in your overworked sitting room," he said, his eyes lively. "Her little son wasn't happy with me, but his mam was, to the tune of two fish called coley that I am not familiar with. Stew for supper tonight?"

"Aye, Mr. Bowden."

He leveled a stare down his nearly too long nose at her.

"Douglas," she amended. "I was planning on leek soup but was short a fish or two."

"Then here you are. This miracle is almost out of St. Michael's gospel. What's mine is obviously yours, since I haven't a kitchen." He handed her another wrapped packet. "Mr. McLaren says it is butter and insists he still owes me for that little dab of surgery on his pretty daughter's face. I assured him I was paid in full."

"You'll never make your fortune in Edgar," she teased, knowing he had no plans to stay.

"I hadn't intended to," he replied, which made her sad somehow, even though he had made his thoughts on the matter amply clear. "And look, Miss . . . Olive: we have the first roses of May simply because I stopped to admire them, and Mrs. MacDonald assures me she doesn't mind Englishmen."

Olive laughed out loud, which made Maeve open the door to the kitchen and stare at her.

"It appears you don't laugh enough, Olive," Douglas remarked, when Maeve closed the door. "You're frightening the help." He turned serious then. "Pardon me for prying, but I suspect you spend a lot of time worrying over what was probably your late father's flock."

"Aye," she said. "Them and now the Highlanders too."

He handed her the fish, butter, and roses. "I'm going upstairs to check on my patient . . ."

". . . whom Annys Campbell is sitting with." She couldn't help herself. She touched his arm. "Douglas, she is still eating here! I could not be more relieved."

Just as briefly, he covered her hand with his own. "You're everyone's keeper, aren't you?"

She nodded, too shy to speak. He gave her a wink, which made her face go hot. Then he went up the stairs, his hand on his ribs. He turned around. "When I come down, I want to tell you what I learned on my little walk."

"I'll be here."

"And I want you to tell me just what has happened to Edgar."

A brief glance at Tommy assured Douglas that Mrs. Campbell had matters well in hand. She had even managed to scrub some of the built-in grime from Tommy's face and arms. Any fear that Tommy would resist and resent Mrs. Campbell vanished with one look. Still sleepy from the effects of generous doses of laudanum, the boy's eyes followed the woman as she gently wiped down his face and neck, as trusting as a small child. Douglas doubted anyone had ever treated Tommy Tavish with such care.

Douglas hated to interrupt the peaceful scene even with the most cursory of examinations. He apologized to them both before he loosened the bandages, pleased that Tommy did not flinch from pain. He rejoiced inwardly to see no redness and less swelling.

"Another day as good as this one, and I will replace your long splint with a short one," Douglas promised. "There is a rumor afoot that one of Miss Grant's diners is making you a crutch."

"Just for me?" the boy asked, still unable to fully grasp what a good pasture he had landed in.

"Aye, lad. I predict that inside of a week, you'll travel faster than gossip," Douglas said.

"But where will I go? What about me mam?" Tommy asked, the worry returning to his eyes.

"A good question," Douglas told him. "It's one for me to worry about and not you. How old are you, lad?"

"Seven, sir."

So small for seven, Douglas thought, remembering the boy's infant sister and his mother's malnourishment. He was reminded of any number of men and boys recruited from England and Scotland's villages, probably much like Edgar, who were scrawny and short, the result of over-work and starvation rations. It astounded him that some of those sailors actually gained weight and inches on what passed for food in the Royal Navy. In an academic way, he had wondered what their homes were like if they could grow healthy on salted beef and ship's biscuit. Here in Edgar, he finally understood.

"Seven? Then what happens to you is definitely my concern and not yours," he said firmly. "As I see it, your job is to worry less and heal faster. Am I clear?"

"Aye, sir," Tommy said, the worry still evident. "But me mam—"

". . . is in Mrs. Cameron's capable hands. I've been checking on her too. I tell her pretty much what I tell you." Douglas turned his attention to the old seamstress, who had just finishing squeezing out the washcloth. "As you were, Mrs. Campbell. I greatly appreciate the way you have assumed nursing duties and freed Miss Grant for her own work downstairs."

"She's even providing me some meals," Mrs. Campbell whispered to Douglas as she followed him into the corridor. "I couldn't eat if I didn't earn them."

"Of course you could," he replied. "She wants to help."

"Where is she getting her money?" Mrs. Campbell asked. "Her father was only our minister."

It was another good question. Douglas gave an inconsequential reply and walked downstairs, wondering why Edgar was becoming his problem. *I'd better find a solution soon*, he told himself. *I only have a few days.*

Chapter 11

*O*LIVE WAS JUST ADDING THE COLEY TO the leeks when he went to the kitchen. A dab of butter went in next, followed by another dab, until she was satisfied.

Douglas peered into the pot. "Maybe someone else who has a cow will need a surgeon between now and supper," he teased. "I like a bit of cream with my fish and leek soup. I could do a shoulder resection and claim the whole cow. But only if the patient doesn't die."

She laughed out loud, not one of those missish laughs, but a hearty sound that made him smile just to hear it.

"That is wicked humor," she said.

"On the contrary, Miss Olive Grant, it is surgeon humor. What do you do when everything is going wrong and you wish yourself somewhere else?" he asked, and then it struck him: all the years and all the men he could not save. He sat down with a thump.

The smile left her face and she fixed those marvelous eyes on him. What he saw beyond the beautiful color was a deep well of compassion. She understood exactly what he had just said. She sat down, too, and nearly touched his hand.

"Mostly I take a few deep breaths and think of Psalm 37, which begins, 'Fret not.'"

"And that makes everything better?" He couldn't help the sarcasm; he just couldn't.

She reflected on his angry question a moment, her lips pursed. "Not really, if I am honest. What it does is make me better." She handed him a small ceramic jug. "Mrs. Aintree next door has a cow. I usually promise her lemon curd, but you can do better than that." That smile returned. "In fact, I will wager—"

"Your late father would be shocked . . ."

"Wretch! I will wager that she might just offer you a year's worth of cream. Take a good look at her when you see her."

Chastened but puzzled at the same time, Douglas took the jug from her and walked next door. He knocked and was charmed when a pleasant lady of ample years opened the door. He started to explain who he was, before he remembered how small Edgar was.

She took his arm and pulled him inside her house. "Such a laddie," she said. "Everyone knows who you are." She peered closely at his face. "That dreadful scoundrel really planted you a facer."

He laughed to hear such cant coming out of an obviously genteel mouth. "In his sorry defense, I have to state for the record that I hit Joe Tavish first with a stick."

"Good! Too bad you didna hit him harder. Would you be wanting some cream?"

He nodded, at home with Mrs. Aintree. "Olive . . . I mean, Miss Grant . . . is making leek and fish soup and I told her I wanted cream in it. Since it was my idea, I'll happily pay for it."

She took the jug from him, and then he knew exactly what he could do for Mrs. Aintree.

"Set down the jug and let me look at your hand."

She did as he asked, no question in her eyes, because

she knew too. She held out her hand and he lifted it, looking closely at the ring finger and little finger.

"How did this happen?" he asked.

"The silliest thing! Last year I spilled hot oil on my fingers." Mrs. Aintree looked at him apologetically, as if it were her fault there was no medical care in Edgar. "I cleaned it as best I could, and bandaged the two fingers together. Alas, they grew into one finger." She couldn't look him in the eyes. "I should have known better."

Edgar needs me, Douglas thought. *I swear it does.* He tried to wish the thought away, but it hung around his shoulder like a guardian angel wanting to perch there, but hesitant.

"How were you supposed to know?" He turned over her hand, such a dainty one. "I can fix this."

Tears filled her eyes. "Really and truly?"

"Really and truly. It will be painful, because I have to separate your fingers, stitch up the open sides, and wrap them independent of each other. And then when that heals, you'll have to keep flexing your hand, because the muscles have surely atrophied. That part might not be successful, but at least your fingers will be separate again."

He gave her an inquiring look and she nodded, with no hesitation. "Do this for me, Mr. Bowden, and darling Olive will have cream whenever she wants it."

"Done, madam!"

Her face fell. "I won't be able to milk my cow, will I? Twice a day, without fail, Lucinda must be milked."

He smiled inwardly at Lucinda, remembering a sweet girl of the same name that he had mooned over when he was ten years old. "Probably not for a while." He thought a moment and felt that guardian angel land and nestle near his ear. "I have a solution. Young Tommy Tavish is about ready for a half-splint. With that in place, there is no reason he cannot sit on a milking stool and do the honors."

"I doubt he knows how to milk," Mrs. Aintree said,

which told him everything he needed to know about her concern for—ahem—Lucinda. "I doubt the Tavishes have ever had a cow. They are from the poorest part of Scotland."

"You will teach him. When he is good enough for your satisfaction—and Lucinda's, I don't doubt—then I will perform this little surgery."

"It might be a week or more. Lucinda must be taken care of properly. And then I pray you will remain here to make certain my hand is properly healed."

"I fully expect this to take at least six weeks," he replied. "I never leave my patients before I am confident all is well. We must be certain there is no infection, and that you can hopefully bend those fingers."

Mrs. Aintree nodded, satisfied at last, as Douglas wondered about the workings of fate. Man proposes, God disposes. He remembered one of his captains booming that from the quarterdeck after every reading of the Articles of War on Sunday, followed by a miniscule sermon more threat than encouragement. The captain also shouted that after a battle, and generally while facing a French or Spanish foe.

He stood there contemplating his immediate future, while Mrs. Aintree took the jug into a back room. She returned with cream for the leek and fish soup, plus a small sack. "I made a nice soft cheese yesterday."

He took the items with his thanks and let her open the door for him. "I'll tell Tommy of our arrangement for his future."

"I could pay him a visit," Mrs. Aintree said.

"Delightful. Every convalescent likes to be remembered."

Douglas was silent through the fish and leek soup, which had enough cream to please him. He sat in the little dining room and watched Olive Grant and little Maeve serve the pensioners. A few paying customers came in, but so few. He knew it wasn't his business how she managed to keep the tearoom open, but it began to dawn on Douglas Bowden that he now found himself in the middle of life in Edgar. Nowhere was it written in any surgeon or physician's oath that he was responsible for everything, but he knew himself well. He had his own credo, which had served him well aboard a ship: If it moved and breathed, and, in the case of sailors, swore a lot, he was accountable to God above that it kept moving, breathing, and swearing in good health.

A visit upstairs and bowls of soup for Mrs. Campbell, Tommy, and Duke confirmed his confidence that Tommy could not have a better nurse. He was cleaner and more alert, without the bewildered look of someone in pain and mental turmoil.

Duke thumped his tail in approval of the leek and fish soup. Even the dog looked cleaner. A questioning glance to Mrs. Campbell made her blush. "He didn't mind a good brushing and a little water, think on," she admitted.

An inspection of Tommy's sutures proved satisfactory. "I'll craft a short splint today," Douglas said. "I see no reason for you to not begin walking about."

"Then I could help Miss Grant, couldn't I?" the boy asked, hopeful.

"Aye, lad, but there might be something else for you to do," Douglas told him. He patted the boy's shoulder, wishing he had more meat on his bones. "Rest some more today, and I'll apply that splint tomorrow morning."

He walked down the stairs slowly, knowing that he needed a surgery for Mrs. Aintree and a place for himself. Olive Grant deserved better than to have her little parlor full of bloody lint and bandages and smelling of camphor and alcohol. He fingered the coin in his pocket, the one he had been tossing for heads or tails and then ignoring.

At the foot of the stairs, he tossed the coin again. *Heads I stay in Edgar for at least two months*, he thought. *Tails I stay in Edgar even longer*. There. He had finally quit fooling himself.

The coin went up and over, rolled a bit, then came to rest on its edge, leaning against the carpet. "I need a new coin," he said as he pocketed buggy-eyed George III.

Luncheon was in full swing, so Douglas helped himself to leek and coley soup and slapped down that coin on the kitchen table, through with it. Olive stopped long enough to look at the coin and murmur, "You're overpaying me," before she edged out of the door with a tray of bowls and chunks of bread.

When he finished, Douglas stood in the dining room a long moment, hands in his pockets, nodding to the meek members of Miss Olive Grant's dining society. They remained a mystery to him. He would have to commandeer Olive to explain them and what ailed Edgar.

Most of the people took a second bowl of soup and more bread, which told him that luncheon was probably their first meal of the day, perhaps their only meal. He recognized the pale skin, rheumy eyes, and air of futility that he had seen on the faces of prisoners—him among them—languishing in a Spanish prison. He saw no hope on their faces.

He made up his mind. When Olive and Maeve came out to gather the empty bowls, he helped them. "Can you enlist some of these old dears to do dishes? You and I need to talk."

He saw the surprise in her colorful eyes and then apprehension. "I'm not leaving anytime soon," he assured her, pleased to see surprise replaced by relief. "In fact, I also need you to tell me how I can rent that empty house by the bridge."

Without a word to him, she touched two ladies on their shoulders and gently herded them toward the kitchen, where Maeve stood scraping bowls that didn't need scraping because no one left anything uneaten. The door closed. When it opened, Olive wore a chipstraw bonnet and her plaid shawl.

He fell into step with her as she walked toward the bridge. They paused at the empty house. He smiled to see Olive peer into a dirty window, almost as though she wanted to see the pitiful place pass muster before she agreed to his scheme. *Are you determined to nurture all of us?* he thought.

"I have heard it is haunted, but I suppose it will do," she announced finally. "You could have an office on the first floor and a surgery. I know there is a large-enough cupboard—see there?—for your medical supplies."

He came closer and peered into the window too. He looked where she pointed. "There is a kitchen?"

"You can cook?" she asked.

"No. I can compound medicine and roll pills in a kitchen," he told her, then looked at her freckled, earnest face, so close to his own as they looked through the window. "I was planning to take my meals at Miss Grant's Tearoom, if I can work out a paying arrangement with the proprietor."

She smiled at that, and he admired her crooked incisor. Amazing how a woman with so many interesting and varied elements to one face could look so charming. Douglas wondered again what was wrong with the men in Scotland. Didn't they understand that absolute perfection becomes tedious?

"We can do that," she said, stepping back because he probably was standing too close.

"Who owns this house?" he asked.

She pointed across the river to the mansion just below the castle ruins. "Lady Telford." She glanced back at her tearoom. "Matters are well enough in hand there. I like to give Maeve more responsibility. Let us pay a visit on Lady Telford."

"We will walk slowly, because I want to you explain to me what is wrong with Edgar," he said, flattered by her concern and knowing her well enough in their brief acquaintance to know that idle moments with Olive Grant were few indeed.

She nodded, and he saw the trouble return to her eyes. She pointed to a stone bench on the other side of the bridge. "We can't walk that slow, sir. I have such a story for you."

Chapter 12

"WHAT DO YOU KNOW OF SCOTLAND?" she asked, after he had wiped wet leaves off the bench and she seated herself.

"A broad question," he began, smiling a little, until he saw how serious she was. "Not much. I am from East Anglia—Norfolk—and my father was a cooper. I went to sea at twelve years, and my life has been taken up with war ever since."

She gave him a look of great compassion, which made him wonder if Olive Grant's role in life was to do battle with all the evil in the world. He knew that was impossible, but something in her expression assured him that she was going to spend her life trying.

"Olive, I am fine," he assured her.

"No, you are not," she said just as promptly. "Are you even aware that I have been in your room every night since you arrived and put my hand on your shoulder until you are quiet again?"

He felt his face go hot. "I remember the first night. I do apologize."

"No need," she said. "What control can you possibly

have over your mind when you sleep? Don't tell me tales, Douglas Bowden. Don't ever do that."

He nodded, sufficiently chastened. All the more reason for him to find his own dwelling quickly, no matter how temporary. To his relief, she plunged immediately into the story he wanted.

"Have you at least heard of the Clearance?" she asked, turning slightly on the bench to give him her entire attention.

"Vaguely," he began, not a little embarrassed by his lack of knowledge. "Something about landowners far to the north of your country changing from cattle to raising to sheep? It sounds simple enough."

"Who tended those cattle?" she questioned.

"I don't know." He shook his head, chagrined at his ignorance. "I obviously know more about splinting legs than I do about Scotland."

"For centuries, the Highland clan chiefs parceled out land, small holdings their people rented, to raise cattle and paltry crops. Somehow, through the years, the chiefs came to control the land and kept their own people in near bondage."

"I didn't know," Douglas said.

"No one pays much attention to the poor," she said. He saw a militant look in her eyes, which told him worlds about her father and his ministry in the Church of Scotland. "Yes, the Highlands were overpopulated, and yes the people were more ignorant than we are here in the Lowlands, but nothing can excuse what happened next. It is still going on, even as we sit here."

A seagull swooped close to the bridge and screamed. Douglas jumped.

"I've watched you around sudden noises," Olive said.

He knew better than to comment. She had him. Between sudden noises and nightmares, she had him.

"It all comes down to power and land," she continued,

not giving him the chance to feel embarrassed. "People in power passed the Enclosure Acts, which drove the crofters off their little holdings entirely. Let us add money to that unholy brew. Sheep make more money than cattle and require only a few shepherds and some dogs to control them."

She frowned down at her hands then. When she spoke, he heard the tremble in her voice. Whether it was anger or tears he could not tell.

"Some were given a mere week's notice to vacate their homes. If the people objected or dragged their feet, the houses were burned down, some with people still inside. Or so I have heard."

Silence. She swallowed a few times. Her voice became so soft that he had to lean closer to hear her.

"The poor folk of the Highland clans were rounded up like their cattle, stuffed into ships, and dumped here in Lowland Scotland. Some were sent to Canada and Australia, whether they wanted to go or not."

Shocked, he thought through the matter, looking with new eyes on the hovels at the other end of town where no one tended roses or had a cow that gave excellent cream and butter. He thought of the Tavishes and Mrs. Cameron, and the others that flitted around like wraiths, not even seeking his medical help for anything because they had no hope. He had ignored them too.

How to phrase this? Olive obviously belonged to the tending-roses faction of Edgar, the people who had lived here for a century or likely more, modest but comfortable. "I gather that the good people of Edgar were not eager to see their own Scottish brethren from the north dropped on their doorstep," he commented. "Pardon me, but in Edgar you do have a small pie to divide amongst your own."

"That may be, but it does not excuse what happened. It is our everlasting shame that some of the townsfolk turned a deaf ear to the sermons my father preached about charity being kind and not puffed up," Olive said.

"When did this begin?"

"Some years ago," she answered. "We in Edgar have only been affected by the more recent clearances. I regret that any help given to them was provided grudgingly. Some of the women work on the dock cleaning fish. A few of the men went to sea and never returned. A few of the men are scavengers."

"Scavengers?"

Spots of color bloomed among her freckles. "They clean the vaults under the necessaries, when they grow full and start to reek." She paused to let him absorb that one. "Some Highlanders took to drink, like Joe Tavish. My father did all he could to feed them." She bowed her head and her voice became scarcely audible. "He died about the time the first Highlanders straggled here two years ago. I have continued his work."

He knew Olive was a plain speaker. He was too. "What happens when you finally run out of your own money?"

His blunt question did not seem to surprise her. "I have another year or two before that happens," she said, and no more. That was her answer. She looked straight ahead then, avoiding his eyes.

"What about the empty dry dock or shipyard?"

"The men with skill to run it moved to Glasgow, and some to your country, to build man o' wars to challenge Napoleon. The fishing fleet is greatly diminished because press gangs came this far north to kidnap seafaring men for the Royal Navy. They have never returned either."

He winced inwardly, knowing the truth of what she said. As a ship surgeon, it was his duty to pass judgment on the general health of those men clubbed into the navy by press gangs. Some were too feeble and he dismissed them. Where they went after that, he did not know, but it seemed unlikely that the Royal Navy escorted them home again to Scotland. He looked at Olive Grant with even more respect because some sense beyond the usual six told him that if Olive had been on the docks in Plymouth or Portsmouth, she would have fed those forgotten men and gotten them home somehow.

"Why do you do this?" he asked her.

She seemed surprised by his question, even flustered, which he found endearing. And when she spoke, he felt the tiniest grain of hope squeeze into his heart. "I'm the same as you," she told him. "We just try to do some good wherever we can."

He felt his face grow warm. "Olive, I have always been paid for doing good," he reminded her. "You appear to be going through your own inheritance to do good."

"No one paid you to mend Tommy Tavish's leg," was her quiet reply.

"But . . ." He stopped, knowing full well that he had money and she did not. He couldn't pursue this discussion, so he stood up. "Come, come. I am looking for a house to let. Lady Telford awaits, even though she doesn't know it," he told his . . . his what? He considered the matter, suddenly bowled over with the unvarnished reality that he had a friend in Edgar. "See here, Olive Grant," he said impulsively. "Will you be my friend?"

Her smile could have lit a lighthouse, which flattered him right down to his shoes. "I'd like nothing better, Douglas Bowden."

She meant it. Olive tried to recall her last chum, which meant scrolling through her brain for ten years, as she had watched her childhood friends flirt, marry, have children, and discover they had nothing in common anymore. She had become an afterthought to those who had invited her to parties and teas and who had swung with her in the swing behind the vicarage.

A friend at thirty would be a different sort of friend. She also knew he had no plans to stay long. Still, even a temporary friend was better than none at all. The retired surgeon would be a friend to remember long after he was gone.

"Good," he said. "Bring on this Lady Telford. What should I expect?"

How to describe Lady Telford? "She is crabby and complains a lot, according to Maeve Gibson's sister, who works for her," Olive said, not one to mince words, which had probably cost her at least one suitor. "There is an air of pretension about her because the late Sir Dudley was a baronet and we are remarkably common."

"Any lingering, mysterious illnesses that I can save her from and earn her undying gratitude?" Douglas joked. "Or is that what only happens in bad novels?"

"Bad novels," Olive agreed. "She likes money, I have heard, so she will overcharge you for that house."

"Can I appeal to her better nature?" he persisted.

"She has no better nature. I am sorry to disappoint you," Olive assured him. "Prepare to be cheated on the rent."

"How do you know all this?"

"Gossip," Olive replied, which made him laugh. "She keeps to herself, and we don't interfere."

"Coward."

Oh, this was good. No need for him to know that she had a few qualms about the visit, not the least of which dated back to the time Lady Telford scolded her father for wasting so much of his resources, not to mention his strength and energy, on people who would never appreciate his efforts. Olive felt braver already because she wasn't fighting this little battle by herself. She had a friend now.

"She frightens me a little," Olive said, just to warn him.

"My dear Miss Grant, I have been hip deep in a sinking ship, with a wounded man on my back, trying to take him topside to a cutter. I can probably survive being cheated on the rent."

He stopped with her outside the iron gate, looking dubious. "Does she . . . does she have patrolling watch dogs?" he asked.

Olive laughed out loud. "Hip deep in sea water and what else was that?"

"I don't care for dogs," he said. "Give me a cat any day."

"I won't tell Duke," she teased as she pushed open the gate. "I'll protect you."

And she did, stepping in front of the surgeon when Lady Telford's fat and waddling, thoroughly nondescript geriatric dog threw himself off the stoop and lumbered toward them, wheezing, his tongue hanging out. As the surgeon chuckled, the dog flopped on the walk at Olive's feet and bared his stomach to her.

"Do you feed him, too, at Miss Grant's Tearoom?" he asked, crouching down beside the brute to scratch his stomach.

"Upon occasion. He seems to know when cod is on the menu. Lady Telford calls him Xerxes."

"That's a heroic name," Douglas said. "Perhaps overly ambitious. This is the kind of dog I like—too fat to run and too old to feel so inclined."

Olive scratched Xerxes, too, which made him sigh in an almost human way. "The surgeon here is saying terrible things about you," she told Xerxes, who belched loud and long.

Douglas leaned back and shook his head as though to clear it. "That fragrance would evacuate a room," he said. "I suspect dental decay, but I will not make him a patient of mine. He couldn't even pay me in butter or cream."

Olive laughed out loud and let the surgeon help her to her feet. "Brave man," she said. She mounted the steps and wielded the doorknocker. She listened for footsteps and stepped back.

"Maidie," Olive said. "Is your mistress in?"

A plain, honest face grinned back at her. "Tha knowest t'auld biddy is in," she whispered. "Who in Edgar is her equal to visit? But I'll go look. C'mon in, Miss Grant."

Olive glanced at Douglas, who was doing his dead level best not to laugh. His lips were pressed tight together, but his eyes were merry.

"Douglas, this is Maeve's sister Maidie Gibson. We'll wait in the hall."

The maid put her hand to her mouth. "I keep forgetting." She opened the door wider and drew herself up. "Wait right here, dearies." She hurried off in a purposeful lock step as Xerxes waddled along behind.

"I gather it was hard for Lady Telford to get reliable staff to move to the wilds of Scotland?" the surgeon asked as soon as Maidie was out of sight.

"Rumor says that no one from an employment agency lasts more than two weeks," Olive whispered.

She looked around the entranceway, wondering what Douglas Bowden thought of the homemade entry table flanked by two chairs carved to resemble Anubis, an Egyptian god.

He stared at the thin and menacing wooden dogs, then up at the barely dressed plaster nymphs in the ceiling. "Words fail me," he said at last.

"Just as well," Olive whispered back. "Lady Telford prefers that guests be seen and not heard."

She could have said more, but here came the lady in question. Olive made a sufficiently deep curtsey, and the surgeon surprised her with an elegant bow. Impressed, she watched him, which meant she saw the sudden surprise on his face when he took a good look at Lady Telford.

"Mr. B . . . Bowden," Olive stammered, wondering at the man's wide eyes and sudden bloom of color from his neck up. "Do allow me to introduce Lady Telford."

Out of the corner of her eye, Olive thought she saw a warning stare directed at Douglas Bowden from the baroness, followed by bland complacency.

What have we here? Olive asked herself.

Chapter 13

*D*OUGLAS KNEW A WARNING GLARE when he saw one, however brief. He inclined his head again. "The pleasure is mine, Lady Telford," he said smoothly.

And it was. Of all the scaff and raff from his decidedly lowbrow upbringing in a cooper's shop in Walton, Norfolk, he never thought to lay eyes on Elsie Glump again. But there she stood, still about as round as she was tall, her hair covered in a hugely unflattering turban. He remembered her from Glump's butcher shop, where she had held forth years ago, measuring out bits of beef with one finger on the scale, the old sneak.

The warning stare Elsie had leveled at him told him all he needed to know, and he was willing to play along. Why not? "Thank you so much for letting us occupy a few minutes of your time, my lady," he told her.

She nodded and gestured most gracefully toward the sofa, where he and Olive sat. A glance at Olive suggested that her curiosity had been aroused, probably because there wasn't anything Douglas could have done to stop the unruly flush that even now continued to heat his forehead.

Better to see it through; he could explain later, if he wasn't flopped out on the roadway, paralyzed by laughter.

Douglas wondered briefly if Lady Telford would lay tea for them, then decided that was too optimistic. He remembered her husband, the sort of butcher who never gave an extra ounce of even humble cuts, the kind the Bowdens' ate. Tea and cakes to drop-in visitors? Out of the question.

"Yes? Yes?" Lady Telford demanded, which assured Douglas there would be no tea and cakes. Just as well; he had no faith in his acting abilities. The sooner this was over, the better.

"Lady Telford, I am a surgeon recently retired from the Royal Navy. I wish to let that stone house by the bridge that Miss Grant here tells me is your property." There. Straightforward and economical, much like a report to a captain on the condition of men in sickbay.

"For how long, Mr. Bowden?" she asked, looking anywhere but at him.

"No more than two months."

He heard Olive sigh, which made him wonder if that period of time was too long or too short. "Miss Grant, that is enough time to see Tommy Tavish well on the mend, and Mrs. Aintree's trifling hand surgery sufficiently healed," he reminded her. "I would really like to be settled somewhere before winter."

"I suppose," Olive replied, sounding surprisingly noncommittal for a woman of firm opinion.

Douglas Bowden approved of philanthropy as well as the next man, but he did have his mind determined upon some sort of medical practice that paid better than fish and cream. When he thought Olive's attention was devoted to Lady Telford, he regarded her for a moment, well aware that he had neither the inclination nor the courage to stake his entire livelihood on tending to the needs of the constantly poor. *Olive, I am not the person you are*, he thought, which did him no credit.

Lady Telford cleared her throat and named her price.

"That is highway robbery," Olive Grant said firmly, determined, apparently, to fight his battles just as she fought those of the meek folk who ate at her tearoom. Perhaps it was an automatic reflex. She hadn't given him time to open his mouth. He sat back, wondering how this would turn out. Maybe having someone take up arms on his behalf wasn't such a bad idea. He had the time, and apparently Olive Grant had the will.

Undeterred, Lady Telford named another price. Olive also refused it and named a lower amount, which made Lady Telford utter something between a gasp and a growl.

Silence. Olive sat a little taller. She leaned forward until Lady Telford had no choice but to follow her lead.

"I am of the certain opinion that if you accept my last offer, Mr. Bowden will relinquish the house completely clean and free of vermin," Olive said. She leaned even closer, signaling to Douglas that this was the coup de grace. "Besides, I have heard from a creditable source that the house is slightly haunted."

She sat back, satisfaction on her pretty face, as Douglas stared at her.

"Haunted?" he asked, feeling little cold fingers run up and down his spine.

"Only slightly," she assured him. "You can get a watchdog."

Her lips twitched at that, and Douglas had to turn his head and pretend a cough.

Lady Telford went down in defeat. "Very well, I will settle for this ridiculous offer, if Mr. Bowden here has the sum on hand. If not, someone else will have it."

Who that would have been not one of the three could imagine, if Douglas were to peer inside the brains of each determined woman. He personally knew that no one wanted to locate to Edgar, he among them. He pulled out his wallet and counted out the modest amount that would rent him a house for two months that was only slightly haunted.

"Is there a key, Lady Telford?" Olive asked.

"Under the flower pot by the front door," the baroness said.

"Is there any furniture in the house?" Douglas asked. He replaced his wallet and wondered how many Romeos and Juliets in Edgar already knew about the key.

"I believe there is a bedstead upstairs, although I would not depend upon a mattress," Lady Telford said.

Certainly not in a house where probably every sport in town could gain entrance, Douglas thought, not certain if he was appalled or amused. *It's a good thing I have medical knowledge of diseases of the amorous variety. I cannot catch something that easily.*

There was no more business to transact, thanks to the expert dickering of Olive Grant. All that remained now was to retreat in good order, ask himself what he had gotten into, and try not to laugh until they were out of earshot.

They all rose at the same time, Lady Telford not meeting his eyes. She turned and swept out of the room, more humorous than dramatic, because she hadn't the shape to sweep anywhere.

They were down the walk and close to the iron gate, Xerxes their affable if ineffective escort, when Douglas started to laugh. Once the gate creaked shut behind them, Olive pounced on him.

"You recognized her!" she declared. "And she was happy enough to get rid of you. I demand to know what is going on."

Laughing, he tugged her down the slope, across the bridge, and sat her down on the same bench they had previously occupied. He gave himself over to mirth, something he hadn't done in a decade or more.

Olive kindly let him, although what she could have done to stop him wasn't readily obvious. Finally he sat back and accepted the lacy handkerchief she handed him. He gave her a sideways glance, wondering if she thought him a complete idiot.

What he saw reassured him. Her own eyes were lively, as if she had enjoyed his complete surrender to laughter. He could tease her or tell her. Because he was a smart man, he chose the latter.

"I knew her years ago in Walton, Norfolk, as Elsie Glump," he said, when he could speak. "I know she recognized me."

"If ever a pair of eyes threw daggers, it was hers," Olive said, then started to laugh. "At least she did not sic Xerxes on you!"

"You are never going to let me forget that I was afraid of a fat dog, are you?"

"Probably not. Life is far too serious a matter in Edgar to squander one moment of hilarity. I do promise to keep this our secret, however," she assured him, completely unrepentant. "Glump? Dear me."

He had her measure. He would have to think of a way to get her back someday, that is, if he planned to spend much time in Edgar beyond the two months he had just committed himself to. "Imagine her in a dirty dress covered by a dirtier apron, if you can. Picture globs of fat and gristle in her hair."

"I'd rather not, Douglas."

"Coward! Elsie Glump cheated her customers regularly. Her husband Dudley was a butcher. Olive, Lady Telford is as common as kelp."

If he thought to startle her, he was mistaken. It was his turn to look puzzled at someone's reaction. Now her eyes registered something close kin to triumph.

She touched his arm. "Douglas Bowden, you have added the missing link to our chain," she said. "Shall I fill you in?"

"Please do," he said, mystified. "Apparently she labors under the misapprehension that everyone in Edgar thinks her to be Lady Telford."

"Which she is. We suspected Sir Dudley Telford of all manner of misdemeanor, but not a butcher," Olive said. "We had heard that he owned a valuable piece of property somewhere . . ."

". . . more than likely Norfolk . . ."

". . . which he sold to a consortium buying up land for a canal. It made him amazingly rich. He invested in some fly-by-night scheme that made him even more wealthy." She waggled her finger at him. "This meant that he came to the attention of the Prince Regent."

"Prinny himself," Douglas interjected. "I shudder. Would this have been around the turn of the century? It was common wardroom knowledge in the fleet that our Prinny was constantly in debt."

"Sir Dudley loaned him quite a sum of money, which Prinny repaid by giving him a knighthood. Though why Telford instead of Glump, I do not know."

"Let me inform you," Douglas said. "If I recall correctly, that butcher shop was on Telford Lane, just off the High Street in Walton. You will concede that Telford sounds more dignified than Glump."

"Decidedly."

Douglas considered the matter and arrived quickly enough at the logical conclusion. "From the look she gave me, Elsie Glump thinks no one knows. How then . . ."

". . . do we know?" Olive asked. "Someone heard it from someone else. So many people have had a hand in the telling, that I wasn't certain it was true."

Something else struck him, and it touched his heart. "You all know?"

"Certainly."

"And everyone in Edgar continues Elsie Glump's little charade?"

"Aye, Douglas," Olive said. "You may not know this about us yet, but on the whole, Edgar is a kind village." She sighed. "With the exception of what to do for the Highlanders dumped here. We're a poor village, made poorer by the war, and yet poorest still by the clearing out of northern clan holdings, which really should not have affected us at all."

"Being kind to Lady Telford is an easy matter, compared to your greater issue," Douglas said.

Olive nodded.

They sat together in silence, and then he had to ask: "Slightly haunted?"

He wasn't certain which eye he preferred better and decided on the brown one, simply because his own were brown. Both eyes shone with good humor now, even though he suspected that Edgar's worries were never far away from Olive Grant.

"I may have exaggerated," Olive admitted. "Mrs. Campbell claims she sees lights in the upper rooms now and then."

"Hardly surprising, since the key under the flower pot is likely common knowledge," Douglas said. He slapped his knees and stood, giving her a hand up too. "I can temporarily solve some of Edgar's problems right now. Miss Grant, would you organize a working party to clean out that house? I pay very well."

"Bless you," she said quietly.

"I assume you know somewhere I can get a mattress, and somewhere else I can find a man handy enough to make me a table and chairs, and a surgery table?"

"Aye and aye," she said.

They started toward the road. He tried to look at Edgar with new eyes, but he still saw the same shabby village. Worse, the tide was out and the odor ferocious.

"Anything else, sir?"

"I'll make a list."

The road was slick and muddy so Douglas crooked out his arm. Olive twined her arm through his, even though he knew she was capable and in no danger of slipping. He walked slowly, so she did too. He thought about the letter he would write to Mrs. Fillion, requesting his trunk and that box of shells. He knew there would be a visit to Dumfries soon to round out other needs and wants for a short stay in a slightly haunted house.

He also knew he had to do something about Edgar.

*P*RECISELY HOW HE KNEW THAT, Douglas Bowden couldn't have said. He did know this: the more thought he devoted to Edgar's problems, the less his nightmares bothered him. Olive had said as much at the end of the week, with only a little tinge of rose to her complexion. She blushed and confirmed what he suspected.

"There has been no cause for me to keep half an ear open for you," she had told him one morning as he finished his coffee and prepared to tackle his house again. "See there? Edgar is good for you."

He nodded, although he did not agree with her. She saw that too, commenting, "You're a wee bit too skeptical, Mr. Bowden," as she retreated to the kitchen. He already knew she only called him Mr. Bowden when others were present or when she had a bone to pick. She was an easy woman to feel comfortable around.

Olive Grant had been as good as her word. In the time Douglas had taken to re-splint Tommy Tavish's leg and compliment the lad on his courage and stoicism through the ordeal, Olive had assembled a working crew in the dining room. By the end of the week, he was ready to move in.

Douglas decided that "slightly haunted" was probably one of Olive Grant's few attempts to stray to the shady side of truth. When he teased her about it, she merely smiled.

"I don't object to a little fib now and then," he told her. "The thought of 'wee hants,' as Mrs. Campbell said, apparently was enough to tip the scales in my favor."

He had to admit that the house by the bridge suited his temporary needs completely. With the key safely in his pocket now, he felt a certain pleasure each evening after the cleaners left to walk through the rooms and realize that he had a place of his own, one that didn't shift about at the whim of the ocean or the Royal Navy.

He even wondered if the long-empty house had been built specifically with a surgeon in mind, although Olive told him it was not. The small kitchen off the back of the house was perfect for compounding and rolling pills. To his surprise, the room he had designated for his combination office and surgery already had that wall of built-in shelves and drawers. Even the minister, perhaps chagrined that he hadn't been Christian enough to say a few words of comfort over Tommy's tiny sister, found a suitable desk and chair for that room. Once the man who had crafted crutches for Tommy finished the surgery table, the room looked like exactly what it was, right down to the smell of carbolic, part of his haul from Dumfries' apothecary, which took him away for a day of scouring the town to furnish his surgery.

Between Olive, Mrs. Aintree, and other neighbors whose aches and pains he had addressed, he soon had chairs enough for a waiting room adjacent to the surgery, plus a threadbare but clean carpet underfoot.

Upstairs was his own area, complete with sofa that could easily convert to a bed, if he had a patient who needed closer supervision. Mrs. Aintree insisted she had no use for a handsome wingback chair and small table. "It's a chair for a man," she said, her tone of voice brooking no argument. (*What is it about Scottish women?* he asked himself.) "Mr. Aintree has been gone long years now. He'd be pleased to see it put to good use."

After some rudimentary lessons on the management of crutches, Tommy made a halting beeline to Mrs. Cameron's hovel and spent the afternoon with his mother. As shadows began to lengthen across Edgar, Douglas walked to the hovel to retrieve Tommy and to think about what he saw there. Only that day, Olive had told him more about the Highland Scots from the Duchess of Sutherland's district who literally washed ashore two years ago, the Tavishes among that number.

He had gone to her kitchen to beg the loan of some tacks to anchor a rug that had appeared on his doorstep. A better rug than most, he wondered out loud if Lady Telford had seen to its arrival that morning. It was too good a rug to have crawled there to die, he had joked to Olive Grant as she kneaded bread.

"Please don't use that phrase," she had said, giving the dough an extra punch and wallop. "You are reminding me of the first of the Sutherland crofters only two years ago."

"Tell me," he said, wanting to know more.

Her gentle face still registering the horror of that day, she told him of the storm that had capsized a small vessel already dismasted by a fickle spring storm. "It happened at night, and none of us knew anything until the next morning." She stopped her kneading and stood there, wrists deep in dough. She looked at him and her eyes filled with tears.

"Douglas, we could have used you then." She passed her hand in front of her eyes, leaving flour on her forehead.

Douglas promptly took a damp cloth and wiped her face. He didn't imagine that she would lean into his shoulder, and he didn't object. He put his arm around her. *I have done this to many a patient*, he thought. *None of them smelled this good, though.*

She moved away so he released her. "Papa was still alive then. He opened the front door, and there they were, a few survivors, crawling down the street, too wounded and weary to cry for help."

He shook his head, thinking that such sights had been his lot in wartime, but in England? "Where were they going?"

"They didn't even know," she said, giving the dough a savage punch. "Several of them spoke only Gaelic. My father could understand them, but just barely. From what he pieced together, these crofters from somewhere in the Grampion Mountains had been herded to Fort William and told they were going to Prestwick south of Glasgow, to take up the fishing trade. Fishing! They knew nothing of fishing."

She slammed the dough into a pan and covered it, then sat down with a thump, her eyes bleak. "They had never even been on a boat before, so you can imagine the seasickness. And then a spring storm came up, and the captain was blown south and sought shelter in our estuary."

She couldn't say anything else. Douglas sat beside her. He fingered his taped ribs and felt sudden pity for Joe Tavish, one of hundreds overwhelmed by misfortune not of his own making. And if he was honest, and why not, he could remember some heavy drinking after he lost three amputees in a row.

Bless Olive Grant's kind heart; she seemed to know what he was thinking. She nudged him. "Everyone has reasons," she said.

"Yes, but my ribs still ache and my eye is almost as

colorful as yours," he teased. "Still, I wonder where Joe has taken himself."

No one had stopped by his surgery, but he tacked a "Returning Soon" sign to his front door because he was conscientious. The fishing fleet still stood off the mouth of the River Dee, but the afternoon hour told him that soon the little boats would dock at Edgar and the women who cleaned the fish would arrive in force. After what Olive had told him, he wondered how many of the women were Highland cattle herders' wives, transplanted unwillingly to strange southern shores.

The Tavish house looked even worse, with the front door flapping open, and someone's chickens wandering through like spectators judging one family's misery.

He knocked on Mrs. Cameron's door.

"Come!" said a cheery voice.

He opened the door and saw what he had seen before, with one difference: There was food on the table, which had been covered with a neatly patched cloth. A loaf of bread sat almost proudly in the center of the table, with a knife placed just so, and a jam jar.

"I didn't mean to interrupt your meal," he began, but Mrs. Cameron hushed him with an upraised hand.

"We're eating later," she said. "T'bread is there in case someone should stop by—thou, for instance."

With sudden, blinding realization, he knew what he was looking at, and it humbled him. The coins he had left with Mrs. Cameron had been turned into Highland hospitality.

"You have other loaves and maybe some herring?" he asked, hopeful there was more.

"A wee dab of butter too," she said, beaming at him. "Some eggs and some mutton and potatoes for a stew."

He took her hand and she did not try to pull away. "Mrs. Cameron, you are a providential housewife and a kind neighbor to Mrs. Tavish. Where is she?"

She patted his hand and pulled him into the next room, where Tavish mother and son sat close together on the bed. Occupying the room's only chair was Mrs. Aintree. His tail wagging hard enough to nearly overset him, Duke leaned against Tommy.

This was more than he had dared hoped for, considering that Olive had told him of bitter feelings of Edgar's long-time citizens, trapped in their own more genteel poverty, against the Gaelic-speaking, mostly illiterate Highlanders dumped on them.

Neither a look nor a glance suggested that Mrs. Aintree suffered embarrassment to be found in such a place. A casual visitor who didn't know better could have been forgiven for thinking that the two women were the dearest of friends.

Mrs. Tavish might not have considered herself a patient of his, but she offered no objection when Douglas touched her wrist to feel her pulse, and then rested the back of his hand against her forehead. He saw that she was clean and her hair tidy. She wore a nightgown that looked well worn, but came with a delicate sprinkle of embroidered flowers on the yoke. He turned inquiring eyes on Mrs. Aintree, who blushed.

"How many nightgowns does a widow need?" she asked. "Tommy said his mam had n'more than a shift, and that will never do. I found some other things, for when she feels better."

"You're a good neighbor," Douglas said.

"It's overdue," Mrs. Aintree said simply. "Besides that, I had to tell Mrs. Tavish what a fine job her boy is doing of milking my Lucinda."

Tommy smiled at that bit of praise. "Mr. Bowden, Mrs. Aintree says that I am ready to milk all by myself."

Mrs. Aintree held up her hand with the fused fingers. "Mr. Bowden, you let me know when you are ready, because I will be too!" Her face fell and the worry returned. "I don't know about Tommy lifting the milk pail, but . . ."

"We'll find someone," Douglas assured her. "Give me another day or two to make things right in my surgery, and we'll do the thing." He turned his attention to Mrs. Tavish, who lay in bed, her face composed and the strain gone from her eyes. He even thought her face looked less pinched and hungry. "You'll be up soon, too."

She nodded and said something in Gaelic, which made Tommy beam. It needed no translation. Douglas nodded to them all and returned to the front room, where Mrs. Cameron held a slice of bread—glory, but it was still warm—slathered with plum jam. She held it out to him, and he took it, enjoying the bread and jam, but even more, the kindness.

When he finished, he left more coins on the table. "Keep up what you're doing, Mrs. Cameron. Your kind of nursing is the true balm."

Satisfied, he left the hovel, wondering at what point it had turned from a miserable pile of boards barely holding its own against rain and wind into a home. He took a good look and understood what had changed.

He had.

He sauntered slowly past the row of hovels, suddenly understanding that inside each wreck was a family. Some had already been to see him in his temporary surgery in kind Miss Grant's sitting room. Many more probably needed his help, but pride and poverty kept them indoors.

"Wait up there, lad."

Douglas turned to see Mrs. Aintree making her deliberate way toward him. He waved a hand and waited, thinking of battles at sea and wounded men tumbling down the companionway to his overcrowded, overworked sick bay. That was one kind of medicine; this was another. Might as well do all the good he could here, before he found a better place to spend his days. *I'll perfect my bedside manner, where never I had needed such a luxury before,* he thought with some amusement. *I'll experiment on the people of Edgar.*

He nodded to Mrs. Aintree and decided to start with her. He offered her his arm, which she took with a blush. "You are kindness itself, Mrs. A," he said. "I doubt Mrs. Tavish has ever worn anything with embroidered flowers."

She pinked up further, probably amazed that a man would notice, and looked back. "It's hard there," she said.

"Not as hard as it was a week ago," he told her. "Tommy is on the mend, and you have given him something to do. I will do what I can for you, and I think that is how things work on land."

She chuckled at that. "Nobody has much say at sea, do they?"

"None at all," he assured her. "Not those patients. Now these—I'll have to coax some of them to come to me with their troubles."

"No coaxing from me," Mrs. Aintree said. She patted his hand for emphasis. "I can pay you, of course."

"I have a better idea," he told her, deciding there was no time like right now to see if he possessed even a spoonful of negotiation skill. He stopped, took both of her hands in his, and looked into her eyes. "Mrs. Aintree, would you consider paying me by opening your home to Tommy and his mam?"

She stared at him, open-mouthed. "Surely not."

He thought she would say that, but he had time on his side. He started them both in motion again. "It was just an idea. You have a large home, and I imagine you enjoy the peace and quiet there."

"I do," she said with some emphasis, which set the feathers in her bonnet nodding.

"I was just thinking how convenient it would be to have Tommy there to milk morning and night. With a little advice from you, I suspect that Mrs. Tavish would keep your place tidy, while your arm is in a sling."

"A sling?"

"Have to hold your hand still and not bump your fingers on anything," he said. He shrugged. "Perhaps you will figure out how to do all your housework by yourself. Ah! Here we are at your place, Mrs. Aintree." He gave her a little bow and she took her hand from his arm. "Thank you for all you have done for Mrs. Tavish."

"It was just a nightgown," she said. "Well, maybe a few other things."

He tipped his hat to her. "I do like the good ladies of Edgar. Good afternoon to you now."

Smiling to himself, he walked across the street toward his own house and surgery. He looked back before he opened the door, secretly pleased to see that Mrs. Aintree still stood there. He would have given a year's retirement pay to know what she was thinking.

Chapter 15

*D*OUGLAS BOWDEN HAD ALWAYS taken pride in his medical education: two years at London Hospital, courtesy of one of his captains, followed by a year of ward-walking in Guy's Hospital, and then surgery under fire at Trafalgar. He hadn't thought he was a man given to pride, not the son of a cooper from Norfolk. Or maybe he was.

What he learned about medicine the next day equaled every hour, every anguish, every triumph, and every failure. And he learned it from little Flora MacLeod, six years old and small like the other Highland children, bearing a huge burden.

He began the day flat on his back, staring at the novelty of an overhead deck that did not move. There were no bells to summon him, no grabbing of his shoulder by the pharmacist mate with bad news, always bad news. No drummers beating to quarters. He let the day come, and with it came wrens and robins and the warbles of the morning lark. The tide was in, and with it the lapping of water against the bridge supports.

His bedchamber was long and narrow. The bedstead

mentioned by Lady Telford was worth nothing except to be broken up for firewood. At first, he had toyed with the idea of screwing two hooks into opposite walls and just slinging a hammock. When Olive offered to sell him her parents' bedstead and mattress, he hadn't argued, mainly because he was acutely aware how little she made from her tearoom. She objected when he overpaid her, but he ignored her.

As it turned out, the bed was a capital idea. He could lie in the middle of it and touch each side of the mattress, which was better than scrunching into a hammock. There was one thing about a bed: there was room in it for some-one else too. The idea of a wife had never been more than a luxury, and luxuries were always in short supply in the Royal Navy.

Hands behind his head, he contemplated the novelty of marriage, probably brought on even before the purchase of his bed. The acquisition of a house had opened the door on the idea. It swung wide last night when he was called to the home of the grocer, whose wife was in the middle of a labor going nowhere.

Douglas had no trouble reassuring the skeptical but desperate grocer of his obstetric abilities. He had delivered a moderate number of babies aboard ship, mainly the chil-dren of the rare captains whose wives refused to remain on shore or the less-exalted sons (and daughters) of the guns, delivered to drabs sneaked on board and discovered too late to return to shore before a lengthy voyage.

Red-faced and determined, Mrs. Grocer had surren-dered without complaint to the embarrassing novelty of a man taking charge. He had the right tools: a small-enough hand and a reassuring manner. In a mere five minutes and two contractions, the grocer's first child squinted, wailed, and saw the light of dawn.

"Same thing happened two years ago," the grocer said as he wiped his tears and held his son. "No doctor then."

Douglas left the three of them an hour later, satisfied and thinking that he could have banged on a drum and somersaulted out of the room and the parents wouldn't have noticed, so deeply were they looking into each other's eyes. Little Grocer Junior completed the tableau as he stared at both of them, wondering.

Once he had deep-sixed the idea of a wife, Douglas hadn't considered children of his own, either, not until this morning. His medical satchel slung over his shoulder, he strolled home and crawled back in bed, content and discontent at the same time, wanting what he did not have. He came to no immediate conclusion, other than that he would postpone all matrimonial enterprise until he was permanently settled somewhere. He did know this—he wanted a wife as kind and cheerful as Olive Grant.

Over breakfast in the tearoom later, Douglas told Olive about Edgar's newest citizen. He was too circumspect to say anything about his epiphany.

"You have no idea how they grieved two years ago," she told him as she slid another cinnamon bun on his plate. "I'm glad you're here, Douglas."

It was praise simply said, delivered in that no-nonsense, honest tone that he had already come to expect from Olive Grant.

He arrived in Mrs. Aintree's cow bier in time to pour the full milk pail into a deep pan and set it in a dark corner. Mrs. Aintree had already showed Tommy how to take off the cream from last night's milking.

"She didn't need to show me," Tommy said as he expertly skimmed the settled cream. "Been doing this since I was four." His eyes lost their lively gleam. "Da had cows in Sutherland."

"How long have you lived here?" he asked, wondering just how many people in Edgar were victims of the Great Emptying.

"Two, maybe three years," Tommy said with a shrug.

"Men came with torches, fired our house, and drove off Da's cows. We spent three nights in a graveyard until they drove us away from that too."

He spoke in the matter-of-fact way of children made old too soon. Douglas felt his blood run in chunks. "How . . . how did you get here?"

"I don't want to say no more." And Tommy didn't, turning his attention to teats already wiped clean. He sniffed and wiped his sleeve across his face, but he didn't turn around.

After a few words with Mrs. Aintree about fixing a date for her surgery, since Tommy was so capable, Douglas walked back to his house, head down and hands stuffed in his pockets—his usual pose—wishing that Mrs. Aintree had agreed to take in Tommy and his mother, but not surprised that she hadn't.

He didn't see the little girl sitting by the stoop until he was practically on top of her. He stepped back, startled, and then crouched down beside her. "You're early, little miss," he told her. "Surgery hours don't start until nine of the clock."

When her brown eyes filled with tears, something told his heart that he was looking at another child of the Great Emptying. It wasn't so much the tears as the desperation, easily as great as that on the grocer's face last night— grown-up desperation on a child's face.

"There's no reason why we can't start surgery hours right now," he told her. "Where do you hurt?"

She shook her head and lifted the shawl end from the tartan she wore. Two dark eyes looked back at him, eyes filled with pain and pleading. One meow, then two, and the kitten lowered its head and tried to burrow deeper into the girl's lap.

"I don't doctor kittens," he told the child, even as he wondered just what was wrong with the little thing. "Who are you?"

"Flora MacLeod," she said, and his heart melted just a bit around the edges with the loveliness of her Highland brogue. He was beginning to tell the difference.

"Well, Flora, I really don't . . ."

She did something then that melted his heart more. Careful with the kitten in her lap, she knelt in front of him, and looked at him with eyes as pleading as the kitten's. She said nothing, only looked.

Silently, too, he lifted her back to the bench. "What's wrong with your bonny little kitten?" he asked.

Carefully, so carefully, she pulled the shawl end away again and he saw the kitten's mangled front paw. "I think it was a dog," Flora whispered. "Gran tells me just to drown it in the river." The tears spilled from her eyes now, and she cried without making a sound.

In his long and painful career in the Royal Navy, Douglas had seen silent sobbing like that among young refugees fleeing one army or another. When his Spanish was good enough, he asked a fleeing mother about it. "To make noise is often to die," the woman had said. "We train them to suffer in silence."

MacLeod. MacLeod. He already knew it was a Highlands name, because he had doctored MacLeods from the island of Skye, serving in the fleet. And a name like Flora told him one of the child's not-so-distant ancestors had been a supporter of Bonnie Prince Charlie, who had fled Scotland with Flora MacDonald's help.

"Flora MacLeod, let's see what I can do. Come in."

He ushered his patient's mistress into his surgery and spread out a towel on the table. "Lift it out and onto this," he directed. He slid over a wooden box so Flora could at least see onto the table.

She stepped up and set down her bundle, her eyes serious. Gently, he lifted the kitten from the shawl to the towel, where it tried to burrow under the fabric. Flora ran her thumb and forefinger on the spot under each ear, which told Douglas that she knew cats and what pleased them.

While she was doing that, Douglas lifted the bloody paw with his own forefinger, observing the crunched bones. *I can do this*, he thought. *I can take the foot off at the joint above the paw. A stitch or two and done.*

"I'll fix . . ." He lifted the kitten's tail ". . . her."

Why in the world did little Scottish girls have such beautiful, heartbreaking eyes? He knew what she was going to say.

"I hae nowt t'pay thee," she whispered.

He looked into her pretty eyes, dismayed to see they were sunken. He saw how tight her skin was stretched across her face, and the fact that her dark hair looked brittle. He asked himself who was his patient and broke his own heart.

"Let's worry about that later," he said.

She shook her head. "We'll worry 'bout it now," she said and her head went up. He saw the pride in her face then, and it gave him heart. She was a game little girl. If he was so smart, he needed to think of something, and fast, because Flora was smart too. He could buy a little time, though, and kill two birds with that single proverbial stone.

"I do need to be paid, Flora, but right now, I need to take care of your kitten, and time's a-wasting," he said, reaching for a sheet of paper. "I'm going to send you across the street with a note for Miss Grant. Do you know who she is?"

Flora nodded. "The kind lady."

Douglas felt his eyes tear up. Gadfreys but he was an easy mark. "The very one. Pay close attention: Your kitten needs some food, and soon. Sometimes that's as important as surgery." He started writing. "Take this to Miss Grant. She'll know exactly what to do."

"Because she takes care of wee kittens too?" Flora asked.

"Most certainly," he said, perjuring himself without a qualm. "Now you do exactly what she tells you." He reached in a dish on the counter next to his surgery table and took out two coins. "Two pence should do the job."

"But I told thee I . . ."

"I'll add it to your bill of receipt, Flora," he told her and broke out the firm voice he hadn't used since his Royal Navy days. "You have to do exactly what Miss Grant wants. Your kitten is depending on you." And Scotland expects you to do your duty, he nearly added, knowing the late Lord Nelson would approve.

He finished the lengthy note, hoping at first that Olive could read his chicken scratch, and then confident she would know what to do, even if she couldn't read the note. He wrapped the paper around the coins.

Eyes full of determination now, Flora took the money and hurried out the door, closing it quietly behind her, as her gran had probably taught her. He turned back to his other patient. "All right now. Better we do this while your mistress is across the street."

He picked out his smallest capital knife and threaded a needle with catgut. *Excuse that*, he thought and chuckled. He put on his surgeon's apron and stuck the threaded needle into a handy spot easily within reach. The kitten objected to the alcohol swab, but was too weak and hungry to struggle.

Douglas lit his lamp and pulled it close, then moved aside the box Flora had stood on. "I have got to stow away some boxes," he told the cat. "Mrs. Fillion—you'd like her—sent me my trunk and other things I forgot I had." He looked down at the box labeled "Shells" and wondered why he had collected so many from foreign beaches. He toed the box under the table.

Some pledgets of cotton completed his preparations. He poised the bistoury over the wounded paw, then moved it higher, seeking the joint. "All right now. If you scratch me, I'll . . ." He chuckled again. "I'll be scratched. Better than the time that powder monkey bit me. Here I am talking to cats. Take a deep breath and think of something pleasant like mice."

Chapter 16

*F*LORA, WHAT A WELCOME SUR-
prise!" Olive Grant said as she opened the
door. All she knew about the MacLeods came
from Maeve, who was cutting up onions right now.

"You'll never see them in here," Maeve had told her.
"They're MacLeods from Skye and even prouder by half
than the Sutherlanders."

And yet here stood the smallest MacLeod, orphaned
because her da had been one of the Highland soldiers who
fought at New Orleans in America. Her mam had died
of abuse that none of the others would talk about, as they
were cleared out of their homes in the Highlands.

She had a sweet face and those round eyes that usually
don't linger long after infancy, except in the lucky few who
keep them forever. Olive could not overlook the worry and
the tight-lipped mouth that suggested Flora MacLeod was
only just keeping a lid on her feelings.

Flora held out the folded note. "Two pence from the
good doctor across the street and down a bit," Olive said.
"Let me take your shawl, my dear. Sit here, and I will see
if Maeve has a biscuit."

Flora should her head. "Gran said I was not to ask for anything."

"You didn't, did you? Here you are."

The biscuit went down in a hurry, which told Olive worlds about the child before her and helped explain the portions of Douglas's note that she couldn't quite decipher. She read it again and understood just what kind of a sly man had taken up temporary residence in Edgar. She pocketed the note and gestured to the kitchen.

"Mr. Bowden attached the utmost importance to what we do, and it must be done right." Olive poured a combined cup of water and milk into a saucepan and set it on the Rumford, luckily still fired up from breakfast. "We'll let that boil." She held out the note to Flora. "It says here that the oats must be of the right size and consistency or your kitten will not eat."

"Her name is Pudding." She sighed, forgetting herself. "Mostly because I wish had some."

I wish you did too, Olive thought, and she turned away because there must have been a little soot from the Rumford lodged in her eye.

"There now. I will add some oats and stir." Olive stirred, then requested that Flora pull over a stool and be ready to help.

Her eyes serious, Flora was soon stirring the oats round and round, and dabbing at the saliva at the corner of her mouth. Olive looked away again.

"There now. I believe we have it." Olive took the pan from the cook top and uttered an exclamation. "Oh, dash it all! I wasn't paying attention, Flora. Mr. Bowden most distinctly asked for fine-ground oats, and look what I have done."

Flora looked and drew in a deep breath of the fragrant oats, her eyes closed in pleasure.

God forgive me when I complain that my lot in life is not

easy, Olive thought as she watched the little girl. *I am not an orphan from the Highlands.*

She knew that Flora would not argue about what came next. Olive poured the gruel into a small bowl, sugared it well, and added cream. She stirred it as Flora watched her every motion and then set it on the table. She took Flora by the hand and sat her down in front of it.

"I'd be a pretty poor Scot if I just threw out these oats, Flora," she said, her voice as firm as she could make it, when she wanted to throw her apron over her face and sob at all the injustice and cruelty in life. "You had better eat this. I'll try again."

She turned away as Flora picked up her spoon and dug in. Olive poured in more watery milk and slightly finer oats in the pot and returned to the Rumford. Flora ate quickly and with little sounds of pleasure that made Olive lean her head toward the warmth of the cooking stove and draw one deep breath after another.

Olive glanced at Maeve, who had finishing chopping onions and withdrawn to the sanctuary of the pantry, her shoulders shaking, as she murmured something about "tears from onions."

Her back straight, her admiration of Douglas Bowden growing by the second, Olive stirred another pot, declared it not fine enough for little Pudding, probably undergoing surgery right now, and placed the second rejected offering before a little girl only getting started.

Twice more Olive failed on purpose, and then turned out fine oats that any kitten could manage. How fortunate that her success coincided with Flora pushing back her last empty bowl and declaring, "I hope you get this one right, Miss Grant, because I am full."

"I believe I did, Flora. Let's put it in a small container. You carry that. I will bring this wee pitcher of cream." *What else, what else*, she thought. "Oh, and this. I know that Mr. Bowden likes my plain biscuits." She held one out. "They have been in the cupboard for two days at least, though, and I am skeptical. You try it, Flora. Tell me if it's something I should take across the street."

Flora ate with no hesitation, rolling her eyes. "He'll like it, Miss Grant."

"Good. I will carry this plate and the pitcher, so you must open the door."

They crossed the street and walked toward the house by the bridge, Olive's heart so full that she knew she would have to have a good cry later in the day, if she could find the time.

Douglas opened the door and wiped his hands on his apron. Flora held out the container.

"It took a while, because Miss Grant wanted it to be just right, Mr. Bowden."

"Perfect. Your little kitty isn't up to eating it right now, but I'll keep it here in a good place and let you feed her later."

Flora peeked in the door of the surgery and her face grew solemn. "Where is Pudding?" she asked, a quaver in her voice.

"Pudding, is it? She's in a box that I lined with another towel. Go through that door and you'll see. I built a little fire to keep her warm. The kitchen will be quieter, and she needs the solitude. Go on; it's fine."

Olive followed Flora to the door of the kitchen. She watched Flora kneel by the box and hold her hand just over what remained of Pudding's bandaged front leg. Her hand hovered there a moment, and then Flora gently rubbed her first two fingers on that spot on top of a kitten's head, between her ears. Olive winked back tears to hear a purr enormously out of proportion to the size of the patient as Flora crooned to her Pudding in Gaelic and became a child again.

Olive went into the surgery, where Douglas was returning his knife to a wicked-looking case of knives. He tossed the bloody lint into the fireplace, and then held out his arms as she walked into them, sobbing.

"I ruined the oats four times before she was full," she managed to tell his shirt.

"You're not a very good cook," he teased, but she heard the unsteadiness in his voice, much like hers. "God have mercy on us, Olive. What in the world can we do here?"

We. She swallowed and thanked the Almighty for answering one of the many prayers that surely came his way every day from Edgar.

He seemed to have no inclination to release her, which relieved her, because she had no inclination to move away. She had borne this burden so long, fighting a battle she could not win. Did he just seem to know what she needed, the same as he knew what Flora needed? The Royal Navy was minus an excellent surgeon now and maybe even a greater healer. Olive wondered if he had any idea of his own gifts.

But she couldn't stay that way forever, even though his hand rested on her back now, gently rubbing that spot between her shoulders that was always a tight knot. She raised her head from his shoulder.

"And now your shirt is wet," she said.

"Won't be the first time," he told her, backing away now. He untied his surgeon's apron and hung it back on the hook by the fireplace. He sat down at his desk donated by the vicar and indicated the chair next to it. "I'm going to keep Pudding with me for a few days, and insist that Flora visit you every day for more gruel."

Olive shook her head, amused, now that the edge was gone from her sorrow. *I have an ally*, she wanted to shout, but she knew he was serious. "You can count on me to have more trouble getting the proportions right on that dratted porridge," she assured him.

He grinned at her, a wonderfully boyish grin that seemed to scour away a layer or two of professional propriety. He turned serious soon enough. "See if you can burn a little fish or beef, while you're at it. There are properties in fish, swine, and beef that strengthen."

"Beef is too dear, but I can get fish," she said. "We'll see about pork."

"I like beef too, and I've decided to become your steady customer, as long as I am here," he said. "I'll buy a haunch of venison at the butcher's, if he has any. Venison has more iron in it than beef, from the smell of it."

"You'll get a more varied bill of fare at the Hart and Hound, where the coach stops," she reminded him.

"True. Maybe I'll go there a time or two. I like the convenience of eating in Miss Grant's Tearoom, if she'll have me. I pay in advance too."

There was nothing in his voice even hinting she could protest or act missish, which told Olive everything she ever needed to know about his handling of people in his sickbay aboard ship. "Aye, then," she said.

He looked less sure of himself then. "I have a dilemma, Olive," he said. He yawned and ran his hand across his face, which turned red. "My apologies! Babies are about as unpredictable as the Spanish fleet used to be. The least the grocer can do is name his son after me. I lost half a night's beauty rest."

Olive studied his face in mock-serious fashion. True, the bags under his eyes were more pronounced, but his hair didn't look any grayer around the edges than it had the day before. He had such nicely chiseled lips, something a Scottish lady seldom saw north of Hadrian's Wall. For some reason, Scotsmen had thin lips. Not Douglas Bowden, born and raised in Norfolk. He had a way of stretching out and unlimbering himself, probably the exact opposite of how he sat in cramped quarters in the Royal Navy.

As far as she could tell, Douglas Bowden had not suffered from his pre-dawn visit to the flat over the greengrocers, and so she told him. "Apply some damp tea leaves to the bags under your eyes, and you should sparkle again," she teased. "Mama told me once to apply buttermilk to my freckles."

"They're fading nicely," he said, which gratified her. Who knew he would even have noticed them? "Do you credit the buttermilk?"

"I daren't. I drank more of it than I applied, and Mama was none the wiser."

"Seriously, they are a pleasant color," he said, then stood up, his hands back in his pockets. He stood in front of the window that faced the river. "I'm stalling. Flora insists that she pay me. I told her I would think of something, but I have not yet."

He half-leaned, half-sat against the front of his desk now, closer to her.

"Maybe after a night's sleep I'll have something. Would you think I had taken entire leave of my senses if I told you I want something that will put money in Flora MacLeod's pocket, so she and her Gran will visit your tearoom once a day?"

She had no answer for him, but she did recite what she knew of the MacLeods, how Flora's father had stood firm with the 93rd Highlanders at New Orleans, America, only last year, where he died and was buried.

"I doubt Flora ever knew him," Olive said. She didn't even try to mask her own bitterness. "The 93rd was the Duchess of Sutherland's own regiment, raised by her father in her honor! And what have she and her husband done but drive out the families of the men who so loyally served King George to the death."

She hadn't meant to raise her voice. She put her hand over her mouth and looked toward the door, hoping Flora had not heard anything. Douglas got up and walked quietly to the kitchen door, peering in.

"She's singing to little Pudding," he reported.

"Forgive my outburst," Olive said when he returned. "It was unmannerly and uncalled for."

"And true," Douglas concluded. "So it's Flora and Gran?"

"Flora's mother had been ill for some time." It was Olive's turn to cover her eyes for a moment. "I have this from one of the other Highland families, but apparently Gran pleaded with the Countess's factor to let them stay until Annie MacLeod passed away. Apparently it would have been only hours."

"No luck?"

"None. Neighbors helped Gran get Annie outside on her mattress. Soldiers burned down the cottage as the MacLeods watched. Apparently Annie died that night, lying on a mattress in the rain."

She watched Douglas's head rear back as if someone had slapped him. "And all this for sheep," he murmured.

"More pound per animal than cattle. Those tiresome Highlanders who have been raising cattle for centuries can . . . can do something else," Olive said, suddenly not caring how angry she looked or how shrill she sounded. "They can stop speaking Gaelic, discard their kilts for trews, and forget bagpiping."

"The world is not a fair place," he said as though to remind her. "My father worked so hard on his barrels, each one near perfection. One shire over, an inferior cooper who married into a scrap of money set up his shop and undercut my father at every turn."

"At least no one burned down your family home," she countered, unwilling to be placated.

"True, but inferior barrels did send me to sea at twelve years of age. There was no future in quality."

He sighed and she felt shame at her hot words. "Edgar used to be a bonny little town, where everyone cared for his neighbor. With the dry dock falling apart, and fishing not what it was, and the young men gone, things changed. And when Highlanders fleeing their troubles landed here . . ." She couldn't finish.

"And you're trying to carry the whole burden?" he asked, but it was no question.

He crossed the room, gave her a hug, and kept his arm around her shoulders as he walked her to the kitchen door, where they watched Flora singing to her kitten, her cheek on the floor, her eyes on her pet.

"Don't give up, Olive," he whispered in her ear. "It's too soon to give up. I haven't thought the matter through yet. Don't give up."

Chapter 17

*O*LIVE STAYED A FEW MORE MIN-
utes, after making Douglas taste one of the biscuits she had brought.

"I told Flora to test one and see if they weren't too stale,"
Olive said, when Flora was sitting up and listening to her.

"It's fine," the child said, her eyes on the bag. She took
one out, looked at it, and handed it to him. "You try one,
Mr. Bowden."

Douglas took the biscuit. Out of the corner of his eye,
he saw Olive give a slow wink with one of her heterochromatic eyes. *You are a sly one*, he thought. He took a bite
and recoiled. He held it out to Flora.

"I have never really enjoyed biscuits made with anise,"
he told her. "Begging your pardon, Miss Grant, but Flora
is going to take these home to her gran."

Olive sighed. "Flora, do me a favor and take them. If
your gran complains, she can take it up with me."

"She won't," Flora said in a small voice.

He could tell Olive wanted to stay. He wanted her
to stay, but there were probably social rules that made
her give him a bright smile and close the bag. "Don't

forget these, Flora. Mr. Bowden, I'll think about what you told me."

"Do it."

He saw her to the door and watched her cross the street. She waved at him from her own stoop. He stood there a long moment, looking down the street to see Tommy Tavish making his way to Mrs. Cameron's house, rollicking along at a clipping pace on his crutches. Douglas turned and looked at Mrs. Aintree's tidy place next to the tearoom, wishing he could convince the woman to do a great service for a little family hanging on by a thread.

He thought of Mrs. Campbell, who had sat with Tommy when he couldn't and whom Olive paid with meals. Tommy managed on his own now, and Mrs. Campbell had returned to her own cottage, back to meals of weak tea and toast. And he knew that for one Mrs. Campbell, there were others in want, and not just the Highlanders. Life was less complicated at sea.

Maybe Olive was right, and why not? She knew her village better than he did. Maybe everyone in a poor village would look with suspicion on their own countrymen from far to the north until the refugees died off or crept away to become someone else's challenge. The pie only had so many slices.

Flora proved to be an excellent nurse, petting her little patient, singing to her, and then feeding her the thin gruel. He stood in the doorway and watched Pudding lap up the gruel, then curl up in her blanket-lined box and go to sleep.

"Flora, I have something you can do to help me," he told her, holding out his hand to her. He walked her into the surgery and pointed to two boxes on the floor. "I'll carry these into my waiting room, where I want you to organize them into piles."

She nodded and followed him back into the waiting room. He pried up the box top and indicated that she come closer.

He enjoyed her sharp intake of breath.

"Mr. Bowden, where did you get these?" she asked, touching the shells with the same delicacy she had used on Pudding.

"When I was only seven or eight years older than you, I started collecting shells," he told her. "Before us are shells from all of the seven seas." He set down three squares of ship's cloth. "Small, medium, and large will do for now, until I figure out what to do with them. Will you help?"

"Aye, but it's not enough to pay my debt for Pudding," she said, and followed that announcement with a solemn shake of her head.

"It will do for right now," he assured her.

He saw three patients that day, two of whom were able to pay his modest fee, and the third who brought him fish, which did perk up Pudding for a brief spell. He took a thoughtful walk to the greengrocer's to find mother and son doing well.

Lunch was fish soup at the tearoom, where he sat in the corner and watched Olive Grant with her diners. They paid so little, but Olive smiled at each one, stopping to chat before she went to the next table, and the next. He had enough left of his own luncheon to share with Flora across the street in the kitchen that had become Pudding's convalescent home.

Only with difficulty could he convince Flora that Pudding needed to stay overnight and that she should return home. He walked her down one of Edgar's narrow closes and into a row of decrepit stone shelters barely deserving the title of homes. Olive had told him those were the poor houses, provided by the Church of Scotland.

Flora hung back, her eyes apprehensive, as she took a scolding from Gran.

"I told her to drown the wee beast," Gran said and shook her finger at Flora. "She was not t'bother thee."

"No bother," Douglas assured the old woman. "I'm not too busy yet, and it seemed a pity to drown a perfectly good kitten."

"There's always more where that one came from," Gran told him with a sigh. She lowered her eyes, and Douglas felt the shame that filled the little room that appeared to be parlor, bedchamber, and kitchen for Gran and her dead daughter's child.

He felt a sudden burning anger at the Duchess of Sutherland and her progressive estate managers, who had convinced her that her Highland holdings could be squeezed for profit. He knew enough about the woman to know that her husband, the Marquess of Stafford, was England's wealthiest man. He wondered if the countess had any idea of the misery she had unleashed on her own people, many of them now as helpless as the kittens he saw kneading and nursing the equally tired mother cat in a corner of the room.

He swallowed his anger, determined that Flora not think he was angry at her. "You have a fine granddaughter," he told the old widow. "She took good care of Pudding after I finished."

"We'll pay you when we can," the widow murmured, her eyes still on the dirt floor.

"I'll think on the matter and find a way for Flora to pay me," he said. He touched Flora's shoulder. "And you'll report to Miss Grant tomorrow morning for more porridge for Pudding."

Flora nodded. "Thank'ee," she whispered. "I knew you would help me."

He had spent a lifetime helping men with great and unmanageable wounds. He had heard other heartfelt thanks, which he had brushed off because he was too busy and too hardened by suffering to dare them to sink in. An old surgeon ready for retirement had told him when he was newly back in the fleet as a surgeon that it wouldn't do to get too close to his patients. "If you care too much, you'll go mad, laddie," the surgeon had told him.

And here he was, caring with all his heart, and his patient was a kitten. He shook his head at his own folly. "I was glad to help, Flora. Good night to you both."

He stood a long while on the bridge, looking up at Lady Telford's mansion, where one wealthy woman lived, and then down the river toward the fishing docks, where the boats had been buttoned up for the night. He looked at his own place and then across the street to the tearoom.

A breeze came up and set the wind chimes outside the door to Miss Grant's Tearoom in motion. He smiled at the sound, thinking of years of creaking timbers and violent motion in his other homes. He recalled the high-pitched whine in the rigging when the wind was stiffening and the crash of waves onto the deck during storms at sea. All told, he preferred Olive Grant's wind chimes, both soothing and predictable.

Inside his house, he assumed the duties of mother cat and cleaned up his little charge. Pudding offered only a squeak in protest before sinking back into the kind of sleep he was familiar with, that of patients lying in their hammocks in that stupor of the wounded. He gathered up the kitten and box and carried them upstairs because he was a conscientious surgeon who had spent many nights in service to his patients.

He raised the window because the upstairs air needed to circulate. He didn't bother with a light as he stripped and pulled on his nightshirt, happy to surrender to the mattress again. With his hands behind his head in his thinking pose, he considered what to do about Tommy Tavish, who had pleaded with him only that morning in the cow bier to be allowed to return to his mam in their wretched cottage.

Douglas thought he had won that round, firmly telling

the boy that his stitches needed to come out in a week, but not in a place as dirty as the Tavish hovel, where foul humours and infections ruled. "I won't have you undoing all my work," he had told the boy. Whether Tommy listened to him remained to be seen. Other patients had ignored him, usually with lamentable results.

He rehearsed in his mind the surgery planned for Mrs. Aintree's fused fingers. At least her house was spotless and far less susceptible to germs. Once she was on the mend and her wounds healed, he could leave Edgar in good conscience, knowing he had helped.

Why did the knowledge have no appeal? Tommy would be healing, Mrs. Aintree as well, and Flora would be happy that little Pudding would be gimping about on three and a half legs. The grocer's wife had friends and relatives to assist her if she needed help, which he doubted. Women and mother cats had a fine instinct for child care. Miss Grant would smile her patient smile and wave goodbye, even as he knew she was staring down her own ruin in a year's time when her legacy ran out, all because Olive had a conscience and the Duchess of Sutherland did not.

Discontented in the extreme, he sat up and looked out the window, elbows on his knees, chin in his palms. He listened to the mellow chimes and suddenly had an idea so brilliant that he flopped back on his bed and laughed at the ceiling.

It was a modest idea, one so tiny and inconsequential that he knew if he over-thought the matter, he would toss it onto the ash heap of ideas better left to die aborning.

He padded downstairs to his surgery waiting room, where Flora had left his three piles of shells. He sat down cross-legged on the floor, wincing a bit as his bare parts met the cold wood. The moon shone on the shells, rendering them all white and gleaming, where he knew them to be multi-colored, exotic, and a far cry from a place as tired as Edgar.

He selected three shells, large, medium, and small, and took them into his surgery. He lit the lamp and searched until he found his smallest drill in his trephining kit, knowing in his heart that he would never tell Olive where he got it, even as it made him chuckle, thinking of the times he had used it to drill tiny holes in skulls.

He did a quick inventory of his catgut before he unrolled a modest length from the spool. Largest first or smallest first? He debated, then drilled holes through the largest shell at the top and bottom, then ditto with the others. He threaded through the largest shell, catgut behind, and made a small knot before he repeated the steps. One more trip to the waiting room and he had three threaded shells.

For want of anything better, he hung the three-shelled strands from the little hearth broom, using more catgut. Then he set it swaying. The sound bore no resemblance to Olive's metal wind chimes; it was a tantalizing rustle. He knew when the light struck his shells in the morning that the colors would glow, some almost iridescent, others pale and mysterious.

He held out the impromptu chimes and announced, "Flora, you are going to pay me with wind chimes. You'll make one for the kind lady too. And then we'll see who else wants them."

Olive rubbed her eyes and sat up in bed. She yawned and opened her eyes. There was the sound again, pebbles against her window. *I'm too old for pebbles against the window*, she thought and would have gone back to sleep, except for the "P'ssst! Olive!" that came next, a whisper in a lower register that she couldn't ignore.

She looked out the window, laughed, and opened it, astounded at the sight of Douglas Bowden, dignified surgeon, standing there in what looked like his nightshirt, holding out something that glittered in the moonlight.

"My blushes, Douglas," she whispered and tried not to laugh. He obviously had no idea that moonlight did curious things to cotton nightshirts. Luckily no one else was out at midnight. It wouldn't do for the constable to call Douglas up on charges of indecency or insanity or both.

Olive pulled on her robe, didn't bother with slippers, and hurried down the stairs, careful not to waken Tommy and Duke in the next bedchamber. She let herself out the front door and stood in the street with a lunatic.

He was nearly hopping up and down in his excitement. She just stared at him.

"It's a wind chime, or sort of!" he said, holding out the hearth broomstick to her. "Well, it will be when I have Flora and other children find just the right lengths of driftwood. I'll have her make me one to pay me back for Pudding's surgery."

"I want one too," Olive said, admiring the delicate shells and trying not to stare at the surgeon's hairy but handsome legs. For certain she would never stare at his nearly thigh-high nightshirt. Well, maybe just a peek.

A quick glance, and then she looked into his eyes, because that was safer. He had an inquiring expression, as though he expected her to think his thoughts. Amazingly, she did. She put her hand to her mouth because the idea was so audacious.

"We can get Flora and maybe other children to make more," she said, "and—"

He interrupted her in his enthusiasm. "—take a few to the Hare and Hound, where coach riders and the touring trade will see them—"

"—and want one of their own as a souvenir! Douglas, you are a genius."

"Not yet," he declared, taking back the shells. "If she only makes a few pence a day, it'll keep her and Gran fed and their pride intact."

He continued to look at her in that inquiring manner. "You have something bigger in mind, don't you?" she asked.

"I just might."

He seemed to have recalled where he was standing and in what stage of undress. "Beg your pardon, Miss Grant." He started to back up. "Flora's coming over for oats tomorrow . . . well, this morning. Can you ruin some more porridge?"

"Mr. Bowden, this is a strange conversation," she said with a laugh. "I will ruin some more porridge."

He gave her such a grin then, the boyish kind she had seen earlier. He gave her a salute, turned on his bare heels, and walked back across the street. She watched him go. If he was going to caper nearly naked in the street at midnight, she might have to suggest flannel.

Or not.

Chapter 18

*D*OUGLAS CAME ACROSS THE STREET in the morning for breakfast, fully clothed. The high color on his cheeks suggested to Olive that he might have taken a good look at himself in that nightshirt and wondered if he ever dared show himself in the tearoom again. Better put him out of his misery.

He opened his mouth, probably ready to apologize, but she spoke first. "My lips are sealed, sir," she said. "Would you like porridge or porridge?"

"I believe porridge would be best," he replied. "Do forgive last night's enthusiasm, but I had been wondering what to do. Will Gran require convincing?"

"Let's find out. When breakfast is over and I have ruined sufficient porridge for Flora's sake, let us see if Flora can put the chimes together."

"I should find a piece of driftwood," he said after he finished breakfast. He stood up to drink his coffee, which told Olive worlds about his busy life during the war. She wondered how many meals he ate sitting down.

"Nothing simpler. If you haven't already noticed, it piles up against the bridge."

He raised his cup in salute and hurried away, a far cry
from the man who had walked by her place only yesterday,
head down, hands clasped behind his back, dejection written everywhere except on a placard around his neck.

Feeling more optimistic than usual, Olive surprised
Maeve by instructing her to add more fish to the noonday
stew and be generous in slicing the loaves of bread.

Flora came into the kitchen like a breath of spring,
desperation gone from her face. She came right up to
Olive. "Miss Grant, I stopped to see Pudding first and she
is moving around! Please may I have some more thin porridge for her?"

She handed over the penny that Douglas had surely
given her and made no comment when Olive's first batch
of porridge was too thick. She ate it with no objection,
likewise the second, which took longer for her to eat
because she wasn't starving today. Flora concluded breakfast with bread from Maeve, who said she hadn't meant to
slice it so thick.

Her eyes widened to see butter on the bread. Olive's
breath caught in her throat when Flora clapped her hands
at the sight of butter. Olive watched, tears just below the
surface, as the little girl tested it with her tongue and gave
a small sigh. Olive decided that tomorrow there would
be eggs, although what excuse she could give for them
escaped her at the moment. Deformed yolks? Three minutes instead of four? Olive took a page from the surgeon's
book and decided she would think about it later. No sense
in rushing into prevarication. Perhaps a good fib was like
fine wine and needed to age.

"I nearly forgot," Flora said as she waited for Olive to
spoon Pudding's thin gruel into a can. She darted outside and returned with a piece of driftwood. "Mr. Bowden
wanted you to see this."

She held it out and Olive took it, turning the nicely
weathered wood over in her hands. "Brilliant."

"I don't understand," Flora said. "He wants you to come with me, and that it is all he would say."

"Very well, Flora. I have a little time before I must start luncheon."

They were almost out the door when the greengrocer stopped by with a basket of onions, leeks, and potatoes. Olive took a moment to savor the happiness in the man's eyes, even though he appeared to need sleep. He looked like a new father.

He held the basket out to her. "I paid Mr. Bowden, but I wanted to do this too. Since he's eating here, he said you should have it, Miss Grant."

She took it with thanks, mentally adding more potatoes to the as-yet-unmade luncheon, which in a stroke went from fish soup to fish stew.

He held out a smaller basket, this one with eggs nestled in oats so they would not crack. "And here are these."

"I appreciate your kindness," Olive said simply. After the greengrocer left, she took the food past Maeve and into the pantry. She touched the eggs, pleased to see two brown ones. *I can tell Flora tomorrow that people would rather eat white eggs than brown ones*, she thought.

Douglas met them in the waiting room. He had carried Pudding's box into the room, where kitten watched them with interest.

"I have to keep several layers of bandage on that limb because Pudding licks it," Douglas said. "Thank the Almighty that none of my Royal Navy patients licked their sutures."

Flora laughed out loud, which made Douglas smile. When Flora turned her attention to Pudding, he leaned toward Olive. "What would you wager that she has not laughed like that in ages?"

"I never wager," she replied, struck again at the great care Douglas took of his patients, and their owners in this case.

While Flora made certain her pet licked the porridge instead, Douglas enlisted Olive to help him. "I have drilled holes in the shells of appropriate size, and here is my spool of catgut. Did you like that piece of driftwood?"

She held it out to him. "I could wish we could take a bit of glass paper to it to smooth the rough surfaces, but I believe the rustic quality is what you were looking for."

"Precisely. This is to be my set of chimes and that is what I wish. Flora, I need your complete attention now," he told the child. "This is how you are going to pay me back for the surgery on Pudding."

In less than a half hour, Flora proved to be adept at stringing shells. Her eyes full of accomplishment, she held up the chimes and gave them a gentle shake. "'Tis magic," she whispered.

"I believe it is," Douglas agreed. "I am going to hang it outside my front door. Flora, this is magnificent." He bowed, and she curtseyed and then giggled.

"I would like one as well," Olive said. "I will pay you for mine."

Flora stared at her.

Olive looked beyond Flora to Douglas, who held up three fingers. "Three pence," she said.

Flora nodded, so solemn. After a moment of quiet consideration—who knew what a six-year-old thought about money?—she pointed to the three boxes of shells. "Which ones would you like, Miss Grant?"

Olive made her choice while Douglas hung his shells on a nail outside the front door. Flora let her help, and soon Olive had her own chimes. She handed three coins to Flora, who stared at them in her palm.

Olive closed her fingers over the little girl's hand. "Put them in your apron pocket, and keep them safe." She glanced at the surgeon, who nodded his approval. "Mr. Bowden, I have a good idea. Flora, would you make three more of these?"

"One for me and Gran, but who are the others for?" Flora asked. "Do you know, Mr. Bowden?"

Olive appreciated his fine instincts, where children were concerned. He squatted on his haunches so he was eye to eye with the girl. "It's this way, Flora: surgeons haven't much business sense. I believe Miss Grant has a lot of good ideas. She and I both think you can make these little baubles and sell them to traveling visitors."

Flora was silent again. Olive could nearly hear the gears turning in her brain, but what she saw humbled her. Nothing in Flora's face even hinted at discouragement; instead, there was barely suppressed excitement, an energy that seemed like a candle catching fire and growing taller. The child patted the coins in her pocket and gave the surgeon such a look of admiration.

"People will really buy them?" she asked him.

"They really will, Flora," he assured her. He got up, sat in a chair, and motioned for her to sit in the chair next to him. "I have traveled to so many places."

"Farther than Dumfries?" Flora asked. Her face grew solemn, all the light and energy gone. It was as though some cosmic hand had snuffed glowing hope. "I traveled too, only it was not fun."

"My travel wasn't fun either," he said, and Olive saw his struggle to remain in control of his own emotions. She could tell he saw the sudden difference in Flora's demeanor. "But some of those places were beautiful and I wanted to remember them. People do that when they travel. They want to take something home from their adventure. Your shells will be just the right touch."

Flora nodded, still so serious. "They will pay me? They won't just steal the chimes or break Mam's mirror or drive off the cattle or . . . or kill my dog or shout at us?" She put her hands over her ears and scrunched down small, her breath coming faster and faster.

Olive grabbed Flora and sat the child on her lap, holding

her close. She took in Douglas's shocked expression as he understood what was happening to this little one who was suddenly more his patient than Pudding ever could be. His arms went around them both as they sat close together on the two chairs. The only sound was Flora weeping.

"My poor, poor wee one," Olive whispered, wondering if Flora had ever allowed herself the luxury of tears for her own cruel uprooting.

"Gran and I, we couldn't keep Mam warm, not with the rain and the wind. And then that soldier! No one helped us! We needed a little help!"

Olive didn't try to stop her own tears as she wished with all her heart that someone, anyone, had at least held a blanket over Flora's dying mother. *I would have*, she thought, frustrated because it was such a small, puny thing.

"What have we done?" she said to Douglas.

"Us? Nothing," he replied, speaking into her ear as Flora cried between them. "The better question is what are we going to do now?"

In a few minutes, Flora's tears subsided into sniffs. Douglas disentangled himself and went into the next room, returning with squares of cotton. "Blow," he commanded them, and they did.

With a sigh, Flora leaned against Olive, whose arms tightened around the child. "Gran says crying never solves anything."

"Actually, it can, Flora," Douglas said. He dabbed at Flora's face and then Olive's. "Whenever you feel sad, come here or visit Miss Grant if I am not here."

"You don't have a pill for this, do you?" Flora asked.

"I don't, but you may weep all you wish. And when you're done, we'll sit here and make shell chimes."

Flora nodded. She got off Olive's lap and went to the table where she had laid out Olive's shells. In another minute, she was humming to herself and stringing shells.

"Give me your hand," Douglas said.

Olive held out her hand, and he took it in his firm grip. She moved closer on her chair. "What just happened?" she whispered.

"Life just happened," he said. "I've seen it over and over—men mourning the loss of a limb, men just exhausted from a victory when they should be over-joyed." He looked beyond her shoulder. Something told her that if she turned around and looked too, she would see an unknown universe, a place inhabited by men at war. "These are the hardest wounds of all to heal," he told her, when she didn't think he was going to say any-thing. "I have my fair share, but Flora has too many. Her mind can't handle what happened because she has no basis of fact to comprehend why anyone would treat her cruelly."

"I can't handle what happened," Olive retorted.

"I disagree; you can, and you're doing splendidly," Douglas declared. The pressure of his hand increased.

He hesitated then, and she knew what he was going to say. Why was it that she already knew him this well? "Go ahead and say it," she told him, "or I will. What will I do when my legacy runs out and I cannot feed anyone else?"

"That's close," he admitted. "Edgar needs to become a paying concern again, which will lift your burden."

He was right; she knew it. "Do you have any . . . any . . ."

"Solution yet? Alas, no. I'm thinking, though."

She sat with the surgeon, supremely unconcerned that they were holding hands like giddy people. *Human touch*, she thought. *How I've needed it. I'm tired of being the adult.*

"I took on some burdens and I can't get out of them," she told him, hesitating herself, because the words sounded weak to her ears. "I mean, not that I want to . . ." He didn't need to know how many nights she stared at columns and figures, wondering how to squeeze out more income. She was already wondering where she would go when the money ran out.

She looked into his eyes, which made him smile, because she already knew his opinion of her colorful eyes. He saw one thing, she saw another, looking into his brown eyes. She saw a depth and breadth that took her breath away. This man, this retired surgeon, was far from retired. Whether he liked it or not, and she wasn't certain how the matter stood, he was always going to be a surgeon. He was always going to care more than the average man. She took a deep breath.

"Sometimes at night I stare at columns and figures, and it frightens me," she said softly, testing the words, hoping they were firm enough to prove that she wasn't a coward.

"I've wondered how you manage," he said and shuddered elaborately. "It would give me the willies."

She couldn't help a little laugh. "What can I do?" she asked, squeezing his hand in turn.

"We can find a way to involve others," he replied. "How many Highland families were dumped on you or wandered here?"

"Twenty, but the number has shrunk. I swear some of the women simply died of homesickness," she said, as her eyes filled with tears again. "They wouldn't eat. They just turned their faces away and died."

He dabbed at her eyes with his cotton square. "How many people then?"

She blew her nose. "Maybe forty. Of that number, fifteen or eighteen men. Some have cast aside their pride and come to me for food at least once a day. Some, like Gran, are simply too proud. I fear for them most of all."

"And well we should."

There it was again. Every time Olive said *I*, he said *we*. In that case, "What should we do?"

"Done!"

Startled, Olive released Douglas's hand to see Flora standing triumphant by the table, holding out her shell chimes. "This is yours, Miss Grant," she said, tears forgotten, eyes bright.

Olive held it up, admiring the play of colors and the gentle swishing sound when she shook it. "Flora, you are a wonder."

"I like doing this," Flora replied, obviously not a child requiring much praise. "Mr. *Bowden*, if I can sell these, Gran and I will have enough money to eat in Miss Grant's Tearoom, won't we?"

"You will," he agreed, his voice not quite firm, but firm enough to satisfy a child. "Do you know another little girl or boy who might like to be a partner? You could make twice as many that way."

"Aye, we could. Sally MacGregor," Flora said decisively. "She and her sister have to share a dress. They could buy material and Gran could sew it."

Share a dress? Olive thought, appalled. She put her hand to her mouth.

"That is a wonderful idea, Flora," Douglas said. He moved in front of Olive to stand closer to the child, but Olive knew he was shielding Flora from the horror he saw on her face. She took a deep breath and another.

"That's right, isn't it, Miss Grant," Douglas was saying smoothly. "You two can make a few of these this morning. I would help, but I have to visit the greengrocer's new son, and stop by the docks and check on Captain Fergusson's sprained ankle. Nasty affairs, sprains. When I get back, and after luncheon, we'll visit the innkeeper at the Hare and Hound."

"I may come?" Flora asked.

"Most certainly. You are the merchant, Flora," he said promptly.

He fetched his medical satchel from inside his office and hurried away. Olive pulled her chair closer to the table, where Flora had already arranged the shells for the next souvenir that traveling folk might buy this summer as they journeyed through their little corner of Scotland.

Oh, please let them come and buy, Olive thought. She threaded a shell and tied the first small knot. *Please, for Flora's sake.*

Chapter 19

*D*OUGLAS CHOSE THE NAME FOR the chimes that weren't strictly chimes, the shells strung on catgut by a Highlands child who wanted to eat and not feel like a charity case.

After taking a good look at wee Davey McDaniel's umbilical stump and a quick listen at his lungs, then a rewrapping of Captain Fergusson's sprained ankle and a further admonition, probably fruitless, to stay off it, Douglas found Olive and Flora in the tearoom.

Tommy sat with them, discreetly scratching at his sutures. *At least he does not lick them,* Douglas thought. He nodded when Olive put a bowl of fish stew in front of him, thick stew with onions and leeks and speckled with butter. A thump on the floor meant that Duke was not so patient.

"I had a visit from Johnny McDaniel, the greengrocer," Olive said. "He said the onions and leeks were for my kitchen."

"He already paid me, and he asked what else he could do," Douglas said and laughed. "His eyes nearly glittered when I told him that Miss Grant's Tearoom could use whatever seconds he doesn't need. Or maybe he was just tired from staying up late with little Davey. I mean, wee Davey."

Flora cleared her throat and looked at him in so pointed a fashion that Douglas had to wipe his mouth just then so he would not laugh. *This is a businesswoman*, he thought, with considerable admiration. *I think I am wasting her time.*

"Tommy says we need a name for this," Flora said and looked from one person to the next, reminding Douglas of an old sailing master getting the attention of midshipmen for a hated lesson on navigation. She had amazing poise for a six-year-old. "They aren't really chimes."

"No," Tommy agreed. "Just something pretty to look at."

Olive put in his two pence worth. "I like the swishing sound."

They all looked at him, which Douglas found flattering. And there was little Flora, drumming her fingers on the table. Her serious expression touched his heart. As young as she was, this child of cruelty and misfortune knew exactly what was at stake with the little whatchamacallits.

"I collected my shells from the seven seas," he said, "and they were too charming to pitch overboard. I hauled them from the Baltic to Australia." He looked at each face, startled at how dear they were becoming to him. "Seven Seas Fancies, since they aren't really chimes. What do you think, Flora?"

He knew who was in charge. A glance at Olive's smiling heterochromatic eyes told him she understood too.

"I like it. How do we—"

"I have some stiff paper in with my ordinary stationery," Olive said. "If we cut it in strips, poke a wee . . ." She flashed those marvelous eyes at Douglas again. ". . . a little hole and then tie it on with yarn or twine, that will do. We can write the price on it too."

The others nodded. "What should we charge?" Flora

asked. "I know we should pay you for your shells. Without them, we couldn't do this."

Where is this enormous love coming from? Douglas asked himself. He had never felt anything like it before, not in his life of war and wounds. He could no more charge Flora for his shells than fly.

"The shells are a gift, Flora," he said simply. "I've never met a braver child than you."

Other than Olive's intake of breath and another kind look, the room was silent and the conspirators motionless. Slowly, Flora put out her hand. He took her small fingers in his, grasped her hand, and gave it a shake.

Her hand still in his, Douglas answered the question he thought he saw in her eyes. "I can get more exotic shells like these. I know a kind lady in Plymouth who has wanted to do me a favor for years."

Flora swallowed and seemed to feel no inclination to let go of his hand. He knew there had never been a father in her life, that man who stood firm with the 93rd Sutherland Foot and died at the Battle of New Orleans. He tugged on her hand. "Flora, come sit on my lap."

With no hesitation, she did precisely that, leaning back with a sigh that made him wonder how he could keep breathing, he who knew so much about respiration.

"What should we charge?" he asked and looked around. Everyone looked back at him. "Well?"

He realized that none of them, probably including Olive, had much experience with money. "Four pence," he said decisively.

Flora and Tommy gasped. Even Duke, who had insinuated himself into the dining room thumped his tail. Olive seemed to be considering the matter, but mostly she was just smiling.

"Too much? Not enough?" he asked.

Again the blank stares.

"Four pence," he repeated. "If the cost is too dear, no

one will buy. We're going to ask the innkeep at the Hare and Hound . . ." He looked at Olive.

"Jamie Dougall."

". . . Jamie Dougall, if we can display your fancies in his front window. The coaches all stop there."

He felt Flora nodding against his chest and knew he had an ally. The little minx did understand business. "And we will suggest to Mr. Dougall that he sell Seven Seas Fancies for five pence, with him getting the extra pence for his troubles. What say you?"

"Aye," they all said, and Duke thumped his tail harder.

"Very well. We'll put five pence on the label. Flora, you need to find your little friend and show her what to do. Make her your business partner." Another nod. "Tommy, can we send you to the bridge for more driftwood? Tell me no if your leg won't manage it with crutches just yet, and I'll go."

"I'll manage," Tommy said. "Mrs. Aintree doesn't need me 'til evening now."

"I'll cut those strips for the charms," Olive said. She frowned. "I am no great shakes at penmanship, but the minister's wife is good at lettering. I'll take these to her."

Tommy shook his head. "The minister wouldn't even read a scripture at my wee sister's burial."

"Then we will give his wife a chance to make amends," Olive said smoothly. "I believe in repentance, even if the minister is shaky on the matter." She looked at Flora. "What do you think?"

"Minister's wife."

"Well, then? We all have assignments. Hop down, Flora, and get to it," Douglas said. He certainly hadn't forgotten his warrant officer voice of command.

Flora hopped down and handed Olive back one of the pence she had paid for her fancy. "Some fish stew for my gran and Sally MacGregor? If she doesn't have the dress today, we can put these together at her cottage."

Olive hurried to the kitchen for a can. Douglas followed her, knowing what he would find. Her marvelous face a study in control, she leaned on the kitchen work table, trying not to weep. He clapped his arm around her shoulder, gave her a squeeze, and said he was off to drill more holes in shells.

"You'll appreciate this as few women would, I think," he said, eager for a smile, if not a laugh. "I'm using the smallest drill in my cranial kit."

She gasped and threw a dish towel at him, which Douglas Bowden counted as complete success.

"Imagine what I could do with my dental key."

"You are a wretch."

They reassembled at four o'clock, Flora carrying six Seven Seas Fancies. The minister's wife had been more than willing to use her prettiest calligraphy on the labels, going the extra mile to scallop the edges of the paper. Even Tommy approved.

Olive dredged up some ribbon from her late mother's sewing basket. "I never have time to mend anything," she confessed. "Thank goodness I am easy on stockings." She blushed and laughed out loud when Douglas covered his face with his hands and peeked between them.

Flora was smiling; so was Tommy. Douglas waited for the tail thump from Duke, and there it came. "We are quite a corporation," he said.

Olive had already run the ribbon through the labels. She tied one on a fancy, and Flora watched and then finished the others. Maeve brought a pasteboard box from the pantry and Flora arranged the six ornaments.

"Here we go," Douglas said. "I can carry the box. Olive, do you have time to accompany us to the Hare and Hound?"

"I'll make time. We're having some of your venison haunch tonight, Mr. Bowden," she informed him. "It's roasting in the Rumford. Flora, you will like it. Tommy, you may join us too."

He shook his head. "Time for me to milk. C'mon, Duke." He thumped handily to the door, adept on his crutches. He stopped and looked back and said with real pride. "Mrs. Aintree watched me milk Lucinda for a whole week, but now she lets me alone. She even fixes me supper and gives me enough for my mam and Mrs. Cameron."

"We're getting nicer here in Edgar," Olive said after Tommy left. "I give you the credit, Mr. Bowden."

There it was again, that feeling of another sort of pride, the kind that comes as part relief and part competence. "I'm just doing what I was taught," he said. "You know, to help where I can, same as you." He touched the fading green and yellow skin around his eye. "Better give the credit to that rascal Joe Tavish. If he hadn't broken his boy's leg, I never would have stopped in Edgar."

"He's still a rascal," Olive said as she took her bonnet off the nail just inside the kitchen. "Now let's see if we have any friends at the Hare and Hound."

"At least the innkeeper doesn't see Miss Olive Grant's Tearoom as competition," Douglas said as they walked up the street, Flora between them, her eyes serious and her hands knotted into fists with thumbs tucked inside.

"Mercy, no! You've seen my afternoon tea and coffee customers who all clear away before I start serving the less fortunate among us. Jamie Dougall has the commercial trade in town."

Whatever the complexities of the argument, the Hare and Hound was empty, with the innkeep wiping off his already spotless counter. Douglas knew the coach he had taken from Dumfries arrived at midday, and another followed around six o'clock. He had eaten at the Hound once, a beef roast just the proper shade of pink, with fat laced through it, accompanied by the best dripped pudding he had ever eaten. He looked down at Flora and wondered if she could even comprehend such a meal. He doubted it.

"Mr. Dougall," Olive began. "I believe the only person here you do not know is Flora MacLeod." Olive knelt beside her. "We have a business proposition to make. Mr. Bowden?"

Douglas set the pasteboard box on the counter and took out one of the Seven Seas Fancies. He stared at it, trying to see the brave little trinket through the eyes of Edgar's best businessman, certainly its most critical. He felt his courage head directly toward a lee shore. *Don't you dare laugh at us*, he thought. It would ruin Flora. He glanced at Olive Grant, a woman he already knew who wore her heart pinned on her sleeve. Flora knew her as the kind lady. Her lips were set tight, too.

A slight smile on his face, Jamie Dougall turned the fancy over and gave it a little shake. The soft rustle made him nod his head. He looked down at Flora. "Did you make these?"

Her eyes wide with fear, Flora swallowed and stepped forward. "Aye, sir. Tommy Tavish gathered the driftwood, Mr. Bowden gave us his shells from every, every sea there is, and Miss Grant had some ribbon." Her voice grew stronger as she warmed to her subject. She touched the catgut that held the shells in place. "Mr. Bowden says this is catgut, but he tells me he never uses real cats." She looked up at Douglas for reassurance. "It's not . . . it's not . . ."

". . . not the Royal Navy way, Mr. Dougall."

Jamie Dougall laughed out loud and spoke over his shoulder. "Brighid, you'd better come out here. We have a business proposition you'll want to see."

A red-faced woman with a floury apron came out of the kitchen, tucking her stray hairs under her cap. She took in the sight before her, but her eyes rested the longest on Flora MacLeod.

Mrs. Dougall nodded while her husband explained the strange visit. She turned over the label. "Five pence?"

Flora nodded. "That way you can keep one pence out of all the Seven Seas Fancies we make."

Mr. and Mrs. Dougall looked at each other. Flora must have known it was the critical moment. "You see, if we keep four pence, that's enough for Gran and me to eat at Miss Grant's Tearoom, and not feel . . ." Her voice trailed away. "Poor." She brightened. "And there will be enough for my partner Sally MacGregor and her sister to each have a dress. They share one now."

Flora stepped back, looked from Douglas to Olive, saw what she needed, and turned her face into Olive's skirt to hide herself.

"I said too much," she whispered when Olive dropped to her knees to hug the child.

"What you said was right and true," Olive said. She stood up, her arm around Flora, whose face was still turned into her skirt.

Silence. Douglas reminded himself to breathe.

"We had a wee daughter once," Mrs. Dougall said. She wiped her apron across her face, even though more flour clung to her cheeks now. She looked at her husband, and there was something in her eyes remarkably close to Flora's eyes.

"We have enough room in the window for such a bauble," Mr. Dougall said finally. "I'll put up a little sign. We get enough visitors on the coach trade through here in the summer. There's no guarantee in wintertime, but we'll worry about winter later."

When I'm far away from Edgar, Douglas thought and hated himself for the reminder. "Thank you, Mr. Dougall," he said.

Mr. Dougall lifted the hatch in the counter and came out to face them. He touched Flora on the shoulder, and she looked around, her eyes dark and worried.

"We'll take all you can make, Miss Flora MacLeod, you and Sally MacGregor. And mind you, we don't need the profit. You can keep all five pence."

Flora burst into tears, which meant that Mrs. Dougall followed suit. Douglas looked at Olive, who was biting her lip to keep back her emotions. He swallowed down his own, grateful that none of his former patients he had bullied unmercifully to take care and follow instructions were there to point at him and hoot.

Mr. Dougall put his arms around Flora. "Business ladies don't cry. Dry your eyes now. Make me five more and bring them over tomorrow. We'll see how they sell. No promises, mind."

Flora dried her tears on her plaid shawl, so many sizes too large that it had to be Gran's. She nodded and held out her hand to the innkeeper, just as she had held out her hand to Douglas.

Jamie Dougall had no proof against that, the same as Douglas, hours before. His lips quivered, but he shook hands with Flora MacLeod.

Chapter 20

*T*HAT'S AS CLOSE TO A LEE SHORE THAT I ever want to float," Douglas told Olive as they left the Hare and Hound. "I swear I'm getting too old for this much drama."

"You'll be happy enough to push on in a few months and find a peaceful place that needs a surgeon, and that's all?" Olive asked.

"Well, yes. I've had such a life. I have earned a peaceful practice," he told her.

"You've only been here two weeks," she said, which made him stare at her.

"It feels like three years since I snatched Tommy Tavish out of his mother's arms," he said. "Only two weeks? Olive, I'm just tired."

She didn't know Douglas Bowden well, but she doubted he meant to use such a petulant voice. "And you think I am not?" she wanted to say. Then to her embarrassment, she realized she had said precisely that. She opened her mouth again to apologize but then closed it. Edgar was her village. Its problems were her problems and she knew them well. She was wrong to think anyone else would care as much as she did, even a surgeon.

They stared at each other. She looked at every wrinkle around his tired eyes, and the tightness of his lips, and the way he carried his shoulders so high. This was a man so tightly wound that she had no words for that much exhaustion.

They stood in the street and she watched his eyes as he looked around, almost as though anticipating where the next crisis would begin, trying to identify it and buy himself a few more seconds to cushion himself against whatever the crisis might be. Was this what it meant to go to war? She could probably apologize from now to the twentieth century for living in a shabby village in Scotland that needed him so badly. Douglas Bowden had already given every last ounce of his strength to a country at war for a generation; he was done with misery. What right did she have to complicate his life when all he wanted was peace and quiet?

"I am so sorry," she began, "so sorry. I . . . We needed you and we took from you without even asking. We won't ask any more."

She did something then so forward, right there on the street. She kissed his cheek, patted his shoulder, and gave him a little push toward his rented house.

"Go to bed, Mr. Bowden. If I could sing you a lullaby, I would."

He smiled at that, so Olive knew she hadn't completely fractured whatever sort of friendship this was.

"You left out the part about warm milk and biscuits," he said, the ragged edge to his voice receding now. "Did you ever have those?"

"Once or twice. My mother was the kind sort." She put her hands on her hips when he continued to stand there. "I mean it. Go to bed. Flora is going home to plan world domination, for all we know. Tommy is busy in Mrs. Aintree's cattle bier. I will bring over some of your venison that you so kindly paid for, and see that Flora and Gran get some too."

"The neighbors will talk, if you come bearing food."

"Maeve will come with me. Seriously. Go on." She turned on her heel and went into her tearoom, touching her metal chimes to set them in motion and make a little music that she suddenly needed. She closed the door behind her and didn't look out the window until she was certain he had to be inside his own dwelling. And when she looked and found the street empty, she felt a little sad that he had done what she bade him do.

The noon meal was the big one, so Olive took her time with supper. Unable to resist a nibble at the crusty layer on the venison haunch, she cut off a corner, and then a little more, unable to remember something as delicious as meat, with potatoes and onions nestled shoulder to shoulder and treading broth thickened by a little flour.

Her few diners were wide-eyed with amazement. The fragrance must have traveled down the street because others came to the tearoom, people of modest means but still able to pay for their portions. The minister's wife dropped by more of her exquisitely printed labels, sniffed the air, and stayed to eat.

"Poached deer?" the well-mannered lady asked, her eyes lively.

"No, I roasted it," Olive teased back.

When the last customer left, after tipping his hat to her and hinting for venison sandwiches tomorrow with lots of sliced onions, Olive prepared a plate for Douglas Bowden. She saw no lights in the upstairs rooms, so she called Maeve away from the dishes.

"We're taking food across the street," she said. "When we're done there, we'll take some to the MacLeods."

Douglas must have been watching for them, because he stood in his open doorway, his shirttail out, his neckcloth a distant memory somewhere. He took the food with thanks and set it on the table in the surgery waiting room, among a pile of books that appeared well-thumbed. What looked like strips of twine marked the pages.

"It's oakum," he said, following her gaze. "You know, the old rope that sailors unravel to use for plugging leaks."

She didn't, aware that she probably knew as little about ships as the bewildered crofters from the Duchess of Sutherland's Highland holdings.

She looked at the book open on the table, with its diagrams of hands. "I haven't tried to unfuse fingers," he admitted. "I have no doubt I can do it, but it's nice to consult the experts. I always study, no matter how many times I have done a procedure. Well, if time allows."

"You're supposed to relax, eat, and go to bed," she reminded him as he sat down with no ceremony and started to eat, the book propped close by.

"Don't you know it's rag manners to order someone about in his own house?" he asked, his eyes tired still, but with humor lurking around his mouth. "You're as troublesome as Napoleon."

"I am a managing spinster," she said.

He shook his head. "No, Flora has it right: you are a kind lady."

Embarrassed, Olive glanced at Maeve, who appeared to be hugely enjoying this whole exchange. "And now we are going to see Flora and Gran. Maeve?"

Someone knocked on the door. When Douglas rose to answer it, Olive silently thanked her own wisdom in taking Maeve along on an errand that required no assistance. She didn't need the person on the other side of the door to spread the sort of gossip that a village where nothing happens sometimes craved.

With relief, Olive saw Mrs. Aintree standing there, a small pitcher of milk in her hand. She gave it to Douglas. "For your dinner, Mr. Bowden." The widow looked around. "Do you have a moment?"

"We were just leaving," Olive said.

"No need, lass," Mrs. Aintree said. "You should know this, too."

"Tommy hasn't been giving you troub . . ." Olive said at the same time as Douglas said, "Tommy's leg is . . ."

Mrs. Aintree laughed. "Listen to the two of you." She looked first at Olive. "No, my dear, Tommy is all I could ask for in a milker." She turned to Douglas. "He keeps scratching those stitches."

"It's time they came out," Douglas said. "Soon, I promise. What . . . what is it?"

Mrs. Aintree took a deep breath and looked toward the ceiling, as if shy to speak. "I have two empty rooms over my kitchen," she said finally, and she spoke fast, as if trying to keep ahead of her own natural reserve, a commodity well-represented in Edgar. "No reason that Tommy and his mam can't move in there. I can use her help, Mr. Bowden. I don't know why I didn't think I needed it."

Olive watched with gratitude in her heart as Douglas Bowden's shoulders relaxed. *Two problems solved*, Olive thought. *The Tavishes will have a home, and Mrs. Aintree will have help with housework and cooking, following Mr. Bowden's hand surgery.*

"I haven't mentioned it to Tommy yet," the widow said. She looked at the surgeon now, the hard work over as she acknowledged her needs and let go of her bit of unnecessary pride. "I wanted you to know first."

"He'll be delighted," Douglas said. "I know I am. Mrs. Aintree, I predict that Mrs. Tavish will be most grateful and ever so attentive in her duties, once you explain them carefully to her. All she wants is a place for her and her boy to live without fear."

"There's a bed in each room and lots of sheets and blankets," Mrs. Aintree said. "I have so much. In fact, if you need some, you know, when winter comes . . ."

"I'll be gone by then," he told her. "But I thank you for the offer."

"You really should just stay here," Mrs. Aintree told him.

"He has other plans," Olive said quietly. "We're grateful he is here now."

Mrs. Aintree nodded. "I'll tell Tommy, and we'll walk together to tell his mam."

"Would you like me to come along?"

"No, laddie," she said, her eyes kind. Olive wondered if Mrs. Aintree saw the exhaustion too. "It's a woman's job. Tommy is all the escort I need."

When she left, Douglas let out his breath in a sigh of satisfaction. "I haven't prayed in years, but I tell you, Olive, I was about to give it a try, before Mrs. Aintree knocked on my door!"

"Heaven forbid that you should be forced to summon deity," Olive joked. "Did you forget I am a minister's daughter?"

He shook his head. "I'm off my feet, my stomach is about to get full, a problem is solved, and I feel a glimpse of returning good humor. How simple is man."

Another knock.

"We are busier tonight than Wellington after Waterloo," Douglas said. "I'll have to tell people to form a line to the left."

Two people stood there. Olive had eyes for one, and from the way he reached forward, Douglas had eyes for the other.

She stepped aside while he gently reached for the good arm of Edgar's cobbler. She sucked in her breath to see a bodkin driven straight through his wrist.

"What did you do, man?" Douglas asked, impressing Olive with the sudden calmness in his voice, and of all things, more than a hint of a smile.

She realized what she was seeing and wondered how

the Royal Navy had ever let such a doctor actually retire. *My stars*, she thought, wondering if such things were taught in medical school. As soon as Douglas Bowden sees that some wretched wound isn't going to be fatal, he has a remarkable facility for putting someone at ease.

Sure enough, the terror left the man's face, even if the pain did not. "You're looking at a clumsy fellow, Mr. Bowden. Can you fix me?"

"Without question, Mister . . . Mister . . ."

"McIntyre. What a poor excuse for a cobbler I am. I was going to stitch up a pair of boots. Got on a wooden box, a shaky wooden box let me add, to reach for my larger needles and the bodkins. I'd shake your hand but . . ."

The surgeon chuckled. "Some other time. Go right in there," he said, opening the door to his surgery. "Let me help you. Just tell yourself it looks worse than it is."

"Crivvens, but he is a cool one, is our surgeon," the innkeeper's wife said.

Our surgeon, Olive thought, touched to her heart's core. *I wish that were so.* "He is. Since he is occupied, may I help?"

Mrs. Dougall silently held out three small dresses. Olive swallowed hard and took them in her arms.

"I said we had a daughter once," Mrs. Dougall said, her voice so low that Olive could barely hear her. "You'll find a good use for them: one for little Flora, and two for the MacGregor sisters."

"Thank you," Olive said, trying to be as cool as the surgeon, when she wanted to give the innkeep's wife a great hug and then dance around the room with Maeve.

"I have others too, and a bonny cloak for winter," Mrs. Dougall said. She hesitated and then cast aside her Scottish reticence much as Mrs. Aintree had done. "Some of us have not been as welcoming and kind as we could have been, have we?"

Olive had no trouble finding excuse for her fellow villagers. "We already slice a thin oatbread here in Edgar,

Mrs. Dougall. Sometimes it's hard to see how we can help others, when our own lot is skimpy."

"That can change," Mrs. Dougall said. "I think it must." She left as quietly as she had come.

"Oh, Maeve, we had better get ourselves to the MacLeods," Olive said.

"Will Gran see these dresses as charity?" Maeve asked.

"Happen she might, but I can be a bit of a martinet, if needs must," Olive told her.

"Miss Grant? You?"

She turned around at the surgeon's voice, to show off the dresses. "Yes! Don't quiz me. So much for your peaceful evening. How is Mr. McIntyre's wrist?"

He shrugged. "The scariest thing is the hematoma, which I will lance. Blood pools under the skin when things like this happen. Toss in a suture or two and Mr. McIntyre will be on his merry, and hopefully wiser, way. The venison will keep and I will eventually find my bed." He fingered the fabric of one of the dresses she held. "This yellow one will look good on the impresario of Edgar, Miss Flora MacLeod herself."

"My thought precisely. Come, Maeve."

He put his hand on her arm and gave it a little shake. "Miss Grant, it appears I may have underestimated your village."

Chapter 21

*D*OUGLAS DECIDED THAT THE earth's axis had somehow shifted under Edgar, and he was quite willing to give the credit to Flora MacLeod. He had mentioned that epiphany to Olive, who had looked at him a long time down her nose.

"I believe she must share the credit with you, Mr. Bowden," she assured him the next morning when he stopped by to see Flora's most recent crop of fancies. "The people of my village are already calling you their surgeon. I know! I know! You have no plans to stay."

"I don't," he had said, trying to sound firm, but failing, in his critical estimation. "Thank you for understanding my own need for peace and quiet."

"I understand perfectly, and they don't need to know, sir," she said. "You can vanish some night, once you have solved all of our problems."

She was such a tease. They laughed together, and Olive even agreed to assist when he unfused Mrs. Aintree's fingers.

"I can train you to be an excellent pharmacist mate," he told her. "You can learn to handle any number of minor crises."

The fishy look she gave him suggested that her heart wasn't entirely taken up with medicine, as his obviously was, since he couldn't even get through a Scottish village without stopping to heal its inhabitants and maybe walk on water.

He accepted the fact that he was an easy mark, which would have astounded his Royal Navy colleagues, who knew him only as a hard-eyed, single-minded surgeon lacking even a flyspeck of sentiment.

Fools, they have never met Flora MacLeod, Douglas decided as he walked across the street later for luncheon with Olive. The little girl had already burst into his house earlier that morning after the early coach had stopped at the Hart and Hound. She wore that yellow dress from an earlier decade, held in by a length of twine.

"Ah! Lovely!" he had said before she even had a chance to speak. "Twirl around."

She did and then opened her fist to show him ten coins. "Mr. Bowden! Two charms to the same lady!"

"That's what I thought might happen, Flora," he told her. "Travelers want more than one to share with friends."

He sent her on her way with little Pudding, who was bobbling about and disinclined to remain in the box where she had convalesced. "He needs that fine oatmeal several times a day," was Douglas's prescription. "Buy two pennies' worth of oats at the greengrocer's and feed Mama cat as well. I'll be over in a few days to remove her sutures."

Satisfied, he watched as Flora carefully picked up her kitten, wrapped her into a length of Gran's shawl, and left at a more sedate pace. She looked back in the doorway and he gave her an inquiring glance.

"Mr. Bowden, you are good with kittens," she said, her eyes kind. He looked for anxiety and distrust and saw none. He was no fool to think that Flora MacLeod would never have another nightmare or frightening turn, but he could not deny the gentle mantle of peace that had settled on her young shoulders. For now, he would count it as a blessing.

By the time he made the trip across the street to luncheon, Flora had found her way to Olive's tearoom with the MacGregor sisters, who now had a dress apiece.

The smaller sister, introduced to him by Flora as Euna, stood on a table in the corner of the tearoom as Mrs. Campbell pinned the hem. "Euna and Sally MacGregor," Flora said. "They will help make our little fancies. Miss Grant says we have formed a corporation."

Douglas laughed. "You'll have to declare a name, register it, and pay taxes to the crown."

"We're not paying the crown a single penny," Flora assured him.

"I wouldn't either," Olive said. She sat hemming one of the dresses.

"A revolutionary," Douglas warned. "*Aux barricades!*"

She shook her finger at him and returned to her hemming, looking as content as he had ever seen her. He looked round the tearoom, where Olive's usual customers chatted quietly and ate what looked like venison sandwiches. *And when was the last time anyone here ever had meat*, he asked himself, pleased.

"The girls are paying me a penny each to alter their dresses," Mrs. Campell said, speaking around the pins in her mouth, which made the surgeon in Douglas Bowden give a silent yelp. Why did women do that?

"Mrs. Campbell is a treasure," Olive said softly, after clearing off a spot for him to sit. "I sold a lot of that venison haunch last night to some of my neighbors who don't always stop in. I was able to buy some squares of cloth from the dry goods store this morning for more serviettes. Mrs. Campbell will hem those too."

"I see commerce all around me," he told her. "Flora, I have written to Plymouth and you will have more shells soon enough. Have you and your . . . your board of directors made more fancies?"

"Done and done," Flora told him. As she turned

around, Douglas noticed that the twine belt had been replaced by a lovely length of yellow cotton, probably bought at the same time as the material for serviettes by the kind lady he sat next to, the one with the deep red hair in its now-familiar disarray, pins poked here and there, because she was too busy thinking of others to give a minute to herself. He hesitated only a second before he tucked in one of those pins about to lose its moorings. She flashed him a smile that did something funny to his heart.

"We're starting small, here in Edgar," Olive said. "We need a bold stroke, Douglas. You can't leave until we have one."

"Leave? Who is . . . Oh, yes, I am."

He ate his venison sandwich in thoughtful silence, watching the girls peacock about in dresses given to them by another kind lady. None of them wore shoes, but it was spring now. He doubted they had worn shoes this past winter, but some knowledge deep inside him assured him that they would have shoes by the time cold returned to Scotland. How he knew, he couldn't have said. It was absurd to think that he was changing too. He was an adult quite set in his ways.

A brief consultation with the kind lady assured him that she would meet him in the surgery with Mrs. Aintree, once the dishes were done.

"Do you mind?" he asked. "I am starting to assume that you are a willing accomplice. Doesn't everyone love surgery?"

She wagged her finger at him again. "Mr. Bowden, you're stretching it."

Stretching it or not, she knocked on his door that afternoon and helped in a pale Mrs. Aintree and a delegation that warmed his heart a little more.

Mrs. Tavish and her son came in too. Douglas closed the door firmly on Duke. "We will expect the beast to guard us," he told Tommy. "Outside."

He looked out the window to watch Duke turn around

a few times and then sink down, as dejected as only a gregarious dog could look.

"We're here to provide comfort," Mrs. Tavish said, with nothing in her tone suggesting that she would leave until Mrs. Aintree was safely back in her own bed.

He made his own swift assessment of Mrs. Tavish, amazed at the difference a few weeks, a little hope, and a home of her own could make. "Do you feel able to tend Mrs. Aintree?" he asked, mainly because it was a doctor thing to ask.

She gave him a little smile, the kind of smile he never saw at sea, because he did not see many women aboard Royal Navy vessels. He had seen it enough in Edgar, though, the smile that suggested men had no idea what women were capable of.

"Aye, Mr. Bowden," was her answer, delivered with sufficient steel to guarantee that although Mrs. Tavish had fallen on hard times, she had not remained in them. The set look to her lips and in her eyes reminded him of other Highlanders he had doctored through the years. He knew them as people who did not complain because they were already well acquainted with the cruelties of life.

"Sit here with your boy," he told her and indicated the mismatched chairs in his waiting room.

He turned to Mrs. Aintree and took her by the hand. She looked at him with all the trust in the world. He had seen the look before, even in times when he felt less adequate than a barnacle. It had moved him the first time, and it did not fail to move him now.

She had brought along a nightgown as he had asked. "I just want you comfortable," he had told her last night when he had spent time in her parlor.

She had asked last night why he could not separate her fingers in the ease of her own home, and he had explained about the light. He could tell she was skeptical but a polite lady. She looked around his surgery and nodded.

He had borrowed two lamps from Olive, who had talked the minister's wife out of two more.

"I understand now," Mrs. Aintree said, looking around with understanding. "There's not much light comes into my chamber, tucked there under the eaves."

"I like to give myself every advantage." Douglas pulled the curtains closed. "Please allow Miss Grant to help you change. Knock on the door when you are ready, and I'll come back."

He went into the waiting room, surprised to see Mrs. Campbell and the minister's wife sitting there, too, as well as two ladies he did not recognize. The press of well-wishers reminded him of an outdoor surgery in the South Pacific, surrounded by tribesmen all too close to their cannibal roots, watching every nervous move he made. He had been called up to amputate an infected leg of a sailor who had deserted the Royal Navy years earlier. He thought of the chorus of "Ah's" from that unholy bunch as he pulled the diseased leg away and set it in a bucket. He had turned back to his patient to finish the job, peering around a few minutes later to find the leg gone, and the cannibals looking more than usually satisfied, if such he could divine from their expressions. The memory of that amputation made him smile.

But this was Edgar, and his patient was not a heathen but a lady. His tongue felt paralyzed. He was wholly inadequate to conduct idle chatter, which, he realized, with a sinking feeling, must constitute some necessary portion of a private medical practice. He sat there, ill at ease, aware that no one in his waiting room would appreciate his little South Seas story. Probably no lending library, even Edgar's, owned a book that would explain idle chatter.

Olive's knock on the door put him out of his misery. He bounded up, which made Mrs. Campbell chuckle, and began the business at hand, confident of his skills.

Wearing serviceable flannel and a solemn expression,

Mrs. Aintree stood in her stockinged feet, her face rosy. "No man except Mr. Aintree has ever seen me in a nightgown," she informed him primly.

"You're fetching, my dear," he said. "I know you wonder why this is necessary, but I assure you that you'll be easy for me to carry across the street and pop you into your own bed, without having to suffer raising your arms to remove your garments then. Allow me, Mrs. Aintree."

He took her hand, and with Olive assisting, helped his patient onto the surgery table, which he had earlier padded with Mrs. Aintree's own blankets. He raised the clever hinged board that the author of Tommy Tavish's crutches had crafted only last night. He situated Mrs. Aintree, stretched out her arm on the board, and then bound her to it with bandages.

He heard a muffled sob and looked back, startled, to see Olive in tears.

Mrs. Aintree looked too. "Olive Grant, you are made of sterner stuff!" his patient said. "Buck up."

Pray don't faint, Olive, he thought. "You were a stalwart when I operated on Tommy Tavish," he reminded her.

She nodded and chewed her lip. "I am no stalwart," she said. "Af . . . after you finished with Tommy I went into the alley behind my tearoom and . . . oh dear."

Mrs. Aintree raised up on her elbow. "Douglas Bowden," she commanded, "give our Miss Grant a little cuddle!"

The advice was excellent and Douglas gathered Olive close. His good humor reasserted itself. "You're a thousand times more fun to cuddle than a pharmacist's mate," he declared, which made her chuckle. She murmured, "I should hope so. Surely you never . . ."

"Certainly not, Miss Grant!" he said, which made him laugh out loud. He rested his hand on her neck, because she had a fine neck. "Just be a stalwart for ten minutes, and I'll hold back your hair over the basin myself."

"Such an offer," she said, with some vestige of her sharp humor. "You don't give a person a chance to back out or disagree, do you?"

"No." He led her to the surgery table. "I never could afford to, then or now. Mrs. Aintree, meet Olive Grant, my excellent assistant. And here you thought she only ran a tearoom. She is going to hold your good hand and we will be done in less than ten minutes. Ten minutes. Keep that in mind."

Mrs. Aintree nodded. She closed her eyes, which Douglas took as his signal to proceed. He poured a dab of laudanum on a bit of cotton and squeezed a few drops into Mrs. Aintree's mouth. "It'll take the edge away, but not much more."

He watched a moment until her shoulders relaxed, knowing they would tense again when he made the first cut. He moved Olive across the table from him and put her hands on the widow's stomach. "Just keep her steady."

Olive turned terrified eyes on him, which meant he had to touch her face and look into those eyes.

"There, now."

He opened the curtains, turned on the lamps, and began slicing between Mrs. Aintree's ring finger and little finger, fused because there had been no surgeon anywhere near Edgar to offer sensible advice a year ago. Mrs. Aintree shuddered but Olive held her still. He cut and dabbed, secure in the knowledge that this little bistoury, a favorite of his, had been honed as sharp as he could make it.

"Syncope would be nice about now, Mrs. Aintree," he murmured, when she moaned.

"What is syncope?" Olive asked through chattering teeth.

Suddenly Mrs. Aintree relaxed. Her shoulders drooped and her head drifted to one side as she fainted. "That," he said.

He knew he had just a little pain-free time, so he worked faster, separating the two fingers and dabbing away, pleased with what he saw. He threw in several looping sutures, careful not to bind anything too tight, because there just wasn't enough skin.

"My hope is that the area will granulate and eventually allow for skin growth," he explained to Olive as he worked, talking her through what he was doing, simply to distract her from the blood. He had done this before with other pharmacist's mates, but he had been teaching them. He just wanted Olive to bear up.

He dipped gauze in a sweet-smelling solution he had concocted during a rare bit of calm near Australia one year, and bound Mrs. Aintree's fingers.

"That smell!" Olive gasped.

He glanced at Olive, her distress made manifest as she sniffed the fragrance he had always enjoyed. She swallowed several times, so he grabbed a basin. She snatched it, turned away, and heaved.

"I like that fragrance."

"You are a lunatic," she declared and turned away again.

He knew this was no time to laugh, but he couldn't help a little smile. Maybe he was relieved to know that the kind lady had her moments too.

He sat Olive down on the stool he had occupied, holding her hair back as she heaved again.

Her eyes filled with tears. "I'm sorry," she whispered. "You expected better."

"You did what I needed." He fingered her lovely hair, wondering how she kept it so soft. He turned his attention to his patient, whose eyes were wide open and watching him with something close to amusement, despite the pain he knew she was suffering.

"Mrs. Aintree, welcome back," he told her.

With her good hand, she gestured him closer. "Thank you for my fingers. In just a few weeks, and you can be on your way," she whispered.

"On my—"

"Aye, lad," Mrs. Aintree said. She closed her eyes against the pain, but her voice grew stronger. "You found a job and home for Tommy and his mam; little Flora has her South Seas Fancies, and I have fingers."

"I wouldn't be so hasty," he said. "Your hand will bear watching, yet a little while."

"She is right, Mr. Bowden," Olive said, as she stuffed pins back in her hair. "We've tried you sore enough and you have been so kind."

"Don't hurry me!" he protested.

"I would never," said the kind lady. "Would we, Mrs. Aintree?"

"Heaven forbid! A man ought to know what he needs, and so you have told us a time or two."

"I have, haven't I?"

Chapter 22

$\mathcal{A}$FTER PLACING MRS. AINTREE'S arm in a sling, Douglas carried the little lady across the street as a host of villagers watched and offered advice, something he was beginning to recognize as the Scottish way. The kitchen was full of food, reminding him how hungry he was.

Brighid Dougall presided over the already weighted down table in the kitchen, with able assistance from Flora MacLeod and the MacGregor sisters. He stood still a moment with Mrs. Aintree in his arms, watching Flora. He bore too cumbersome an armful to drop to his knees in appreciation for what he saw: Flora was not focused on the food. *You're not hungry*, he thought as gratitude filled his heart, even in those dusty corners that never showed up in medical textbook illustrations.

"You have a houseful of friends, Mrs. Aintree," he told the widow in his arms.

She turned her face into his chest and sighed. "Get rid of them," she whispered. "Turn Mrs. Tavish loose on them."

A few quiet words to Rhona Tavish, and a few quiet

words of her own was all it took. By the time he laid Mrs. Aintree down on her bed, silence prevailed. He sat on the bed, satisfied that the little splint firmly bandaged on top and underneath her now-separated fingers would stop any movement. He checked the barely visible, V-shaped bit of wood at the base of the two fingers, there to ensure they would remain separate.

He had done all he could. What remained was to dose her with just enough laudanum to put her asleep and keep her that way, then find a comfortable chair and begin his night's watch.

He began his vigil and ended it five minutes later, when Rhona Tavish informed him that she and Tommy could watch as well as he could. He objected and she ignored him, reminding him forcefully that Rhona Tavish was the first person he met in Edgar as she ran into the road holding out her bleeding son.

"You have done quite enough for one day," she informed him. "Up tha' gets, ridire."

There she stood, a veritable Boudicca—capable and determined. He knew he could argue, but what would be the point?

"Mrs. Tavish, if I argued with you, would you just reply in Gaelic and pretend not to know any English?"

She grinned at that. A word to Tommy, and the two of them tugged him upright and ushered him out the door.

"If anything—and I mean anything—concerns you, send Tommy," Douglas said. He indicated the laudanum on the table and the small silver cup beside the bottle. "If she starts to moan and toss her head about, pour laudanum to that lowest marked level and give it to her."

"Aye, Mr. Bowden," she said, and sat down in the chair from which he had been evicted. "Tommy, show him our little home over the kitchen. Good night, Mr. Bowden."

And that was that. Douglas followed Tommy to the kitchen, snatching up a slice of shortbread from among the many neighborly offerings still on the table. Treat in hand, he followed the boy up steep steps, marveling how well he managed his crutches.

A small landing boasted two doors. Tommy opened the near one and held it grandly open, pride everywhere on his face. Douglas saw a room with a table, two chairs and a bed. He knew the wind had picked up outside, but the windows in Mrs. Aintree's house did not chatter and shiver like his grudgingly rented domicile. He saw a rug on the floor and heat registers, where the little rooms could receive warmth from the kitchen below.

The next room was much like the first. Everywhere he saw calm and order, a far better prescription for what ailed the Tavishes than anything he could suggest. The winds could blow and the rain pelt, but Rhona and Tommy Tavish were safe here. Silently Douglas thanked the Deity he mostly neglected.

"My own room," Tommy said simply. "And t'aud widow doesn't mind Duke. I've seen her feed him scraps, even though she swears she wouldna." His head went up, and Douglas saw the pride of the Highlanders, battered and pummeled to be sure, but still alive and on fire within. "She tells me that anytime I want something from the kitchen, I needn't bother to ask permission."

"I hope you will be careful on your crutches and take your own rest," Douglas said, even though he knew Tommy would do precisely as he felt best.

"Aye, sir," Tommy said promptly, "although I have wondered lately—I hear noises by the cattle bier. When I go downstairs . . ." He shrugged.

"I can inform the constable."

"Nay, sir!" Tommy assured him, the fear back in his eyes. "Not him."

Douglas clapped his hand on the boy's shoulder and gave him a little shake, understanding that look, and the one like it in Flora MacLeod's face a few days ago. "No constable."

In the kitchen, he took a larger piece of the shortbread and let himself out the door. He stood a moment leaning his arms on the fence, watching Mrs. Aintree's cow chew cud with an expression of indifference. "I could sit and watch you all night," he said, then looked around to make certain no one had heard him.

He rolled his eyes when he heard a smothered laugh.

"Olive Grant, go to bed," he said, without looking to see where she stood. He knew that voice. "Are you waiting for someone?" he asked when she said nothing.

"I was just curious to know how long it would take Rhona Tavish to run you out of Mrs. Aintree's bed chamber."

"You make that sound highly salacious," he commented, starting across the street to his house. *I have a bed in there*, he thought, tired down to his toes. *It is calling my name.*

"Brighid Dougall wanted to wager on the matter, but I don't wager," she said. She cleared her throat. "There is a slight matter."

Why did words like that make his heart start to race and his breath come faster? He had thought his days of sudden alarm were done. Apparently not, if something as innocuous as "a slight matter" was enough to set every nerve on edge.

"Uh, what?" he asked, groaning inwardly at how stupid he sounded. Stupid tired, more like.

"I told Lady Telford that your house was haunted, so you could get a better deal," she reminded him.

What was she up to? "You are a rascal."

"Take a look over there in the shed," she said, lowering her voice. "A good look."

He looked, straining his eyes to see into the midnight gloom, compounded by that dratted light mist that seemed to be Edgar's lot in life and geography. He looked, squinted, and saw the flickering light.

"Should I wake up the constable?" she whispered.

No, let's allow the poor fool to get his rest, he wanted to say, but he didn't. Olive Grant probably meant well. "Not if it's ghosts," was the best he could come up with.

"Aren't you concerned?" she asked.

He wasn't. "Mostly I am tired, Olive Grant, kind lady," he teased. "Let's take a look."

He walked across the street to the stone shed close to the bridge and behind his house that Lady Telford had assured him was his property too, for the next two months. The way the bank slanted, he wouldn't have noticed the light.

He opened the door and his life changed again.

Joe Tavish stared back at him, his eyes dark with misery. Olive sucked in her breath and prudently stayed behind Douglas. The man held the stare for an uncomfortable, silent time, then sighed and returned his attention to what looked like a small pile of black oats. By the light of that single flickering candle, Douglas watched in horror and then in deep compassion as the silent man finished stirring something dark and sludgy around in a hole he appeared to have dug into the dirt floor of the shed. He had no bowl or spoon, only a dirt hole.

"Throw me out when I'm done," Joe Tavish muttered, his voice rusty, as though he had not spoken to anyone in a long time. He dipped his hand in the nasty mess and ate. He gagged, but he did not stop.

Remembering his last beating, Douglas hesitated. He watched Joe's dirty hand as it shook, traveling the short distance from the hole to his mouth. "I could probably push him over with one finger now," he whispered to Olive. "Olive?"

We are two easy marks, he thought, listening to Olive sniff. He reached behind him and took her hand.

"Go get him some food," he said, loud enough for Joe Tavish to hear.

Joe's shaggy head went up. Even in the gloom of the shed, Douglas saw that same expression of pride that he had seen only minutes before on his son Tommy's face.

"No charity," he spit out.

"Ya bowfing, dighted dug!" Olive burst out. She scrambled out from behind Douglas before he could stop her and grabbed the front of the startled man's shirt. She gave him a good shake as Douglas stared, open-mouthed. "Aye, it's charity! Did no one ever tell you hardheaded Highlanders that charity is the pure love of Christ?" She gave him another shake for good measure, then shook her finger at him. "You're going to eat what I serve you if I have to push your face in it! I'll thrash you myself if you give me grief!" She leaped up and ran from the shed.

I should do something, Douglas thought, shocked, until it dawned on his fuddled, sleep-deprived mind, that Olive Grant's brand of Christianity had trouble suffering fools gladly. *I will keep my mouth shut*, Douglas decided, not certain if he was more appalled or more entertained by the surprising sight of the kind lady pushed past her limit. He knew he never wanted to cross her.

Joe stared at the open door. He put down the mess and just sat there. Douglas looked closer and swallowed when he realized what the dark mess was. Tommy had probably heard his own father bleeding Mrs. Aintree's cow, the last resort of a desperate man.

He took a deep breath, which wasn't so wise, considering that the man reeked. He reminded himself that he had spent a quarter of a century working in dark, stinking ships. Was he that big a milky boy?

He considered what he could say to a man reduced to the lowest common denominator, someone on the brink of starvation, someone who had not had a good day in several years. Shame washed over him and he knew what to say.

"I owe you an apology, Joe, for striking you," he said. "Forgive me, please."

Tavish raised dark eyes to his, held his gaze briefly, and lowered his head. "I'm the one what gave you the black eye and maybe a bad rib," he muttered.

"I started it," Douglas insisted.

"Oh, listen to the two of you barmy moonflies!" Olive declared, obviously still not over her rage. She held two bowls and had stuck a loaf of bread under her arm. One bowl went to Tavish, and the other to Douglas. "Eat something, both of you, and remind me why I shouldn't slap the two of you silly!"

Joe stared at the bowl in his hands. When it started to shake and fish stew washed over the edge, Olive took it from him gently now and spooned it into his mouth, which he opened obediently as tears streamed down his face.

"There now," she said, sounding perfectly reasonable. "Hold it with both hands and drink it. I have bread for dunking too."

She tore the loaf into hunks and handed one to Douglas. He dipped it in the bowl he held and ate because he was hungry too.

"After Trafalgar, I operated for two days straight. My feet swelled and I stood in blood to my ankles. That smell! He was eating raw oats mixed with cow's blood."

Olive nodded. She took the bowl from Douglas and dipped chunks of bread in it. She handed it to Joe Tavish when he stared down at his now-empty bowl. "I would call you resourceful, Mr. Tavish," she said. "I doubt this surgeon would have thought to eat oats and cow's blood."

Douglas knew what she was doing and it warmed his heart. "You have me there, Miss Grant," he admitted.

Joe Tavish understood too. He looked from one to the other. "Aye, right," he said, his scorn unmistakable. "Don't ye dare make me a figure of fun."

"I'd rather you tell me what has happened to get you and your friends to this state," Douglas said.

"So you can laugh at us too? Laugh at the ignorant Highlanders?" Tavish challenged.

"So I can figure out what to do," Douglas told him.

"Do? Do?" the man burst out. "Go away!"

"Not yet!" Douglas shouted back, painfully aware that he had not raised his voice since he had taken a stick to this same wretched man weeks ago. Joe Tavish seemed determined to bring out the worst in him. "I have a two-month lease on a house in this miserable village and look there, your arm is a mess." He tried Olive's admonition and shook a finger at the startled man. "I have some salve and by h . . . he . . . Hadrian's Wall, you're going to let me tend you and try to figure something out."

"T'pure love of Christ?" Joe shouted back.

"Nothing that kind," Douglas replied. "One angry, put-upon surgeon, more like. Now shut up and don't you move until I get back with my satchel."

Chapter 23

*O*LIVE FOLLOWED HIM FROM THE shed. "By Hadrian's Wall?" she asked, just on the edge of mirth. "Are we both certifiable?"

"You're generous to include yourself," he said as he went into his surgery and grabbed his satchel.

"I've never been so irritated with a man as with Joe Tavish," she started, and then she turned all Flora MacLeod on him and burst into tears. "What have we come to in Scotland?"

He grabbed her in a fierce embrace and kissed her smack on the forehead. "You're all crazy here north of Hadrian's Wall. That is my new curse word. Olive Grant, we have work to do. Get me some blankets and a pillow. He's crawling with lice and he's not coming in here." He clung to her another minute apologizing all the while, babbling something about being tired of doing so much by himself, wishing he could drop himself into the middle of the Canadian wilderness, and sick of endless misery. Appalled at himself, he finally stopped ranting and stepped away from the comfort of Olive's arms. And here he thought he was holding her; quite the opposite.

"What came over me?" he asked, embarrassed.

Olive appraised him as professionally as he might observe the sick and the wounded. "You're just tired of working and working and seeing no end in sight. So am I," she said simply. "We need a bold stroke here in this miserable town."

"Oh, about that . . ."

"Nay. You're right. Hush and let me finish." She put her hands on his shoulders and he saw the fight in her eyes, banked but not even remotely extinguished. "We have to think bigger than either of us have ever thought before."

She leaned forward and rested her forehead on his chest for a brief moment, too brief to suit him.

"Poor man! All you wanted was to pass through Edgar and get somewhere else. We'll let you go, because it is perhaps illegal to hold someone in our village against his will, but we need you first. That's the truth of it."

Silently, he agreed that it was. "All right then. I'm going to clean off that wicked-looking abscess on Joe's arm and give him blankets to bed down right where he is. Tomorrow I'll find a way to either douse him in the river or stuff him into a tub. He reeks and I won't have it."

They walked toward the shed, Olive carrying blankets and Douglas with his satchel. He stopped. "Suppose that man has scarpered off?"

"Then we'll hunt him down and fix him," Olive said.

He felt a measure of his good humor returning. "Even if he doesn't want to be fixed?"

"Especially if he doesn't want to be fixed," Olive teased in return. "He should be on a leash, more like."

But there Joe Tavish was, leaning against the wall of the stone shed and shivering. He seemed surprised to see them again, as though everyone had failed him for so long that he couldn't imagine anything going well. He appeared to be looking over Olive's shoulder for someone else.

"There will be no constable," Douglas told him, interpreting the gaze. "Let me look at your arm."

Douglas expected a struggle, but Tavish did as directed. He hadn't the strength to hold it out, so the surgeon rested the forearm on the man's upraised knee. The cut looked raw and angry, but with laudable pus, thank goodness.

Olive must have gone across the street to her tearoom because she came back with a brass can of lukewarm water. "The Rumford has been extinguished for hours, so this is the best I can do," she apologized.

She poured the water into a basin and Douglas dipped in a square of gauze, cleaning the area around the wound, caused, he suspected, by a small cut that became infected.

"It was just a scratch," Tavish said as he leaned back, as though trying to distance himself from his own stink.

"In a cow bier?"

"Aye." He sighed.

Douglas wiped the wound clean and then looked over in surprise of his own as Olive washed Joe Tavish's face. Douglas nearly told her not to waste the water, but he saw Joe relax as the grime came away from his face.

"I always feel better when my face is clean," she told Joe, who actually smiled at her. With the exception of his forearm, bandaged now, and his face, Tavish was as filthy as a man could be. Funny how a clean face made a world of difference. Olive understood what Douglas had forgotten.

He dressed another inflamed cut and wrapped it, at a loss of even where to begin tomorrow in resurrecting this man. He leaned back himself, exhausted and disheartened with the enormity of cleaning Joe Tavish, never mind trying to help so many. He stared at the wall and what he saw touched his heart—a drawing of a crofter's cottage, perhaps done with a burned stick, with mountains towering behind it, and another drawing of a woman and small boy.

Tavish watched him with a wary expression, as if daring him to make fun of the little works of art, which they were, no matter the medium. He looked at Joe Tavish with new respect.

"I recognize your wife and son," Douglas said. "The other one?"

"Glen Holt, near Inchnadamph," Tavish replied as his voice took on an unexpected softness. "We Tavishes lived there for two hundred years, minding our own business, raising a few cattle, growing a few crops." He turned away with another sigh and stared at the wall with no drawings.

"What happened?" Douglas asked. "I . . . I ask not to dredge up a wound, but I truly don't know." He put away his salve. "I've been so long away." *Maybe in more ways than I even know,* he told himself.

Douglas did know, because Olive had told him, but he also understood, perhaps better than most, the emotional value of conversation. He thought of the times he had done nothing more than sit at men's bedsides and listen to them. At first, he had sat out of sheer exhaustion. What he learned when he listened opened up a new side of medicine to him.

He thought Tavish might not speak, because the man continued to stare at the empty wall. With a groan and an oath, he carefully lifted the drawing of Rhona and Tommy Tavish from the nail and held them in his lap, as though deriving comfort from the mere images. He traced the outline of his wife's face.

Douglas exchanged glances with Olive, who moved closer to him, still out of reach, but closer.

When Tavish shivered, Douglas put a blanket around his shoulders. Olive followed that with a pillow. When she sat down again, she was even closer.

They waited in silence as Joe Tavish—a forgotten, wounded, hungry, misunderstood man—marshaled his puny forces. "We weren't doing anything out of the ordinary, but one day two men came riding into our glen, one by the name of Patrick Sellar."

Olive started in fright when Joe Tavish spat.

"Sorry, mam," he said. "I hope Patrick Sellar dies a painful death some day, but likely he will only grow richer. If I didna know then how the world works, believe me, I know now."

"What did he do?" Douglas asked.

"You really don't know, do you?" Tavish asked. He shrugged. "Neither did we." He took a deep breath. "How can I forget? I was outside the croft, mending a chair when he walked up my lane and handed me a writ." He grunted. "Just like that. He gave a little salute and walked back down my lane." He voice broke. "I see him walking yet in my dreams, but he grows taller and taller with each step until he is looking down on us from our own crags and mountains, like an awful demon." He shuddered.

I do understand dreams, Douglas thought.

The story poured out of Joe Tavish then in a monotone, as though he were living the events through someone else's eyes. Three months to leave his beloved glen, and go where, how, and with what?

"Why?" Douglas asked.

Joe tried to speak. His mouth opened and nothing came out. Olive put her hand on Joe's arm. "This much I know," she told Douglas. "The Countess of Sutherland decided that her Highlands land would pay far more in taxes and revenue if she ran sheep."

"But surely those are clan lands. I know that much," Douglas said, genuinely puzzled. "Have people like Joe no rights?"

Joe picked up his own story. "At one time, aye, we did. Through the years, the clan chief began to look on us as free labor."

"But the Countess of Sutherland?"

"Scottish landowning is a murky matter," Olive said

when Joe fell silent. "The clan chiefs became landlords, if you will. After the Battle of Culloden Moor, more land ownership was shuffled around until the Gordons owned most of the Highlands. Elizabeth Gordon and the Countess of Sutherland are one and the same."

They sat in silence. No one had an answer, because Douglas knew the three of them were the little people, be he from Norfolk in his case, Galloway in Olive's, or the Highlands in Joe's.

"And the writ was an eviction," Douglas said finally. He knew that it was impossible for blood to run cold, but his did as he stared at the pain in Joe Tavish's eyes. "Did . . . did anyone leave the glen as Sellar demanded?"

Joe shook his head. "From time to time, Sellar came back with other agents, who assured us that we could find work along the coast, cleaning and gutting fish. Fish! No one wanted that so we ignored him."

Except that the writ didn't disappear, did it? Douglas thought. "And then they returned and brought troops?"

"Aye." Joe looked him in the eye briefly, then bowed his head on his chest, as though ashamed of his own gullibility. "'We told ye three months ago,' Sellar shouted at my door. 'Thirty minutes now or we fire it with you inside.'"

"He wouldn't," Douglas said.

"He did. Rhona and Tommy and I grabbed and ran, but t'deaf widow next door, an old ancient of days . . ." He shook his head vigorously, as if trying to throw out the image lodged there. "I'll hear her scream until I die."

Joe wrapped his arms around his updrawn legs and hugged himself for comfort.

Olive reached out her hand and touched his arm, but he shook her off. "Lice."

"This can wait for another day," Douglas said.

"Nay, you'll have it all now because I won't speak of it again," Joe told him. "All over the glen, cottages burned. Sellar and his troops set so many fires that the air was smoky. We got away with our clothes, a Bible, a few dishes, and two candlesticks. They herded us like dogs toward the coast."

Olive leaped to her feet and ran from the shed. Joe retreated inside himself again. Douglas remembered coastal Spanish and Portuguese towns where one army or the other displaced ordinary people with the misfortune to be caught in the middle. A more compassionate captain had set him and his pharmacist mate ashore near Gibraltar to tend to the bruised, battered, and bewildered who had taken refuge in a convent. He had tended to their physical needs but was powerless to calm their minds or give them a reason to live. He still had nightmares from watching perfectly able-looking young women and children simply slide sideways and drop dead.

He looked up from contemplation of his hands to see Joe Tavish staring at him.

"What, no sympathy? No advice to read our Bibles and take comfort that things are better in heaven?" Joe asked, his voice thick with bitterness. "That's w'the English told us on the docks. Smug and sanctimonious the lot 'a ye."

"Give me some credit, Joe," he snapped. "Lapdogs in English sitting rooms are treated better than you were. Don't paint me with that brush because I do not deserve it."

Carrying a dark green bottle and small glasses, Olive let herself back into the shed. Tight-lipped, she poured them each a drink. "Smuggler's brandy," she announced. "Papa said we would use it to toast me and my husband when I married someday. That never happened, and we need a wee dram now."

They drank, Joe throwing his drink down his throat and breathing a sigh of relief. Olive swirled her little portion around in the glass, a slight smile on her face, so wistful. Maybe she was thinking of events in her life that hadn't turned out the way she wanted. Douglas took a small sip and another, thinking of various wardroom toasts through the years, from "Glorious war" to "Beauty ashore."

"No more," Olive said. "Let's save the rest for a happier occasion."

"Finish the story, Joe," Douglas ordered. "You were on the docks."

"Aye, and such a scene that was." He ran both hands across his face, digging in his nails. "The soldiers just herded people aboard until the captains protested. Some were bound for Canada, and the rest for Timbuktu, for all we knew." He keened then, a low moan that set the hairs at attention on Douglas's neck. "A remember one mam, calling and calling for her little boy—he couldna been a day over five—who was left behind on the dock. She pleaded for someone to help her. No one did. The wee fellow jumped in the water, desperate to reach his mam. Sank like a stone, he did."

Olive sobbed out loud and Douglas gathered her close. He resisted the nearly overpowering urge to gather Joe Tavish close too, the man who had blacked his eye and dented a few ribs. From the look of him, bleakness hovering over him like a foul odor, Joe Tavish was beyond any comfort an English surgeon too proud of his skills could provide.

"They sailed, that ship and two others," Joe continued in a voice hushed now, almost as if he couldn't believe the horror of what he had witnessed. "Someone on the ship— heaven only knows how he smuggled'm aboard—unlimbered his bagpipes and played 'Flowers of the Forest.' We wept, they wept, and no one helped us." Joe keened again.

"What . . . I don't understand," Douglas whispered to Olive.

"'Tis played at funerals alone," she whispered back, her voice ragged. "Some call it 'The Lament.'" She sang softly into his ear. "'The Flooers o' the Forest, that fought aye the foremost, the pride o' oor land lie cauld in the clay.'" Her sigh was three parts sob. "We Scots are a tragic lot, Douglas. Remember when Flora said, 'We needed a little help'?"

"Now's the time, Olive."

They sat in silence, listening to Joe Tavish lament the loss of everything, and all for the Countess of Sutherland's sheep. When he finished, Douglas covered him with a blanket, tucking it around him.

"Sleep now, Joe," he said. "We'll sort out what we can in the morning."

"You'll make it all better?" Joe asked, his voice so bitter, and with good cause.

"Would that I could." Douglas squatted beside the blanketed figure. "What I aim to do, and you will help me, is find some sweet revenge."

"And how are we to do that?" Joe's sarcasm was unmistakable.

"Ask me tomorrow night, for I intend to have a plan. And you will help me."

Chapter 24

AWN WAS COMING, BUT A FULL moon still lit the sky. They stood in silence together outside the shed. Olive knew it was well past time to drag herself upstairs into her own bedchamber, but she knew she would only stare at the ceiling until she heard Maeve laying a kitchen fire below and another day would begin.

Maybe Douglas had the same idea. He looked at her, his face so serious, and crocked out his arm. She tucked her arm through his and walked with him to the bridge.

"I'll never sleep tonight," he said a minute later as they both leaned their arms on the railing and watched the River Dee below.

"I have a feeling that you have seen yourself coming and going on many a morning," she said.

"Aye. I rather thought those days were done, but here I am." He stared downriver toward the docks where the fishing boats were neatly tied. She looked where he looked, thinking of their ordinary days in Edgar, one following pretty much the same. She thought of Joe Tavish in Glen

Holt, where the sameness of two centuries had ended in eviction, flames, and death.

"It could happen to any of us," she said. "We think it will not, but what proof do any of us have against people such as the Sutherlands?"

No answer. Douglas stared at the boats. Slowly, he stood upright again, his eyes still on the distant view, as far as she could tell, except that he seemed suddenly alert.

"Let's go for a walk, Olive Grant," he said. He crooked out his arm again and she twined her arm through his. "The moon is full and the sun is coming up anyway, so let's take the path along the river."

They walked in silence behind the row of houses like his with their back walls to the River Dee and then walked onto the fishing boat dock. He kept walking past shabbier homes now. Somewhere a child cried, which made him stop and listen for a moment and then continue on.

They walked until they reached the outskirts of Edgar, and she suddenly knew what he had in mind. *Is this even possible?* she thought. *Evidently I do not think big enough.*

They stood at the abandoned shipyard and dry docks. He tucked her arm closer to him. "Do you remember when the shipyard was active?" he asked.

"I must have been about ten years old," she replied, after long thought. "I was never allowed to come down here. Papa said it was dangerous, and besides, he didn't want me hearing such foul language."

"Like Hadrian's Wall?" Douglas teased, and she laughed.

"Oh, especially that one." She looked across the yard. "Two really large bathtubs, eh?"

"As near as," he replied. He looked and then nodded, as if pleased with what he saw. "The brick ones like these are called graving docks." He pointed to the massive open gates. "A ship needing repair would sail in here, and the gates would close. Big pumps would take off the water and leave it dry. Talk about our modern age—the pumps in the Plymouth yards are steam-powered now." He pointed to the uniform rows of open space in the masonry. "The shipwright runs in long poles that, in essence, balance the ship upright. Carpenters go down there once the water is gone and commence repairs. When it's done, the gates open, water flows in and the ship sails away."

He pointed to the second graving dock beyond, and the long wooden structure behind it.

"It's probably full of mice and birds now, but that's the shiphouse. You could build a right fine vessel in there, out of bad weather, and then slide it down the ways into . . . into the bathtub, and then out to sea, once it was masted and rigged. Nothing huge, mind, no frigates, but . . ." He stopped and his chuckle was self-deprecating. "You probably think I am a lunatic."

"No, I do not," she assured him.

"It shut down because . . . ?"

"We could ask Mrs. Aintree, or maybe even Lady Telford. Sir Dudley bought the whole thing, plus some other houses." She hesitated and then realized that grand ideas shouldn't be strangled at birth. All she had to offer was gossip, but there was probably some truth in there somewhere. "The talk about the village said that the shipwright, a man long dead, got into a fearful row with some of the fishing fleet captains. They took their repair business elsewhere—Dumfries, I think—and that was the first nail in the coffin."

"And then the war probably enticed what builders remained to go to Clydeside near Glasgow," Douglas suggested. "I do know that shipwrights in Plymouth and Portsmouth commanded a respectable wage, likely better than anything Edgar could offer. It was probably the same in Glasgow."

She nodded and leaped closer to Douglas when a

whole fleet of bats—one was too many—flew swiftly into the shiphouse. He put his arm around her.

"Only bats," he whispered in her ear. "Aren't you the brave lady who just shook Joe Tavish's teeth until they rattled, bullying him into taking Christian charity?"

"Don't remind me. That was not my shining moment," she said, trying for dignity. "Bats are different."

"I will concede that bats are different," he said. "Just think, Olive: This shipyard and dry dock could employ a lot of men. Granted, our stubborn Highlanders might prefer to remain proud and starving."

"Not if they see others making good money and working."

He turned to face her. "Tell me honestly, Olive Grant: Is this going to look like a stupid idea once the sun is up and I have had some sleep?"

"It might," she said cautiously. "No! It is a wonderful idea."

He yawned. "I believe I could almost curl up among the bats . . ."

"Hang from the ceiling?"

"I suppose not." He yawned again. "Such rag manners, Olive. Two hours of sleep, if I'm lucky, will enable me to check on Mrs. Aintree, then delouse Joe Tavish—horrors—then visit Lady Elsie Telford."

"Do you know a shipwright?"

He started walking back, still holding her close. "That is the only sure entity of this decidedly sketchy plan. I know three. I also took a good look at the shipyards in Devonport before I left Plymouth. The demand has certainly dropped off, now that Boney is cooling his heels on St. Helena."

She bid Douglas good night, or maybe it was good morning, from the middle of the street. She went up her own front steps and watched in amusement while Douglas just stood at his door, key in hand, as if wondering what his next move should be. *Just go inside and lie down*, she advised, from her side of the street. She smiled as he stared at the key in his hand, as if it had suddenly grown lichen, and then finally turned it in the lock.

Two hours was just enough to fool Douglas's brain into thinking he had enjoyed sound sleep. A few minutes later, he stood over Mrs. Aintree, her eyes half open (matching his), her hand free of overmuch swelling.

"Are you ready to take a stick to me because I am the author of all your pain?" he asked her. "Give yourself a few days to feel better."

The widow shook her head. "You left me in good hands. Oh, dear, that is amusing." She laughed and then closed her eyes and slept again, while Rhona Tavish tidied up the already spotless room.

He debated for a long moment whether to say anything to the Tavishes about Joe, then he decided he couldn't leave them ignorant. After helping Tommy with the milk pans, he gathered them into Mrs. Aintree's kitchen.

Mrs. Tavish surprised him. Her arm around Tommy, she listened to the whole story, sniffing back tears when Douglas described her husband's mean supper of oats and cow's blood, mixed in a bowl of dirt. When he finished, she looked at her son.

"Well, lad?"

Tommy nodded. "We'll clean'um up, Mr. Bowden. He's still Da, and he needs us."

"I'm not so certain that Mrs. Aintree will allow him here," Rhona Tavish said.

"No worries. He can stay in my shed for now."

"I'm not even certain that I want him here, either."

"You're quite entitled," Douglas said.

She shrugged. "For richer or poorer, although we've only been poorer. I'll see if Mrs. Aintree has some clothes that might fit." She left the room.

"Tommy, did you know he was back?" Douglas asked. Something in the way the boy wouldn't look at either of them had made him suspicious.

"Aye," the boy said in a small voice. "One morning Lucinda had already been milked and the milk put in pans."

"Anyone could have done that."

Tommy dug into his pocket and pulled out a scrap of paper. He held it out to Douglas, who wondered if he would ever fathom the human heart. Joe Tavish had sketched Olive's backyard and his daughter's grave. "Only one man did this."

Satisfied, Douglas had his usual bowl of porridge in Miss Grant's Tearoom, disappointed because Olive did not make an appearance, but grateful that she had better sense than he did and still slept. He thought about the times—he really had no idea how many—that she had come into his room and given his shoulder a shake firm enough to dislodge his bad dreams, but not wake him up entirely.

Flora MacLeod nearly tackled him as he crossed the street to return to his house. She tugged his arm and announced that she and her business partners had sold four Seven Seas Fancies yesterday. She tugged his heart next. "We have enough money to eat all week, and it is only Tuesday," she told him. "My partners and I have decided to give some of it to the Hannays and the Elliotts."

I am surrounded by the kindest people, Douglas thought, and then he sobered. *Let us see if I can include Lady Telford in that number.*

A visit to Lady Telford should have included a bath beforehand and clean linens at least. The Tavishes had already borrowed his tin tub, so Lady Telford would have to be satisfied with just a clean neckcloth.

Whether she would even see him, when her maid announced his rumpled presence at the front door, gave him cause to worry. He knew precisely who she was, making him likely the last person she would invite into her sitting room.

"Brace yourself," he said to his mirror as he tied his neckcloth. "The enterprise will die right here if you cannot convince one old woman that you are not an idiot."

It was not a sanguine observation. And why in the world should he suddenly feel ten years old again and unsure of himself, facing Elsie Glump across the high counter in the butcher shop? Come to think of it, why was he doing any of this?

He thought about that as he took another look at Mrs. Aintree, who was being watched over by Mrs. Campbell now, and who gleefully informed him that the girls made two more sales of fancies just this day.

"We're getting low on shells, mind," Mrs. Campbell said.

He assured her that his shell source in Plymouth would rise to the occasion, which earned a grunt from Mrs. Campbell and a pithy remark best rendered in Gaelic and never translated.

He knew he would find Joe Tavish in the shed, sitting with no good grace in the tin tub on loan from his house. Tommy managed to balance himself and sweep out the shed, or at least lay the dust on the dirt floor. Rhona kept up a wicked-sounding scold in Gaelic as she scrubbed her husband's back. *Ah, blissful marriage*, Douglas thought as he smiled at them all and closed the door on Rhona Tavish's pointed remarks.

Still, there they were, three people tossed into a murky stream like wood chips, to bob or sink on their way to the ocean. They were not as alone as he was Douglas had to admit. True, Joe Tavish was probably getting a well-deserved trimming. One couldn't really tell with Gaelic because it always sounded harsh and peremptory to Douglas's ears. If Rhona Tavish had felt nothing for her louse-ridden, defeated husband, he'd be sitting in dirty water in an empty shed.

He stood a long moment on the bridge, looking uphill to Lady Telford's manor, thinking what an excellent hospital it would make, once the current occupant quitted the place. He shook his head over that piece of folly, wondering if every doctor had similar thoughts.

And here he stood at the front door, scarcely aware how he had got there. He looked back at Edgar, smiling (and a little flattered) to see Olive Grant on her front stoop looking at him. He waved to her and she waved back. He directed his gaze toward the abandoned shipyard, thinking that if he squinted hard enough, he could see a yacht under construction and workers swarming about.

"I'm not asking much," he said out loud, wondering if this constituted a prayer. In case it did, he said "Amen," and knocked on Lady Telford's front door.

Chapter 25

*M*AIDIE, IS YOUR MISTRESS HOME?" he asked Maeve's older sister, who dropped him a curtsey.

"Aye, Mr. Bowden, she is always home," Maidie began. She put her hand to her mouth. "Blast and dash! I am supposed to say, 'I will inquire within.'"

He kept his smile to himself. "I am here to tell you, Maidie, that if she insists that you inform me that she is not at home, I'm going to stay here anyway."

"Is it a matter of grave importance?" the maid asked, her eyes wide and worried.

Was it? Douglas decided the answer was yes, if Edgar was ever going to regain even a speck of its prominence. "I believe it is. Yes, I am certain. And you had probably better tell your mistress right away," he added gently, when she appeared transfixed by the idea of anything of grave importance ever happening in Edgar.

"Oh, aye," she said and bounded off, without showing him to the sitting room. Douglas doubted that Lady Telford had overmuch company, considering how little Maidie knew what to do.

Douglas stood in the entryway a long moment. He was staring up at the elaborate plaster whorls in the ceiling when he heard a massive throat clearing behind him. Odd how that sound could transport him back some three decades.

He turned around and there she was, Elsie Glump, wearing an even more colorful turban today, and a dress in which someone much younger would appear to great advantage. *Do I pretend I don't know who she really is?* he asked himself, suddenly at a loss.

She solved the dilemma for him. She executed a perfunctory little bow for someone who still considered herself far superior to the little son of a cooper.

"Dougie Bowden," she exclaimed in that booming voice he remembered.

I can play this too, he thought as he gave her a better bow. "Mistress Elsie Glump. I never thought to see you on England's far side. I remember you last in a butcher shop not too far from my father's cooper yard."

She gave him a thoughtful stare, and heaven help him if he didn't start feeling younger and less confident by the moment. He remembered that stare, especially during a hard time in the barrel business when the Bowdens were eating little meat and only the cheapest cuts. He stared back gamely and watched the hard light leave her eyes.

She indicated a seat, plumping herself down. He followed suit.

"I thought you must know who I am," she said finally.

He didn't think he imagined the glimmer of fear in those eyes now, just a small glint, but enough to suggest that the road between Glump and Telford might have been unexpectedly rocky.

"I do."

"Then I thank you for not giving me away to Miss Grant," she replied.

"Not I," he said, unwilling to ruin the woman's life by

even hinting that everyone in Edgar already knew who she was. "I came here for two reasons. The first is that I am concerned about the way your eye droops. It looks more pronounced than on my first visit here."

"I have a physician," she informed him, obviously inclined to toss out a better title than mere surgeon. "Sir Rodney Follette of Edinburgh, who sees quality clientele."

"I am relieved," he said, wondering what game she played. "I would suggest that you pay the man a visit soon."

He could tell she had no intention of doing that. He also thought she had no real desire to talk to him, which made him wonder why she had agreed to seat him in her parlor.

"And your second reason?" she asked, her tone frosty.

"It can wait," he said, even though he knew it couldn't. "I really would like to know the happy set of circumstances that took you from a butcher's shop to Lady Telford." He gestured around the overdone room. "You and Sir Dudley have evidently done well."

Her eyes filled with tears. Whether that came from his mention of her late husband or some other source, he couldn't be certain. From what he remembered of Dudley Glump, a coarse and overbearing bully, he thought it must be the latter.

But she was a woman suffering from something, and his bedside manner overpowered his hesitation. He joined her on the sofa and took her hand. "Lady Telford, kindly tell me what is bothering you."

"Nothing," she said immediately, but she did not withdraw her hand from his. Never mind. He could wait her out. "Perhaps there is something," she said, after only a short pause, "but you must swear yourself to secrecy on that . . . that hypocritical oath."

"Confidentiality is for medical matters," he explained, as he swallowed down a laugh of epic proportions, "but I will never tell anyone anything, if that is your wish."

"Aye, it is." She looked around elaborately, perhaps making certain that no enemy agents or members of the peerage lurked. "Dudley—Mr. Glump—sold a boggy piece of property to a gent buying up land for a canal scheme."

"Plenty of boggy land in Norfolk," Douglas agreed. "Did Mr. Glump buy more land then and increase his fortune that way?"

Lady Telford shook her head so vigorously that her turban shifted a bit on its axis. "He wanted to, but I told him about a joint stock company in the slave trade, name of the Royal African Company, and made him put it there." She looked at him, triumph in her eyes now. "We made a pile of money."

On black men and women's bones, Douglas thought, more than a little disgusted. He recalled one memorable afternoon when their frigate had come upon a slave ship becalmed in the doldrums. The stench across the water had been unbelievable. The ship had run up signals requesting a surgeon, and his captain sent him aboard. He did what he could among the dead and dying, felled by dysentery and starvation, but mostly loss of hope. Months passed before he could close his eyes and not see mothers chained to the deck and holding out their dying babies to him.

"I suppose you did," he said, merely because she seemed to expect some commentary. "Made you wealthy, did it?"

"More than," she crowed, and the satisfaction on her face turned to something less joyful. "This brought Dudley to the attention of Prinny, himself."

And he needed money in the worst way, Douglas thought, recalling wardroom stories about the Prince of Wales's constant penury. "Let me guess: Mr. Glump loaned him a healthy sum, in exchange for a title."

"A baronetcy," Lady Telford said. She looked at him expectantly, as if waiting for him to congratulate those shrewd Glumps.

"Why Telford?" he asked, unwilling to congratulate

her on a title handed out by the Prince Regent like sweets at Christmas, all to cover his own debts and with no regard for the country's well being.

"You remember that pretty manor house near Walton," she said.

"I do. Name of Telford. I remember the street with that same name."

"We even paid the Telfords for the name, and they disappeared from the district," she declared. "They had fallen on hard times and were only too happy to take our money."

Douglas sat back in the sofa, knowing precisely where this tale of sudden riches and greed was heading. He had known some titled men in frigates and men-o'-war —most of them good enough at their duties, some even exceptional, but through their veins ran, in addition to blood the same color as everyone else's, a vast superiority that had no equal in the Royal Navy. They took his skills when they needed them, and otherwise ignored men like himself.

Lady Telford was silent now, vulnerable. Douglas began to pity her, an ignorant woman shrewd and unprincipled enough to know how to make shady money, but unable to command anyone's respect with a mere purchased title. She and coarse Dudley no longer belonged among their own kind in decidedly unfashionable Norfolk and certainly not among the titled people they so wanted to impress.

The only sounds in the room were a clock ticking and Lady Telford's labored breathing, which smacked of congestive heart failure and not in the distant future. He considered all the angles before he spoke because he did pity her. Thank the Almighty that his own ambitions ran to becoming a surgeon second to none and not a toady of the titled. He knew his merits and his limits.

"You tried to enter their society and they laughed," he said, keeping his voice low.

She nodded, her eyes glistening again. "Right to our faces, drat their hides," she said, with considerable venom. Her head came up and he saw her pride. "So we moved here and bought this mansion. Dudley bought up property, and no one is the wiser about our beginnings. They believe we are Quality."

So you think, Douglas told himself. "Do you . . . do you mingle at all with the people of Edgar?" he asked.

"Mercy no," she scoffed. "After all, I am Lady Telford."

"I don't think you are happy," he said, after more consideration. "Everyone needs friends. There are some fine people in Edgar."

It struck Douglas that he had found friends aplenty in Edgar, friends he would miss, when he left.

She had no answer for him, no retort. She was too proud to admit that he was right and she needed friends. Everyone did.

"Lady Telford, would you be interested in leaving a wonderful legacy right here in Edgar?" he asked. "The kind of a legacy where word would get out to other towns and shires until no one in places like Edinburgh or London would ever laugh again?"

She gave him a suspicious stare and her hand hovered over the bell, perhaps to summon Maidie and have him shown out.

"Of course, I can understand if you have someone to leave your fortune to, or another way to be remembered with real affection, long after you are gone," he added, sitting back.

She put her hand back in her lap and raised her head enough to look down her nose at him. He smiled inside because he no longer felt like Dougie Bowden, sent to the butcher and clutching a small coin, ready to palm his dignity for some below-standard meat. He was Douglas Bowden, surgeon, Royal Navy retired, and it suddenly felt so good.

"What do you have in mind?" she asked.

"Your unused shipyard, Lady Telford. I have some money, courtesy of Napoleon, I suppose. Every man aboard a Royal Navy ship is entitled to shares in the purchase of captured vessels and cargo. As a surgeon, I have one-eighth of a share for each such transaction. This added up to a more-than-comfortable sum."

He glanced at Lady Telford, pleased to see he had her attention. Dudley certainly had not been the brains of their marital partnership. As repugnant as Douglas found her willingness to make money on African slaves, he had to admire her ability.

"My money resides with Carter and Brustein in Plymouth, making me more money." He took a deep breath. "I propose that you and I form a corporation and call it the Telford Boat Works. We will build yachts and fishing vessels and employ the less fortunate folk of Edgar. This would include the Highlanders dumped here and left to rot by those titled gentry and nobility who laughed at you and Dudley Glump."

She sat back, her mouth open. He saw the shrewd gleam in her eyes, one of which had a cataract. He knew he had her when she asked, "Why not the Telford-Bowden Boat Works?"

"I have no plans to remain in Edgar, beyond tending to some patients of mine, and seeing that an enormous wrong is righted, at least here," he said. "All I want is a peaceful country practice in a charming village somewhere."

She smiled then, and he was struck by how such a simple shift of muscles shed the years from her puffy face. She even leaned toward him like a conspirator, which he found a wonderful omen. "We will agree that Edgar is not charming."

They laughed together.

Her shrewd look skewered him. "Dougie, I know that everyone wants a reward. I applaud your desire to help these people. What is it you want?"

"Am I that transparent?" he asked, deciding that he had underestimated Lady Telford.

"Perhaps," she hedged. "I have had some experience in making money, which sometimes involves looking deep. What else do you want?"

"I intend to find other investors in the Telford Boat Works," he said, "but I want a guarantee that Miss Grant's Tearoom will be funded so she can feed the workers and their families, without having to dip into her inheritance, which I fear is slight."

"You like her, don't you?"

It was a woman's question. He could be honest. "I do. She is charming and kind and heading to the poorhouse herself by feeding people."

"That is all?"

"For now." He could be cagey too. He had started this trip north to find a place to settle, not anticipating so many complications to a simple quest. He felt the warmth begin somewhere around his pectoral muscles and spread north to his forehead. He saw the growing amusement on Lady Telford's broad and plain face, and he felt like Dougie again.

But that was silly; this was a business proposal and nothing more. He smiled at her, thinking he would do almost anything to convince Lady Telford that his scheme was a good one, for whatever reason. No, for the reason that Flora MacLeod's kind lady deserved someone to watch over her.

He looked at Lady Telford; she stared back at him, the warmth in her eyes touching his heart. "It's a legacy worthy of the wife of a baronet," he told her. "This corporation will change lives for the better. What say you, Lady Telford?"

She did not hesitate. She put out her hand and he shook it.

His hand still in hers, he said, "You are certainly

capable of drawing up terms. Do that. In a day or two I will go back to Plymouth and find us a shipwright. When I return, we will sit down with your solicitor and go over this contract between you and me."

The pressure on his hand was firm. "Will you find such a man?"

"I will. This I do not doubt." He looked at his time-piece. "I leave you to think about the matter. I have a patient who needs my attention."

She showed him out herself, her hand on his shoul-der, which he found oddly comforting, even if she was an old rip who had frightened him as a child. He was no child now.

Chapter 26

MRS. AINTREE'S HAND SHOWED NO signs of infection, to Douglas's relief. Mrs. Tavish's solicitous care of the lady impressed him. Tommy's sutures came out easily. Mrs. Aintree had insisted that Douglas perform that bit of business right there in her room so she could watch, which told him worlds about the widow's growing interest in the Tavishes.

Tommy was stoic and steadfast as Douglas cut and tugged, probably because his mother and Mrs. Aintree watched him so anxiously. Douglas gave him a wink the women couldn't see and told the boy to keep breathing, which made him laugh.

"That is it," he said as he applied another bandage, encasing Tommy's leg from knee to ankle as before, and attaching the splints again. "You will continue to exercise some caution," he admonished, knowing full well that Tommy had no such plans.

"Aye, sir," the rascal said.

It was time to lower the boom, probably past time, but Tommy Tavish was an engaging rascal, and Douglas admitted to other distractions. He stood up, giving himself at least the advantage of height. He had no trouble remembering his Royal Navy days, because it hadn't been that long ago. He tapped the boy's chest to gain his full attention, looked down his nose, and frowned.

"Listen, Thomas. If, in my professional opinion, I see you disregarding all caution, I will reapply that splint that ran from your ankle to your armpit. Don't even try me."

Tommy gasped. "You wou . . ." He stopped and saw no sympathy in anyone's eyes. "You probably would," he admitted.

"I can guarantee it. Do we understand each other?"

"Aye, sir," Tommy said most reluctantly. He sighed, very much a small boy again, and left the room with considerable dignity, muttering to himself.

Douglas turned his attention to the women in Tommy's life. "Ladies, if you see any infractions, just let me know. I will do as I promised."

He sat down again and turned Mrs. Aintree's hand over gently, pleased with what he saw. He tried a different tactic with the widow and kissed her cheek, which made her blush like a maiden.

"And you, dear lady, stay in bed another day. Tomorrow is soon enough to try out the sling and move about." He smiled. "I trust you considerably more than I trust Tommy."

Mrs. Tavish walked him down the stairs. He spent a quiet moment with her in the kitchen, inquiring after Joe Tavish.

He watched her eyes for wariness or disgust and saw none. "Thank you for tidying up that man of yours, Rhona," he said, unsure how to proceed because he had never been married, and certainly never gone through anything resembling the Tavishes' experience. "I prefer that he remain in the shed, but if you have other ideas . . ."

"Not at the moment, although he is my husband and I care a great deal for the man, as difficult as he may be," she said honestly. "I'll see that he has food from Miss Grant's Tearoom, unless Mrs. Aintree feels charitable enough to include him in her kind stewardship."

He gave her a bow, grateful for the ladies. He doubted that he would have been so forgiving.

Flora MacLeod grabbed him in a monstrous hug as he entered Miss Grant's Tearoom. She held out a little draw-string bag that she said Brighid Dougall had presented to her. Flora made him heft it, delighting him that his first modest enterprise in Edgar was bearing good fruit, if the weight of the pouch was any indication.

"Mrs. Dougall put up a bigger sign in her window too," Flora said. "Both MacGregor sisters are helping me now."

He handed back the pouch. "Keep it safe, Flora. Maybe give it to Miss Grant. No, give it to Mrs. Dougall for safekeeping."

Flora nodded. "I think she likes me."

"Flora, who wouldn't?" he asked and felt his heart grow larger—a medical impossibility.

Happy with that homely victory, he went into the kitchen. Her face flushed, her hair curling everywhere because of the steam, Olive stood over that evening's stew. She looked at him, and he was struck with the kindness in her eyes. He liked to think it was for him, but he knew she was kind to everyone.

On wild impulse—Maeve was watching, after all—he took Olive's hand and pulled her out the back door and into the yard. When she was down the stairs, he put his hands on her shoulders and told her everything he had done at Lady Telford's. Her hand went to her mouth and tears came to her eyes.

"Your tearoom will become the corporation's dining room," he concluded. "You will have an ample allowance for food and more staff."

She closed her eyes and nodded. "I have been praying about this. Doug, I am nearly without funds."

"I feared that," he said, flattered to his heart's core at his nickname.

He looked into her honest, true, multicolored eyes and knew he needed to lighten the load a bit. He was getting almost sentimental. "Olive, I find myself looking more into the brown one than the blue one. Odd, that."

She laughed and slapped his head, which made him grab her and kiss her, not on the forehead this time. Her arms went around him as though they did this every day, and they stood together in a tight embrace.

She drew away first; he had no immediate plans to ever move. "My goodness, but I react boldly to good news," she said. Her face was fiery red now, and he supposed his was too. "I should perhaps apologize?"

He shook his head, dazed with feelings he had thought belonged to a younger man. *You're not eighty, you dolt*, he scolded himself, struck by the fact that for the first time in decades, he didn't feel eighty. This bore some private thought.

"I don't think it's necessary for either of us to apologize for exuberance," he said, acutely aware how stupid he sounded. *Great gobs of monkey meat, I am Dougie again*, he thought, thankful that Lady Telford wasn't watching. "Besides, I started it." He tugged her curls. "And I have no plans to apologize. Olive, Edgar's fortunes are looking up."

Maeve giggled when they came back inside, and he knew she had watched out the window. All a man could do was forge ahead and pretend nothing had happened. He sat down for stew and ate quickly. "I'll take some of this to Joe Tavish, along with whatever of that stiffer paper that remains. Do you have a pencil or two?"

She did and fetched it as he finished eating. "I hope he is feeling better this afternoon because he needs to sketch the . . ." He paused as the enormity of the project suddenly landed on his head like an ostrich egg, cracked, and dribbled down his temples. ". . . the Telford Boat

Works. Hadrian's Wall! I'll take the drawings with me to Plymouth and see how persuasive I am."

"I have no doubt that you will convince any number of shipwrights to follow you up north to this country," she said.

After that kiss in the garden, he saw no reason to be suddenly coy. "Olive, I don't do things like this! I don't create corporations or make grandiose plans. I'm a surgeon, for heaven's sake."

"Have a little faith, Doug," she said simply.

He spent the rest of the afternoon removing a splinter from the palm of a child who wanted nothing to do with him, and then making an emergency house call to the grocer's. Maintaining a calm sort of professionalism when he wanted to slap his knee and laugh, he reassured a worried Mrs. McDaniel that, yes, indeed, the umbilical cord stump was supposed to fall away just like that.

The walk back to his house meant stopping to chat with the fishmongers again and then taking tea with an elderly lady whose name he could not recall, who just wanted to talk. He listened, offered a little advice about dry, itchy skin, and returned home with a smile on his face.

He lay down then and tried to sleep because he couldn't remember when he had last done such a thing. This enforced stay in Edgar was beginning to resemble a fleet action.

He dozed, fearing bad dreams as usual, but instead enjoying the pleasure of Olive Grant's breath on his neck and the edgy comfort of her softness. He imagined her wearing nothing but a shimmy, which meant he had to get up and walk around a bit, wondering about himself.

On the tenth back and forth pacing, he stopped and looked into his shaving mirror, as though to ask himself, Who is this man? The usual face looked back at him, but the mirror Douglas Bowden smiled.

He spent an hour with Joe Tavish in the shed, which had been swept clean and equipped with a cot found somewhere. He tended the infected wound on the man's forearm, happy to see it no worse today, and told Joe what he needed and why.

"I want you to come with me in the late afternoon to the old shipyard and sketch it." To Joe's unasked why, he told him about the Telford Boat Works and his plans for the corporation to employ every man in Edgar who wanted to work.

"We aren't carpenters or shipwrights," Joe argued. "We're crofters and cattlemen."

"Can you change?" Douglas asked. "The man I have in mind to manage the yard is a fine teacher. The corporation will pay you well as you learn a new trade."

"But it's not—"

"—and it never will be the Highlands again," Douglas snapped, out of patience. "And, no, I'm not doing this for Olive Grant!"

"I didn't say—"

"I see it on your face," Douglas said. "Stop your nasty leering! I'm doing this because I hate the waste of human life. I held little Flora MacLeod on my lap while the horror of her experience took over her brain and she told me through her tears, 'All we needed was a little help.' I have no proof against that, Joe Tavish. I need your sketches and I will pay you for them. Whether you want to work in the boatyard is your business. Just don't get in my way."

He knew he had spoken too loud because the Highlander stared at him, his face drained of color. "It's not for a woman?"

Douglas considered the question. "I admit it is, as well. Do any of you realize that Miss Grant has used up nearly all of her inheritance to feed people?"

"I didn't know," Joe mumbled. "I . . . maybe I just thought she was lording it over us, making us feel poor."

"Olive Grant hasn't that capacity, and you know it," Douglas said, suddenly weary of arguing with an idiot. He picked up the paper and pencils. "I need your help and I need it now. Don't hem and haw and turn away because things have not gone your way, Joe Tavish!" There he was, shouting again. Who was this shrill man occupying his usually calm body? Douglas took a deep breath and another, not trusting himself. "If you will not help me, I'll draw my own sketches."

He left the shed, angry with himself for shouting at someone as beaten down and demoralized as Joe Tavish. Maybe the only thing he would ever accomplish in Edgar was Seven Seas Fancies. He had never thought of himself as a leader; maybe he wasn't.

Shadows were lengthening across the empty shipyard when he arrived there, out of breath and angry. He stood still a long moment, trying to decide where to start, he who had not one single ounce of artistic ability in his whole body. *Do it for Flora. Do it for Olive*, he thought and took heart.

He walked around the graving docks—Olive's bathtubs—until he felt less like throttling Joe Tavish. He reminded himself to ask Lady Telford for the key to the enormous padlock on the one-story stone building that ran nearly the length of the yard.

The tide was in and water filled the one graving dock where the massive wooden gates remained open. *I can see it in my mind*, he thought, at odds with himself. A yacht so sleek and stylish being built right here. *If I touch the pencil to this paper, my sketches will look like cats mating.*

He decided to begin right where he stood. He could probably sketch the graving dock with some portion of the shed behind it, so the Plymouth shipwright he had in mind could get some clue about the yard's layout. He poised a pencil over the paper, nearly paralyzed by his inadequacy. *Give me an amputation any day*, he thought and began to sketch.

"Nay, Mr. Bowden. The light's better here. Give that to me before ye waste a sheet of paper. Paper is dear, don't you know?"

Douglas looked up, startled. Joe Tavish stood there shaking his head.

"'Tweren't joking. Thou really doesn't have a drawing bone anywhere."

"Not one." Douglas handed over the paper. "I want to get this graving dock with the shiphouse in the background."

Joe nodded. He looked over his shoulder to a row of men who hesitated by the long shed. "I'll draw that while you talk to them."

Douglas looked, too, striving to be casual and matter-of-fact when he wanted to click his heels and dance around like a maniac. As he walked toward the ragged men, some of them in trousers, others in kilts, he saw more Highlanders joining them, some with their wives. Joe must have gone calling.

Douglas perched on the low stone wall that surrounded the abandoned . . . No, the Telford Boat Works. "Come closer," he said, gesturing. "I have this plan . . ."

Chapter 27

*O*LIVE GRANT SAW DOUGLAS BOWDEN off on the morning coach a day later, a pasteboard box full of drawings tucked under one arm and his ever-present medical pouch slung over the other. She saw the resolve in his deep-set eyes and she loved him.

After he left, she wondered if she loved him for the good he was attempting to do for Edgar and for the displaced families from the Highlands. Was it because he was also trying to save her from ruin? Or did she love him simply because he was Douglas Bowden, the man she had waited to give herself to, after all these years; the man she wanted to make her children with; the man she knew she would do anything for, if he only asked?

These were new emotions, easy enough to brush off because nothing remotely resembling this had ever happened to her before. Maybe she was confusing love with pity or earnest effort. How would she know? When had something like this ever happened to her?

She stood on the steps of the tearoom long after a simple wave of the hand would have sent most people inside again, especially since it was raining. She stood there, back straight as always, watching as the coach took the little curve that followed the bend of the bay. To her delight, he looked back on that curve, and she waved again. She laughed when he took off his hat and waggled it out the open window.

Even then, Olive didn't want to go inside. The girls had spread the remaining shells across three tables, with hunks of driftwood occupying a table of their own. She wanted to walk somewhere and think about what she felt.

She thought it had begun with the totally impromptu kiss in the backyard, when her arms had so naturally circled his body, pulling him close as he did the same. Papa would have looked askance to see no space between one body and the other; Mama would probably have smiled and then taken her quietly aside for a discussion on what usually happens next when two people did that. That thought made her smile, because she had an excellent idea of what happened next.

But it had begun much earlier, maybe even in the first days when she barely knew Douglas Bowden, and he had started to talk in his sleep, his voice deepening in intensity until he whimpered. A simple hand to his shoulder had ended his nightmare each time and usually led to deep, peaceful sleep, his cheek resting against her hand, until she moved it and returned to her own narrow bed. He had thanked her once in that straightforward, clinical way of his, and then never mentioned the matter again because he was too busy taking care of too many people and dealing with issues he had never encountered at sea, unless the dratted Countess of Sutherland had found a way to ruin lives on-board vessels of the Royal Navy too.

Olive had quickly discovered him for what he was because he said so: a retired surgeon looking for a trouble-free place to establish a country practice. She knew he had earned such a place because his nightmares told her so. She wanted such a place for him, up to the moment when she knew that if he left Edgar, she would never be the same again.

Reading the occasional novel had suggested to her that finding the right man led to tranquility and harmony. The reality was far more wrenching, especially if the right man for her had no idea what he wanted.

"You have to leave it at that," she advised herself in the mirror that morning. She knew she must tell herself that every morning, up to and beyond the inevitable morning when he climbed aboard the coach and left for good. She would probably tell herself that every morning and watch the woman in the mirror grow gray and wrinkled. She had found the man she loved; there was never any guarantee that such a fellow would reciprocate. The kiss indicated strongly that he might, but there was a much bigger issue at stake in Edgar, and they both knew it.

And drat the matter, she was a reticent Scot, disinclined to ask advice of such an intimate nature from anyone. Just as well, because she could think of no one to confide in, the irony, of course, being that a woman ought to be able to talk to her doctor about anything.

The only solution in sight was to work harder. After the coach left, carrying away the man she adored, whose mind was completely occupied with finding a shipwright and saving Edgar, she went into the kitchen and banged away at bread dough. Maeve wisely made no comment.

Olive began to feel more satisfaction after lunch, in which she counted more Highlanders eating her beef roast, dripped pudding, and hot bread. The roast had been a gift from the butcher, who showed her the carbuncle Douglas had lanced only yesterday. "Look at that, Miss Grant," he had said, until she was forced to look.

Once the butcher had left and relieved her of exclaiming delights over his carbuncle-free hand, her heart truly had lifted to see Joe Tavish hesitate at the door and then

come inside, Tommy with him. He put down a conspicu-
ous coin and asked for beef roast.

"I think our doctor overpaid me for a handful of
sketches," he whispered to her.

"He knows the value of your drawings, Mr. Tavish,"
Olive assured him. "They will very likely tip the balance
in favor of finding a shipwright."

He nodded at that, shy now, but with a certain quiet
pride that seemed to radiate from him. Olive felt certain
such a feeling had not come his way in several years, if
ever. She served father and son and calmed her heart.

Blissful afternoon. A quick visit to Mrs. Aintree found
the widow sitting up and looking cheerful. Rhona Tavish
had put the widow's arm in a sling and sat by her bed,
darning stockings.

"Joe and Tommy ate beef roast in my tearoom for luncheon," she said.

"Our surgeon paid him well for those sketches," Rhona
said. She looked so kindly at Olive and taught her worlds
about marriage. "I like to see them together, father and
son. Nothing changes here right now, except that we're
breathing a bit easier, Miss Grant."

Anyone would, Olive thought, *who is not teetering con-
tinually on ruin*. She wished with all her heart that Douglas
Bowden, Edgar's "our surgeon," knew what it was like to
breathe easier.

All was equally well at the Hare and the Hound, with
Brighid Dougall selling a fancy to a tall woman, all planes
and angles. Brighid gestured her closer.

"Mrs. Fillion, this is the lady you have been inquiring
about, Miss Olive Grant," she said.

Olive curtsied, wondering where she had heard the
name before. The unknown traveler took Olive's hand in
hers, to Olive's surprise, but not her chagrin.

"Miss Grant, I was supposed to mail a box of sea
shells from the Drake in Plymouth to a certain surgeon

we know. My son reminded me that that I have not had a holiday since forever, and I am decidedly curious about what Douglas Bowden is doing. And so I am here."

Ships pass in the night, Olive reminded herself. "He has mentioned you. We would let him tell you in person, but our surgeon has scarpered off back to Plymouth."

Mrs. Fillion's startled look was certain proof she was not a Scot. This was not a lady to hide her light under a bushel. "Well, take out me eyes, scrub them, and put them back in," she exclaimed. She took a close look at Olive. "He wrote me that he looks more at the brown one than the blue one. Miss Grant, what is this man up to?"

"How is it that you know about my eyes?" Olive asked, her guard down as she listened to words spoken in the soft burr of the West Country, so pleasing.

"Miss Grant, he has written me all about you, and this village, and a sweet child named Flora, and . . . and . . ." She held up the little trinket she had just purchased and gave it a little shake. ". . . and Seven Seas Fancies. I have known that man for years, but not this man."

Olive leaned closer. "Did he tell you about the man he struck with a stick and who thrashed him and gave him a black eye?"

"He didn't!" Mrs. Fillion put her hand to her mouth.

Mrs. Dougall leaned over the counter and gestured Olive closer. "You should take her to your tearoom and give her an earful."

"P'raps I should," Olive said, curious to know what else Douglas Bowden had told this woman about her. And why should she seem so surprised about the man of action that everyone in Edgar knew? "Mrs. Fillion, may I offer you tea? My tearoom has turned into a factory for Seven Seas Fancy production, so you can meet Flora MacLeod and her confederates."

She carried the box of seashells for Mrs. Fillion, who walked beside her with a traveling satchel to Olive's tearoom, where Maeve was ready with green tea and biscuits.

"You'll stay here too," Olive said. "I don't rent my rooms above, but I know it is quieter than the Hare and Hound. You will be my guest."

Mrs. Fillion's eyes were on the three little girls who had created workstations as soon as the luncheon eaters finished. They had looked up when Olive and Mrs. Fillion entered the tearoom. A quick glance satisfied them and they returned to aligning and threading the shells.

"Nonetheless, I will pay you," Mrs. Fillion said, in a voice that brooked no disagreement. "You can call it my contribution to the drink and victual fund. Aye, miss, Douglas wrote me about that, too."

Mrs. Fillion touched Olive's hand. "I was wondering what he would find in Scotland."

"He hasn't found it yet," Olive told her with a shake of her head.

"I rather think he has," the woman replied. "Up these stairs?"

Midafternoon was Olive's favorite time of the day. The luncheon rush was over, and whatever more modest items she had prepared for dinner—lately, these had been less modest—were either cooking in the oven or simmering on the hob. She had sent Maeve to the greengrocer with a list and a basket over her arm. After a shy introduction, Flora and the MacGregor girls had taken their own basket to hunt for driftwood. The tearoom was blissfully empty and the green tea the right temperature.

Mrs. Fillion understood the unspoken need to explain herself. She told Olive about the Drake, a three-story hotel and dining room located in Plymouth's old Barbican, home to a generation and more of Royal Navy officers back from the sea, if only briefly. They both chuckled over the perpetual whist game that never seemed to lack for players.

"Was Mr. Bowden among them?" Olive asked.

"Never. He would watch and sit with fellow officers, but he did not play and he never gambled," Mrs. Fillion said. "Douglas is a careful man." She took a sip of tea and regarded Olive over the rim of the cup. "I cannot imagine him actually striking a man and engaging in any kind of rough and tumble."

Her own tea grew cold as Olive told the interested woman of Tommy Tavish, bleeding with a compound fracture, carried by his mother, nine months gone with child, into the path of the coach.

"Those who saw it told me that Mr. Bowden was out of the carriage before it even stopped, tugging at his neck-cloth to quench the bleeding."

"That he would do," Mrs. Fillion agreed. "I never saw a man quicker to react than our Douglas."

She spoke with such a degree of familiarity that Olive wondered at the connection, then asked herself why it was any business of hers.

Mrs. Fillion seemed to know what she was thinking. She rested her hand on Olive's for a moment, just a gentle touch. "Miss Grant, you must understand that these exalted officers were all my boys." She swallowed and her eyes filled with tears. "They came, they slept in my hotel, they played cards, they drank, and they went back to sea where many died in battle or drowned in storms."

She must have felt that the burden of those wartime years needed to be lighter because she laughed and shook her head. "And you tell me that Douglas beat the boy's father? That is not our Douglas."

Olive could tease in turn. She had to, because her heart was near to breaking, just hearing the wistfulness and affection in Mrs. Fillion's voice for men gone too soon. "I rather believe it is the same man—tall enough, brown hair with considerable gray in it, brown eyes, and a flat East Anglia accent? He grinds his Rs?"

"The very one," Mrs. Fillion agreed. "A true Anglian. The same one who assured me that he was going to find a village far from the ocean."

"He will yet find it," Olive said, keeping her voice light because she did not want to weep before this near-stranger. "He reminds me that all the good he is doing here will last until he feels satisfied that Edgar is a better place. Let me show you what this quiet man you speak of is doing."

They walked to the dock and on toward the empty shipyards.

"Oh my," Olive said as she looked upon a ragged little army busy cleaning the place, hauling off debris. Supervising the cleanup was the MacGregor girls' father, dressed in rags but obviously in charge. He waved to her and walked in their direction.

"Miss Grant, our surgeon set me onto this work before he left." He looked around and Olive saw the pride in his eyes, this man who had herded cattle in a Highlands glen and was now remaking himself. "Told'm we'd have it shipshape by the time he returned with a builder." He touched his hand to his cap and returned to his equally shabby crew.

Olive took a deep breath. "And that quiet man you speak of has endowed my puny victual and drink account with enough funds to feed the workers and their families as a condition of their employment." She dabbed at her eyes. "I was running out of my inheritance, seeing that the Highlanders dumped here and left to die at least had food."

"I suppose I do know this side of him," Mrs. Fillion said, her voice equally soft. "He saved my son Michael's life, he did, when the boy developed pneumonia."

"I'll wager he did not leave the child's side."

"Not once, until he was breathing better." Mrs. Fillion looked back where they had come. "My boy became a sailor, too, and those are Michael's shells."

"Please tell Michael how much we appreciate them," Olive said.

"I wish I could. He died at Trafalgar," Mrs. Fillion told her, holding tight to her hand. "My older son helps me with the Drake now. He stumps about on one leg, but he lives."

The two women stood there with their arms around each others' waists. They started back toward the docks, where the first vessel of the fishing fleet was tying up.

"All of your boarders—your sons?" Olive asked. Her heart was full as the entire cost of war landed on her. "You knew them better than most."

"I felt that way about them," Mrs. Fillion said, when she could speak. She tucked her handkerchief back in her sleeve. She stopped, faced Olive, and sat with her on a bench by the poorest end of town.

"I have never told anyone this," she began and then looked down at her shoes. "I would walk the halls of my hotel at night. Well, the officers' wives who were able to meet their husbands in Plymouth—I put them in quieter lodgings on the top floor and did not venture there. My, you can blush!"

Olive touched her warm cheeks. She had long resigned herself to spinsterhood, but she could see those rooms with closed doors. She imagined couples behind them, relieving themselves of worry and war, even if for a brief time, taking a moment to fall asleep in each others' arms, and then leaving too soon, as duty called and the tides and winds made their own demands.

"I shouldn't tease you," Mrs. Fillion said. "I walked the other halls late at night, listening to sleeping men singing drunken songs, some of them. Others were in the grip of different nightmares. Some wept. Some seemed to be arguing with fate or the French. Douglas talked, quietly at first, and then louder. I think he woke himself up and managed to put himself back to sleep. Others did the same. There was no one to fix them."

I touched his arm a few times and we kissed, Olive thought, *but that is my memory and I will not share it.*

Mrs. Fillion looked up, her face so worn, telling Olive without words how much she must have cared for her self-declared sons of the Royal Navy through years of national alarm. It was Olive's turn to take the woman's hands in her own.

"I wanted to gather them up in my arms, every one of them, but it was not my place to do anything of the sort. I ran a hotel, after all, and not a hospital or a confessional. And so I wore myself out walking down my halls, cursing Napoleon and counting a cost so high that I could not see the end of it."

They sat in silence then. Olive thought of all the ways that war had touched every small village and large city in Britannia. She thought of the indifferent cruelty leveled on the Highlanders, many of whose sons had served king and country through war. Her heart recoiled at all the evil in the world, and she was not surprised at her own weariness or that of the woman sitting beside her.

"We've pretty much forced Doug to pick up our burden here in Edgar," she said, not caring that Mrs. Fillion heard the familiarity of his name. "All he wants to do is get away, and we haven't let him. We are wrong, I suppose, but we are desperate."

"He is used up," Mrs. Fillion warned.

"I know, but our need is so great," Olive said quietly. She waved her hand toward the shipyard, where change was coming. "He'll be here with a shipwright, I have no doubt. There will be order, and he will leave us."

"Are you so certain?"

"That he will succeed?"

"No, Miss Grant—that he will leave you. My dear, he wrote about you to me."

It was past time to be cautious. Olive tightened her grip on the woman who had come so far with shells because her life was entwined with her hotel patrons.

"I love Douglas Bowden," Olive confessed. "I don't know what he is thinking, though, beyond the need to be gone from here and to find a quiet medical practice that probably does not exist."

"It may be that he will have to keep looking before he realizes what was right under his nose in Edgar," Mrs. Fillion suggested.

Olive considered her words, wondering if she could bear the pain of waving good-bye to Douglas Bowden, "our surgeon," as the people of Edgar already called him. And once he was gone, would he think twice and return? As much as she would wish it, she knew that people seldom returned.

"Life was easier when I had no expectations," she admitted to Mrs. Fillion. "If this is love, it is not a pleasure."

Chapter 28

Mrs. Fillion remained another day in Edgar, walking with Olive to visit Flora's Gran and Mrs. Aintree. The hotel keeper spent an afternoon in the widow's comfortable bedroom and then in Elizabeth MacLeod's one-room hovel, sipping tea and eating biscuits with one, and drinking cold water and oatcakes with the other.

Mrs. Fillion admired Flora and gave her advice on managing a business. Olive wished Douglas could have been there to watch Flora on Mrs. Fillion's lap, paying close attention to advice from how to keep the money safe to what to charge when a customer wants more than one fancy—"If you discount her a penny each for a dozen, she will buy more." He also could have seen how Flora's eyes drooped and how she then slept with Mrs. Fillion's arms enveloping her.

Olive took Mrs. Fillion along with her on a summons to Lady Telford's manor, precipitated by a note on heavy embossed paper. The note contained a veiled threat or two of the variety that sent Mrs. Fillion into whoops.

"Really, Olive"—they had progressed quickly to the

Olive and Nancy stage—"Lady Telford seems to regard the drawing up of corporate papers as something close to Magna Carta."

"It might be causing her severe palpitations to have to deal with me in Doug's absence," Olive told her as she stared at the note. (They had also abandoned Mr. Bowden and gone beyond Douglas.) "We're common as weeds, you see, but at least he can find her pulse." She pointed to the last line. "'Attire yourself appropriately.' I suppose this means I must remove my apron and wear matching shoes."

"Without a doubt," Nancy Fillion agreed. "I recommend a new bonnet too."

There was no place in Edgar that carried bonnets, which meant a trip to Dumfries, and a glorious day spent in the heady dissipation of looking in actual store windows until she found the right hat.

Olive couldn't remember a jaunt like this. Maeve had assured her that she could manage the day's meals. Annys Campbell had been hired to assist in the kitchen, under Douglas Bowden's same financial umbrella that was seeing the shipyard cleaned. Olive had her own growing pile of coins, which meant choosing a bonnet because she liked it, not because the thing was cheap.

By the time the day in Dumfries wound down, Olive had no objection to resting her feet—matching shoes—in a solicitor's office.

"I have a bit of business which cannot wait," Mrs. Fillion told her and Olive had no objection. She reminded herself that this was just a simple day in nearby Dumfries and not her first outing in well beyond a year of work and worry.

As she waited, Olive took the three white ribbons from their brown paper twist and admired them, thinking how lovely the Seven Seas Fancies Corporation would look on Sunday. There were drawing pencils for Joe Tavish, a thimble for Rhona, and a small carved elephant for Tommy that the shopkeeper vowed came all the way from the "distant mists of the great Ganges." As to that, Olive had her doubts, but the carved creature, reared on hind legs with ears back and trunk upraised, might remind the boy that he was still a child.

She lifted her reticule, pleased to feel the weight of coins left over from their modest bolt to a bigger town. Only a week ago, she had sat in her cramped office next to the kitchen and cried because she had so little left of her inheritance. Now she sat in the waiting room of a solicitor's office and asked God to bless Douglas Bowden for his generosity. The surgeon might not be one to bother the Almighty, but Olive was.

Sleep came easily that night, easier than some nights when she worried about Douglas Bowden and the lights on across the street, long after everyone else was abed. Her bedroom faced the street, the same as his did. Because it was summer, she had opened her window. A light sleeper, she heard even the quiet knocks on his door, signaling someone in town in need of a man who had already given everything he could to king and country. Before she slept, she smiled to think of his leaning out the window in his nightshirt, elbows on the sill.

She slept peacefully that night because she had seen to Mrs. Aintree, well and truly tended by Rhona Tavish, and exclaimed over the ten new fancies that Flora took to the Hare and Hound. She already knew that Brighid Dougall would have a pasty for the child, or warm milk, which they would sip together. Even Mrs. Fillion had exclaimed over the absence of debris in the shipyard. As she lay in bed, Olive thought she heard faint bagpipes and singing somewhere in town.

The morning brought sunshine, a rare enough occurrence, but pleasing to Olive, because she need have no fears for her new bonnet. She chose her dark green wool, mainly because there wasn't much decision involved, not with only two good dresses. She mourned briefly over her lack of fashion sense, personally aware that cotton work dresses and sensible aprons suited her better. There was no one to impress.

Maeve and Mrs. Campbell were perfectly in control in the kitchen, which warmed Olive in a way that a fire in the hearth never could. She felt a slight portion of her responsibilities slough away, leaving her optimistic, even though Douglas Bowden would return soon, install a shipwright, check Mrs. Aintree's healing hand, and probably take the next coach from Edgar. *You are building castles in the sky*, she scolded herself, and the burden returned.

Mrs. Fillion had followed her downstairs and joined her in the dining room for porridge and tea.

"You've been too polite to ask why I have shouldered my way into this visit with Lady Telford," Mrs. Fillion said.

"Probably because I welcome your company," Olive admitted. "Lady Telford is a testy old rip."

They laughed together. Olive assured Maeve that whatever Lady Telford wanted surely wouldn't take long, considering how little the baroness had to do with Edgar's citizens, each as ordinary was Elsie Glump was, even though Lady T remained in ignorance of their knowledge.

Putting on her new bonnet required kitchen assistance, with Maeve shaking her head and retying the bonnet's bow until it was located under her ear.

"I will look like a coquette," Olive protested.

"And what is the matter with that?" Maeve asked, not about to be cowed.

"You know there is no one in Edgar to . . . to coquet for," Olive insisted, even though she did like the effect in the mirror, when Maeve dragged her in front of it.

"Then call it practice," her servant said, unperturbed.

The fishing fleet had already left for the day, but Olive

stood a moment and looked toward the docks, and then beyond to the clean but quiet shipyard. She remembered the shipyard sounds and the fun of standing by the graving dock as the shipwright—long since gone to work in Glasgow—knocked away the wooden supports and the new fishing boat slid sideways into the water.

She thought of the extreme expense and wondered if Douglas Bowden was waving farewell to all of his retirement funds, whatever they were. "We just can't do this," she said out loud. "It's one thing for me to go destitute in Edgar, but why should the surgeon who hadn't even meant to spend any time here lose his shirt? I own that I have very cold feet right now."

Mrs. Fillion turned her purposefully from the docks toward the bridge spanning the Dee. "I had a moment exactly like this, my dear," she said, and started Olive in motion. "It was during the Peace of Amiens, when few ships sailed, and the officers were cast ashore on half pay. I needed to make some essential repairs to the Drake, which would drain my account." She sighed with the memory. "And I had few lodgers."

"Did you pray for a renewal of war?" Olive teased, happy to think of someone else's misfortune for a moment.

"Very nearly!" Mrs. Fillion teased back. "I stood in front of my mirror and took a good look at a woman who had started out in the Drake's kitchen as a scullery maid."

"Surely not," Olive murmured.

"Oh, yes. It's a lengthy story, but the place became mine." Her voice softened. "I stared just long enough to trust myself. I began the repairs and war was declared again a month later."

"I suppose if Douglas Bowden wants to spend his money this way . . ." She let the words trail away. "He is helping us beyond any reason."

"Have you ever considered that you and the people of Edgar might be helping him more?"

They were across the bridge now and walking toward Lady Telford's manor. "Does he even know that?" Olive asked.

"You will have to ask him someday."

There was no backing out now. Mrs. Fillion gave the doorknocker a sharp rap. Olive nodded to Maidie when she opened it. "We're here."

Maidie dropped a clumsy curtsy and led them down the hall. She opened the door on what was a bookroom. Seated behind the desk was Lady Telford, who scowled to see someone besides Olive.

"And who, pray, are you?" she asked, not rising.

"Nancy Fillion," Nancy said. She gave a little curtsy. "I am a friend of both Miss Grant and Mr. Bowden, from Plymouth."

"I suppose it doesn't matter," said a stout fellow dressed in unrelieved black. "I am Frederick Hornby, Lady Telford's solicitor." He indicated that they sit, when Lady Telford seemed disinclined to observe the courtesies.

He handed Olive a sheaf of papers. "Take a look through these if you wish, but I will draw your attention to the part of it that affects you and your tearoom." He pointed to the page marked by a scrap of paper.

She began to read, touched at the generous provisions for the tearoom, where everyone and their family who labored in the boat works would eat for a mere penny each a day. Her hands nearly started to tremble, just looking at the monthly sum that would be hers to buy food. She had to dab at her eyes to see Douglas Bowden's last stipulation. "Miss Grant, owner of the tearoom, will be paid an annual salary of fifty pounds a year, until such point as her depleted inheritance has recovered."

"I think that is exorbitant," Lady Telford said. "I tried to remind the surgeon that you had undertaken to spend your inheritance of your own free will and choice, but he wouldn't have any of it."

"Bravo, Douglas," Nancy Fillion said under her breath, then turned innocent eyes on Lady Telford.

"Aye or nay?" the solicitor asked, his eyes merry, but only since his head was turned and he knew Lady Telford could not see his expression.

"I should really argue with Dou . . . Mr. Bowden," Olive hedged.

"He would only ignore you," Mrs. Fillion said.

"Aye, then," Olive said. She sat there amazed at one man's generosity. Until Douglas Bowden had come to town, she had faced certain ruin. Now she need fear for nothing. Still, this was only a portion of a much greater outlay, and she cringed inside that he would impoverish himself to help her. She thought of his kiss in the garden and felt the tiniest grain of hope.

"Very well," the solicitor said. "Initial here and here, and I will incorporate this into the document."

She did as he asked, dazed at her good fortune, where none had been expected. She turned to Mrs. Fillion, who seemed to be enjoying this cut and dried legal wrangle. "I suppose we can leave now."

"Not yet." The owner of Plymouth's most prosperous hotel took a sheet of paper from her reticule. She handed it to the solicitor, who read it, his eyes even livelier now. " 'Pon my word, Mrs. Fillion, you intend to become an investor in the Telford Boat Works!" He looked at the paper, which Olive could tell had been crimped by a notary. "And for a . . . my, my . . . a tidy sum."

Olive gasped and grabbed Mrs. Fillion's hand. The woman squeezed back and her eyes became tender. She swallowed and pressed her hand and Olive's to her bosom.

"Douglas Bowden sat with my little boy for hours. He did everything he could. As it turned out, he bought us another ten years of life together as mother and son. Could I do any less?" She bowed her head over their twined hands.

CARLA KELLY

Olive leaned against her shoulder. "You don't even know these people, these Highlanders, you are helping," she whispered.

"I know they are little people, as we are," she said. "They are common and frightened and angry and deserve so much better. Do I need to know anything else?"

Olive shook her head. She swallowed her own tears as she saw, in her mind's eye, Joe Tavish grubbing in a hole in a dirt floor for oats and cow's blood to keep him alive one more day. She heard Flora's plea for someone to help her and her mother and Gran. She could almost see Patrick Sellar and his troops driving out hardworking crofters from their glens and slaughtering their cattle, all because the Countess of Sutherland wanted sheep.

She waited a long minute, glancing at Lady Telford to see eyes less hard now. From the sound of the solicitor, deep in his handkerchief, he was not a man inclined to cynicism.

She had to try, which meant several breaths, and the deepest wish of her heart that Douglas sat there too. "Before my father died, he told me to wait upon the Lord," Olive said. Her voice cracked like a schoolchild's, but how could that matter? "I did not understand what he meant. I do now."

Chapter 29

*D*OUGLAS BOWDEN CLOSED HIS EYES against a headache so powerful that everything from his neck up seemed to throb. He knew it wasn't a migraine. It was just the kind of headache that had been his lot after days of battle and surgery and no rest, and shirt and trousers, despite his apron, soaked with other men's blood.

He had swallowed the anchor by retiring and assured himself as he left London that those days were done. *I am an idiot*, he thought.

Perhaps he was too hard on himself. All he had to do was look across the narrow space in the post chaise to contradict that he was far from being an idiot.

Even now in a bumpy chaise, Homer Bennett, shipwright, was sketching plans for a yacht. And farther back on the Great North Road, Homer's two journeymen and one apprentice were making do on the mail coach. Under Homer's directions, Adam Pine, first journeyman, had been given the assignment to locate the other two, promise them more-than-adequate wages, and point them north to Scotland.

Homer had batted away Douglas's worries that the men might not wish to inflict Scotland upon themselves. "Look here, friend, and make no mistake: As disagreeable as war was, at least it employed all of us."

That same man—the competent, even-keeled Devonport shipwright Douglas had known for years—had confessed to Douglas in the quiet of his bookroom that retirement was proving to be a harder mistress than war. "But don't tell Amy," he had whispered, even though his wife of some thirty years was playing piquet with her best friend three blocks over on Granby Street. "She thinks I am satisfied to be home and doing next to nothing. Blast and dash it all!"

Despite his headache, Douglas had to smile at another whispered conversation he had that same evening with Mrs. Amy Bennett herself, begging Douglas to find something for her husband to do. "He wears a hang-dog expression all day, and mopes, positively mopes, and overeats," she had told Douglas, after swearing him to silence on the matter.

Since he knew nothing of marriage politics, Douglas had cut through the Gordian knot by taking both husband and wife by the hand and sitting them down in their own parlor, where he explained his need for a shipwright in far off Edgar, small village in the shire of Kirkcudbright. "Homer, you are bored," he had said. "Amy wants you to be busy. Admit to each other what you have both disclosed to me."

Both husband and wife had stared daggers at him and he had stared back, arms folded, wondering if Olive Grant would ever resort to such silliness. He decided she probably could, because most females had a curiously devious nature, rather like cats. The matter was moot, however, because he would never be bored. The scope of his thoughts took his breath away, because his mind was wandering farther afield than ever before. What had Olive

Grant to do with his happiness? Never mind; the matter at hand was to get the Bennetts on the same even keel.

He had faith in good friends. In a few moments, the thought-daggers lobbed his way had mellowed. Douglas knew Homer Bennett to be a realistic man. How could he have been otherwise, when for years he was saddled with relentless deadlines upon which the fate of the nation seemed to hang?

"He's right, Ames," Homer had said finally to his wife. "I am filled to the brim with boredom. Not with you," he hastened to add and then sighed. "It's harder than I thought to let go of a career."

Amy Bennett was a bright woman. Douglas thought she could probably read frigate blueprints as well as her husband. Heaven knows that shipbuilding had probably been the chief discussion around the Bennett dinner table during years of national emergency.

"He's not a young man," she had said to Douglas, by way of preamble. "He shouldn't have long hours."

"Indeed no," Douglas had assured her. "This is strictly an eight to six o'clock day. He'll be building and teaching at the same time, which will require the patience of Job."

And then the Bennetts were holding hands and listening as he laid the dubious charms of Edgar—misty days, horrendous odors when the tide was out, and nowhere of interest to shop—side by side with the utter need of hardworking men rendered impotent by expulsion from their distant glens to find meaningful work. "Amy, your man will be busy, paid well, and providing a desperately needed service."

He could tell from the expression on her face that she hadn't heard any word beyond "busy." He knew the Bennetts were comfortably well off, thanks to war. Homer didn't need the work, except that was precisely what he did need. Idle days stretching into idle weeks could put a man into the grave almost as fast as gas gangrene.

By the time bedtime rolled around, Homer Bennett had agreed to resurrect Edgar's shipyard and train his workers. Before she closed the door to the bedchamber she shared with a much happier man now, Amy Bennett had kissed Douglas Bowden's cheek.

"I'll be there as soon as a house is ready," she assured the blushing Douglas. "Truth to tell, I am bored too. A lady can only play so much piquet."

"Doug? You're woolgathering," he heard from the man seated across from him in the post chaise. "Twice now I've asked you about lumber."

"Beg pardon. I will suggest that when your number one journeyman arrives, that the two of you spend several days in Glasgow. Olive—Miss Grant—tells me there is a mighty rope works there, as well, to answer your rigging needs. They'll provide you with no false leads, since the Telford Boat Works is no competition." *So I hope*, he thought, and crossed his fingers.

"I know a few ship builders Clydeside who will help, now that you mention it," Homer said and returned to his sketches. "I have heard they are even experimenting with steam power in Glasgow."

Douglas sat back, contemplating the wonders of this modern age. More than that, he wanted to contemplate the wonders of Olive Grant, and not for the first time.

Not for the first time, some sense assured him that once Olive dug herself out of the financial pit her own generosity had placed her in, she would change in no way. He would probably have to keep an eye on her to make sure she didn't take herself back down the same path. She had the heart of a servant, probably much as her parents before her. She wasn't a woman to shirk hard things.

And how was he to keep an eye on her, except to marry her? There, he had thought it, even though he knew Edgar was not the place he had in mind during lazy days at sea when he had time to lie on deck in the sun and contemplate a future beyond war.

That had been early in his career, on long voyages to the South Pacific, when he was still optimistic and before war stretched from one year to the next and finally had no end in sight. He had stopped imagining anything but war. And so dreams died.

First things first, he told himself. There was a shipyard to make fully operational. He had put off his own wants and desires for so long that he did not know how to introduce them into his life. Maybe they were better left alone, to be considered later, when he found his ideal medical practice. Maybe he didn't even remember what they were.

They spent the last night away in Dumfries, where Douglas replenished his medical supplies and pharmacopeia in the morning. He followed Homer Bennett into a stationery store and watched as his shipwright bought many tablets and pencils, and single sheets of stiffer paper.

While Homer made his purchases, Douglas wandered next door to a shop simply titled "Clothier." Trust the Scots to be frugal even with signs. The shop seemed balanced evenly between apparel for ladies and gentleman. He bought him a pair of gloves, banking on winter eventually returning, and then found himself drawn to the ladies side of the store.

"Something for your wife, sir?" asked a young woman in a black dress.

"Oh, no, I . . . Yes." What was the point in trying to explain his relationship to a shop girl he would never see again?

"Do you have something in particular in mind?" she asked.

"I'll know it when I see it," he assured her, hoping she would leave him to roam alone.

He did know it, a fringed shawl made of silk—if he

could trust his fingers—woven into little kidney shapes of yellow, red, and orange design, with splashes of royal blue. He had seen something like it in the Persian town of Qerm, in the Straits of Hormuz, where they had once taken on water and vegetables.

"Beautiful, isn't it?" The shop girl had materialized at his elbow without his being aware of it.

"Aye. What do you call it? I saw something like it in Persia once."

"Paisley," she said. "There is a town named Paisley not far from here where the weavers use those Persian designs."

Maybe she wanted to spare his feelings. He was wearing one of his new suits, but he had been traveling in it for days. She leaned closer and whispered. "It's rather dear, sir. I can show you something less expensive and more practical."

"No matter. The lady I wish to buy this for has had her fill of practicality. This will do."

She named the price. He winced inwardly but forked over the money. She wrapped the impractical bit of cobweb in prosaic brown paper and knotted it with twine. He was out in the street, purchase tucked under his arm, when Homer emerged from the stationery shop with his more substantial burden. Douglas took on his share of the load as they ambled back to the waiting post chaise.

Purchases stowed, Douglas could barely understand why he looked forward with such eagerness to Edgar; he knew what Edgar was: worry and work.

But there Olive was, standing on the stoop of the tearoom as the post chaise swept past and deposited them at the Hare and Hound. The day was cool and she had bundled herself in her Grant tartan. He waved to her as they went by and she clapped her hands, either pleased to see him, or pleased to see that he had not returned alone. He hoped it was both.

He directed Homer Bennett inside the Hare and

Hound, where Mr. Dougall took charge, his broad face wreathed with smiles. Telling Homer he would return, Douglas went outside and nearly ran into Olive, who was coming up the steps. He took her by the shoulders to steady her and walked her back down to the street.

"I did what I said I would," he told her, his hands still on her shoulders even though she was perfectly capable of standing on a sidewalk without his assistance.

"I knew you would," she said. She touched his face, then withdrew her hand quickly when she must have realized how forward that was. "There you go! Which eye are you looking in?"

"Both at the same time. I'm talented." He held out the brown paper package. "A little trifle for you, alas, from nowhere farther than Dumfries."

As she hurried to open the package—her delight so abundant that he wondered when anyone had ever given her a gift—he teased, "What, you're not going to say 'You shouldn't have?'"

"Not I," she replied quite stoutly. "I love presents."

She sighed when she pulled out the paisley shawl, which looked like butterflies exploding into the misty afternoon. Wordless, but with her eyes expressing every particle of her gratitude, she handed him her old plaid and draped the pretty thing around her shoulders.

"I don't know where I will ever wear it," she said, "but, oh, thank you."

"Save it for the christening of the yacht that Homer Bennett, his crew—they're coming—and a lot of Highlanders are going to build," he replied, wondering if he had every seen anyone as beautiful as Olive Grant.

She took his hand in hers so gently that he had to remind himself to breathe. "Douglas, you have done the thing." She leaned forward and rested her forehead on his arm. "Come by tonight for supper, and I will tell you all about Mrs. Fillion's visit."

"I have some ideas. I stayed at the Drake and her son told me she had gone north. He told me you would have a sur . . ."

He was facing Olive, but now she was looking over his shoulder at the street. "Oh, dear, it is William Lacey from the *Maid of Galloway*," she interrupted, back to business as she took her old plaid from him and draped it over the paisley shawl. "He has worry in his eyes and I think your village needs you again. Poor Douglas. You'll tire of us yet."

Chapter 30

HIS WAS HARDLY THE TIME TO HEAR about Olive's visit with Mrs. Fillion, not with the first mate of the *Maid of Galloway* lying near death, his skull fractured when a mainmast yardarm gave way in yesterday's squall and landed on him.

It was the kind of injury that Douglas hated because the outcome was invariably death. He drilled a few small holes in the poor man's skull, grateful that he was unconscious, but doubting that he would ever wake.

"His brain will swell, and this might relieve some of the pressure," he said to Rhona Tavish, who had not hesitated when Olive asked her to help. "It might not, too."

"What do you do now, Mr. Bowden?" Rhona asked as she gathered his medical tools. He had already extracted a promise from her to wash them in scalding water, dry them, and return them to their proper places in his surgery.

"I will sit here with our patient. Thank you for your help, Mrs. Tavish," he said as he pulled up the chair closer to the bed. "You didn't flinch and you don't look green."

She allowed herself a tiny smile. "We all know that

Miss Grant is too tender-hearted for this sort of thing. I was glad to help."

After a few quiet words with the poor man's wife, Rhona Tavish, exiled Highlander and a woman with her own problems, let herself out of the house. Douglas covered his eyes with his hands, an old sea habit, that gave him a second's worth of privacy. He knew no one ever bothered him when he did that, and it gave him time to work through everything he had done and ask himself if there was something more, some little thing he could do, to change the probable outcome. He could think of nothing, but he kept his hands in front of his eyes a little longer, enjoying the peace.

When he removed them, Olive Grant sat on the other side of Brian Hannay's bed. She did look a little green, but her presence gave him heart. Maybe she had known it would. He knew she had no love for the sickroom.

"Am I the last person you expected to see here?" she asked, studiously avoiding looking at the dying man, even as she held his limp hand. "You know I am not much good for the cutting part, but I don't mind the vigil part. Does he have even a chance?" She said this last in a whisper, because Brian's wife stood just beyond the open door, her children clutched to her.

He shook his head ever so slightly. "I'll be here until the end."

Olive reached across the bed, and he held her hand briefly, giving it a squeeze.

"Why are you here?"

"You need to know what Mrs. Fillion did." She looked at the unconscious seaman then, her gaze so tender. "She said you did not leave her son, during all the struggle for his life."

He shrugged and looked away. "He died ten years later at Trafalgar. I wonder how the whole turn of events did not render her bitter."

"You don't know mothers, do you?" she asked. "She told me how grateful she was that you gave the two of them ten more years that they would not have had otherwise. And she invested eight thousand pounds in the Telford Boat Works."

"Such a sum," he said, when he had fully absorbed the enormity of her gift. He leaned back in his chair, his eyes on Olive, who looked back with the same tenderness. "I merely did what any surgeon would have done."

"I doubt that, Doug," she contradicted. "You're just the best man."

She said it with no sentimentality, as though she merely stated a fact. Her face had gone a bit rosy because it wasn't something a woman without a commitment, tie, or promise said to a man. In a sense, she had opened her breast, removed her heart, and held it out to him. He had never been so flattered in his life, and humbled, at the same time.

"I'm sitting here, staring at failure, and you say that."

"You canna cure them all, Douglas Bowden," she replied, her tone a little sharp now, which was precisely what he needed. She gestured to the man lying between them. "If by some miracle he survives, what then?"

He lowered his voice even farther. "He will never be Brian Hannay again, not the Brian they remember."

"Does he know you are here?"

He shook his head.

"And yet you stay," she said in a voice close to wonder now. "I stand by my statement."

Why he should suddenly feel better, he could not have told anyone, let alone himself. He thought of all the dreary watches just like this one that only ended in death. On the surface of it, this was no different. In actuality, he felt at peace simply because Olive Grant stood the watch with him.

"Stay here, will you?" he asked, feeling needy.

"That was my intention. I have finished all my chores in the kitchen. Anything else can wait for morning."

Speaking quietly, he told her of his trip to Plymouth and finding Homer Bennett, retired and disgruntled. "I didn't even have to mount a major campaign to get him to agree," he told the woman seated across from him. "I perjured myself and promised him a tidy house."

"No perjury there. The wives of the men who have been cleaning out the shipyards have done duty on the house. I had some furniture and Lady Telford had more pieces." She couldn't help her chuckle, there on Brian Hannay's deathbed. "Yes, Lady Telford! She has even been to the Hare and Hound for tea."

"My word," he said, sufficiently amazed.

"Of course, the chairs and table in the shipwright's house are from that horrible Egyptian period; you know, the one following Lord Nelson's Battle of Abukir Bay."

"Horrors," he said. "I was there at the battle, a newly minted surgeon, but none of us encouraged the furniture."

She was ready to laugh, but Mrs. Hannay, her face ghost-white, her eyes huge in her head, tiptoed into the room, one baby in her arms and a serious little boy grasping her skirts.

Without a word, Douglas relinquished his seat and found a footstool for the Hannay's son. He walked around the bed and pulled up a chair beside Olive.

Mrs. Hannay looked at her husband, gently touching the bandage on his head, and then turned her attention to Douglas. "T'captain said t'mast was unstable. Drat the man! Why did he sail?"

The question couldn't be answered by anyone in the room.

Mrs. Hannay continued, as if she were talking to her man lying there before, the one who couldn't speak and would likely not make sunrise. "Brian, ye told me there was something owt with the mast and yardarm, and that

Captain swore he would take the *Maid* to Dundrennan for repairs next week." She sobbed out loud. "Because there is no shipyard here!"

She bowed her head over her infant. Olive motioned to the little boy, who came around the bed and climbed onto her lap. Olive kissed the top of his head and held him close.

They sat in silence. The only sound was the suckling baby, once Mrs. Hannay opened her bodice, after a look of apology in Douglas's direction. When the boy in Olive's arms slept, she carried him through the open door and into the arms of an older woman. Olive returned, standing behind Douglas and resting her hands so gently on his shoulders. Too soon, she gave him a little pat and sat down.

When Mrs. Hannay left to put the baby to bed, Douglas turned to Olive. "A shipyard would have made the difference," he whispered.

"It will for others," she assured him in her forthright way. "Don't borrow a problem that never was yours."

She was right. "Easier said than done," he admitted.

"Tell me more about Plymouth," she said, her eyes on Brian Hannay, who had begun breathing deeper and deeper, and then stopped, before resuming more shallow breaths.

"He will do this now until he dies," Douglas whispered. "Plymouth? The most amazing thing happened. I paid a visit to Carter and Brustein's Counting House, wanting to shift around some funds. I told old David Brustein himself about the shipyard, and do you know, he is now an investor too." He smiled. "Obviously as certifiable as Nancy Fillion. I asked him why, and he said that Jews know something about being driven from their homes and killed. Ten thousand pounds, Olive. Ten thousand! And now Nancy's eight thousand, plus some of my own. I believe we can do this thing."

She took his hand, which meant he had to lean closer and kiss her cheek.

"Stay with me, Olive," he said again.

She stayed with him until after midnight and into the middle watch, that time when, from his experience with death, fiercely wounded men seemed to give up. At Douglas's mental two bells, a pause, and two bells more, Brian Hannay's shallow breaths turned into one long exhalation that went on and on until it wore itself out.

Douglas looked at his timepiece from habit. "I call it at two of the clock," he said to Mrs. Hannay, who had returned hours earlier, both children asleep. "I am so sorry I could do nothing." He gestured toward her husband's wide-open eyes. "You or me?"

When she shook her head, he closed the first mate's eyes. As the new widow began to shake and weep, Douglas took his prescription tablet from his satchel and wished he could brush down the hairs standing tall on his back at the fearsome sound. He scribbled date, time of death, and cause, signing his name. Mrs. Hannay could take this around to the minister when she felt up to it, and he would record in parish records the conclusion of Brian Hannay's too-brief life.

His services were no longer needed. In mere minutes, the female relatives of Brian Hannay assumed command. He assured the widow that she owed him not a pence, which news brought relief to her ravaged face. He stood another moment by the still form, wishing with all his heart that men did not have to die this way. He did what he always did and planted a kiss on the man's forehead.

"It would surprise you how many men called out for their mothers at the end," he remarked to Olive, trying to sound casual, even as his heart broke for the thousandth time. "I always do that."

Olive took his arm as a matter of course when they left the Hannay's tidy home. He looked up at the moon, the same moon he had stared at from a frigate's deck. It had become his habit to come on deck when he could, after death, to contemplate the moon and stars and know that other surgeons like him probably did the same thing, wanting to howl out their frustration at too much injury, not enough skill or medicine. He couldn't have explained the moon's cleansing power to even someone as bright as Olive Grant. Only other surgeons like him, working in a tiny sickbay with death all around, could understand the curative powers of the moon.

She tugged him toward his house, but he tugged in the other direction, until they stood at the entrance to the shipyard, tidy now, free of debris and other decade-long clutter. Both massive gates to the graving docks were closed, keeping out the high tide. All it wanted was a shipwright, and he had found one.

"Lady Telford gave me a huge key to that long building there," Olive said, pointing. "I opened it—well, Charlie MacGregor did—and what do you think we found?"

His mind was mush; he shook his head.

"Lumber, and lots of it. Probably not enough for a yacht, but enough to begin."

He clapped his arm around her shoulder and her hand went around his waist. "You're awfully free with your charms," he teased, and by all that was holy, it felt good to tease.

"Oh, shut up," she said in a gruff voice. "May we kindly stumble home now?"

He wished she meant what she said. She would go to her chaste side of the street, and he to the other. With any luck at all, no one would need him for the rest of the night, except his usual assortment of demons and dead men. "Very well, if we must."

"I have neglected Mrs. Aintree fearfully," he said as they strolled along.

"No fears. Rhona Tavish is a remarkable nurse," Olive said. "I find that quite a relief."

"Coward."

"Truer words were never spoken," said the bravest lady he knew. "When you feel able—and it had better be by noon—Lady Telford wants you to peruse the corporation papers that her solicitor has drawn up. Charlie MacGregor—Doug, he is a brilliant leader—wants to hold a meeting with the shipwright and the men who have agreed to work in the yard."

"Are you my secretary?"

"Mostly I am your friend. Good night."

Chapter 31

ITH NO MORE FANFARE THAN that began the best summer in Olive Grant's memory. The two journeymen and one apprentice arrived, stiff and rumpled, on the local bone-cracking carriage, young, experienced, and ready to do battle in a long-abandoned shipyard. Even though nothing was ready yet, Homer Bennett and his Devonport crew repaired the faulty mainmast yardarm on the fishing boat, Homer's face set and determined, which told Olive everything she needed to know about the man's commitment.

When the boat was repaired, everyone in Edgar went to the funeral for Brian Hannay. The Church of Scotland was crammed to capacity for the first time in years, according to the bewildered minister. Scots and Englishmen mourned together the loss of a good man. They stood shoulder to shoulder, filled with a resolve that Olive had not seen in Edgar in years.

Douglas sat next to Olive. She saw the sorrow on his face and understood only the tiniest part of his suffering for every patient of his that he could not save. He took death personally, and Olive prayed for his comfort, as well as comfort to Brian's wife and children. He was in his own little world until she took his hand and held it until the funeral ended. *Propriety be hanged*, she thought, filled with her own resolve.

Immediately after the funeral, Homer Bennett and Andrew Pine took that same bonecracker to Glasgow. When they returned in a week with contracts for lumber, masts, and rope, Mrs. Bennett had settled into their house overlooking the yards, and the Devonport builders had their own quarters, more rudimentary, but carrying the promise of steady meals at the tearoom.

Homer Bennett, an immensely capable man, had insisted the Highlanders wear blue canvas trousers and cotton shirts, which meant the Telford Boat Works corporation hired all the needlewomen in Edgar to cut and sew. "This way, I know their clothes won't catch on anything." He gave Olive a solemn wink. "Besides, Miss Grant, I've heard tales about what Scots do or do not wear under those kilts. Don't want any such injuries, not this man."

Douglas, the traitor, just laughed, and Olive felt her face go crimson.

The need for good workmen's shoes meant that Edgar's cobbler had too much work, so he hired another cobbler from Gatehouse of Fleet. And this meant the new cobbler and his wife needed a place to live, which meant the fledgling corporation hired more men and women work. Andrew Pine had whispered to Homer that his wife was wanting to come north too. Could they find a place in Edgar?

In no time, another of Lady Telford's empty houses was rented out and prepared for Mrs. Pine, who, from the looks of her as she got off the carriage, was going to put Douglas to work in a few months. "I am discovering that delivering babies is the best part of my job," Douglas said as he eyed Mrs. Pine's gentle rotundity.

"Cobblers, seamstresses, house cleaners, kitchen help,

retired surgeons: All of this means extra pay all around," Olive announced to Douglas one evening when he slid into the tearoom after everyone else had finished for his own bowl of something and excellent bread. "And you're busier than you want to be, Doug."

He was Doug now, but only to her. Doug nodded and leaned back in his chair at a precarious angle. "That's how it works, Miss G." He rubbed his hands together and she saw the happiness on his face. "Do you know, I was even paid in coin for a baby I delivered today in Wigtown no less, and piles I tended. Not the baby's. Pardon that, Miss G."

"Did Rhona Tavish assist?" she asked, determined not to be overly embarrassed by plain speaking. "She went to Wigtown with you?"

"She did," he said. "I had to convince Mrs. Aintree that I couldn't do without her, and she reluctantly gave permission. By the way, Mrs. Aintree can move her fingers just a little. We might eventually have full recovery there." He stretched his arms over his head, and she could almost feel his satisfaction. "I intend to sleep tonight. If you chance to see anyone heading toward my house in the middle of the night—providing you are awake—shoot them for me."

As it turned out, Olive would have had to shoot herself. Lately, she was awake long past her usual bedtime, nothing new of itself even though the reason was. No more for her the sleepless nights, worrying for her own future as her legacy from Papa dribbled away. The tearoom had become the dining hall for the Telford Boat Works, which had meant hiring another cook and two girls to assist Maeve in the scullery and in serving hearty meals three times a day to workers and families.

True, Olive contrived just as hard to squeeze every penny until it yelped in pain—she would always be frugal. The difference was she knew there were more pennies.

What wasn't covered by the penny each worker and family member gave her for every meal was cushioned by her generous monthly allotment, spelled out so specifically by Douglas Bowden in the corporation bylaws.

She stayed awake now because she found herself alternating between the euphoria of love and its irritation. Since that memorable kiss in her garden, Doug had not attempted another such liberty. He teased her, told her his worries for Edgar, and strolled with her arm in arm to watch the steady work of a forgotten shipyard turning into a business again, but he did not kiss her.

She had no experience with love, beyond that of child for parent, but she knew, as sure as it rained every morning, that she was in love with Douglas Bowden. At first she had wondered about her faint uneasiness when the man was nowhere in sight, followed by the great lifting of her heart when he came through the door of the tearoom, more and more now in the company of others. He always gave her a wink and never minded when she bullied him about eating more, or wearing the same shirt over and over, or any number of little things. He had become essential to her peace of mind. If that wasn't love, then she would never understand the emotion.

She realized quickly, no ignorant lass she, that he was still determined to move on in search of the perfect place for his medical practice. She saw it in his eyes as he stared at the progress in the shipyard, calculating just when things would move on their own and he could decently leave.

He even ticked off the progress on his fingers one night, after the evening meal was done and tidied, and she had a moment's leisure to sit in her "wee parlor," as he liked to tease her, and knit.

"Mrs. Aintree stopped me today on the street just to show me how well her fingers moved," he said, his feet propped on the fender of the unlit stove. Olive loved the way he could relax so completely and so quickly, probably a result of taking advantage of every leisure moment aboard ship. "I set her some hand exercises, and she is diligent in doing them, for which I credit Rhona Tavish."

He leaned over and touched her arm, lowering his voice at the same time, even though Maeve and her assistants were long abed. "The shed is empty now, and Mrs. Aintree blushed to tell me that the Tavishes are sharing a bed again."

She nodded, relishing her own delight to see Joe Tavish always beside Homer Bennett, sketching what the shipwright wanted. "I heard Mr. Bennett say that he had never worked with a finer draughtsman. Joe smiled and looked so pleased."

Doug gave her arm another gentle tap. "Tomorrow's the day I remove Tommy's splints. He's been pestering me for a week, but I've been busy." He kept his hand on her arm. "And Flora and her colleagues have a tidy business."

"I know," Olive said, enjoying the warmth of his hand. "She came to me only this morning in near-stupefaction and holding a pound note. Apparently Lady Telford herself has requested an . . . an extra-fancy fancy made of scallop shells in graduated sizes. She was quite specific and Flora is over the moon."

He nodded and said what Olive had been dreading. "I've done what I set out to do here, or nearly so. Homer has the names of several men who might be interested in buying the yacht. Two are in Edinburgh. He wants me to take Joe's sketches and test that interest. I can easily do that after I leave Edgar, perhaps as early as next week."

She couldn't help the tears that welled in her eyes and only hoped the room was dark enough to hide them. It wasn't.

"Olive, I had no plans to stay in Edgar," he reminded her, after a painful silence. "I'll certainly come back and visit now and then, but . . . ." He shook his head. "I'm still looking for the ideal medical practice. I just need to look a little more. It's out there somewhere."

She nodded and tried to swallow her misery. Her traitor tears continued to fall. All she could do was wish him a good night and leave him sitting in her parlor with a frown on his face.

She heard the door close a few minutes later and looked out her bedroom window. Hands shoved in his pockets, Doug crossed the street. He stared at his house for a long moment, then passed it and walked to the bridge, where he stood for a long time, watching the water. Discouraged, she went to bed, certain she would not sleep.

She resolved in the morning to write to Nancy Fillion in Plymouth. There was no one in Edgar she could talk to, and Mrs. Fillion seemed to understand what made men like Douglas Bowden tick. She stared at the ceiling for a long while, wondering what on earth she would say in such a letter that wouldn't sound like whingeing.

He simply isn't as interested in you as you are in him, she thought at last, and decided there was no reason to write to Mrs. Fillion. A spinster she was and a spinster she would remain. Her tears slid from her eyes to her pillow. "I do not want to be a spinster," she said out loud. It didn't sound like whingeing to her self-critical ears. It sounded like a sensible woman realizing that as much as Edgar might change, she would not.

She must have slept then, because when she woke, the room was full dark. The moon had not yet risen. She lay in bed, uncertain why she had awakened.

There it was again, someone knocking on her door. She crossed to the window and looked down to see Flora MacLeod, wearing a shift that barely came to her knees.

"My dear? What do you need?"

The child looked up. "It's my gran," she sobbed. "She fell out of bed and I canna lift her back in. And her eyes are rolling around. Oh, please."

Olive grabbed her robe and ran down the stairs. She threw open the door and Flora tumbled inside, reaching for her. Olive knelt beside her on the floor, holding the child close, feeling the rapid beating of her heart.

"I didna want to bother Mr. Bowden," she sobbed into Olive's shoulder. "Ye said earlier how hard he works and how tired he is, but Miss Grant, it's my gran."

She sat Flora down. "I'm going to dress and I'll be right back," she called over her shoulder as she took the stairs two at a time.

She threw on her clothes, despaired of doing anything about the hair so wild around her head, knowing that Gran was more important. After stuffing her feet into her shoes, she ran downstairs to see Flora with her head down on the table, looking as alone as anyone could. Olive put her own shawl around the child and took her hand.

"Let's go wake up Mr. Bowden."

They crossed the empty street, Flora pressing close to her. She wondered what terrors the child was revisiting, to walk in the dark by herself.

"I believe Mr. Bowden keeps his house unlocked," she said. Sure enough, the door opened at her touch. She sat Flora on one of the chairs in the first room that had become his surgery waiting room.

She took her own deep breath and went up the stairs quietly, startled to hear Douglas talking. She recalled the few times she had wakened him from his dreams in her own house, when Tommy lay so desperately ill, and he had his own bruises and black eye.

Olive listened a moment to a reasonable man talking to patients. As she listened, her terror gave way to compassion. She wondered how many dead men came to him each night in his dreams, pleading for his help, demanding his services. She stood there with her hand on the doorknob as she finally understood this complex man who only wanted some peace. Treaties could be signed, Napoleon sent far away to St. Helena Island, and navies and armies reduced, but Douglas Bowden's war still raged.

"They don't ever let you alone, do they, Doug?" she whispered. "How do you even dare close your eyes?"

Chapter 32

"Doug?"

He sat up in bed, mentally hushing the scores of patients that had grouped themselves around him. He almost told Olive to mind her steps so she did not tread on any of the wounded, but he woke up fully before he committed that felony which could probably get him tossed into an asylum.

No one else called him Doug. He shook his head to clear the mental fog, and saw Olive Grant before him, dressed, but her hair wild, curly, and magnificent. "What in the world . . ."

"It's Flora's gran," Olive said. She didn't come any closer, which should have relieved him but didn't. For one irrational moment, he wanted to grab her, sit her down beside him, and babble out his own night terrors about patients that refused to let him alone.

"I'll be downstairs in a moment. Get my satchel. You know where it is," he ordered, in control again. He was out of bed and looking for his trousers before she even left the room.

He stuffed his nightshirt into his trousers and scuffed

his sockless feet into his shoes, thinking of the many times throughout his life that he had wakened from terror, only to find himself in greater terror. Living or dead, he was doomed and condemned to be a surgeon. Hopefully, Olive had not heard him pleading and cajoling his stubborn corpses.

He ran down the stairs, snatching up the satchel that Olive held out to him. He gave her a quick glance and saw something disturbing in her eyes. He wondered if she had heard him talking and figured out just who he was talking to. Well, never mind. He would be leaving soon enough.

He touched Flora's head and told her he would do his best and ran to the hovel that Gran shared with Flora, Olive and the child right behind him.

He dropped to his knees beside the dying woman. He could tell from the door that she hadn't long, simply by hearing her tortured breathing, with its gaps and rattles. All he could do was cradle her head in his arms, and he did that, holding her close, hoping she was beyond terror now and fixed on a more peaceful place. He hoped it was her beloved highland glen, before eviction, soldiers, and fire arrived.

As soon as he held her, she relaxed and sighed. Death may have marched beside her, like troops harrying her family away, but she burrowed closer to him.

"We have you, Gran," he whispered. "Flora is here, and by all that is holy, we will keep her safe. Come closer, Flora."

Olive gave the child a gentle push forward. Flora hesitated and then sat down beside Douglas. In the space of a few more breaths, Flora rested her head on Gran's stomach. Gran couldn't move her hand, but Olive picked it up and placed it on Flora.

"You can't . . . ," Olive began, her voice soft and close to his ear.

"No. There is nothing I can do but hold her and watch

her die," he whispered back. "All my skills are useless at this moment."

Olive surprised him then, as he already knew she had the capacity to do. She had been surprising and delighting him from the first day he threw himself at her mercy, an injured boy in his arms. "Hush, Doug," she said, her lips on his ear now, which gave him a pleasant thrill, oddly out of place in the middle of an old woman's dying, but suddenly vital to every breath he drew. "Almost the first thing you told me was that the hurt and wounded just want a calming hand. Sometimes that is all the medicine a body needs."

She was right. For the first time in his busy life, he wanted desperately to apply the remedy to himself. He couldn't, because Gran needed him right now. He glanced down at Flora, who clutched her gran, the only person in the world she thought could help her. He had seen children like her in war-numbed areas, nearly incapacitated when their only sure rock and anchor died before their eyes.

"Flora, look at me," he said.

She raised tear-filled eyes to his.

"Know this: When your gran is gone, you will not be left alone."

"It happened before," she said, her voice so soft he could barely hear her. "No one helped us."

"Those days are over, my dear. There is an entire town that will help you now."

He made the mistake of glancing at Olive. She was watching his eyes, his face, not Flora's. "You will not be left alone," Olive said, but she wasn't looking at Flora.

She knows, he thought. *By all that's holy, she knows. What must she think of me?*

His anguished question remained unanswered because Gran stiffened in his arms, tried to reach for Flora, and died. He closed her eyes, and Flora shrieked and began to shake the old woman. Olive took her by the arms, but instead of pulling her away, she enveloped the child in her arms and included the dead woman in their embrace.

"How is it that you always know to do the right thing?" he asked.

Olive looked up at him. "Prove it to me. Trust me," she said.

He broke their gaze, too ashamed to look at her or say anything. He just sat there holding the old woman who had borne too much, with her granddaughter and the kind lady holding her too. With painful clarity, he realized he might be the most wounded of them all.

Flora began to keen then, the high-pitched sound similar to something he had heard in North Africa. Gently, Olive pulled the child away from her grandmother and into her own arms. She rocked back and forth until Flora was silent.

Grateful he had something to do, Douglas picked up the woman and set her on the bed. He arranged her hands, sorry to the depths of his heart that she could not have died in her own bed, in her own glen, and not in a distant town.

He turned to Flora, who watched him with dull eyes now. "When morning comes, I will ask Mrs. Tavish to take care of Gran. Right now, though, where would you like to go, Flora?"

He was so certain that she would speak Miss Grant's name that he was momentarily taken aback when she whispered, "Mrs. Dougall."

Olive was much quicker than he. She hugged Flora and said, "That is a wonderful idea. Would you like Mr. Bowden to fetch her?"

Flora nodded. She turned anxious eyes on him. "What will she do?"

Douglas touched the child's cheek. "I think she will knock me down and trample me in her hurry to get here and hold you, missy. I also believe she will include Pudding, her mother, and the other kittens."

Flora smiled at that image, as he hoped she would. He drew the coverlet over Gran. He stood there a moment looking down and wishing that life was fair and kind, and then he went across the street to the Hare and Hound. He saw a light on and wasn't surprised to see Brighid Dougall peering back at him through the window by the door. He knew the first coach arrived shortly after six o'clock from Dundrennan, and her yeast buns, hot and drenched in melted butter and sugar, certainly didn't make themselves.

She let him in, giving him her full attention, even though he knew she was busy with predawn preparation. Her eyes misted when he told her what had happened. When he told her of Flora's request, her lips began to tremble.

"I had a wee lass once," she said. "But you already know that. You've seen Flora's dresses."

"I think you are going to have another wee lass, if it won't be a burden."

"No burden," she assured him, all business now. "You bring her over here with her clothes and her kittens. I'll have her help me finish these buns. Then we'll find a nice room." She sat down suddenly as though she had lost all strength and put her hands over her eyes. "Have you ever prayed really hard for something, Mr. Bowden?"

He couldn't think of a time, but he knew it wasn't a question that needed answering. He left her there and went back to Gran's little place, a house that he knew belonged to the Church of Scotland, one of several hovels parceled out to the Highlanders who straggled south.

Flora was dressed and ready to go when he returned. Her few possessions were tied in a sheet that she kept lifting to her face to dry her eyes. She sat on Olive's lap in the room's only chair, looking young, small, frightened, and far from Edgar's most engaging entrepreneur. Olive had rounded up the kittens and mama cat into a basket.

Douglas knelt by the chair. "Mrs. Dougall didn't

trample me down only because she is making her buns for the six o'clock coach."

His reward was a tiny smile. "Does she need some help in the kitchen? I helped her once before."

"So she told me. Aye, she can use your help. And then she'll find a nice room for you. Shall we go?"

He stood up and held out his hand. She hesitated only a second before putting her hand in his. She tugged on his hand. "Gran got me to a good place, didn't she?"

"The best place. We'll take care of things here."

The door to the Hare and Hound was wide open, with both Dougalls standing there. "It's early but you're welcome here, lassie," the innkeeper said, his voice none too steady.

Whatever resolve Flora had mustered dissolved at the sight of Brighid Dougall's open arms. With a sob, she dropped her bundle and threw herself into the woman's embrace. Douglas stood there a moment, relieved beyond words, as Brighid picked her up and murmured words of comfort. *Olive, do that for me*, he thought, then banished the idea. He was a grown man, after all.

He stood in the street, tired down to his toenails. He knew the morning would bring the women to Gran's place to wash her body, try to find a dress that wasn't in tatters, and prepare her for the long sleep. He wasn't needed there; this was now the women's domain. He wondered if Flora would spare him one of the other kittens, then reminded himself that he was leaving.

He glanced at the tearoom, seeing lights on. Probably despairing of any return to sleep, he imagined Olive was in the kitchen, preparing for a new day. He wanted to talk to her, to make light of whatever she had discovered about his dreams, but he knew any woman as smart and practical as Olive Grant would see right through his paper-thin disclaimer.

There was nowhere to go but back to his house. He

couldn't face a return to bed. Just the thought made him break out in sweat, maybe even afraid that if he opened the door, his dead men would tumble out. No, better to remain below deck and wrap bandages or inventory his medicines.

He sat on a chair in his surgery waiting room and dozed until he could go to Olive's tearoom with a crowd of workers and their families, preparing for a new day of work in the newly resurrected ship yard. He could sit with them and not have to face any look of concern or pity on Olive's pretty face.

She knows, he thought in misery, *she knows*.

Chapter 33

WRAPPED IN HER YELLOW AND black plaid with red strands, Elizabeth MacLeod was buried the next day in a small patch of sunlight quickly replaced by misty rain. She was far from her glen in the Highlands but now cradled on another silent shore that the minister assured everyone was far better than this one. No one disagreed.

Olive felt her heart lift when one of the Highlanders in Charlie MacGregor's crew piped "Flowers of the Forest" for Gran MacLeod.

"If I'm not mistaken, that's the same air that he piped for Brian Hannay a week ago," Doug Bowden whispered to her.

"Aye, it is," she whispered back. "I told you before, 'tis our funeral song."

He nodded and directed his attention back to the crude coffin. Olive could nearly feel the embarrassment that radiated from him, but somehow, he had been drawn to stand beside her anyway. She knew she could ignore the matter, as he may have wanted to in some portion of his troubled mind, or she could do what she thought he really wanted. She held his hand, giving it a brief squeeze before letting go.

It was left to the men to walk Gran's coffin to its new Scottish home. The women and children returned to the tearoom to complete preparations on the modest meal they would serve when the men finished.

Her expression set in stone, Flora MacLeod brought out the plates of food. Every now and then, Olive heard a sobbing breath from the child, which always brought Brighid Dougall to her side, even if only for a light touch.

You have a fine instinct, Brighid, Olive thought, envying her for the smallest moment. A less kind Olive Grant would have demanded that the innkeep's wife give the child to her, she who would never have children of her own, the way matters stood. An even less kind Olive would have reminded Brighid Dougall that she once had a daughter and she still had sons living, albeit far away in India in service to the king. Couldn't she at least share Flora MacLeod?

But Olive was none of those Olives. She kept silent and worked, the only remedy she knew for a heart broken.

And there matters would have stood, if Brighid had not come to her for advice a few days later, after Edgar returned to the business of rebuilding itself.

Brighid had made it a habit to bring over any extra cinnamon buns remaining after the morning coach came and went. "They never keep," she had said when she began the habit, even though all the grateful recipients of the delicious treats saw right through her. Olive even suspected the woman of making another batch, just so she could say she had leftovers to share.

Brighid brought along no pretense this morning. She handed over the buns and found the man she was looking for.

"Mr. Bowden," she said to the surgeon, as he rose with

the others to leave in a group and not have to face Olive. "I have a dilemma. You're the surgeon."

"So I've heard," he said, even though Olive saw no smile on his face. "Sit down. Tell me."

The others left. Olive sat, too, which made Douglas Bowden tighten his lips. She knew he wanted no audience but she ignored the look. Brighid, on the other hand, flashed her a relieved smile and patted the bench next to her.

"It's this, sir: Poor Flora cries herself to sleep, and then she wakes in the night in tears. I hurry to her room, and all she can do is cry and say there is no one to help." Brighid patted her generous bosom. "I tell her I am here to help, but it does not bring her comfort."

"She must be remembering when the soldiers came and put her dying mother out of the house, to lie on a mattress while they burned down her home," Olive said. "She told us that one day. Don't you think that is the problem, Mr. Bowden? She has terrible memories and they haunt her." *So there*, she thought. *I don't care if you think I am a managing woman, Douglas Bowden. You are a sore vexation to me.*

The sore vexation sighed and stared beyond the tearoom wall into a place she was not invited. "Charlie MacGregor has told me the same thing about his daughters," he said, still not looking at either of them. "I think if I were to ask all the Highlanders, they would tell me the same thing. The fathers might be working now, but there is a greater problem, a sore trial of the mind."

He surprised Olive by addressing her directly. "Miss Grant, would you gather all the children of the Highlanders here? Those above, say, three years of age? How many would you think that is?"

"Maybe fifteen. Boys and girls?"

"Yes. Everyone up to thirteen years or so."

"That makes it sixteen. When?"

"Now."

With no explanation, he got up and left the tearoom. She looked out the door to see him walking toward the boat docks, then beyond to the shipyard.

"Something is wrong with our Mr. Bowden," Brighid said.

"Very wrong," Olive agreed, "but let us do as he asks."

To Olive's surprise, no parents questioned her. All she had to do was tell them that "our Mr. Bowden" wanted the children in the tearoom. She wondered if the surgeon had any idea of the vast respect that the Highlanders and people had for him. All he seemed to see were his own flaws.

In less than half an hour, she and Mrs. Dougall had rounded up the children. From some magical place, more cinnamon buns emerged, which brought out smiles all around, even among the restless.

Olive took a good look at the restless ones, watching their eyes rove about the room, as if looking for an escape route. Maeve dropped a wooden bowl in the kitchen, which made some of the children jump up, then look around, hopeful they had not been noticed. They slunk down in their chairs then, seeking invisibility.

If there was a name for what confronted the children, she did not know it. Their mothers and fathers were stretched past bearing to find food and work and a place to lie down at night. With such huge worries, it was easy to overlook the children.

When the children were seated and through eating, the door opened. She turned to see Douglas carrying sheets of paper and a handful of pencils. She had watched Homer Bennett and Joe Tavish working over a table in the shipyard, instructing and drawing on similar paper.

He set down the paper on one of the tables and did nothing more to get their attention. He commanded respect and he got it, no questions asked.

"I want you to tell me something," he began, "and you must be honest."

The children looked at each other, then back at the surgeon, their eyes wary now. He sat down to be on their level and motioned them closer. Soon his arms were around two of the little boys, and the younger MacGregor girl was on his lap. Without needing a cue, Olive sat down too, with the same result. Mrs. Dougall was not slow to follow. Flora MacLeod nearly leaped into her lap.

"It is this, my little friends. How many of you are troubled with bad dreams?"

Silence. One hand went halfway up, then another and another. The girl on Olive's lap turned her face into Olive's breast.

"You went through a terrible time," he said, his voice soft. He looked at Flora, who sat on Mrs. Dougall's lap, her eyes so troubled. "There was no one to help you, but you survived and you have my deep respect."

Again the children looked at each other, but there was something in their eyes besides fear now. One of the young boys sat a little taller.

"I want you to do something very hard now." Douglas took a deep breath. Olive found herself breathing with him because she understood too plainly what this cost him.

"I want you to draw what happened there in your homes."

Two of the girls gasped and Euna MacGregor on his lap began to cry. He cuddled her close.

"I told you it would be hard, but you need to do this," he said, when Euna was silent.

No one questioned why. They seemed to understand exactly what he meant. Olive looked to the older children, a wordless prayer in her heart, as they were first to obey, taking a piece of paper and then a pencil. She thought they would sit together at the tables, but they scattered to the corners of the room, their backs to each other, seeking a private place for their misery.

Sixteen children began to draw. Douglas went to the window and looked out, giving their privacy dignity. Olive and Mrs. Dougall went into the kitchen and closed the door.

"He wants them to face their terror, doesn't he?" Brighid asked quietly.

Olive nodded.

"There's more to this, though," the woman said.

"Much more." Olive could barely get out the words. The two of them held hands.

Time passed. The tearoom was silent except for the scratching of pencils, and an occasional sob. Brighid put her hands to her face.

"We could have been kinder to them when they first came here," she said. "We could have been as kind as you, Olive."

"Never mind that," Olive said. "We here have learned our lesson too. We know better now. Maybe many of them speak little English and have strange Highland ways, but we are all Scots." She touched the woman's cheek. "Let's not forget that."

Nearly an hour passed, during which time Olive and her helpers who filed in through the back door finished preparing soup and bread for luncheon. Olive heard firm footsteps cross the room and a knock on the kitchen door. She opened it to see the children all seated again, their faces so serious, but with the addition of pride. Not the pride that speaks of power or ownership, but the pride of shared experience and survival.

Douglas held the pictures. He shook his head as he looked at them and even grew pale. He placed one on top of the pile. Olive stared at the picture, a crude drawing, but explicit. She held her breath to see a croft on fire, troops outside, if those stick figures held muskets and bayonets as she thought they did, watching a woman burn to death inside.

"Mary MacKay," a little boy said. "We watched and no one helped her."

"She wouldna leave her home," a small girl chimed in. "My da, he tried to tell the soldiers she wasn't right in the head and mostly deaf, but they only laughed."

"That should never have happened," Douglas said. "Who wants to tell me about this picture? And this one?"

His gentle questions opened a floodgate as the children took turns with their own pictures, describing cattle slaughtered, chickens with their necks wrung, fathers and uncles beat down to the ground when they tried to resist, and other soldiers herding women and children like animals. His face more serious than a judge, Tommy had drawn a tarpaulin draped over tombstones as he and his mother cowered within. It was a good rendering of misery of the acutest kind; Joe Tavish's artistic talent had touched his son.

Flora sat on Mrs. Dougall's lap again, her drawing in her hands. The child had drawn a woman lying on a mattress, with streaks of pencil rain pouring down. Olive looked closer in horror and then turned away, her mind reeling. Another figure lay on top of the dying woman. She thought at first it was Flora, but it was a soldier with a musket beside him. She caught Mrs. Dougall's wild-eyed glance and held it.

"He blacked my eye just like yours," Flora was whispering to Douglas, who knelt beside her now. "I tried to pull him off Mam, but he wouldn't listen. Mam screamed and screamed, but he didn't care." She drew a breath that caught and became a sob. "Then he left her and he laughed at us." She put her hands on Douglas's cheeks, drawing him close. "We needed help! Where were you?"

Chapter 34

*D*OUGLAS KNEW HE WOULD NOT sleep that night, which came as something of a relief. He was tired of his own demons, the ghosts of men he had tried to save and failed, as they raised their arms to him night after night, seeking what he could not give. He sometimes tried to reason with them, speaking in calm tones as he described the ferocity of their wounds, and explained logically why a man cannot survive with half a head, or with most of his entrails lying next to the guns on the deck.

They weren't interested in logic, his wraiths and haunts. They only wanted to live a little longer, to return to their parents or their wives and children all in one piece, not sewn into their hammocks, weighted with lead shot and slid off a board into the ocean, after a prayer and a verse. He had sat with each one of these men and watched them struggle for one more breath. He had closed their eyes, called the time of death to his pharmacist mate, who carefully wrote it into his medical log. John McIntyre, Scotland, carpenter's mate, Nov. 18, 1815, off the coast of Spain. Cause of death: perforated bowel. And on and on through years of war. His logical brain reminded him occasionally of the many more sailors and officers who owed their lives to him. He knew it was so, but always standing behind them were the dead, not so much accusing him, but sorrowful that he could not have done more.

He sat alone in his surgery and grew angry at those ghosts. "You do not understand that I wish I could have done more," he said, his voice firm. "There was not enough medical science to cure you. If there had been, I would have."

He couldn't possibly appease his demons. He never wanted to face Olive Grant again, she who knew what his dreams consisted of and who probably thought him a maniac and a weak man. He understood how much he loved her, the kind lady who fed people and risked her own inheritance. The woman with a blue eye and a brown one, and red hair and freckles, and a heart so big that it just might include him, if he weren't so cursed by his own dreams. He could never wish that on a wife. Wouldn't such a woman grow weary of sharing her bed with ghosts? Would love turn to disgust? Better not to chance it.

He slept finally, simply because the body craves sleep after too many hours without it. Mercifully, he slept alone this night, beyond the occasional shriek and mutter from the more persistent ghosts. When he woke, his bedroom was empty as always. He dragged his timepiece from the table by his bed, amazed that it was nearly noon.

He lay there on his back, staring at the ceiling as he used to stare to the deck above, thinking through his duties of the day, and reminding himself of one more remedy he might attempt, one more procedure. This time he thought about his patients in Edgar, his friends now. He shook his head, thinking how they called him "our Mr. Bowden," possessive already.

Mrs. Aintree's fingers would continue to heal. He had watched her move them yesterday, pleased to know that there was enough skin to permit the joints to bend. Rhona Tavish would keep her exercising those fingers.

He had removed the splints from Tommy Tavish's leg two days ago and unwrapped the stiff bandages. Tommy had been reluctant to put his weight on the leg at first, but with a little coaxing from Olive the kind lady, he put down some weight and then more. Douglas had told Rhona exactly what to do there too. The boy who had been the reason for his several months in Edgar was on the mend.

The grocer's wife would probably always be a little worried about her baby until she realized that he was fine and healthy, and destined to live. Maybe all new mothers were that way. She would learn. Just yesterday morning he had seen her talking so earnestly in the store with a Highland mother of four. All was well.

He wanted to do more for Lady Telford, but he didn't know what it would be. She was aware she was failing, and that her little bouts of apoplexy would only increase. Maybe the best cure for what ailed her was something she had begun to do already of her own volition. More than once he had seen her leaning on Maidie's arm and walking to the shipyard, where Homer Bennett always seated her in a prominent place and let her watch the growth of the yacht. If he had time, Homer would escort her to Miss Grant's tearoom for green tea and biscuits.

He thought of Olive Grant, the woman he wanted to marry and have his children by. Better he spare her the complications of life with Douglas Bowden, retired surgeon who could not let go of his ghosts. He knew her hopes for finding a husband were not sanguine, not because she wasn't pleasing or kind, but because she was thirty and had no real inheritance now, thanks to the Countess of Sutherland, determined to improve the little people right off her land because sheep were more profitable.

Not many men would look as deep as he had and see

the kindness and quality that made Olive Grant the best of women. He had needed her help from the beginning, even though she was no great shakes in the surgery, and he needed her still, for reasons that were his alone.

That was his dilemma. When he was much younger and the blood flowed a little faster, he had fantasized about the woman he would marry someday. For a while they all seemed to look like Spanish ladies, then Polynesian women, and even a blonde and blue-eyed Dane he'd met in the Baltic.

But then he had clapped his tired eyes on Olive Grant and he knew, he just knew. She was no fantasy. She was a practical Scot with more character and principle than most small countries, especially Mediterranean ones. She was the woman he wanted, if only he had been a better man. If only he had known that Edgar, with its troubles and sorrows, was the perfect place to practice medicine. But no, he had yammered on about how quickly he could leave Edgar and find the ideal place, which he understood now was Edgar. She had probably known it all along and knew him to be a complete jackass.

"I am an idiot," he said as he packed.

Packing took no time at all. He stuffed his medical satchel full of his usual assortment of sharp hardware and nostrums. He looked around, feeling a pang to leave his growing store of medicines and that wonderful surgery table that one of Edgar's formerly out-of-work carpenters had built. Perhaps some other surgeon would venture into Edgar and not be such a fool.

Bags packed, ready to go, he stood in the surgical waiting room and talked himself out of going to the tearoom for a final meal before catching the bonecracker to the next small town. He could eat at the Hare and Hound after he stopped at the shipyard for one last look, and to pick up some of Joe Tavish's sketches of the yacht in the covered shiphouse, boasting only a keel right now. All he had to do was travel to Edinburgh and speak to the two men that Homer Bennett suspected might be interested in such a thing as a yacht, sleek and nimble and built by men learning the trade.

That was the plan. It changed the moment he walked into the little antechamber, built to shelter anyone coming inside the house from a typical drizzly Scottish rain.

Someone had pushed a sheet of paper there, the very paper he had borrowed from Mr. Bennett, along with pencils, to coax the children into drawing out their eviction experiences, in the hope of expiating their demons. There was a note attached, so he picked up the paper for a closer look.

Draw your own experience, Douglas Bowden, he read. *Heal yourself before you don't care anymore. With fine regard, Olive.*

He stared at the note, written in Olive's careful handwriting, wondering if he had read the words right, or if they had jumbled in some odd order to produce sentences that suggested someone cared enough for him to demand self-examination.

A fool would have considered her demand impertinent and forward. Staring at the note, Douglas Bowden decided he was tired of being a fool.

"If that's what you want," he said out loud. "I'm no artist." He returned to his waiting room and dragged a chair up to the little table where a collection of old newspapers, religious tracts, and political pamphlets had taken over.

He started to shake before he even touched the pencil to the paper. He put his hands over his face for his quiet time. When his hands were steady, he picked up the pencil again.

Do I feel any different? he asked himself an hour later. Perhaps not, because the first thing he did when he finished was turn the paper over so he didn't have to look at it. Maybe he could slide it under Olive's door before he bid farewell to Edgar.

He remembered his errand to the shipyard and spent a pleasurable moment there chatting with Joe Tavish. The Highlander gave him the yacht sketches done up in a pasteboard sleeve to keep them wrinkle free and dry, plus the addresses in Edinburgh, and then held out his hand.

A handshake wasn't enough. Joe grabbed Douglas in a fierce embrace, reminding the surgeon of the man's strength and his own black eye and unhappy ribs.

"I wish you weren't leaving," Joe told him after they stepped back and both of them tried to be sly about wiping their eyes.

"I've done what I set out to do here," Douglas said, but it sounded so feeble to his ears.

"Ye have not," Joe told him flatly.

"I know my own mind," Douglas replied, waiting to be irritated so he could leave without a regret, but feeling dismal instead. What if Joe was right? "I have to give something to Miss Grant. Then I'm off."

Joe's blank look should have warned him. "Good luck to ye finding her. She's scarpered off on the early carriage, with a grim look and those pictures from t'infernal regions tight in her grasp." He shuddered. "Ye don't want to see a grim look from the kind lady."

Douglas stared at him as the words seemed to register slowly. "Wh . . . where did she go?"

"Edinburgh. T'kind lady saw a wee notice in a broadside about the Countess of Sutherland"—Joe paused to clear his throat and spit—"and her husband holding court at their residence in the city. Petitioners' claims, 'tis called." He spit again. "Ye won't see them doing that at Dunrobin Castle in Ross-shire. They'd be burnt out."

"What in the world is Oli . . . Miss Grant . . . hoping to accomplish?" Douglas asked, suddenly fearful.

Joe shook his head, not a mere shake, but a dramatic

waggle from side to side. "I guess even the kind lady has her limits. I sent along one of my drawings, too, 'ta one with that evil witch's factor, Patrick Sellar . . ." Another spit. ". . . watching old Mary MacKay burn to death in her hut." He closed his eyes against the memory. "I could have drawn more, but time was short."

"I'm going to Edinburgh," Douglas said.

He turned to walk away, but Joe took him by the arm. "Wake up, man! I know ye're going there. Ye told Mr. Bennett ye'd take the drawings of the yacht I just gave ye."

"Yacht? Yacht? What drawings? I'm going to find Olive Grant," Douglas said.

Joe gave his arm a little shake, which meant that Douglas felt his teeth rattle. "That's the right answer. Maybe ye're going to be smart yet, for an Englishman. Hurry now. No folly or foul play now."

"Not from me."

"Not ye! From the kind lady! Don't let her do something she'll regret."

Chapter 35

*D*OUGLAS WAS THREE DAYS getting to Edinburgh. The city is not a great distance if a body was a crow, but if the body was a surgeon and he had the misfortune to stop his post riders at the sight of a coach wreck, three days it was.

As he waded into the mess on the highway, sorting frightened people and limbs and pressing yet another neckcloth into service as a tourniquet, Douglas had reason to curse Hippocrates for being such a stickler about doing his duty.

The reward was sweet, however: No one died. The old people in the carriage were so grateful they would have adopted him if they could have, which amused his post riders no end. When Douglas finally handed the injured off to the care of their own physician and extricated himself from tears of gratitude, he was two days behind.

He also had reason to curse his lively imagination as he pictured the woman he loved cast into the dungeon at Edinburgh Castle for preaching rebellion and mayhem. Or maybe she was awaiting transportation to Australia for spitting on the Countess of Sutherland. There was no telling what a truly indignant woman would do, so he worried.

On the third day, disheveled and wearing no neck-cloth, Douglas paid his post riders and bid farewell to the post chaise that had grown smaller with every mile as his concern grew larger.

He paid off his post riders in front of a mansion that a reliable source—an Irish street sweeper one of the post riders hailed—swore belonged to George Granville Leveson-Gower, second Marquess of Stafford, third Earl Gower and Viscount Trentham, and husband to Elizabeth Gordon, nineteenth Countess of Sutherland.

"Aye, boyo," the man said as he pointed to the mansion. "She's a fat one, and he's got a beaky nose and stupid expression." He shrugged and gave them all an impish grin. "They probably hate t'Irish, 'cause everyone does, but they hate their own people too. No accounting for the rich."

To Douglas's gratification, the post riders argued about just leaving him there. He argued back that he had held them up because an overturned carriage needed him. The riders compromised by insisting they would remain for another day in a posting house on High Street at Nicholson and to sing out if he needed them.

So there he stood at the door to a mansion, luggage in hand, like a long-lost relative coming for a visit. There was nothing to do but proceed and hope that Olive hadn't finished her business and returned home, or been arrested and tossed into prison for being an angry Scot.

He remained a minute longer, wondering at the course of the last few months since he had separated from the Royal Navy. Nothing had worked out as planned, not a single thing. His quest for a quiet country practice had died aborning. All he wanted now was to clap his eyes on the kind lady and see if he had the slightest chance of regaining her regard, if he had any in the first place. And he was to do it in a den of thieves.

The footman seemed not surprised to see him, giving Douglas hope that some petitioners still remained. He received permission to leave his luggage in an alcove off the foyer, but he kept Joe Tavish's yacht sketches with him. Perhaps Lady Stafford, Countess of Sutherland, would be pleased to know that someone was looking out for the Highlanders scattered by her own orders.

He followed the footman into a narrow hall where five petitioners were seated. He counted; there sat Olive Grant in the first chair of a row of ten, of which five were occupied. Relieved that he had not missed her after all, Douglas watched her, feeling amazingly like a thirsty man eyeing a well.

She wore her new bonnet, with the bow tied so charmingly under her right ear. His heart did a drumroll to see that she wore the butterfly-colored paisley shawl he had bought her on a whim. He was already familiar with the trusty green wool dress, plain as can be, that he had seen on several occasions. He even dared to hope that she might choose to expand her wardrobe if things fell out in his favor and he could convince her that part ownership in the shipyard hadn't driven him into the poorhouse.

He took a closer look at her and saw a sweet face with not an ounce of hope anywhere in sight. She looked down at the parquet floor, so solemn. He wondered how long she had been sitting there.

"Hugh MacReady. Rise and make yourself known."

To Douglas's surprise, the man seated in the number two chair stood up and followed another footman into what must be the audience hall. Douglas stayed where he was, watching, curious why the number two petitioner was called before Olive.

The petitioner came out quickly enough, his expression sour, which suggested that Lord and Lady Stafford

were hard to please. Douglas waited now for the footman
to call Olive's name, but he passed her over again.

"Why isn't the lady called next?" Douglas whispered
to the footman standing beside him.

"Word from the butler is that she is a troublemaker,
petitioning on behalf of the Highland wretches," the footman whispered back. "She has been there for two days and
this is the final afternoon. They had hoped she would get
discouraged and leave, but so far . . ." He shrugged. "I suppose we will escort her out at the end of the day."

Douglas's first impulse was to explode in anger at such
poor treatment of the kind lady. He stopped the harsh
words that rose in his throat like bile, knowing that if he
reacted in any way, he would be ignored and never given
permission to step beyond those closed doors, either.

"Sir? Your purpose?" the footman asked.

"I am Captain Douglas Bowden, Royal Navy, recently
retired surgeon," he said, his anger so fierce that he could
barely speak, but using every title he could think of to
keep from being thrown out before he started. "I am part
owner in the Telford Boat Works in Edgar, located in the
old kingdom of Galloway. I have a commercial proposition for his lordship." There. That sounded businesslike
enough for people that obviously didn't give a rap about
ladies waiting forever or sore subjects, like families tossed
away to ruin and death. Douglas Bowden could play this
game.

The footman had produced a small tablet and a min-
iature gold pen. He took down what Douglas said before
ushering him to the vacant chair four seats down from
Olive.

She looked up then, her mouth a perfect O. He shook
his head, barely discernible (he hoped) to the footman
who was even now turning away to examine his finger-
nails. It would never do for the footmen to know any connection between them.

Evidently understanding, Olive turned her gaze to the wall. Douglas settled down to wait, his eyes on the row of paintings that Olive must have stared at for two and a half days now. He wondered where she went at night and how she had managed in such a large city. Her posture, always impeccable, had begun to droop. She sat there, feet together, the folder of terrifying drawings on her lap.

The next petitioner came out with a smile on his face and a spring to his step. The footman called the next man, which meant the others all moved up a chair. Now Douglas was only two chairs from Olive. After the next man was called, he sat next to Olive.

"When they call my name, I'll grab your hand and pull you in too," he whispered. "What folly is this?"

"Mine, or the Countess of Sutherland?" she asked, barely moving her lips to avoid detection.

"Yours is no folly. Joe Tavish tells me you were in a rare state after looking at all the drawings, and you abandoned ship to spread around a little indignation."

"Obviously I will not succeed. I . . . I thought you were leaving Edgar. Why are you here?"

"Because you are."

She sighed. "I feel so alone right now."

"Not any more."

He moved a little closer until their shoulders touched. Olive pressed her lips into a tight line. Her eyebrows came together, and Douglas saw that his touch had rendered her close to tears. He moved away slightly, sad to think what would have happened if he had not arrived in time.

"I would have been here sooner, but we came across an accident on the road and . . ."

"You are an amazing man," she said, interrupting. Her face reddened. "About that paper I slid under your door."

"It can wait. Right now I . . ."

"Captain Bowden, come this way, please."

He stood up and grabbed Olive's hand, tugging her

up with him. The footman walking ahead didn't even notice. To his relief, the footman at the ornate door at the end of the hall had left his post, perhaps because Douglas was the final petitioner, since the woman would never be allowed in.

He released Olive's hand and put his arm around her waist, pulling her close. If the footman realized his mistake and tried to separate them, Douglas wasn't going to give up easily.

They came to the end of the endless hall and the footman opened the door without looking back. "Captain Douglas Bowden, late of the Royal Navy and part owner in the Telford Boat Works," he announced and ushered Douglas forward.

The footman blanched as he realized his mistake too late. To say anything now would expose his own error, or so thought Douglas as he nodded to the astounded man and hurried inside with Olive Grant. He held his breath, but the door closed behind them. *I hope they sack you when they find out*, Douglas thought. He smiled and bowed. Olive Grant performed a magnificent curtsy and they walked closer.

The Irish street sweeper had been right. Two ordinary-looking people sat near each other in gilt chairs on a raised dais. Douglas saw some beauty in the brown eyes and handsome carriage of the Countess of Sutherland, but years and childbearing had given her a double chin and a waist that was only a memory now. She looked bored and ready to be done with petitions and audiences. Douglas thought the reddish tinge to her face suggested elevated blood pressure.

The Marquis of Stafford was of slighter build, possessor of an unfortunate hooked nose and a vanishing chin. Douglas thought the marquess wouldn't have lasted a day on board any ship he had sailed with in the past twenty-five years. His air of disinterest equaled his wife's.

From the way he sat, at a slight angle on his chair, Douglas gleefully diagnosed a case of hemorrhoids.

"What have you to do with us?" the marquess asked. "Is this your wife?"

Douglas took Olive's hand. "Not yet. I am a surgeon retired from the Royal Navy. I am now part owner of the Telford Boat Works, and Edgar's doctor."

Her heard Olive's little intake of breath, and he squeezed her hand.

"We are principally employing the Highlanders, your Highlanders and former tenants who were summarily dumped on Edgar and other villages on the southwest coast."

Other than Lord Stafford's uncomfortable shifting to his other haunch, Douglas saw no discomfort in the complacent people who sat before them. He wondered what might stir them to call for his removal and continued.

"They have no skills beyond those of their glens. They were dying of starvation because some were too proud to eat at Miss Grant's tearoom, where she has been providing modest meals out of her own inheritance."

The countess tossed a benevolent look Olive's way. "No skills. Exactly!" she declared in a triumphant voice that bore no trace of a Scottish accent. He wondered where she had been raised. "We are creating these improvements for their own good."

"Burning their cottages around their shoulders and leaving them to die in the rain?" Olive asked. "How is that for anyone's good except your own, my lady?"

"Oh, now," the marquess began. "We took many of them to the coast and told them to fish for a living."

"Did anyone think to show them how?" Olive asked quietly. "Did anyone provide cottages to replace those torn down and burned? Did it occur to anyone that the residents already along the coast might resent this threat to their own livelihood? I thought not." Her voice had increased in intensity, if not volume, with each condemning question.

The silence was less than congenial. As much as he loved Olive, Douglas wanted to tread on her foot. He turned his attention to the marquess, although he suspected that the countess was really in charge. He opened his folder and took out Joe Tavish's lovely drawings of the yacht in the shipyard.

"I have hired an excellent shipwright from Plymouth, now out of work and not happy to be retired because the war is over," Douglas began. "He agreed to come to Edgar and run the boat works. He brought journeymen, who are training as many Highlanders as want to learn a new trade."

"See there! Initiative is wanting among my people," the countess said. "We decided to stock those glens with sheep, which pay out much better than a few straggly cows and thin crops. Removing them should teach them something."

I'm beginning to dislike you, Douglas thought. *It isn't hard.* He plowed ahead, holding out the drawings to the marquess. "We were wondering if you might be interested in purchasing this first yacht, my lord. It's made by people from the land I assume you control because you married the countess. It would be a kind gesture and a welcome one."

He probably could have withstood nearly any insult, if the marquess hadn't started to laugh. He heard more laughter, and realized for the first time that there were other gentlemen in the audience hall. Maybe they laughed because the marquess laughed and they owed him something. Maybe they were as oblivious and mean-spirited as the hawk-beaked, simple-looking marquess and his stout wife.

"I get seasick in my bathtub," the marquess declared and looked around, pleased with his wit, which made the others laugh harder. He waved away the drawings. "Peddle these somewhere else." He gave Olive a look of supreme distaste. "Are you entirely through? It's late and I have had enough petitioners."

His face warm from embarrassment, Douglas knew he was done, disgusted and ready to shake the dust of Edinburgh off his shoes. He glanced at Olive to confirm her own willingness to leave, and he saw something that alarmed him: the great anger that Joe Tavish swore frightened him.

Olive's eyes had taken on a hard look quite out of character. In alarm, he watched her nostrils flare and then her lips tighten. She took several deep breaths, and he knew she was trying to calm herself.

It was useless. The great injustice inflicted on her dear ones bubbled to the surface and ruffled the calm demeanor of the kindest lady he knew. *Should I stop her?* he asked himself and knew the answer. He moved closer to her instead, not to grab her and hustle her from this awful place where no one cared, but to stand with her. Whether Olive Grant knew it or not, he was her man and he wasn't about to desert her. It had nothing to do with duty or oaths or vows made to higher powers. This feeling was elemental and long overdue in his life and in his heart.

He put his arm around her waist and felt her tremble. "I'm not leaving you alone. Not ever again," he told her. "Say what you came here to say, my dearest."

Chapter 36

"WELL?" THE MARQUESS ASKED, QUITE out of patience.

They came closer, moving as one. Olive took the children's drawings from the portfolio she carried. She quickly sorted through the tragic pictures, drawn by children who had no resources to protect themselves from evil they did not understand.

"I hardly know where to begin," she said, "but I will be brief, since I am evidently taking you away from something more important."

The countess nodded. When she seemed to realize that Olive's words were said in sarcasm and not concern, her eyes narrowed. A glance at the marquess told Douglas that he wasn't partial to nuance. *What a slowtop you are*, he thought, disgusted.

She brought out little Margaret Randall's drawing of a kitten on fire. "Meggie's mother tells me that her daughter cries herself to sleep each night, remembering this. Take a good look, please," she demanded in a voice so compelling that everyone in the room looked.

"The family was yanked from their home and

a torch put to it," Olive said, her voice even, under supreme control. "Meggie's kitten fled the flames, and the soldiers threw the wee morsel back into the burning house. Two times the kitten tried to escape, the last time on fire. She was thrown back into the flames. Meggie Randall still wakes up in terror, hearing her pet suffer and die."

"It's just a cat," the marquess said in a voice so bored that Douglas wanted to pummel him.

"It was a wee child's pet," Olive said and handed the drawing to Douglas. She pulled out Tommy Tavish's drawing. "This is perhaps more serious and is what makes Tommy Tavish shudder and grind his teeth in his sleep. I've heard him do that." She held out the drawing of the Tavish family huddled against gravestones with a less-than-adequate tarp covering them. "They tried to find shelter in the cemetery after their home was destroyed. The soldiers drove them away even from the graveyard. The Tavishes fled with a Bible and two candlesticks." She handed this one to Douglas.

Doug looked over her shoulder as she stared down at Flora MacLeod's drawing. He knew what it was, but his gorge rose anyway.

"Take a good look, my lord and lady, at this pleasant tableau. A good look!" Her voice rose, as though all the pain of the dislocated Highlanders was funneled through her heart and soul. Douglas thought her magnificent.

She showed the picture to the others standing close.

"Apparently it wasn't enough that Flora's mother was dying of consumption and lying on a mattress in the cold rain. One of the soldiers decided to vent his anger in the way that the worst of men do while Flora and her grandmother were forced to watch. Take a good look!"

Her voice rang to the rafters. Doug prepared to grab Olive and run before anyone laid a hand on her, but the audience hall was silent, waiting. From the corner of his eye, Douglas saw other audience members craning to see the picture. More than one turned away.

"Let me add that this tormented, violated woman's husband had fought and died with your Highland regiment, Lady Stafford, in New Orleans, America, brave to the end and fighting for his king and country."

"I have seen quite enough," the countess said. Douglas noted with dismal satisfaction that her face had gone chalk white.

"Only one more then," Olive countered and pulled out Euna MacGregor's drawing. "Little Euna stays awake at night remembering Mary MacKay burning to death inside her cottage because she was old and bewildered and refused to leave it. Don't you dare turn away from this!"

There was something mesmerizing about Olive Grant. No one in the room dared to turn away. He remember the more skillful drawing that Joe Tavish had given him, and which he had stowed in the same sleeve that contained his rejected yacht sketches. He pulled it out and held it up.

"This one goes with that one," he said. "Joe Tavish said this man, this factor of yours, Lady Stafford, watched the whole thing. I do believe his name is Patrick Sellar."

He heard whispered voices and glanced to the source, only to stare in shock at the man in the drawing right there in the hall. "You, sir," he said. "You. Joe told me that when someone objected to what was happening, you said, 'She has lived too long. Let her burn!'"

"That's a lie!" the man shouted. He started toward Doug, but someone restrained him.

"Is it?" Olive asked. Douglas had to hold her back when she started toward Patrick Sellar, her hands balled into fists. "These children and Joe Tavish have sealed these images in their brains."

She turned to Douglas and he saw the tears in her eyes. "This good man is our surgeon in Edgar. Tell them what you told me about these drawings." She put the rest back in their pasteboard sleeve.

"When I . . . when I return to my village . . ." There. He had said it. His village. Edgar was his perfect medical practice and had been all along.

He wondered briefly if Olive Grant really wanted to share her life with someone as slow to get the message as he was. Never mind. They could sort that out later.

"I will sit down with each child. We will talk about their picture. We will talk about it as often as we need to, until they come to understand that the great crime you and you, my lord and lady, have perpetrated on your own people can be overcome with kindness and courage. Olive, let's leave this place. There is a foul odor here."

Olive nodded, suddenly looking exhausted. He thought her superb in her bravery, especially now that both the countess and the marquess were on their feet, shouting their own denials and demanding their removal.

"I don't think we did much good," Olive whispered, "but between you and me, it felt fine."

Douglas laughed out loud, which only increased the impotent fury of those two oblivious, cruel people on the raised dais. He saw footmen coming toward them. "Oops."

He tightened his grip on Olive, pushing his hand down into the waistband of her skirt, determined not to let go of her, no matter what the footmen tried.

"Just one more thing!"

He stopped in surprise, amazed at the calm, splendid protest coming from the only woman he would ever need in his life. She must have taken lessons from watching her father, minister of the Church of Scotland, hold a congregation in the palm of his hand. Silence reigned again.

"Lady Stafford, I wish you would call Patrick Sellar over there to account, but I am no fool. You would probably only hire another factor equally cruel. Shame on you. Shame on you both."

She looked around the hall, slowly eyeing everyone in turn. Douglas watched some of those men of power avoid her glance.

"There will come a judgment," she said, her voice conversational now, but equally compelling. "Someday you, as all of us must, will stand before the judgment seat of Christ. May God have mercy on you."

She turned then, this remarkable woman, put her condemning pictures drawn by little ones under her arm and nodded to Douglas. "Maybe I have said enough."

"You covered the subject," he assured her as they walked slowly from the audience hall, footmen in front of them, in back of them, and on each side.

"Really, Doug," she said, her head held high. He couldn't see a defeated bone in her body, and he knew enough about anatomy to pass any examination.

The footmen let him collect his luggage and his medical satchel from the alcove where he had left them what seemed like years ago. The front door slammed shut behind them.

He realized he still held her skirt in his death grip. He took his hand out, only to have her sink to her knees as if he had been holding her up. He tugged her to her feet and walked her to a nearby bench on the street. She sat down, and to his delight, discarded all propriety and rested her head on his shoulder.

They sat in silence for a few minutes. Douglas gradually felt the roaring in his ears give way to ordinary street sounds. He even thought he heard a robin.

The delightful woman tucked so close to him chuckled. "When that . . . that odious Mr. Sellar started toward you, I was afraid you were going to try to thrash him, and you know you're not good at that."

Douglas leaned back against the bench and put his arm around Olive's waist, not with a tight hold, but because she had a nice waist and he enjoyed touching her. "No, I'm not a brawler. You could have found a better defender."

"No, I couldn't," she said. "Doug, since I am sitting here with my head on your shoulder—I would even put my hand on your knee, but I have a few standards remaining—you won't be terribly surprised if I tell you I love you, will you?"

He closed his eyes with the pleasure of her announcement, amazed at the speed with which he could go from horrible anger and indignation to nothing short of bliss. Medical science treatises suggested that such extreme dislocation of bodily humors would bring on indigestion or worse, but a little upset to his system could be easily cured with bicarbonate of soda. Or maybe marriage.

"Would you be surprised if I told you the same thing? I do love you, Miss Grant."

She kissed his cheek then, which further stirred up those bodily humors.

"Curious," he mused. "I came out of this endless war feeling like a man of eighty. I don't feel like a man of twenty, but will thirty-seven do for you?"

"I'd be robbing the cradle if you felt twenty," she informed him. "Remember my standards?"

"I've been thinking . . . ," he began, then paused, amazed all over again about what had happened in the few months since he stopped in a shabby town to help a little boy.

"Don't quit now," Olive said. "I hope you're planning to ask me a question."

"Eventually," he teased and ducked when she swatted at him. "I was going to make the observation, Miss Grant, that I was seriously disappointed when I came to your country, passed through Gretna Green, and didn't see a single blacksmith marrying anyone over the anvil."

"Disappointed, were you?" She threw caution completely to the wind and put her hand on his knee.

"Yes, disappointed." He took a deep breath and tied

himself irrevocably to shabby little Edgar, and work and worry for the rest of his days. "Let me propose—"

"High time."

"—that we go to Gretna Green and give that black-smith something to do. I have a post chaise located at a nearby hotel, and the post riders said they would remain in my employ until they heard otherwise from me."

"Aye, then," she said. "If that was a marriage proposal, I accept."

He laughed, loud and long until Olive gave him a shake.

"What in the world . . . ," she began.

"It's this, my love," he told her. "I just remembered that I promised Joe Tavish I would keep you from doing something rash in Edinburgh that you would regret." He inclined his head toward hers. "Any regrets yet?"

She appeared to give the matter significant thought, which assured him that he was marrying a woman with a sense of humor.

"Well?" he asked.

She leaned in closer. "Only that Gretna Green isn't just around the corner. I am thirty and ready for misbehavior right now."

"It's not misbehavior if we're married," he assured her.

"Then no regrets, Doug," she said so softly into his ear.

Hang propriety. Anyone passing on the street in front of the Countess of Sutherland's manor would have seen a middle-aged man with graying hair wrapped up in the embrace of a woman a little younger and with red hair. No one could have seen her interesting eyes because they were closed as he kissed her once or twice, maybe more.

They came to their senses eventually and sat in pleas-ant silence. He remembered the other drawing in his port-folio with the yacht sketches. He took it out and handed it to her.

She sucked in her breath as she looked over his sketch

of a man sitting up in bed and staring with wide eyes at a circle of imploring, pleading hands raised all around his bed.

"I see those men every night," he said softly. "I assure them I did everything I was capable of, but it's never enough."

She was silent a long time, looking at the picture, then traced the drawing of the man with fright in his eyes. She kissed her finger, touched his image, and then tore the sketch into small pieces. She threw the pieces into the air and they watched them scatter down the street.

"It's not that simple," he said.

"Nothing is," she agreed. "I believe that we will be bearing one another's burdens after that anvil business. You can rely on me, Doug."

"And you on me."

Then hang propriety again.

Epilogue

AUGUST, 1817

Dear Owen Brackett,

Cross your fingers I have time to finish this letter before some crisis or another demands my attention.

I can't believe it's been six months since I wrote last. If I had suspected that a quiet country practice would be anything but, I might have taken Sir David Care-Less's advice and accepted that assistant superintendency at Stonehouse when he offered it to me. That's a fib of vast proportions, because Edgar suits me right down to the ground.

Olive and I send our congratulations to you on the birth of your third child. Owen, you've been a busy surgeon, indeed. I hope your life in Kent continues to satisfy both you and Aggie. We're a long way from the Royal Navy, eh?

It's finally here: the yacht will be christened today. Homer Bennett (I know you remember him) and his crew have taken longer than usual, but this pretty little ship was done with such care, since it has been the training vessel for new but willing Highland ship builders. Almost without exception, they have proved to be apt pupils. All anyone needs is a chance, and they have succeeded. There is a fishing boat being built now in the other graving dock, and orders for two more. I don't doubt that once this yacht goes down the ways and sets sail, other orders will pour in.

We owe such a debt to Lord Crenshaw. Olive and I were so certain that nothing good had come of our efforts in that infamous audience hall that I wrote you about, and we are happy to be proved wrong. Lord Crenshaw was in attendance and heard us. He sent a letter to Homer and arrived in Edgar a week later to look at more detailed plans, visit the Telford Boat Works, chat with our Highland crew, and make an offer.

He had wanted Olive herself to christen the yacht. After all, he insisted it be named Fiery Miss Grant, *but she begged off. With blushes a-plenty, she told him she felt too self-conscious about christening anything, not in her interesting condition. On Olive's suggestion, Lord Crenshaw chose Flora MacLeod instead. She is over the moon with joy.*

Flora and her own crew have become quite the entrepreneurs. Nancy Fillion (I know you remember the redoubtable Mrs. Fillion) has commissioned Flora to make Seven Seas Fancies to sell at the Drake. Nancy has visited us several times this year. She claims it is to make certain that I am treating my darling Olive well and drop off more shells, but she has her own pleasure in watching "her girls" make the fancies. The Dougalls are parenting Flora well.

On a less sanguine note, Patrick Sellar was acquitted of all charges involving the murder of Mary MacKay. We were not surprised at the outcome. Money and titles have a way of talking so loud that no one can hear the truth. He did have the grace to retire, but I hear that the Countess of Sutherland has advanced James Loch, a lowland Scot, who is as cruel as, if not more cruel than, his predecessor. You're a man of the world, same as I. You won't be surprised to learn that Patrick Sellar is now a large landowner and runs sheep in the Countess of Sutherland's domain.

The Highlands continue to suffer. More of its poor uprooted citizens are taking ship for Canada and the United States. Those nations will someday reap the benefits of Highland courage and strength, mark my words.

On to better subjects. In your last letter, you inquired about the outcome with Mrs. Aintree's digitus annularis and digitus minimus mani. I am pleased to report that she has nearly full use of both fingers. I give the credit to looping sutures, rather than tight ones. And credit must also go to her housekeeper (more of a confidante) Rhona Tavish, who exerted firm control and made Mrs. Aintree obey my instructions. In her gentle way, my kind lady is nagging me to write a "wee paper" on hand surgery for the medical society. What do you advise?

Tommy Tavish walks with a slight limp, but since he is usually running, who notices? Only his surgeon.

Joe Tavish has just recently stopped apologizing for thrashing me. He claims he has not drunk a drop ("nary a bare dram" as he puts it) since he beat me to a pulp. I believe him. He is sober and Homer Bennett's prize draughtsman. And Joe is also to become a father again, so he told me only last week. All is well in the Tavish household.

Oh, and this: Lady Telford invited Olive and me to tea last week. She weakens daily, and there is nothing I can do. But you know the feeling all too well. At any rate, she showed us her latest will (I say latest, because she is a changeable old sort). Currently, Olive and I are to be the recipients of her manor when she passes. She wants us to live in it, of course, and we will appreciate the space, but she also wishes a portion of the house to become a hospital. She is supplying sufficient funds for such alterations as will be required. The rest of her fortune goes to Telford Boat Works.

I am a happy man, Owen. I have fewer nightmares, which is a relief. Olive just holds me close until they go away. Was ever a man more blessed than I? Yes, blessed. Olive has convinced me to go to church with her. There might be something to religion, after all.

Edgar is the best place to practice medicine. There is always something (or someone) here to heal, or plaster, or set, or bleed. I'm thinking about looking for another surgeon because Edgar is growing. The shipyard flourishes, and it has been the means of increasing all other businesses in town. We even have a solicitor of our own. Whether that proves to be a blessing or not, who knows? At any rate, another surgeon would permit me to sleep in my bed for a whole night. (Again, you know the feeling.) A two-man practice would come as a relief.

Must stop. Olive is standing in the doorway, looking down at a little puddle. It's her time. I believe we'll both miss the yacht christening. Let's see if my delivery skills are good enough to take her mind off the pain, considering that her surgeon got her this way in the first place!

(Evening now) A boy! He is red-haired and heterochromatic like his mother, although eye color might change. My only contribution appears to be his plumbing. Olive is fine. Our best to you and Aggie.

Yrs with affection,

Douglas Bowden—husband, father now, and Edgar's surgeon

Afterword

*I*N THE HISTORY OF GENOCIDE AND cruelty to one's own people, the Highland Clearances have to rank somewhere near the top of that most unsavory list. The Clearances began roughly in 1792 and dribbled out by the later nineteenth century. By 1900, the wild mountains and breathtaking glens of Scotland's far north were nearly devoid of people.

The reasons are complicated. Scottish history is no stranger to betrayal by her own. The centuries-old system of small farmers holding land tenancies at the good will of their clan chieftains had devolved into a near serfdom quite at odds with long-held notions of a fiercely independent people.

Beginning in the late 1600s, clan chiefs were required to travel to Edinburgh to account for their clan members' good conduct. Through the years, this annual accounting created a mind-set among the hereditary chieftains that they were landlords and no longer just leaders. As such, clan members were forced to provide labor for their chiefs in a near-feudal arrangement.

Clan members farmed as tenants on unproductive soil

in the harsh climate of northern Scotland. They also raised black cattle we know as Aberdeen Angus, and Highland cattle. They maintained a thrifty existence and mainly spoke only Gaelic, unlike the Scots of the Lowlands, who had more contact with England whose border they shared.

In truth, the Highlanders were poor, uneducated for the most part, and over-populating their breathtaking vales and glens. The hereditary, aristocratic Scots who "owned" this land became known as Improvers. It became common knowledge that running sheep in the Highlands would be far more profitable to them, even though it meant the forcible removal of their clan-tenants. But, those aristos reasoned, surely it was for the benefit of the Highlanders to yank them into a modern age.

Writs of removal (eviction), such as Joe Tavish described, typically gave the bewildered folk three months to vacate their ancestral homes. If they did not move of their own accord, they were driven from their homes on pain of death and forced into exile, no exception. Some were herded to the Highland seacoast, where they were told to become fisherfolk, never mind that they knew nothing of such a livelihood. Other were put aboard ships and sent to Canada, the new United States, and some to Australia. The suffering of a whole people can only be imagined. Although figures are uncertain, 15,000 exiles is the usual estimate.

The utter brutality of the Clearances devastated Highland life and put an effective end to Gaelic culture. A few shepherds from Lowland Scotland, with their black and white dogs, could easily manage huge flocks of Cheviot sheep, an English breed hardy enough to withstand the fierce Scottish climate, and meaty and woolly enough to bring a good profit. The land become devoid of people.

Elizabeth Gordon, nineteenth Countess of Sutherland, was a major Improver. Her husband,

George Leveson-Gower, Marquess of Stafford, and England's richest man, encouraged her to evict her tenants and open the land to sheepherding. If our kind lady, Olive Grant, had known how wealthy the marquess was, she would surely have questioned why he needed more money at the expense of ruining lives. I can nearly hear Olive asking, "How much wealth does one man need, my lord? Is it worth the misery of thousands?"

The greatest beneficiaries of this forced eviction were the commonwealth of Canada and the new United States of America. Many people of Scottish ancestry trace their roots to those suffering but stalwart folk who made new lives in foreign lands. Canada and the United States are richer for the now-distant brutality of the Clearances.

Ironically, the novelist Sir Walter Scott, a Lowlander, became enamored of the old stories of the brave and independent Highlanders. His novels of the Highlands sparked a voracious literary interest in the far north and became best sellers, just as the very people who had lived there were being cleared out.

Today, travelers are awed by the wild remoteness and the fierce beauty of the Highlands. Thoughtful travelers are also aware of the land's great emptiness. The friendly folk who might have greeted them had been driven out on the point of bayonets and swords, their homes burned, their fields flattened and their cattle slaughtered or sold to others. This is one of history's great injustices, and the role of the Countess of Sutherland and her husband, the Marquess of Stafford, remains controversial.

What can one make of such a tragedy? Although it has been more than two centuries, bitterness remains. Again, the kind lady understood something about Judgment Day, when there will be a reckoning.

On a personal note, some of my own relatives were Lowland Scots who lived near Kirkcudbright, disguised as Edgar in my story. In 1867, Thomas Fergusson, a stone mason and my great-great-grandfather, along with other relatives, friends, and their Presbyterian minister, left Scotland and settled around Chatfield, Minnesota. With them was my great-grandfather Samuel. My grandfather Carl, after whom I am named, was born in Chatfield, as was my father, Kenneth Carl.

About the Author

Photo by Marie Bryner-Bowles, Bryner Photography

THERE ARE MANY THINGS THAT Carla Kelly enjoys, but few of them are as rewarding as writing. From her short stories about the frontier army in 1977, she's been on a path that has turned her into a novelist, a ranger in the National Park Service, a newspaper writer, a contract historical researcher, a hospital/hospice PR writer, and an adjunct university professor.

Things might be simpler if she only liked to write one thing, but Carla, trained as a historian, has found historical fiction her way to explain many lives of the past.

An early interest in the Napoleonic Wars sparked the writing of Regency romances, the genre that she is perhaps best known for. "It was always the war, and not the romance, that interested me," she admits. Her agent suggested she put the two together, and she's been in demand, writing stories of people during that generation of war ending with the Battle of Waterloo in 1815.

Within the narrow confines of George IV's Regency, she's focused on the Royal Navy and the British Army, which fought Napoleon on land and sea. While most Regency romance writers emphasize lords and ladies, Carla prefers ordinary people. In fact, this has become her niche in the Regency world.

In 1983, Carla began her "novel" adventures with a story in the royal colony of New Mexico in 1680. She has recently returned to New Mexico with a series set in the eighteenth century. "I moved ahead a hundred years," she says. "That's progress, for a historian."

She has also found satisfaction in exploring another personal interest: LDS-themed novels, set in diverse times and places, from turn-of-the-century cattle ranching in Wyoming, to Mexico at war in 1912, to a coal camp in Carbon County.

Along the way, Carla has received two RITA Awards from Romance Writers of America for Best Regency of the Year; two Spurs from Western Writers of America for short stories; and two Whitney Awards from LDStorymakers, plus a Lifetime Achievement Award from Romantic Times. She is read in at least fourteen languages and writes for several publishers.

Carla and her husband, Martin, a retired professor of academic theater, live in Idaho Falls and are the parents of five children, plus grandchildren. You may contact her at www.carlakellyauthor.com or mrskellysnovels@gmail.com.

SCAN TO VISIT

WWW.CARLAKELLYAUTHOR.COM